# A Pocketful of Charm

# Nick Cree

Copyright 2019 Nick Cree

This book is licensed for your personal enjoyment only. This book may not be re-sold or given away to other people. If you would like to share this book with another person, please purchase an additional copy for each recipient. If you're reading this book and did not purchase it, or it was not purchased for your use only, then please return to your favourite book retailer and purchase your own copy. Thank you for respecting the hard work of this author.

The moral right of Nick Cree to be identified as the author of this work has been asserted by him in accordance with the Copyright, Designs and Patents Act 1988

All the Characters in this book are fictitious, and any resemblance to actual persons living or dead is purely coincidental.

All rights reserved. No part of this publication may be reproduced, stored in a retrieval system or transmitted in any form or by any means, without the prior permission of the publisher, nor be circulated in any form of binding or cover other than that in which it is published without a similar condition, including this condition, being imposed on the subsequent purchaser.

For Bryn and Frank.
Two souls who were stolen too soon.

# Prologue

The answerphone's red light was blinking, incessantly. This particular feature, told Billy Randell, that there were multiple messages awaiting his attention and that was very unusual. He hardly ever received phone calls at home and definitely not during the daytime or early evening. The light had been a steady red when he had left the apartment earlier in the day, so in between now and then, a person or persons unknown, had been trying to get hold of him. A heavy shudder of uncertainty passed up his spine. His mum always claimed this feeling was caused by someone walking over your grave. Right now, Billy felt like someone was dancing a hornpipe on his. No good news ever came when the phone rang in the early morning, or during the day. These were the times for either death, disaster or just plain ordinary bad news. He would have to endure that feeling of dread for a few moments longer, because right now his hands and arms were full with a large bag of groceries. So he kicked the front door of the apartment closed with his heel and shuffled down the corridor to the kitchen. He dumped the carrier bag on the worktop and then shrugged off his backpack tossing it over towards the armchair. The presence of an armchair, indeed the presence of anything beyond essential appliances in the kitchen still seemed a bit odd to Billy. Growing up, the kitchen in his mother's flat, had been no bigger than the alcove now occupied, by the armchair. To have an armchair, a dining table and four chairs, in the kitchen area, was a luxury Billy was still getting used to. Drinking coffee while relaxing in the armchair in the morning was one of his favourite pastimes. It was not a particularly attractive chair, but it was very comfortable and Billy had mentally thanked his landlord many times for its presence as he indulged in the pleasure of sipping a hot drink, while he waited for the toaster to pop up.

For now, Billy flitted around the kitchen putting his shopping away. The cereal box in the cupboard, the milk and other dairy products into the fridge. The tinned stuff he left on the countertop. He was going to use most of them in tonight's gourmet meal experience. The solitary white onion tried to roll onto the floor, but Billy caught it dextrously, and tossed it into the small vegetable basket that currently stood empty. Freakishly, it landed squarely and stayed where it was. Billy raised his arms in triumph as if he had just dropped the winning basket in the NBA Final and then made a lap of honour of the kitchen, high fiving his imaginary team mates, whilst making the noise of a roaring stadium audience. His victory circuit eventually found him back at the worktop, where he pulled the last item out of the shopping bag: a bottle of Hundred Pipers whisky.

He ferreted around, for a clean glass before disappointedly grabbing one from the sink and rinsing it under the tap. Billy couldn't see anything wrong in this. It had been used for whisky the night before, and it had even been the same brand. Last night's empty, stood over on the floor next to the rubbish bin, with several identical bottles, lined up like a small glass army. He really needed another trip to the bottle bank to make a deposit, but that would have to wait for another day.

He flipped the freezer box door down and peered at the ice cube tray. It was empty. He had forgotten to refill it last night when he had taken the last two cubes out. He did so now, sliding the tray carefully into the freezer section as he tried not to spill too much water. For now, he would have to drink the scotch neat. He shrugged his shoulders and poured himself a good-sized measure. Billy thought he felt his hand tremble a little as he raised the glass to his lips. It was a very fleeting tremor, almost unnoticeable. The amber liquid caressed his tongue, slid down his throat and he forgot all about it.

He pulled the pack of cigarettes out of his top pocket and then patted the rest of his pockets for his lighter. He finally found it in the left front pocket of his jeans and lit the cigarette. He grabbed the ashtray off the side, clasped the bottle and glass into the other hand and sauntered into the living room. He placed the ashtray, bottle and glass on the coffee table and collapsed on the sofa. The TV remote was beside the ashtray so he hit the on button and flicked to the channel showing the 7 o'clock News. He watched the half hour bulletin and downed a couple more scotches. His ears pricked up once when a report mentioned sporadic rocket fire from Lebanon into Northern Israel. It appeared that tensions were mounting in the old neighbourhood. As the anchor was signing off with yet another trite feel good piece about some animal with an amazing talent, Billy hit the red button, then sat in silence, before taking a final drag on his latest cigarette, grinding the butt out among the others in the ashtray and necking the last of his whiskey. Time for some supper!

On his way back to the kitchen, he noticed the answerphone with its ominous red light still blinking away, like some malevolent eye. He had forgotten all about it as his focus had, subconsciously or otherwise, been elsewhere. Without thinking he stabbed at the machine and instead of play messages, he hit the outgoing message button. There was a long beep and then they started up. "They" had been a bunch of friends who had arrived back at Billy's flat after a night on the town and after a 'few' more drinks 'they' had decided to record a new answerphone message. Instead of Billy apologising for not being able to answer the call and asking the caller, politely, to leave him a message and assuring the caller that he would get back to them as soon as possible, anybody ringing Billy when he was out was greeted by a group of drunken youths chanting,

"We're not here, we're not here
we've gone for a beer.
Start to speak after the beep,
and make your message clear."

The first few times he had played it back, it had made Billy smile, nowadays he just thought it was embarrassing and he had been meaning to change the message back for several months now. There was just one, small, problem. He had lost the instruction manual for the answerphone and he had no idea how to record a new outgoing message without it. He let the message end and then looked closer so he ensured that this time, he hit the correct button.

When he hit the play message button he was surprised that the message tape took so long to rewind. This meant that whoever had called had left multiple messages or some wag had called and then chosen to not hang up. Eventually the tape clicked and the first message began to play. The familiar voice of his ex-girlfriend came out of the speaker. She sounded pissed off. Over the last few months this seemed to be the usual tone that she adopted with Billy. Melanie Bishop had met Billy on the beach in Eilat when he had been almost at rock bottom. He had been robbed, had his passport stolen and was down to his last few shekels. She had carefully led Billy into the life of being a beach bum in Eilat, showing him the ropes and how things worked. They had become inseparable, first as friends and then in time, as lovers.

After their stint in Eilat had finished, they had returned to Billy's former kibbutz, Tel Boker, and resumed life as volunteers. This change of circumstance had suited Mel perfectly. She had been under immense pressure from her parents to allow them to visit. They were in the dark about her situation in Eilat and had laboured under the mis-conception that she was thriving in the communal lifestyle of a kibbutz. Mel was certain her parents would not have continued to fund her life as a beach bum in Eilat, and would, without doubt, have demanded her immediate return home. Like Billy, she had fallen foul of the membership on her kibbutz and been asked to leave. So this move to Tel Boker gave her the opportunity to invite her family to visit, and they had accepted. Unfortunately for Billy their arrival a few weeks later had sounded the death knell on his relationship with Mel. Although Mel's parents were aware of Billy's existence, again, as with her circumstances in Israel, Mel had not been strictly honest about him or his background. She had, during an interrogation by her mother, claimed

Billy was the son of a respectable dentist from Finchley. When Mel revealed these details to Billy he exclaimed,
"the only time my Dad would have been in Finchley was probably to rob one of the big houses."
The fact Billy didn't know where his father was, or even if he was still alive, did nothing to endear him to the Bishops, so they took a seriously dim view, of their daughter's relationship with Billy. Mel's mother was not prepared to let things rest and run their course. Whilst in Israel, she had made it her sworn duty to drive a wedge between her daughter and in her own words, "that awful boy ..." Her perseverance paid off, as not much more than a month after her parents departed, Mel announced she was returning home to England. She revealed that following her father's advice, she was returning to London to try and secure a place at University starting that following October. She was gone within a couple of weeks and although they had kept in touch by letter, the relationship was effectively over.

Billy had stayed on in Israel for a few more months before returning home. He had reached out to Mel when he had eventually arrived back in London and they had kept in touch, but their relationship had now been downgraded to a friendship; a strained one at that. Billy was not sure why their friendship had soured and asking Mel had proved fruitless, she was always totally non-committal, bordering on evasive. If pressed she would go to some lengths to avoid answering the question, eventually ending the discussion with some comment like, "We are not on the kibbutz anymore." Pressing her for further explanation was pointless, so Billy just gave up.

Billy now listened to Mel's voice on the tape. She sounded bored and fed up as usual.
"Billy, it's Mel, would you please stop phoning here late at night when you are drunk. You scare the living daylights out of my mother if she is in the house on her own, which incidentally, she was, last night. She wanted to call the Police and report you for harassment and it was lucky I came home when I did or you would have been explaining yourself to the Met's finest. Don't do it again. Okay?"
Billy placed his own question mark at the end of her sentence. He was busy wracking his brains trying to remember what he had said to Mrs Bishop that had got her so upset. He had absolutely no recollection of even calling Mel, so he certainly had no chance of recalling the finer details of what he'd said. Given this amnesia the call had clearly been placed late in the evening when sufficient scotch had been consumed to give him enough courage to pick up the phone and make a call to Mel. This was not something he made a habit of doing when he was sober as they only ended up arguing. What improvement the addition of a half bottle of whiskey could have made to the conversation was, in the cold light of day, a mystery to Billy, but deep in his cups last night it must have made some sense to him.

The machine let out another harsh beep and the electronic voice gave him the time and date of the next call. It was dated and timed around lunchtime today, so the message was about seven hours old. A hesitant voice then spoke, the English clearly heavily accented, the accent was European.
"Hello, is that Billy?"
The owner of the voice was obviously uncomfortable speaking to a machine, but the strength of her emotions quickly overcame her reluctance.
"Billy Randell, is that you? This is Greta! Where the hell are you? You were supposed to meet me an hour ago? I am standing here in the rain outside the station waiting for you?"
Her anger at being soaked for an hour, was now clearly colouring her tone, shredding the hesitancy and becoming more strident..
Peep, peep, peep, peep, peep, peep, peep, peep, peep
"I am very disappointed in ..."
The line went dead. Billy was grateful that the pips prompting her to put another coin in the

slot had interrupted her before she was cut off. But he was puzzled? What on earth was Greta doing calling him about a meeting? Greta was one of the ex-volunteers, but she came from Hamburg in Germany. Why on earth was she waiting for Billy outside a station in London? He had to assume it was a London station although he had absolutely no clue which station she was talking about? She hadn't mentioned it in her brief message. It was probably, a safe bet, that it was a station somewhere in London, but if you combined rail and underground together, there were around 500 stations to choose from. He would need a little more information before he could take any action? As the message had been left around lunchtime, he suspected that Greta would not still be waiting, in the rain, for him to arrive, some seven hours later. Greta, during her time as a volunteer on Tel Boker, had not won any awards for her patience.

The next message was also from Greta, but again, left Billy none the wiser about her location? In this message, left about a half an hour after her first message, she was now at the end of her tether. She unloaded at Billy with both barrels, leaving him in no doubt that she would probably rip his arm off and beat him to death with the soggy end, if their paths crossed at any point in the next ten years. When the pips cut in again, Billy heard a stream of guttural German cursing followed by what sounded like the telephone box being taken apart piece by piece, but was probably just the handset being replaced in a heavy handed manner.

Billy hit the pause button on the answerphone and leaned back against the wall. Apparently, he had made arrangements to meet Greta somewhere in London today and then forgotten completely about it. He wracked his brains for even a vague recollection of such a conversation taking place and drew a big fat blank. He placed his glass on the table beside the phone and then unscrewed the top off the whisky bottle and poured himself another generous measure. He took a large mouthful and swallowed it slowly. He turned his attention back to the answerphone and hit the play button again. The electronic voice identified the time and date as today in the middle of the afternoon.

"Billy, this is Tracey Martin. I have just got off the phone with Greta. She is back at my place now and she says you didn't turn up for your meeting today. You have really upset her, as she only has a limited time in London and doesn't have time to waste waiting around for you not to turn up."

Billy hit pause for a second time. Tracey had been Greta's roommate on Tel Boker and although she was British, apparently the East Ender and the Hamburg girl had hit it off. Billy wondered whether there was some shared family history of death and destruction during the war that had managed to forge that bond, as both places had been devastated by enemy bombs. Tracey finished her rant by demanding that Billy ring Greta and apologise or else. She left the number of her flat and told him to ring before seven. Billy glanced at his old, busted up Timex watch that he had been given as a present on his thirteenth birthday. As it was getting on for eight o clock now, it was too late to make the call. He didn't bother to write the number down, he already had it in his address book, written in Tracey's own fair hand on her final evening before she had left the kibbutz to return to London. Well at least he would be able to duck any confrontation for tonight, but he got the horrible feeling that he had not heard the last of this particular incident and he knew that ignorance would be no defence. In truth, though, he could not remember making any such arrangement. He had no recollection of a conversation, nothing, nada. He shrugged his shoulders and pressed play to resume the tape.

The next message was from his boss at work. Billy had been out of the office most of the afternoon as he had been given a specific list of deliveries to make before he could head home. His current employer, Nigel Finch, was one half of the design partnership Finch and McEwan who ran a design studio off Commercial Street near Brick Lane Market. What Billy knew about graphic design he could have drawn on the back of a postage stamp, but the practice needed someone who could move their creations around the city from studio to client and back again. Billy had other assignments from time to time, collecting work from printers, or photographs from photo libraries as well as being responsible for keeping the in-house reference library tidy, which given the messy nature of most of the artistic types in the practice was almost a full-time job in itself. Nigel was ringing to give him an assignment for first thing in the morning. He wanted Billy to go to another studio in Hoxton and collect a portfolio. It made sense for him to go there, straight from home, as it was just up the road from his apartment and then make the journey into the office afterwards. This was really good news as, like most design practices there would be no one in the office until nine thirty, at the earliest, so Billy could enjoy a lazy start to the day. He scribbled 'Design Company' on a Post-It note and slapped it on the front door as a reminder to himself for the morning, then he punched the air in victory and downed the contents of the whisky glass in celebration, pausing only to pour himself a refill before he pressed play on the answerphone for the next message.

The sweet and sexy tones of his current girlfriend Saskia came out of the speaker.
"Billy, I am really sorry. I won't be able to make it this weekend. Dr Chancellor has changed our schedules again and I am on call all weekend. Speak soon, Love you Bye."
The phone went dead. Dr Chancellor was the senior consultant at the hospital where Saskia worked as a junior doctor. She was still in the fledgling stages of her great medical career and therefore at the bottom of the pecking order and the victim every time one or more of her senior colleagues fancied a weekend off playing golf or sailing. She was always quick to point out that as well as having no say in the matter, all these extra shifts gave her invaluable experience. Billy had slowly got used to these sudden changes of plans, although he did notice that they seemed to be happening more often these days. Billy was definitely beginning to question her commitment to him as she seemed to always go missing at the weekends. They still managed to meet up once or twice during the week, but these days never on the weekends. He wondered how he was going to occupy his time over the coming weekend. The next two messages gave him his answer.

The first of these two calls was from his mother. She always sounded funny on the machine as if she was frightened something might go wrong with the recording, so she spoke very clearly and repeated her message a couple of times before the message tape ran out and cut her off. After Billy sorted through the repetition and the asides in her message, he gleaned, she was asking Billy whether he would be coming home at the weekend as she hadn't seen him for a couple weeks. She was offering to cook him Sunday lunch and the bribe of roast beef with all the trimmings was not one he was about to turn down. He could also take advantage of the trip home to avoid the tedious pilgrimage to the local laundromat. Billy was all too familiar with these places, as he had grown up using the one across the road from the flats where he lived, and the owner and manager, Janice, who had a soft spot for Billy so she always took special care of him when he visited.

The local laundromat here in Hackney was run by an absentee manager who was very rarely there. The machines were ancient and most of the time about half of them were out of service. Those that were still working were grubby and the soap trays were caked in gloopy washing powder. Back home, Janice kept her place and the machines spotless. Here, no one seemed to care and on one occasion Billy opened a soap tray to discover it had been used as a bin, now crammed full with orange peel, apple cores, cigarette butts and what looked like a used condom. Billy had slammed it shut and moved his laundry to another machine. He had tried to complain, but his words had fallen on deaf ears, the manager didn't care and for him the idea of a service wash was definitely something from another decade.

The final call on the tape was a potential double edged sword. Mel was back on the line again, but this time she was extending an invitation to a reunion in a pub on Friday night. It appeared that some of the former Volunteers from Tel Boker kibbutz had taken it upon themselves to organise an impromptu get together at a pub in Islington. To see some of the old crowd would be great fun, but Billy was not sure whether Greta and Tracey would be there? If they were then he could end up getting, at the least, a severe ear bashing, or worst some kind of physical violence done to him. He knew that Mel and he would probably speak before the weekend. Even though they were no longer together as a couple, they usually spoke on the phone at least once a day. Billy decided he would remain non-committal and see how he felt on Friday night. These invitations usually came via Mel as she seemed to be more plugged into the ex-Tel Boker volunteers network than Billy was, despite the fact he had spent nearly a whole year longer on the kibbutz. Billy never gave this a moment's thought, he was happy that Mel acted as the filter on these matters. The answerphone had now made it to the end of the last message and the tape stopped and immediately started to rewind. Billy pressed the delete button to scrub the old messages.

    He grabbed the glass and bottle off the phone table and wandered back into the kitchen. He fished out the frying pan, from the sink, gave it a superficial scrub, wipe and a squirt of oil, before clattering it down on the hob. He then proceeded to peel and slice the onion. This was then chucked into the puddle of warm oil. Next, he prised open a can of new potatoes with the blunt can opener, before slicing and sliding these on top of the onion. Finally, he chewed the opener through the top of a tin of corned beef, since the key for the can had gone walkies. The meat was cubed and then dumped into the pan. When the meat had begun to sizzle, he hauled the pan off and tipped about half of the contents onto his plate before smothering it in ketchup. Then he speared his plate with a clean fork from the draw and grabbed his bottle and glass, before settling back down in front of the TV.

## Chapter One

Billy opened one eye and tried to focus on the red light from his alarm clock. The numbers were blurred and illegible, so he tried to lift his head off the pillow in order to open the other eye and gain the extra perspective. The crack of thunder exploding behind his eyes told him that this was not the wisest move, but he needed to know the time, so he winced a little, rode out the pain and opened his other eye.
The numbers swam slowly into focus. 09:45 a.m.
"Shit!"
Billy vaulted out of bed and immediately regretted this violent movement as the whole room span alarmingly around and a wave of nausea washed over him causing him to dry retch. He steadied himself on the bedroom wall and took a couple of deep breaths, willing the dizziness and nausea to pass. He staggered into the bathroom and ran the cold water tap into the sink splashing the cool water on his face and rubbing it vigorously into the back of his neck. He looked up at his reflection in the bathroom mirror. Even he had to admit he looked dreadful. Brown bloodshot eyes, along with his dark hair, which even close cropped as he wore it these days, still had an annoying habit of frizzing up, like a rat's nest. He needed a shave and when he stuck out his tongue, it was an alarming shade of green and had a carpet of fur to rival Messer's Axminster and Wilton. His mouth was dry and his lips were cracked. At some point during the previous evening he had managed to split his bottom lip and there was a small scab over the wound. He knew that he didn't have time for a shower and shave, so he overfilled the sink with warm water and dunked his head below the surface. He grabbed a towel and roughly dried his hair, before smoothing it flat with his hands. Later in the day he knew it would look terrible but it might pass muster until then.

    He stumbled back into his bedroom and hunted around for some clean clothes. His imminent return home could not come soon enough. There were two large plastic bags full of dirty clothes in the corner of the room and he knew that if he didn't make the trip to his Mums' this weekend he would be spending Sunday down the local laundromat. None of this helped him now as he hunted around for a shirt to wear with his cleanest pair of jeans. One of the advantages of his current place of employment was that being a design house, the dress code was informal, but as he was visiting another design practice he felt a casual shirt would be more in keeping with the image he, and more importantly the company, would want to project. He pulled on the least rumpled of his blue cotton shirts and then went through to the kitchen.

    He had left the milk out on the side and it had gone off, so his coffee would have to be black. While he was waiting for the kettle to boil, he grabbed a fork and picked at the congealed remains of last night's meal, which was still sitting in the frying pan on the back of the stove. Cold corn beef hash for breakfast was not exactly appetising, but it filled a hole. He bolted down three quarters of a mug of coffee, the caffeine hit giving him that quick fix buzz and he grabbed his keys and his backpack and left the flat, slamming the front door behind him. Down in the hallway he paused to open his mailbox. There was a single postcard in the box. He flipped it over and looked at the picture, an aerial shot of the Sydney Opera House. He didn't need to turn back and read the sender's name, he knew exactly who it was from. He stuffed the card in the back pocket of his jeans. He would read it when he had a moment. Right now, he had other things he needed to focus his attention on, like finding a cab to take him to his appointment.

    The main road outside his flat, a major arterial route through the East End of London, was crammed with slow moving traffic, lorries, buses and a fair few private cars, but no black cabs, at least none with the orange for-hire light on. He checked his watch and decided to set off walking. The design studio he had to visit wasn't far and he knew a couple of shortcuts. As he walked he kept an eye open, looking out for an empty cab. If he caught sight of one along the way he would flag it down and then ask them to wait while he collected the portfolio. He knew that the cab fare would be refunded to him from the company petty cash, provided he presented a receipt, even if the fare included a short waiting time outside the studio. Luck was clearly against him this morning and he arrived at his destination without successfully stopping a single taxicab. Most of the cabs he had seen were not available for hire or cruising without their orange lights on. The two that he had attempted to flag down had both ignored him and driven past. He had a feeling that today was just going to be one of those days.

The fresh air from the walk had done nothing to help dispel the pounding headache of his hangover, although the food and the coffee had helped to quell the general feeling of nausea he had felt first thing. He was still feeling pretty dreadful as he pushed open the front door for The Design Company and climbed the stairs to their first-floor offices. He had been here before to collect or drop off various pieces of work. He usually either delivered the work in a large leather portfolio or picked up something similar if work was travelling in the other direction. He got to the top of the stairs and paused to catch his breath. One flight of stairs and he was out of breath, he really needed to do something about his general fitness. Back on Tel Boker swimming had been a daily pastime and along with the physical nature of most of the work, had meant Billy's overall fitness was good. A sharp contrast to the way things were for him now.

He straightened his jacket and smoothed down his hair before he pushed open the door that led to their suite of offices. There was another reason he had just made an extra effort. The receptionist at The Design Company was a particularly attractive looking woman and although Billy had done nothing more than flirt with her until now, he had a feeling that if he played his cards right then it would not be too difficult to secure a date with her. When he did turn on the charm the young lady in question was usually rather responsive and Billy took this as a sign that there might be a spark of interest there. He prepared his most dazzling smile as he walked over to the reception desk.

A stranger looked up to greet him. Not the usual receptionist. In her place was a woman who looked to be the wrong side of fifty. Maybe, way back in the day, she might have turned heads, but those days were long past now. She wore her hair in a dated bouffant style, her eyes shielded behind fifties style tortoiseshell horn-rimmed spectacles that were attached to her neck by a safety chain. Her outfit was suitable for her age and was offset by a rather fetching and expensive looking string of pearls. She spent a moment eyeing Billy up and down over the top of her spectacles, as a seriously suspicious look crept on to her face. When she finally spoke her question was a simple,

"Good Morning. How may I help you?"

But it was loaded with enough overtone and delivered in a manner that to Billy's ears it sounded more like,

'What stone have you just crawled out from under and would I be better to call the Police right now and save time later?'

Under such a withering gaze, Billy was speechless for the briefest of moments, as he struggled to remember why on earth he had been sent here this morning?

"I've come to pick up a portfolio for Finch and McEwan." Billy stammered.

The Medusa like gaze didn't soften but was deflected away for a moment as the woman looked down to check the notepad in front of her. This told Billy that her presence was only a temporary appointment as she seemed to have a copious number of notes in front of her, probably delivered to her at a morning briefing with the company office manager earlier.

"I have nothing on my list like that."

She delivered her verdict in a flat monotone that defied Billy to contradict her. Billy ignored the warning.

"Could you check again please? I had a call from Mr Finch last night asking me to come here this morning and collect it."

The woman tutted audibly, as if to request her to check again was an insult of the gravest proportion. She had looked, there was nothing on her list and she didn't make mistakes. Never the less she indulged this foolish boy standing in front of her by reading through her list a second time.

"No there is nothing on my list, so it looks like you have made a wasted journey."

There was a slight smile of satisfaction on her lips as she delivered this last comment. Billy was determined not to leave empty handed, not if there was the slightest chance that the portfolio was waiting for him somewhere beyond the glass partition that framed the rear of the reception area. He mentally scratched his head trying to recall the name of someone he could double check with? He had the name of someone, Spikey, but he felt sure that was just a nickname and he had to wrack his brains to come up with Spikey's real name. His hesitation was not endearing him to the woman behind the desk who was waiting to resume her duties but felt that if she took her eyes off this dishevelled 'time-waster' he would probably make off with the large floral display that dominated the reception desk.

Time was running out for Billy and his hangover headache was not making recall any easier.

"Would it be possible to speak to Brian Reynolds, Spikey?"

He ended up using both names just to play it safe. Spikey was his opposite number at The Design Company. Like Billy he was the general dogsbody, responsible for keeping the place tidy and running messenger errands for the designers. Unlike Billy, Spikey was actually interested in the design industry and had been studying the subject at night school for the past two years, hoping that one day he would make it to his own designer's chair.

Billy had no such aspirations. For him it was just a job. One that paid rather well given what he was expected to do, but just a job all the same. He didn't see graphic design as a career option in any way. His request to speak to Spikey had, however, had a deeply detrimental effect on the woman behind the reception desk. It was if Billy was challenging her very presence, her right to be there and to run the reception desk. The horrified look on her face could not have been more pronounced if Billy had just leant casually on her desk and asked her permission to sleep with her granddaughter.

Despite the fact she was staring daggers at him, she still picked up the phone, consulted the internal telephone list and dialled the number. When it was answered she spoke briefly to the person on the other end to inform them that they had a visitor in reception before replacing the phone in its cradle. If the person who had answered the phone was keen to know the identity of the visitor or the purpose of their visit then they were going to have to come out to the reception and find out for themselves. Having fulfilled Billy's impertinent request, she returned to studiously ignoring him. Billy sensing that the atmosphere in the reception area had turned exceedingly frosty, retreated to the other side of the small area and waited for Spikey to show himself. Fortunately for Billy it was not a long wait. Spikey emerged from the inner sanctum and was clearly surprised to find that Billy was his mystery visitor.

Spikey was a good head taller than Billy and his height and slim stature were emphasised by his attire and footwear. He was clad in a retro style sixties, satin look suit, with a white shirt and slim-Jim tie. On his feet he had a pair of black suede crepe shoes that had been the favourites of the teddy boys of yesteryear. The whole look was finished off by an unruly riot of spiked, dyed red-orange hair and a diamond ear stud. For all his foreboding attire he had an open face and an easy dazzling smile. He stuck out his hand towards Billy, who took it and they shook hands.

"Billy Randell, what on earth brings you to this part of the world?"

"Finch left a message on my answerphone yesterday. He said there was a portfolio to collect this morning. I came here straight from home."

Spikey looked at his watch. It was a heavy looking piece of jewellery, but Billy couldn't see the make or model.

"Late start today?"

There was no hint of condemnation in his voice, in fact Billy might have detected a small note of envy there instead.

"Yeah, I overslept a bit."

"Heavy night last night?"

"A bit."

"Well I am not sure what to say? I know that my boss, after ringing Nigel Finch last night, was f'ing and blinding," he nodded back over his shoulder,

"the work should have been ready, but the lazy sod who was given it, hadn't done it."
Finishing by raising his eyes skyward. Spikey's voice had descended to a low conspiratorial whisper and he cast an occasional glance in the direction of the reception desk. Billy's nemesis behind the desk, was studiously ignoring the pair of them, but Billy guessed that Spikey was keen not to be overheard.

"It was a straight forward enough piece of illustration and I could have done it with my eyes shut and both hands tied behind my back. Anyway, Mr Hargreaves was on to Finch last night asking for an extension until tomorrow. So, it looks like you are a day early. Didn't Finch call you and cancel your trip here?"

"No, he didn't, and I was home all evening."

"Well sorry about that old son. I suggest you give him a bit of a ticking off then, when you get back to the office." Spikey quipped, in an exaggerated Oxbridge accent.

They both grinned, as they knew the likelihood of that happening, was zero.

"Ah well Spikey, you take care of yourself. I'll see you around."

"Yeah. Stop by one evening around five and we will go and have a beer together. We can both have a moan about our lot in life."

"I might very well do that. I'll give you a ring."

Billy turned and went out the door. He made no attempt to say goodbye to the temporary receptionist and uttered a silent prayer that the next time he returned here, normal service would have been resumed, in the shape of the usual incumbent behind that desk.

Back out on the street, Billy began a fresh hunt for a Black Cab. Even though he had no product portfolio to transport and was therefore not strictly 'entitled' to a cab ride, he felt the company owed him the price of the cab fare today, for sending him on a wild goose chase. He finally managed to hail one and get it to stop, but only after several had blazed past, with their orange 'for hire' lights winking like some spiteful eye. He collapsed in the backseat, letting the continued effects of the hangover wash over him like waves. The postcard he had thrust in his back pocket dug into his skin of the small of his back, so he reached behind him and pulled out the card. He studied the picture of Sydney Opera House in the sunshine with the Sydney Harbour Bridge, in the background. It was an iconic image of an iconic destination. He knew exactly who the card was from and he flipped it over to read the message.

Mike Spencer had been Billy's friend since their first day in school. They had shared the same desk and Mike had stepped in during their first break in the playground to prevent Billy getting his head kicked in by a bunch of bullies. From that day on they had been virtually inseparable, a strange feat given their wildly different social backgrounds. When Mike had suddenly announced he was leaving to travel to Israel to work on a kibbutz, Billy who was always flat broke, had put his life on the line to borrow the money, so he could travel with him. Once they had arrived, they both settled into the life of kibbutz volunteers, each finding their niche in the bigger scheme of things.

Life on the kibbutz had not gone smoothly for Billy and he got into a fight with some new volunteers, who successfully conspired to have Billy expelled from the settlement. Unable to return to England and prevented from joining another kibbutz, Billy had drifted down to the southern city of Eilat. After many months of separation, the two friends were eventually reunited when Billy and Mel were invited to re-join the kibbutz. Mike was, by that time, in a stable relationship with a local girl so although the two friends were back together in the same place there was a different dynamic to their relationship. Where there had been two, now there were four people. Luckily all four became good friends. Life had continued on until Mel had returned home to England. As events went, Mel's return to England had been inevitable, and if he was brutally honest given the atmosphere just prior to her departure and the pressure she was under to end their relationship, Billy should not have been surprised when after a few weeks of separation, a letter arrived calling time on their relationship. What did surprise him was the effect that the breakup had on him, emotionally.

He had found the letter in the Volunteers pigeonholes outside the dining room at lunchtime, but recognising the writing and dreading the contents he had pocketed the letter and waited until he was alone in his room after work before opening it. He had read the short letter through to the end, twice, and then tossed it aside, before picking it up and reading it again, a third time. Billy was instantly surprised by how empty the words on the page made him feel. Mel hadn't pulled any punches, although she had chosen not to elaborate on her reasons, merely stating that she felt the relationship had 'run its natural course'. Billy put the letter aside again and went to the fridge. He opened it and reached for a beer, then changed his mind. No, on this occasion beer would not work. He was thirsty. A long shift in the melon fields would do that to a man, but right now it was not just his thirst that needed dealing with.

Nestled in the door of the fridge there was a bottle of Arac and water, ready mixed and he pulled it out by the neck and unscrewed the cap. He took a long pull on the bottle and gulped down several mouthfuls. It was a strong mixture, heavy on the Arac and light on the water, so it hit the back of his throat like a flamethrower and then burned all the way down to his stomach. He went back over to his bed and lit a Time cigarette. He collapsed on the bed and reached over to where the stereo was sitting on the low table. He pushed the eject button and examined the cassette inside. It was one of Mel's mix tapes, so he hurled it across the room and replaced it in the machine with one of his own. The Redskins blared out of the speakers, and he turned the volume up as the lead singer encouraged the listeners to "Kick over the Statues." Yes, their tone and lyrics absolutely matched his mood and he lost himself in the music and slowly drank himself into oblivion.

The letter's arrival was certainly a catalyst, a pivotal point in Billy's life. He told no one about the break up, but found he was suddenly inundated with offers from other female volunteers wanting to occupy a place in his heart or his bed or both. Billy freely cursed Mel aloud, assuming that she had been the source of the leak, possibly relating her decision in a letter written to one of the other female volunteers. Billy never stopped to consider that his sudden dramatic change in behaviour was a clear sign that something had fundamentally altered in his life. Whereas before he had been social and friendly, now he spent most of his free time in his room, alone, either reading or listening to music, while getting off his head on cheap Arac or Vodka. Provided he turned up for work on time, no one seemed to care what he got up to, or what state he got himself in at nights.

Money was not an object, he was still on a retainer from the production company. His agent, the indomitable Miss Tara Shade, had managed to secure him this retainer from the producers. In the contract Billy agreed to be available full time to join the production as and when he was required for shooting. These retainers were normally used to secure and ensure the first-choice actors would be available for filming, so it was testament to Miss Shade's ability, that she had managed to get such a clause written into Billy's contract, considering he was merely a bit-part player. But the clause was there and the contract had been signed, so the retainer cheques arrived regular as clockwork ensuring Billy was able to keep his fridge and liquor cabinet well stocked.

So for now, in the absence of any other distractions, he just wanted to party and occasionally he was able to find like-minded individuals among the volunteers or young kibbutzniks who really wanted to go on a bender, but no-one was able to keep up with Billy for very long, and even those who lasted a couple of days often took themselves off for a detox in the end. When that happened Billy continued on his own. Mike had tried talking some sense into Billy, with little or no real success. As his oldest friend he was clearly concerned about the long-term damage Billy was wreaking on his health. But whenever Mike raised the subject with Billy, the two of them just ended up arguing. Mike was not around much anyway to witness Billy's decline as he was spending more of his time together with his Israeli girlfriend Yara. He was now living with her in her room and they rarely ventured down to the Volunteer blocks anymore.

Billy, in turn never ventured outside the Volunteer compound much after dark. It was not a sensible idea to go roaming around the kibbutz in an inebriated state. It would only lead to scrutiny from the Members, a lecture from Yossi, the volunteer leader, and might ultimately lead to censure, condemnation and ultimately expulsion. What went on in the volunteer area was excusable provided it was confined to the volunteer area.

Despite this caution Billy didn't escape everyone's notice. It wasn't too long before he received a visit from Yossi. Despite the fact that he was the volunteer leader he also saw himself as a having a personal interest in Billy and his well-being. He went to some lengths to point out that his visit was 'off the record' and a sign of his concern before he started on at Billy about the amount he was drinking and how it was not good for his health. Billy, for his part ignored the advice and merely grouped Yossi together with Mike as a pair of 'killjoys'.

As they were leading very separate lives by this time, Billy was not privy to Mike's plans and it was not until Mike dropped by one evening to say goodbye, that Billy discovered that now that Yara had finished her studies, the two were planning to take off together and see a bit of the world. Whilst this should have been devastating news for Billy, instead he found he was secretly relieved, as it removed a constant nagging voice, always encouraging him to clean up his act. With Mike's departure another of the restraints would be removed. Billy even refused to go with the pair and see them off from Ben Gurion airport claiming that he was unable to take time off from work, but he was fooling no one and when Mike and Yara eventually boarded their flight, bound for the Indian capital, Billy was already deep into a bottle of cheap vodka, drowning his sorrows and loneliness.

A few days later Billy was in a similar state when a letter arrived for him from the production company. Billy had been waiting for the letter for several months, expecting the details of the new shooting schedules and any scripts that he would need to read through and learn. The shooting had been suspended, while the producers and the writers battled their way through the preparations required to turn what had started life as a feature film into a thirteen-part television series. The date for commencing filming kept being postponed, and whilst Christian Jensen, his friend and one of the Assistant Directors on the project, kept him regularly informed via letters and postcards of the various challenges they were all facing, it looked like they were not going to be on set anytime soon. The letter in the volunteer pigeonhole looked thinner than he expected, but regardless, he tore open the envelope and pulled out the paper from inside. He unfolded the single sheet of A4 and read past the introduction. The language and tone of the letter were both terse and business-like, merely taking the few lines to inform all members of cast and crew that the project had been suspended forthwith, put into mothballs and that all contracts and retainers were therefore cancelled with immediate effect.

In a conciliatory tone, typical of the entertainment industry, where you never knew from one month to the next, who you would be working with and who's palm might need greasing or arse needed kissing, the production team had thanked everyone for their sterling work on the project. So, that was it. Billy's fledgling career, as an actor was over, in truth, before it had ever really got started. It took Billy several days of phone calls to his agent and to Christian to finally get the facts about what had happened. His agent, now she was no longer handling an up and coming star, appeared to be refusing to take his calls and Christian, even as an Assistant Director, on the project was being kept in the dark. When the rumour mill finally got up to speed, it emerged that a 'Directors cut', made from existing shot scenes had been assembled as a pilot show and shown to various 'focus' groups. It had not been well received and the producers, fearing they were about to produce another 'turkey', had panicked and pulled the plug on the project. It was a disappointing end to what had been an exciting period in his life, but the attitude of the Production company and particularly Miss Tara Shade, Billy's agent, had left him with a bad taste in his mouth.

After a few days mourning the loss of his additional income, Billy came to realise that with Mel and Mike both gone, and the TV series cancelled there was very little left to keep him in Israel now, and with the end of the retainer payments it was likely that the money would now run out sooner rather than later. He estimated that he had enough money to enjoy a few months more and still have enough for the price of a flight home.

But there was still one major hurdle preventing Billy from returning to the UK, in the form of Delchie Matthews. Matthews was a psychopathic loan shark who lived and operated in Billy's home town. In order to afford the initial trip to Israel, Billy had borrowed two grand from Matthews, under false pretences, and had then skipped the country a few days later. Billy had been forced to cut all communication with his mother in an attempt to keep her safe. When he had eventually reached out to her and she had visited him in Israel they had spent many hours talking about the situation. Matthews had, at the start, visited Susie Randell and demanded to know where her son was, but when she had over many months and multiple visits, from the big man himself, and other members of his gang, maintained that she had no idea, where Billy was, he had eventually left her alone.

Secretly, she admitted to Billy, that she suspected that for several weeks Matthews had been intercepting her mail in an attempt to get a fix on Billy's whereabouts, so his silence and lack of communication had merely bolstered her claim to not know where Billy was. She had been worried, and had eventually reached out, rather reluctantly, to Mike's parents. They had, in turn, passed her concerns onto their son. Billy had still refused to write to his mother and it seemed like, with hindsight, he had made a smart decision. Billy still expected that if he returned to his hometown he would most likely end up in hospital fighting for his life, in much the same way as his old boss Pete Hollingsworth had. Billy had had a serious confrontation with Hollingsworth and this had made him, briefly, the number one suspect for the serious assault. A cast iron alibi had saved him from possible prosecution and the police had been forced to pursue other leads.

The dogged efforts of the two officers assigned to the case, DS Harrison and DC Smith, had eventually paid off. They had arrested one of the minor cogs in Delchie's operation, a drug mule, for a driving offence, and then put the frighteners on him. He had rolled over and offered to deliver chapter and verse on the workings of Delchie Matthews's operation. This evidence, coupled with the drug mule's untimely death, in what could only be described as a very suspicious looking suicide, convinced them that they were on to something. It had taken them another seven months of painstaking work to finally build a case and then they had made their move. They had wound up the whole operation in a series of dawn raids and then sat back and watched as various members of the gang tried to escape justice by ratting out the other members of the gang. This cascade of information had only helped them to strengthen their case and when the whole thing had finally come to trial, at the Crown Court it had been pretty much a 'slam-dunk' case.

Matthews was found guilty of murder, conspiracy to murder, and attempted murder, along with a whole wealth of other violent offences, as well as drug trafficking, money laundering, racketeering and tax evasion. He was sent to prison for life, with a recommendation from the judge that he serve a minimum of twenty-five years. Other members of his gang were also handed severe sentences and although Billy suspected there might still be elements of the gang doing business, as it was impossible to totally wipe out these cockroaches, at least he knew that with the main man behind bars, it was probably safe for him to return home.

Suzie Randell had been present in court throughout the trial, not as a witness, not as a spectator, but by some cruel twist of fate, as a jury member. She had tried her damnedest to get disqualified from the panel, citing her previous links to the accused as a former customer of his loan sharking business, and also the fact that her own son had been a suspect in one of the cases that the accused was on trial for, but the judge and the other members of the court largely ignored her pleas. She had sat patiently through all the evidence, shuddering slightly, when the arresting officer described how armed police had dragged the naked Matthews from his bed in the early morning raid. Suzie had her own memories of a visit from the dawn "knock-knock" squad.

Another face present throughout the whole trial had been Mrs Matthews, Delchie's mother. The old lady had sat in the centre of the public gallery, within touching distance of her son, every single day. On some days she was flanked by her friends, all equally colourfully dressed in their Sunday best, on other days she was accompanied by a minister, his clerical collar shining like a white circle of truth from under his greying patriarchal beard. Mrs Matthews sat emotionless, her lined face as fixed as a block of black marble, as the full catalogue of her son's crimes were laid bare. On the final day of the trial a white gentleman had accompanied Mrs Matthews and sat holding her hand as the verdict was read out. When sentence had been passed she had collapsed wailing into his arms. He had remained unmoved throughout the proceedings until his son was being hustled away down the steps. Then he half stood in his seat and his clear cockney tones rang out above the general background noise of the courtroom.

"It's a total fuckin stitch up."

There had been a few supporting hoots from others in the public gallery who obviously didn't concur with the jury's verdict or the judge's sentence.

Susie Randell had taken no pleasure in finding Matthews guilty, but in her heart, she knew that what he had been accused of was largely true. You couldn't live that close to a madman for as long as she had and not have seen something of his true nature. As soon as the case had been concluded and Delchie was safely on his way to jail, Susie had put pen to paper and written to Billy. Her letter arrived mere days after the letter from the Production company cancelling Billy's acting contract.

Billy was still not convinced that a snap return flight to the UK was necessarily the best option. He was worried about how such an action might be interpreted by, of all people, Mel. They had continued to exchange letters and Mel seemed remarkably well informed on developments in Billy's life, leaving him wondering exactly where she was getting her information from. He was certainly not the source, he kept all his letters short, vague and pretty light on details. Her most recent letter had eluded to the cancellation of the film contract and pressed Billy for details of his next moves. When his response was non-committal she kept the pressure up, almost demanding to know when Billy was planning to return to the UK. So instead of a tail between the legs flight home, Billy began to look at other options. He studied the possibilities of a return overland. He had enough names and addresses in his contact book to make for an interesting meander through Europe, but then, in a rare moment of sober clarity, he crossed all the names off the list that belonged to ex-girlfriends and found he was left with only three countries, Poland, Portugal and Greece. It would hardly be the 'Grand Tour' with just those three countries.

He felt he was also behaving in a gentlemanly fashion by removing the ex-girlfriends from his itinerary. If they had moved on with their life then him showing up could be embarrassing for them and if they hadn't and they still held a torch for him, then he would not be around long enough to do their resurrected relationship justice, and he didn't really want his homeward journey to turn into a "Shag-a-thon Tour" of one-night stands. This gentlemanly thought took Billy a little bit by surprise and he wondered whether the end of his relationship with Mel, had left some lasting scars on him? He was certainly still popular with the opposite sex, except when he was deep in the drink, when that occurred, as it did with alarming frequency these days, he found he was generally unpopular with everybody.

Billy had briefly toyed with the idea of following Mike and Yara eastwards and realised that if Mike had proposed that just the two of them make the trip, he would have jumped at the chance, but he was not going to just catch the happy couple up , and play the third wheel. It was not that he begrudged Mike his relationship. Billy was very fond of Yara and he particularly loved the way that she bossed Mike around and in turn the way that Mike played the hen-pecked husband with the accompanying looks of despair and disbelief. The two of them were made for each other. Remembering his old friend's facial expression, however, just reinforced Billy's feelings of loss and abandonment, but with time those feelings began to morph into something new and fresh. Billy was slowly developing a renewed sense of purpose and direction. It was emerging phoenix-like from the ashes and ruins of his life. He had sat on a beach a year or so ago, with no friends and very little money left. He had been robbed and then ostracised from the social circle, cast out like some leper, but he had managed to pull himself up from there and rebuild and there was no reason why he couldn't do the same thing all over again. He just needed to get up off his ass and make a start.

## Chapter Two

The taxi cab lurched through Central London's heavy morning traffic. It would stop and then start, each time the doors clicked as they locked and unlocked, the meter's orange numbers spiralling upwards to dizzy heights. Billy barely noticed the numbers, he didn't care. The company would foot the bill anyway. He just needed to make sure he remembered to get a receipt. The driver had the radio on in his part of the cab, turned down low, so it was a barely audible sibilant hiss in the back of the cab. At one point when they were at a complete stop he slid open the glass screen.

"Looks like there's a burst water main down by the Mansion House. That's what's causing the gridlock this morning. Nothing I can do about it."

He shrugged his broad shoulders as if to emphasise the point before continuing.

"The whole area is locked up solid. Do you want to get out and walk? It might be faster."

Billy looked out the window and took in his surroundings. He recognised the road he was on and estimated that it would take a good half an hour to walk to his office from here.

"No mate you're alright. I'll sit this one out."

He said this to the back of the cabby's head. The driver turned his head slightly, nodded to show he understood and then focused his attention back on the traffic, which had now started to move again, albeit with the same excruciating sluggishness. After what seemed like an hour, but was probably only half that time, the taxi pulled up outside his office block. Billy jumped out and pulled the banknotes required to pay the fare out of his wallet before shoving the receipt, he received back in. He thanked the driver who wished him a good day, before edging his cab back into the traffic, whilst trying to point its nose back in the opposite direction, away from the gridlock. As soon as this opportunity arrived, the black cab lurched away, completed it's U-turn and disappeared in search of another fare.

Billy turned and faced the building that was the office of Finch and McEwan. Earlier, in its long history the building had been some form of warehouse or storage facility. There were large openings in the front of the building's Victorian brick façade, which would have allowed goods to be lifted from street level on cranes and then pulled inside each of the floors. The stub of the large iron jib that would have supported the crane was still in place at the top of the building. When the place had been refurbished and turned into offices the architects had decided to use colourful red painted wood and glass constructions to fill the holes where these doors had been, giving the building a jaunty look. The entrance, at street level, was through some modern looking smoked glass swing doors. Inside beyond the reception desk the main parts of the building retained a gritty industrial edge with naked brickwork walls and the original Victorian pillars and ironwork, although all the bricks had been sandblasted and then glazed and the ironwork painted a contrasting green colour. The original wooden floors had also been given the full treatment, sanded, waxed and polished to a high gloss before being sealed. For Billy, the best part of the whole project, the jewel in the architect's crown, was at the rear of the building. Here they had decided to remove the entire back wall of the property and replaced it with glass. This glazing was like a huge greenhouse that stretched from the cellar up to the third floor, allowing the natural light to flood into each of the studios on the three levels and into the well of the basement.

Billy's first stop was at the reception desk where Suzette, the self-styled 'Company Secretary' had her domain. She was not the Company Secretary in any legal or directorial capacity, but was in fact, the only person employed in a secretarial role by the company. Her argument was that this made her the 'Company Secretary' and given her overpowering and bombastic nature, no one in their right mind ever argued with her. She was a self-styled rock chick and loved to regale the younger and more impressionable members of staff with stories of her life as a teenager growing up as part of the London 'music scene'. If you ever got her started, then her tales of rubbing shoulders with the likes of the Rolling Stones and Led Zeppelin, in the late-night drinking clubs around Soho, would last for hours. All these stories perpetuated the myth of Suzette, the super groupie. She dressed the part, from the back-combed mane of unruly blond hair, heavy kohled eye makeup, and with an abundance of black leather, satin and lace that probably had once looked alluring, but now struggled to contain her voluminous frame, right down to the silver toe caps on her patent leather stiletto ankle boots. She was larger than life and she towered over Billy. However, he knew that everything from her name to her foreboding image, was a front.

One evening in the pub Suzette had asked Billy to pass her the packet of cigarettes from her cavernous black handbag. Billy had delved inside looking for her fags and instead had found her pocket book, lying on the top, open and with her driving licence visible. The self-styled Suzette was actually Susan Chambers from Battersea. Billy had said nothing at the time and merely pushed the pocket book to one side, located the cigarettes and tossed them across the table. Billy had kept this little gem of information to himself, never mentioned it to a soul, not even Suzette herself. These days, however, she seemed to be in a perpetual state of mourning, as one after another, of the drug addled old rockers were shuffling off this mortal coil. Billy wondered whether she had a hotline to the obituaries desk at the NME or Melody Maker, because she was forever sporting a dark armband and solemn demeanour, following the untimely death of yet another 'leading light' of the music scene, most of whom, Billy had never heard of. This morning was no different, as Suzette had this characteristic air, of a recent bereavement about her. She looked up as Billy pushed his way in through the glass doors. Billy waited patiently to discover who the latest rock and roll casualty was and what small, but vital contribution they had made to the history of rock music. He was about to be disappointed. No one had died.

"Billy, where the hell have you been? Nigel has been raging around the place looking for you since eight-thirty this morning."

"Why?"

Billy was now standing right in front of the reception desk with a highly puzzled look on his face as it was not good that there was a potential problem with one of the managing partners. Billy did his utmost to keep those two happy.

"He knew exactly where I was. He left a message on my answerphone yesterday asking me to drop by The Design Company this morning and pick up a portfolio. When I got there the work wasn't finished, so I have just high tailed it all the way back here in a cab."

"We got a call about six last night, saying that the stuff wasn't finished. Nigel took your number home and was going to call you last night to tell you to forget the visit."

"He didn't call."

"Didn't he? That's not like him to forget something like that."

"He didn't call me."

Billy was adamant, although now there were little doubts beginning to creep in. He cast his mind back to the previous evening, the part that he did remember and the messages on his answerphone particularly the one's from Mel about her mother, and Greta and Tracey about the forgotten meeting. Could Finch have called him last night? Bill was sure he would have remembered, written something down, or at the very least removed the Post It from the front door.

"I had better go and speak to him. Where is he?"

Suzette looked down at the huge diary open on the desk in front of her.

"He's in a meeting right now, new clients. He should be free by eleven-thirty."

"Okay, well I will wait until then."

"A bit of friendly advice. Make yourself look busy until then."

Billy nodded his head and then went on into the heart of the studio area nodding greetings to the designers who bothered to look up from their work, hung up his coat and made a beeline for the kitchen to make a cup of coffee. Billy took Suzette's advice and busied himself around the office for the rest of the morning, whilst waiting for his summons to see the big man himself. There was always plenty for him to do, so it was no real effort to lose himself in the work. The reference library, which was situated in the basement well, at the rear of the building, was always in need of attention. As well as the copious bookshelves, stuffed with everything from coffee table books to magazines and pamphlets, there was a large work table, surrounded on all four sides by wooden benches. The table was used by the staff as a canteen table at lunchtimes and as a gathering place for meetings, when the numbers exceeded those that could be accommodated in the main meeting rooms on the upper floors. This table was always covered with abandoned reading materials. The books and magazines were never returned to the shelves after the designers had finished with them, but were instead left on the table, where they had been used, usually still open at the last page that had been read. The books were useful for all things from inspiration to authenticity. For example, if a designer was designing packaging for a product with an Indian theme, then there were books of Indian art and architecture, picture books of the sub-continent or travel brochures and magazines. All of these could be useful for getting authentic colours and shapes for the artists and designers to work with. The books and magazines all had places on the library shelves, but getting a designer to put a book back after use was rather like getting a drunk boyfriend to lower the seat after taking a pee, a fantasy.

With over twenty designers all working on different projects at the same time, the place soon descended into chaos, unless Billy stepped in a couple of times a day and put everything away. It was unfortunate, but this tidiness could, from time to time be the cause of some conflict. If he tidied a book away while a designer had merely left it to go to lunch or take a phone call or attend a meeting, then they might, if they returned to find said book missing, throw a hissy fit. In those cases, Billy relied on his memory to re-locate the book concerned and return it to the table as quickly and with as little fuss as possible. He had also got into the habit of trying to memorise the page numbers of the books, before he closed them, as he knew this would get extra credit, if he could not only return the missing book to the table, but also at the page it had been open at, before it had been abandoned. It was a good mental exercise. Anything for a quiet life.

Billy had to admit that for the most part, he enjoyed his work at Finch and McEwan. It was certainly a dramatic departure from the jobs he had done in the past. He had never seen himself working in an office environment. From leaving school up until now, he had found only warehouse or factory work. Places where you turned up and clocked in, donned a uniform and did largely the same job or function for eight hours, until you clocked off again. Repetitive, mundane, soul-destroying were all words Billy could have used to describe his English working life up until now. Returning from Israel, from his time on the kibbutz, had given him the ability to break that mould. Jobs like lifeguard and film actor certainly made his resume stand out among the others and it had been these two roles that Nigel Finch had been most keen to hear about when Billy had arrived for the interview, that and his experiences in Israel. The arse end of his CV, the three years of factory jobs before he left England were totally ignored, not even mentioned in passing. Israel, the kibbutz and the fact that Billy had experienced both, seemed to give him kudos and he was often asked to recount stories about his time there. Billy had tried to place some kind of filter on his accounts, but inevitably the truth of some events had come out, usually when he was in the pub, late at night and after a few drinks had been consumed.

Maybe this was not the wisest of moves, because some of the extreme behaviour, whilst not always directly attributed to Billy, didn't portray the Volunteer community in the best of lights. But when the beer and wine were flowing the stories seemed to match the mood and Billy had a wealth of those kind of stories to tell. That everyone was not in the same state of inebriation as Billy on those occasions, had never really occurred to him or that anyone would remember the stories the next day hadn't either. What pole-axed Billy was that anyone would use those stories to question his ability to do the job he was employed to do, at Finch and McEwan, but that is exactly what happened.

When he was finally asked to go and see Nigel Finch in his office he found a very different reception waiting for him from the one he normally received from his boss. He maybe should have guessed that something was wrong when Suzette came and found him and told him that Nigel was waiting for him in his office on the third floor. To be invited into the inner-sanctum was not something that often happened to Billy. Normally if Finch was looking for him or wanted to ask him to do something then he came and found him. He never asked Billy into his office. The door was closed when Billy arrived, so Billy tapped on the glass. Finch, who was sat behind his massive desk looked up and waved for Billy to enter.

"Close the door behind you, would you."

Billy complied and then turned to face Finch.

"Take a seat Billy."

Finch waved in the direction of the two visitors chairs that sat facing him across the expansive desk. The desktop itself was devoid of clutter. There was a blotter made of black leather that looked to contain some kind of calendar and a single Mont Blanc pen resting on a carved ebony wood stand. There was no phone, no other items or clutter on the desk except for a plain brown folder which was open. Billy couldn't read what was written on the papers it contained and Finch flicked it closed as Billy sat down. The desktop matched and emphasised what Billy had come to expect from Nigel Finch. He was a neat and precise individual. Of the two Partners at the company, Nigel Finch was the business brain and Simon McEwan the artistic. They were two complementary halves of a whole person. Finch, the hardnosed negotiator, while McEwan was the dreaming artist. It was a partnership that functioned well and had obviously made the two men extremely wealthy. Finch, being the negotiator and the point man, the public face of the company was always flawlessly turned out. He favoured expensive tailored suits in darker fabrics, paired with plain, but colourful shirts, riotously loud multi-coloured ties and handmade Italian loafers. His partner was never comfortable in formal attire and looked decidedly uncomfortable, when situations demanded he don a suit and tie. He favoured jeans, denim shirts and desert boots and on the warmer summer days, could even turn up in a Hawaiian shirt and board shorts with flip-flops hanging off his feet. A look that Billy had never seen Finch sporting, ever.

Even at the most recent summer party, where on a glorious sunny day the staff had assembled at McEwan's house on the banks of the River Thames in Henley, Finch had been meticulously dressed. Whilst most of the staff had opted for shorts or summer dresses, Finch had donned a light-weight linen suit and topped the whole outfit off with a sparklingly white Panama hat. Billy had been expecting a pith helmet, but it seemed that Finch felt the Panama would be more appropriate.

While Billy got settled Finch took a moment to fiddle with the folder, lining it up so that it sat straight on the dark leather blotter. He placed his hands, clasped together, on top of the plain cover before starting to speak.

"Billy I am not sure where to start. I suppose I should ask you where you were this morning?"

Billy looked up at Finch with confusion written all over his face.

"You left a message on my answerphone yesterday asking me to pick up a portfolio from The Design Company this morning."

"That's correct, but I also then called you last night and cancelled that request as we had been told that the portfolio wasn't going to be ready until the following day now."

"Did you leave another message? I must have missed it." Billy feigned innocence.

It was Finch's turn to look puzzled.

"Billy, I spoke to you, and admittedly you did sound a little tired and confused, but you assured me you would be here first thing this morning and then you roll in here about eleven thirty, still hungover and stinking of booze, and it's not the first time."

Finch opened the manila folder and began to study the papers it contained. He was reading down a list, following it with his finger. Billy didn't really have to think too hard to realise what it contained. It was most likely a list of every occasion he had arrived late for work, or turned up the worse for wear.

Billy wondered which one of his colleagues had been ratting him out to the boss. Finch had not come close enough to him all morning to have gathered that sort of information today, so someone had dropped him in it. This upset Billy and he felt the first flush of rage blossom deep in his chest. He had always thought that he was generally well liked around the place, but obviously someone was not a big fan. He didn't immediately suspect Suzette of treachery, so he began to work through the list of other people he had interacted with since arriving at work. It was not a very long list and took only a second to process. In that time though, Finch had moved on to other things. Billy tuned back in to what was being said, just in time to catch the next reprimand.

Apparently, the management team were not happy that Billy had collected the cash for this morning's cab fare from petty cash. Billy wondered why a man like Finch, who must be taking home a six-figure salary was worrying over a paltry twenty quid. He had probably got a wad of crisp new fifties in his wallet and now he was expecting Billy to hand back the two grimy tenners he had picked up from Suzette earlier. He looked up and saw that Finch had his hand extended over the desk, palm pointing upwards. As he watched the hand made a beckoning motion. The message was very clear to even the stupidest person and Billy was no fool. Billy pulled his wallet out of his back pocket and in the process, the postcard from Mike fell on the floor. What happened next had obviously been brewing for a while in Billy's subconscious. He first picked up the card and slid it back in his pocket before he fanned open his wallet and slid out the two ten-pound notes. It was all that he had in his wallet and he had already earmarked them as funds for restocking his liquor supply that evening. Now he would have to make a detour via a cash machine. He stood up closing the distance between him and Finch's outstretched hand. He didn't place the notes there, instead he slammed them dramatically on the desk just to one side, yelling out.

"You know what, you can stick your fucking job where the sun don't shine. I quit."

Billy turned on his heels and bolted for the door. Behind him he heard a sharp intake of breath from the other side of the desk. No one had probably spoken to Nigel Finch in that tone of voice for a long time and it certainly left its mark. Billy heard the strangled coughing start up and he turned back briefly, simply to ensure that the guy wasn't having a heart attack. He had certainly turned a strange shade of red and was struggling for breath or to find his tongue. Billy wasn't sure which. But as he didn't look like he was about to keel over and die, Billy left him and slammed through the door, leaving Finch still sat behind his desk doing a very good impression of a beached cod.

Raised voices, were not something that happened very often on the premises of Finch and McEwan, so they attracted attention and Billy felt every single pair of eyes burning through him as he strode down the central staircase to the ground floor. At the bottom standing between him and the exit was a very worried looking Suzette. She raised her arms to slow Billy's progress.

"What just happened up there?"

"I quit,"

Billy's voice was flat and emotionless.

"I have had enough."

"Billy, are you sure this is the right decision. It was only twenty quid."

So Finch had clearly spoken to Suzette about the pay out before summoning Billy to his office. That's was only to be expected as she was the one who controlled the petty cash tin.

"It's not the money, it's everything. I guess I am just not cut out for this kind of work."

Whether it was the finality in Billy's tone or the determined look on his face, one or the other convinced Suzette that Billy had made up his mind. She lowered her arms and let him pass. Billy pushed through the front door and out onto the street. He stood for a moment outside the building trying to decide which way to go, left or right? One way was to home and the solitude of his flat. Taking that route would only end up with him locking himself away and climbing, alone, down into the neck of a scotch bottle. He sensed that he would find no real answers there. The other direction was the West End, the bright lights and the hordes of people thronging the pavements. He knew he could lose himself in those crowds, be alone, whilst surrounded by hundreds of people. He really needed to gather his thoughts and then afterwards, if he had calmed down sufficiently he would go and find someone to talk to, so he headed up west.


He had wandered around aimlessly for what seemed like hours, no real destination in mind, letting his feet dictate the direction and the speed. Hands thrust deep in his jeans pockets, shoulders hunched, his chin tucked in close to his chest, he must have cut a strange figure as he toured the streets of the West End and Soho. When he reached a junction, he made a random choice in which direction to turn. Pausing on a street corner trying to decide his next move he was distracted by a gentle tug at his sleeve. He turned to face the person. A young and slightly dirty face smiled at him through the layers of makeup.

"You looking for company?"

The voice was high pitched and slightly uncertain, as if the questioner didn't feel totally comfortable with asking the question. Billy looked again, noticing for the first time how young the girl was. She was probably underage, and although she had dressed the part, her frame was slight and waiflike. He cleared his throat to answer and then looked deep into her eyes. There he saw a different story. There he was confronting the gaze of someone old before their time. Billy suddenly didn't trust his voice so he simply shook his head and fled across the intersection, anxious to put as much distance as possible between him and the prostitute. After that, particularly in the side streets around Soho, he tried to avoid pausing on the street corners. Eventually he found himself in a dingy pub where the dark wood and oppressive flock wallpaper seemed to match his mood. He drank a couple of pints of lager sitting alone at one end of the bar. No one approached him, except the barman and he only ventured down to Billy's end of the bar when Billy held up his pint glass for a refill.

When the evening office crowds began to arrive and the place began to fill up with punters, he polished off the last of his pint and hit the streets again. A light rain had fallen recently, just enough to give the grimy pavements an artificial silver gleam. He headed for the underground station at Oxford Circus. He had intended to go down and catch a Central Line train all the way to Liverpool Street and then take a bus from there to his flat, but at the last moment he was overcome with a desire to talk to someone and although he had not arranged anything, instead of heading home he took the Victoria Line train heading in the opposite direction to Green Park and then changed to catch the train to Earls Court. From there he walked around the huge Exhibition Centre building and ended up turning into Mendora Road. The lights were on inside number 48 so he knew that someone was at home. He approached the heavy oak door and raised the brass knocker. It clanged down with a boom which would have been heard all over the house. He knew this for a fact as he had often been startled by the noise when he first started to visit Saskia. It was Saskia herself who opened the door. She was tying the belt on her dressing gown and concentrating on that, so she didn't look up until the robe was secure. The smile on her lips disappeared along with the colour in her cheeks as they turned a deathly white.

"Oh my god, Billy, what are you doing here?" she hissed at him.

"Can't a guy come and visit his girlfriend, surprise her with an invite out for dinner?"

"No Billy you can't just turn up unannounced."

Instead of hissing now Saskia was talking in a louder voice and looking over her shoulder. It was as if she was talking for the benefit of someone else in the house, as if she wanted that person to get involved, which was a little strange as Saskia lived alone.

"You can't come in." Saskia had raised her arm to block Billy's entry into the hallway.

"Why? Are you expecting company?" Billy was half joking but he was beginning to get a strange vibe back from his girlfriend. He had never seen her behave like this before. From where he was standing on the doorstep Billy could see down the hallway towards the kitchen at the rear of the house and about halfway up the stairs. He was therefore a little surprised when he saw a pair of decidedly hairy male looking legs descending the stairs. The bottom half of a second bathrobe appeared and then a male voice asked.

"Saskia, is there a problem? Are you chatting up the pizza delivery boy?"

Completing his descent, a man appeared behind Saskia. Billy had never seen him before, he was not one of Saskia's circle of friends. He took a moment to assess Billy before he spoke.

"You're not our regular pizza guy? Are you new?"

His arms encircled Saskia's waist and he nuzzled the back of her neck.

"I have just confirmed the hotel booking for the weekend."

Saskia's face dissolved in front of Billy's eyes. Her hand dropped from where it had been firmly placed on the doorframe. She took hold of the stranger's wrist and shoved it roughly aside. Twisting out of his embrace she fled down the hallway towards the kitchen. The stranger left alone at the doorway looked confused for a moment at Saskia's rejection, but aware that he was not alone he recovered his composure.

"How much do we owe you for the pizza?"

He looked at Billy, then looked around hoping to see a pizza box resting on the wall or on the adjacent dustbin. Realising there was no pizza anywhere in sight, realisation slowly dawned on him.

"You are not from the Pizza Parlour, are you?"

Billy looked up at the man and started to slowly shake his head. He felt a remarkable sense of calm sweep over him. He didn't blame this guy, had no desire to get violent or aggressive with him. He just folded his arms across his chest in a casual manner.

"No, I am Billy, Saskia's boyfriend, ex-boyfriend," he corrected himself.

"Oh gosh, this is a little embarrassing. You had better come in."

He stood to one side allowing Billy to enter the hallway. Once Billy was inside he closed the door behind him.

"You had better go through to the kitchen."

He raised his arm in a gesture before dropping it to his side.

"Sorry, you probably know the way."

Billy had already started down the hall towards the kitchen. He was grateful when the stranger instead of following him decided to disappear back up the stairs. Billy entered the kitchen. It was a long room with a dining alcove at the far end almost fully occupied by a large oak dining table and chairs. Saskia was sat at the table her head in her hands. She detected movement and looked up. Seeing Billy standing there she looked away. She couldn't meet his eye. She ran her fingers through her hair as she considered what to say.

"I", she stopped, unsure of what to say. Billy intervened.

"Don't say anything. I will just get my stuff and then I'll go. I guess it's over."
Saskia, not trusting her voice merely nodded her head. Billy heard feet on the stairs. Lover boy was back in the hall. Billy could see he had pulled on some jeans and a sweatshirt. He went into the lounge, so Billy took the opportunity to head upstairs and collect his things. He hadn't 'moved in' in any real sense of the word. He had a small overnight bag in one corner of the bedroom with a few items of clothes in it. He tossed the few remaining bits of extra clothing that he could find into the top and zipped the bag up. As he grabbed the handles his eyes were drawn to the bedside table. If he needed any further confirmation of what was really going on between Saskia and the stranger, then the ripped foil wrappers from two condoms lying on the night stand told the whole story.

Billy still felt strangely calm as he came down the stairs. He could hear voices conversing at low volume from the kitchen, but he didn't have anything more to say to anyone, so he let himself out the front door and bundled headlong into the pizza delivery boy. For a brief moment he considered paying for the pizza and then dumping it in a nearby bin, just to let the two people in the house behind him go hungry for a little while longer, but instead he just walked past the young lad. He fired back over his shoulder,

"You will need to knock, but they are expecting you,"
He settled the bag on his shoulder and strode off in the direction of the underground station and the long ride back across the city.

There was an emptiness inside him now that he couldn't fathom. A strange feeling which as he walked along the pavement into the oncoming dusk, he tried to identify. He was not sad. Not in the same way he had been when he had split from Mel. This time it was different, it was almost a relief, like somehow, he had cast off some chains that had been binding him. He didn't wait until he got home. He stopped at an off-licence on the corner of Lillie Road and Jervis Road. The owner or manager looked up as Billy walked in. Billy was not a frequent customer, but he had dropped enough money in the store over the last few months to warrant a smile and a nod from the guy behind the counter. He ordered a bottle of scotch and waited patiently as the bottle was placed in a carrier bag and handed to him along with his change. Outside the shop Billy unscrewed the cap and took a long slow swig from the bottle feeling the harsh spirit slowly burn its way down his throat and then the warmth spread out from his stomach. He took another mouthful, before replacing the cap and setting off again towards Earls Court.

Billy was more than half pissed when he finally got home. He had been taking swigs from the bottle all the way home garnering some strange looks from his fellow passengers on the tube. Some looked at him with disgust and promptly moved away to another part of the train carriage, whilst others looked on with sympathy, they too had probably had a bad day, just clearly not as bad as Billy's. He made an additional stop at his local wine merchants and collected another bottle of scotch. The first one was over half empty by the time he got back to his own neighbourhood. He placed the fresh bottle in the carrier with the half empty one and the two glass bottles made a satisfying clinking sound as he walked the last few yards to his flat.

Once inside, he noticed there was no blinking red light on the answer machine. At least he would not have to listen to some pathetic excuse from Saskia about why she had cheated on Billy and not been woman enough just to tell him it was over and she wanted to move on. That would have been the kinder thing to do. That's what he would have done. He dumped the bag containing his clothes on the floor in the hall and went to retrieve a glass from the kitchen. He then settled down on the sofa to get right royally pissed. He didn't have a job to get up for in the morning, so he didn't have any commitments and could just drink until he either threw up, which would be a waste, or passed out where he was. He poured a double measure into the glass and took a mouthful. So, it was over between him and Saskia Mazur. Eight months of his life wasted.

Meeting Saskia Mazur had been a mixed blessing for Billy. Their first encounter could have gone either way. Billy and Mel were finished as an item, but neither of them seemed to be able to exist without the other. So, it seemed natural that when Mel needed a plus one for an event, she had contacted Billy and asked him to be her date, although she went to great lengths to make it quite clear that this was not a usual date and that they were going together as 'just friends.' The Fresher's Ball was being held at the University where Mel had just enrolled on a Business Studies course. As a Fresher she was expected to turn up, although she had told Billy that there would be plenty of older students, like herself in attendance and it would not just be all the young first year students competing to get completely off their faces in the shortest possible time. Unfortunately, when Billy had met Mel outside the venue, he was already a little unsteady on his feet following an afternoon session in the pub, ostensibly watching the football. She had lost her temper with him and told him that he would fit right in with the more immature members of the first year, who had not learnt how to hold their drink. This had put the mockers on the whole evening and as Mel was in amongst her new colleagues from the Business School, who all seemed to be incredibly staid and boring, Billy had quickly lost interest and wandered off to find someone more interesting and exciting to talk to.

    The subsidised snakebites and purple nasties were definitely taking their toll on some of the patrons and Billy had to weave his way carefully through the staggering crowds to get to the bar. Once he had secured a spot, he decided to stay put, by hooking one of the bar stools over and hoisted himself up at the corner of the bar. His timing had luckily coincided with the arrival of the headline act on stage in the main hall. The bar emptied in an instant leaving behind just a few drunk stragglers and a slightly shell-shocked bar staff who began the laborious process of cleaning up and girding their loins for the next onslaught that would happen when the band had finished in about forty-five minutes. Billy was handed a plastic pint skiff of cloudy looking lager which he dubiously began to sip.

"Band not your thing?" A voice asked from behind him.

Billy swivelled on his stool to greet his interrogator.

"Mark Sampson, third year Middle Eastern Studies. You?"

Billy shook the offered hand.

"Billy Randell, plus one of First Year Business Studies student."

"So, you aren't a student here?"

"No, not me. I work for a living."

Billy smiled. His comment was not designed to be antagonistic, but he was worried it might be taken the wrong way in a place like this. Mark didn't seem to take offence, he simply hooked another bar stool with his leg and then plonked himself down next to Billy. He ordered a lager for himself and the two started to talk. Billy was asking Mark about his course and when Mark mentioned he was studying Arabic and Hebrew, Billy couldn't resist testing the newcomer's knowledge. Billy rattled off a couple of sentences in Hebrew and was surprised when Mark held up his hands and said in very halting and horribly accented Hebrew that he couldn't really speak a word of the language. He continued, reverting immediately to English,

"We mostly study the literature and art of the Middle East. The religion and the history as well. We don't have much to do with the modern languages. You're good though."

Mark, for his part, was really surprised to discover someone in the bar, whose knowledge and command of the Hebrew language was on a par with or exceeded anyone on the department's teaching staff.

"Where did you learn Hebrew? You don't look Jewish."

"Spent a while in Israel recently."

"Kibbutz?"

"Yeah."

"Miss it?"

"More than you can imagine."

This was the first time, since he had returned from Israel, that anyone had asked him this probing question and his answer was almost a reflex. He had not really considered his feelings about his old life, up until that point. Certainly he often spoke with fondness about his time in Israel and he was always happiest when he was relating stories about his exploits and those of others. But after four months back in the country, he had not considered whether or not he actually missed the kibbutz life in any way, shape, or form. Mark's next question, a natural progression in the interrogation, left Billy really flustered!

"Want to go back?"

Billy had to swallow hard to cover the sudden flood of emotion he felt at that question. He had been home in England only a short time, maybe it was just long enough for the memories of bad times to fade and lose their way among the overwhelming number of good memories. He hadn't considered going back. Too much of his focus had been on getting established in his new life, finding a job, a place to live and adjusting back to life in London. Pressed now, he had to dig deep to search his feelings and if he was honest with himself there was really only one answer.

"Yes, I would love to."

Mark was interested in Billy's experiences and the two sat together deep in conversation until the returning hoards signalled that the headline band had finished their set. The return of the great unwashed, hot and sweaty from their recent musical exertions made their spot at the bar almost untenable and the escalating volume made meaningful conversation almost impossible. Billy looked around to see if Mel and her crowd had arrived back in the bar, but there was no sign of any of them. He asked his new friend,

"Is there another bar here?"

"Yeah, the Johnson Bar is up on the next level, why?"

"Just wondering what might have happened to my 'friend' and her crowd?"

"Ah, the first-year students. They might have gone up there or they could be down in the disco. Why? Do you want to find them?"

"Might be a good idea to check in, just to let her know I am still alive."

"You and your plus one, are you two an item?"

"Were. In the past now."

Mark downed the rest of his pint in one long swallow.

"Well onwards and upwards, literally".

He grinned at his own lame joke and pointed up.

"We might as well start upstairs."

Out in the corridor, there was no established flow. Just a huge mass of people either going up or down a spiral staircase. People were just clambering up and down, so you had to make your way up the stairs, occasionally stopping, for people coming down, who were bobbing to the left or right, as they weaved their way through. At one point the crowd stopped completely. Now in front of Billy were a couple of girls, who seemed to be together. The one directly in front, whose rump was at Billy's eye level, was wearing a particularly garish pair of gold and black silk trousers with a pattern of Egyptian hieroglyphs all over them. Billy grabbed Mark's arm and pointed at the girl's backside.

"Do you know what that says?"

Mark shook his head.

"Wide Load."

Mark snorted at Billy's teenage gag, An opening presented itself on the other side of the staircase and Billy ducked under the bannister. Mark followed and the two continued on up the staircase. At the top they joined the throng funnelling through a single door into the bar.

"So you don't speak Hebrew and you don't read hieroglyphs? What are they teaching you youngsters these days?"

Billy folded his arms and looked questioningly down his nose at Mark.

"I know a lot about Islamic art."

Mark added defensively while grinning broadly. Billy's eyes went skywards.

"Useful stuff then."

He grinned at Mark as the movement of the crowd dragged them both forward into the bar area. Mel and her course mates were, in fact, in the Johnson Bar, so Billy introduced Mark to them and then went to the bar to buy their drinks. He hopefully waved a tenner in the air trying to attract the bar staff and eventually one of them noticed him and came over to serve him. He ordered two pints of lager and watched and waited as the drinks were poured. He handed over the note and waited for his change. In the crush and general melee, with people pushing and shoving their way through the crowd to the bar, Billy didn't realise that someone had been tapping him on the shoulder until he collected his change, pocketed it, picked up the two drinks and then turned around coming face to face with the young lady in the Egyptian trousers. It took him a moment to recognise her but she had Billy banged to rights.

"Wide Load?"

Standing there with her arms folded across her chest she looked like she was about to do Billy a physical injury and as he was standing there, clutching two full pints of lager, he would be unable to defend himself.

"You don't strike me as an Ancient Languages expert."

Billy grinned sheepishly. That she had not slapped him hard in the face straight away gave him some small shred of hope that he might survive this encounter unharmed.

"I'm not."

Billy was trying to look contrite. The young lady standing in front of him was actually quite stunning to look at. She had dark brown hair, cut in waves and sharp sensual features, huge dark brown eyes that right now Billy was pleased to say didn't show the slightest shred of anger. In fact if anything they were showing the faintest sign of amusement.

"But I did spend some time in Egypt, Cairo, The Valley of the Kings."

Billy was hoping to change the subject.

"Oh really?"

The girl's voice dripped with sarcasm.

"So, you are a bit of an expert? Well maybe you can help me out. Tell me what this says?"

With that she unfolded her arms and pulled open her jacket exposing her top underneath. She had continued the Egyptian theme in her other garment. Under the jacket she was wearing a rather tight-fitting top in black with several hieroglyphs printed, also in gold. Billy put his head on one side and stared at the woman's breasts. It was not very often in life that women opened their jackets for Billy and invited him to stare at their chests, so in the spirit of scholarship he was prepared to give the task his full attention. Satisfied that he had spent enough time staring he looked up at the girls face again. She was waiting patiently a faint smile was playing at the corners of her mouth. Her look was easy to read.

"Have you quite finished?"

Billy tried to adopt the look of a learned man. One who was about to deliver a pearl of life changing wisdom, as the jacket was wrapped tight around the young ladies torso, her arms firmly folded across her chest in an attempt to restore and maintain her modesty.

"I have seen that particular inscription, it's called a cartouche, by the way, on several temples and tombs in the Valley of the Kings."

Billy was in full on bullshit mode now, making it up as he went along.

"It says in some form or another, 'Beyond lies the garden of Paradise, heavenly treasures await he who ventures inside'".

"Really?"

The young lady's face had assumed a highly sceptical look.

"All that in five characters? Are you sure you're not making it up?"

"Pretty sure. But I might need to have another look to just confirm my translation."

Billy knew he was pushing his luck now, but despite delivering one of his broadest of winning smiles, her arms stayed firmly folded over her chest and the jacket remained closed. Without uttering another word she spun on her heels and disappeared back into the crowd. Billy wasn't sure if he had just blown his chances or had a lucky escape. He went over to where Mark was sitting with Mel and the others and handed over his drink.

He looked around the room searching for hieroglyph girl, but after their exchange at the bar she was now nowhere to be seen. He took an empty seat between Mark and Mel but he was not interested in their conversation. His encounter at the bar had left him distracted. He had felt something during the exchange. At first it had been a slight case of fear. Hieroglyph girl, he didn't even know her name, had looked like she was about to punch his lights out, but she hadn't. Instead she had all but flashed her breasts at him, her top had been silk or some other insubstantial material. Finally, she had turned on her heels and left. No retribution, but no encouragement either. This had left Billy hanging and he didn't like hanging. So, his eyes continued to rove the crowd in the bar looking for her.

His distraction and the fact that he was ignoring his companions on both sides merely forced them to turn to other people for conversation. Mark was in a deep conversation with another of the female first year students. She, in turn, was evidently captivated by Mark and the fact that he was a third-year probably had something to do with that. Billy looked at the two of them. Mark was indeed a handsome chap and his young friend was hanging on his every word.

Mel, on his other side, looked to be in a deep and rather serious discussion with a bespectacled, and rather intense looking chap. He was very animated when he spoke and before he made a response he would take a moment to push his glasses back up his nose. Billy had known Mel a long time and it was clear that she liked this guy. Her body language was open and she was being very tactile, her hands were forever reaching out to touch him, on his arm or his knee. Billy was not the jealous sort. He had learnt his lesson. He knew all too well where uncontrolled jealousy could lead you. His whole life had been turned upside down by one stupid moment of jealous rage. Ultimately it had been in the aftermath of that incident that he and Mel had first met on the beach in Eilat. He took a moment to focus on those days. They were uncertain times, those first few days among the vagrants and vagabonds of Eilat's underclass, but ultimately everything had worked out and he had fond memories and had made some lasting friendships. He wondered what had happened to some of those faces in the past year since the end of filming, where were they now? What were they doing?

Billy was not a great letter writer and he was sure that none of them would even think to put pen to paper. They had other more important things to spend their time and money on, like staying alive. Billy knew that if he wanted to find out what was going on with those people he would have to return and visit them in person. He felt sure that many of them would still be there in the city. He was still distracted by his memories when he realised there was someone standing over him. He looked up and saw the same hieroglyph covered legs. He carried on tracking upwards towards the body, the arms were still firmly folded over the closed jacket, but when he got there the face was smiling down at him.

"Do you want to buy a lady a drink?"

Billy paused for a minute considering his next move. Did he play the fool and make a big show of looking around the bar before delivering one of his witty lines like, 'Find me a lady and I will buy her a drink.' This was a line that worked about fifty percent of the time. It was the other fifty percent that he was worried about now so instead he stood up and smiled back.

"Of course, what would you like?"

"I will have a vodka and tonic, no ice."

Billy walked over to the bar and took a moment to finish his own drink before ordering. When it was his turn he ordered the drinks and turned around. Hieroglyph girl hadn't moved a muscle, but at the same time she was making no move to introduce herself to any of the people Billy had been sitting with. Standing there she looked vulnerable and alone, like a little girl lost. Billy pocketed his change and picked up the drinks. He handed the smaller glass over and then took a sip from his pint. Hieroglyph girl raised her glass to her lips and took a small sip. She smiled and mouthed the words,

"Thank you."

The arrival of a newcomer had provoked a reaction from Mel. Up until that point she had been engrossed in conversation with her new friend and had been studiously ignoring Billy for most of the evening. It was as if she was punishing him for arriving half-cut. Billy, after an evening drinking under-strength gassy lager was now heading back to sobriety at a rapid rate of knots and the presence of hieroglyph girl was an added incentive to keep his wits about him. That Billy seemed to be talking to an unknown stranger meant that Mel was now looking up and over at Billy every few moments.

Billy wondered for a moment what had triggered this rather serious response. He didn't think it was petty jealousy, Mel had made it clear that things were well and truly over for them. He made a mental note to ask her about it another time. For now, he focused his attention on the newcomer. His first task was to make introductions and find out more about her. He realised as he was about to introduce her that he didn't even know her name so he gave her a chance to introduce herself. Once the introductions were out of the way, he found a space for Saskia to sit down and the two began the slow process of getting to know one another. Time flew by and Billy suddenly realised that the bar was emptying out and that Mel was hovering close by, reluctant to break into the conversation. He looked up at her.

"We are all going on to a club in Shoreditch High Street, are you coming with us?"

Billy looked over at Saskia who shook her head slightly.

"No thanks Mel. You go on and have fun. I will call you next week."

Mel, strangely, seemed slightly peeved that Billy had not accepted her offer. But she was on her feet and standing with her coat on and her other friends were already on their way towards the exit. She sniffed once, peevishly, turned on her heels, and flounced off.

"What's the story with you two?" Saskia asked.

"We used to be an item, in another time and another place, but it has been over now for months."

"The place and time may have changed, but I will hazard a guess that she's still in love with you."

Billy didn't respond straight away. There was a certain delicious irony that almost the first conversation he had had with Mel on the day they met had followed similar lines. Back then he had been describing the behaviour of another woman and Mel had reached the same conclusion. He never managed to prove her right or wrong in that case but he had learnt to accept that maybe women had a sixth sense when it came to other women, something that was hidden for blokes.

"That might be the case," Billy said guardedly, "But to tell you the truth it would never have worked out for us. I think her parents have loftier ambitions for her. They want to see her married off to a lawyer or a doctor, someone from the professional classes."

He tried not to sneer as he used the word 'Doctor' and 'Lawyer' but it was hard to keep the note of disapproval out of his voice. The bar staff were making it very clear now that it was time to vacate the premises and were almost aggressively challenging people to finish up their drinks and leave the bar. Billy finished off the last of his pint and placed the empty glass on an adjacent table. Saskia stood up and did the same with her glass. Billy noticed it was still nearly half full. He was tempted to reach over and finish it, but he stayed his hand.

"So, what happened to the people you came with?"

"I told them to go home earlier. All these young freshers, it wasn't really their scene. "

That statement intrigued Billy. Why would Saskia have tried to dismiss her friends? Had she made plans, maybe involving him? Or was it simply that her friends had really not been interested in hanging around with younger students. He thought about this as they made their way down to street level. A quick glance at his watch told Billy that he had missed the last train home, so it would be the night bus or a cab for him. He wondered how far Saskia had to go to get home.

"We've missed the last tube," she said as if she had read Billy's mind. "Is there a mini-cab office around here?"

"I don't honestly know, this is not my stomping ground."

"Well go back inside and ask one of the staff, would you, please?"

Billy turned around and pushed open the door of the venue and walked inside. The place was largely deserted but there was a couple of guys hanging around, one was pushing a mountain of rubbish in front of a broom. Billy figured he had to be staff, so he asked him and was given directions to a mini-cab office about five minutes walk away. He went back outside and looked around for Saskia. She was nowhere to be seen. He spun around twice searching among the few people who were still hanging around outside the venue, either trying to decide how they were going to get home or trying to decide where they were going to go next to continue the party.

Billy felt strangely disappointed that she had chosen to make a run for it instead of making some excuse and letting him down gently. Well at least he knew the way back to Old Street from his current location and from there he could catch a Night Bus home. He still had a half bottle of scotch back at the flat, so he could have a little nightcap, listen to some music and just chill out. He turned his jacket collar up against the cold and thrust his hands in his jeans pockets and started to trudge off.

"Billy Randell, where do you think you're off to?"

Billy spun around. Detaching herself from the darker shadows by the wall Saskia emerged into the pool of light cast by one of the building's exterior lights. She had been leaning on the wall in the shadows.

"I thought you were the one that had done a runner."

"Now why would I do a thing like that?"

"Dunno."

"Did you find a cab office?"
"Yeah there's one just around the corner."
"Lead on."
Saskia moved closer and looped her arm through Billy's and they then headed off together.

The cab office was deserted, except for two drivers standing outside talking quietly and smoking cigarettes. Inside the office the controller was sat behind a bulletproof glass screen. In one corner a black and white TV was showing some late-night film with the volume turned down. Somewhere in the back a radio was tuned to some an easy-listening music show. The controller was in the middle of eating a sandwich and reading a newspaper, so the pair had to wait until he had emptied his mouth before he turned his attention to them. His accent was foreign, possibly Turkish or Syrian.

"Where you go?"

Billy looked at Saskia. Saskia looked at Billy. Neither of them said a word. The silence went on longer than was comfortable. Billy eventually decided it was silly that the three of them were all stuck there in silence.

"Sorry mate," he said to the controller. "Give us a minute, please?"

The controller waved his hand and went back to the second half of his sandwich and his newspaper.

"It might help if I knew whereabouts you lived?"

"Fulham." Saskia said.

"Fulham?" quizzed Billy.

"Yeah Fulham, what's wrong with Fulham?"

"There is nothing wrong with Fulham apart from the fact it's on the other side of London."

"OK clever clogs, where d' you live then?"

"Hackney."

"That's almost as far in the other direction."

Whilst that wasn't strictly true and a quick look at a map would have proved Saskia wrong, Billy was not in possession of a map of any description. He looked around the cab office on the off chance they had one hanging on a wall, but apart from some faded and curled tourism posters for Cyprus, the walls of the cab office were bare of decoration, unless you counted nicotine stained, plain white wallpaper that was peeling away from the walls in certain places as decoration. Unable to prove his point and really unwilling to start an argument which he knew would dampen if not ruin the mood of the night, Billy decided to concede the point and hold his tongue. He, however wanted to test his prospects so he offered a compromise.

"Well, then it's lucky there are two cabs waiting outside. Because I guess sharing a cab is out of the question. A round trip is going to take most of the night."

He was right a trip where they shared a cab, drove to one address first then on to the other would be time consuming and also extremely expensive. Billy could probably afford it, with a quick stop at a cashpoint on the way back, but he was reluctant to waste that sort of money, no matter how sweet and sexy Saskia looked. He also assumed that Saskia, as a student, even one who lived in the more upmarket, London Borough of Hammersmith and Fulham, would not want to waste a large chunk of her student grant paying for a cab ride.

Billy had been raised by his mother and although his early life had been beset by poverty, his mum had always strived to hammer in to him some core values and one of those was that you should never abandon a woman in need, in the middle of the night, not even if she lived on the other side of the city. Billy's knowledge of West London was patchy but he felt sure that like the rest of London there must be some form of Night Bus service that he could catch and that would bring him back to the centre of the city, to Trafalgar Square and from there he could catch his normal night bus service up to Hackney. It would mean that he would be travelling for the next couple of hours and it might be a struggle to stay awake, but at least he knew that the bus out to Hackney terminated quite close to his flat, so if he did fall asleep then the driver would wake him outside the bus garage and he could walk home from there.

So, he resolved that he would at least offer to accompany Saskia home to Fulham. What happened after that, if he was invited in for coffee, offered a sofa for the night or something else then he would accept. In the event that nothing other than a taxi ride across the city was on offer then he would wish her goodnight and beat a retreat to the nearest Night Bus stop and make his way back across the city. At least his conscience would be clear and he would know she had got home safely. He was just about to propose this solution when Saskia spoke up.

"Do you have a toothbrush I can borrow? And a T-shirt to sleep in?"

Billy paused. He couldn't remember if he had any spare toothbrushes at the flat, but he certainly had plenty of large t-shirts.

"Yes, to the second, not sure about the toothbrush though. We can always use some boiling water to sterilize mine if you are worried about germs."

Although Billy didn't know it at the time this attention to oral hygiene was what swung it for the young doctor. Billy was still under the impression that Saskia was a student at the University. He only discovered on the ride home in the taxi that she was, in fact, a Junior Doctor at a hospital in West London, which explained the address on the other side of the city. Billy whispered a silent prayer that he had not been too damning in his comments about doctors and lawyers, earlier on. But along with that particular revelation, also came the information that Saskia was a little bit older than Billy, although she didn't look it. She had completed her university degree and her two-year foundation course and was settling down to do her specialist training in paediatrics.

"Does that make me your toy-boy?" said Billy with a cheeky grin.

"Careful sunshine," growled Saskia in the dark of the cab.

Boy Toy or Toy Boy it made little difference to Billy. They made love most of the night and then again in the morning before she was gone. Billy then didn't see her for a whole week. They talked on the phone most days, but Saskia was back at work in the hospital and Billy had his job at Finch and McEwan to focus on. There was a different intensity to their relationship, which was something new for Billy. He had just spent most of the last two years together with Mel and they had been living in each other's pockets, literally, for most of that time. To now be in a 'relationship' where he did not wake up next to his girlfriend everyday was strange, but Billy also found it liberating. It was like being single without actually being single. He found that he could flirt as much as he liked without having to worry about there being someone standing behind him watching his every move and getting upset by his actions. This was the upside, but there was also a downside. It was caused largely by Billy himself. Every time he smiled at a stranger in the street and received a smile in return he felt a pang of jealousy. What if there was a stranger smiling at Saskia and she was smiling back at him? He was eventually able to reason with himself that in the same way that his smiling never led to anything there was no reason to believe that Saskia would be the same. He had never once considered being unfaithful to Saskia, no matter how interesting another woman had been or how interested she had been in him and he expected Saskia would be the same. She had never given him reason to doubt her fidelity, so maybe that was why the events of earlier in the day had come as such a shock.

## Chapter Three

Billy was still numb from the shock of discovering Saskia's infidelity when he finally came to the next morning still sprawled across his sofa, fully clothed and stinking of whisky. At some point the previous evening he had passed out and from the slight damp patch on his t-shirt and the pervading smell of whisky, he had most likely spilt the remnants of his last glass all down his shirt front. The glass, empty now and undamaged was lying beside him on the sofa. Billy lifted his arm up in front of his face and tried to read the dial of his watch. The light was already streaming in through the lounge window, so the sun was up, but all that meant was that it was sometime after 6 a.m.

Slowly and with extreme effort and some painful concentration the watch face coalesced into a recognisable and readable form as his brain processed what the dial was showing him. It was a bit reminiscent of his childhood sat in front of the television. The big hand is on the six and the small hand is on the ten, which means it is?

Shit! It was ten thirty and he was late for work. He sprang to his feet and yet again regretted his rash action. His whisky consumption the previous night had far outstripped that of any recent evening, so the hangover was equally severe. Standing up so impetuously had caused a reaction that caused him to teeter on the brink of a blackout. He managed to maintain only the most fragile hold on consciousness as the nausea washed over him. He reached out for the surround of the fireplace and used the top of the mantelpiece ledge to steady himself. As the coolness of the tiles slowly penetrated his palm he began to think rationally again. He was not late for work. He couldn't be late for work as he had quit the previous day. He collapsed backward onto the sofa narrowly missing injuring himself on the empty whisky glass. He picked the glass up and then automatically leaned forward and refilled it from the half empty bottle that was sat on the coffee table.

He was probably still drunk from the previous bout of drinking, but he really didn't want to suffer a hangover, so in his confused mind he thought he might as well stay drunk. He polished off the contents of the glass and then reached for the bottle a second time and poured himself another generous measure. He opened his cigarette packet, there were two left, so he extracted one, lit it and then sat back deep into the sofa inhaling tobacco smoke and swirling the scotch around his tongue.

Out in the hallway, the phone began to ring. Billy ignored it as he had decided that the machine was there to answer his calls, which was why he had the volume turned down to zero. If it was someone or something important, they could leave a message. He didn't want to face anyone at the moment. He felt no desire to talk to anyone today. The machine cut in and answered the call. As the tape whirred away Billy began to casually speculate who was phoning him. The fact that he could hear the tape whirring, meant that someone was leaving him a message. If the caller hung up straight away, the machine let out a single, angry, high pitched beep and then you heard the double click, as the outgoing message tape was reset, ready for the next caller. So who was on the line?

It could have been Suzette ringing to demand an explanation for Billy's behaviour the previous day? He didn't expect she would be calling him to offer him his old job back. Mel would expect him to be at work, so she wouldn't usually call him at this time of day, unless she had somehow discovered that he had quit his job? In that case, she would be phoning, like Suzette, to demand an explanation, although being Mel she would dress it up as wanting to hear his side of the story, before roundly condemning him for his actions. There was of course of third possibility. There was an outside chance that it was Saskia ringing. Sufficient time had passed for her to have thought things through and come up with several good reasons, why she had felt the need to betray Billy in the way, she did. Even if they were all cast iron reasons and they bore just a small semblance to the truth, Billy still didn't want to hear them. It really was a waste of time speculating who was on the phone, but right now he had little else to occupy his mind and whoever it was, he didn't want to talk to them. Not now. He heard the machine click as the person hung up. They had left a message. Billy would listen to it later. Right now, he had an empty glass, so he reached for the bottle and unscrewed the cap, tilted the bottle and poured himself another large one. He held the bottle up to the light and calculated he probably had enough for another three drinks, if he carried on at this rate, then he would have to make a trip to the off-licence to restock his supply.

He did just that, polishing off the rest of the bottle, and then heading out to the high street and on to the local wine merchants. He was buzzing from the half bottle he had consumed already that morning and he suffered an embarrassing moment in the off-licence, when he got to the counter and started to slur his words. The old boy behind the counter looked critically at Billy, after he had asked several times for three bottles of Famous Grouse, with varying degrees of success.

"I'll need to see the colour of your money son."

He folded his hands across his chest. He was not going to move a muscle until Billy showed him the cold hard cash. The whisky bottles were lined up on the shelf just behind the shop owners left shoulder, but he was not even prepared to turn around. Billy pulled out his wallet and laid down four new ten-pound notes, fresh from the cash machine the previous afternoon. The appearance of hard cash seemed to mollify the shopkeeper. He reached around behind him and hooked the bottles off the shelf, wrapped them in turn in green tissue paper and placed them in a carrier bag. Billy asked for three packets of Marlboro and they were dropped on top. He handed over the money and scooped up the bag by the handles. He only staggered once on the way back to the flat and made it inside without further incident. He plonked the bag down on the surface in the kitchen, pulled out one of the bottles, a packet of cigarettes and retired back to the living room. He punched the power button on the TV remote and then sat there drinking, whilst flicking through all the crap that was served up on the major channels as daytime television.

He drifted in and out of consciousness for most of the day as he steadily drank his way through the next bottle and smoked his way through endless cigarettes, occasionally switching channels, when he got bored with what was on offer. When he came to, it was dark and the television was still burbling away in the corner. Something had dragged him from his alcohol induced coma. He lay there in the dark and listened. Then it happened again, frantic knocking on the front door. Billy leapt to his feet knocking over the ashtray in the process and stubbing his big toe on the leg of the coffee table.

"Fuck! Fucking Hell! Bollocks!" He hobbled down the hallway. He reached for the light switch as the banging on the door started up again, louder and more violent than before. Billy had no spy hole in the front door, so he had no way of knowing who was on the other side?

"Billy! Billy! Open the bloody door. Now!"

Relief. It was Mel. He opened the door just a few inches and she pushed her way into the flat nearly knocking him flying.

"Come in, why don't you?"

Billy said, standing out of the way, as the front door crashed back into the wall.

Mel was angry. She turned on him as soon as she was inside. Her hands now placed firmly on her hips. Billy could tell from her stance that he was in for a verbal beating and he was not disappointed.

"Do you want to tell me what the hell is going on," she blazed at him, "and why you have not been answering the phone all bloody day? I must have left you a dozen messages in all."

Billy mumbled something non-committal, but Mel was on him again.

"Have you been drinking?"
Billy mumbled again, it might have sounded like,
"Yep."
"Oh, come on Billy, you can't spend your days, in an alcoholic haze."
Mel stifled a small giggle at her rhyming phrase, but quickly regained her stern expression and tone of voice. She pushed past Billy and led the way into the kitchen. Billy followed her reluctantly. When he caught up with her she was standing with her arms folded staring pointedly at the collection of empty scotch bottles, lined up like marching troops alongside the dustbin. Billy grabbed a new packet of Marlboros from the side, peeled off the plastic wrapper, then the foil, before extracting one with his teeth and then frantically spinning the lighter's wheel to light it. He really couldn't be arsed to go and find the open packet from the living room, right now, plus he was worried that letting Mel out of his sight, would only give her a chance to martial her arguments against him, leading to an even fiercer onslaught when he returned. By the time he had the cigarette alight, Mel was on the move again, like a small localised whirlwind, storming around the kitchen: swiping the kettle off the side, filling it from the tap, plugging the power back in and flicking it on to boil.

"I am going to make us both a coffee and you're going to tell me what's happened?"
She was as good as her word, as a minute or so later there were two cups of steaming, strong black coffee ready. She pushed one towards Billy and headed towards the lounge. She gasped, before covering her nose, as she entered into the room.

"Urrgh, for Christ's sake open a window! It smells like a bloody morgue in here."
Billy gingerly placed his coffee on the table, then scooped up the dog ends that had scattered across the carpet, from the upended ashtray. The ash residue he massaged into the pile of the carpet. He got to his feet and crossed to the large sash window, wrestling it open, as its runners squealed out in protest. He took a moment to inhale a lungful of the night air. There was no view worth speaking of from the lounge window, as this part of the flat looked out onto the backs of the other buildings in the neighbourhood. He turned back to face into the room only to find Mel examining the half-empty whiskey bottle. She replaced it on the coffee table and then sat down on the sofa.

"Is that the first or second today?"
Billy was still standing by the window.
"Second."
He said sounding a little sheepish.
"Oh Billy."
Mel sounded bored as well as angry. Billy looked over at his ex-girlfriend. She hadn't changed her overall appearance since they had first met on the beach in Eilat. She still had her hair cut short in a pixie-bob with the back shaved close. And still had all her earrings in her ears. Her clothing had changed, although that was most likely a result of the cooler climate than anything else. When they had first met she had been wearing cotton Bedouin pants and a vest top, now she sported jeans and a sweater. Her feet, shoeless back then, were now enclosed in a pair of black Converse All-Stars. Although outwardly things had changed, Billy got the distinct impression that the Mel of old was still in there, lurking just below the surface. Billy pushed himself off the windowsill, went over to the sofa and took a seat on the other end.

"You have drunk one and a half bottles of scotch today?"
Billy was unsure whether it was a question or a statement, so he decided to err on the side of caution, treat it as a question and answer it.
"Yep."
He was trying not to sound too guilty.
"Have you eaten anything?"

Now he felt he was on safer ground as that was definitely a question. He took a moment to think before he answered, because he guessed that if he answered truthfully then he would be in for another stern lecture. He let the pause drag on for a second longer... ah what the hell.

"Nope."

He answered, honestly and then flinched, awaiting the verbal onslaught. It didn't come, well, not straight away. Billy focused his eyes on the swirls of steam curling up from his cup. He was unwilling to meet Mel's gaze. He knew, from of old, she would be scowling at him.

"Are you just planning on staying drunk the rest of your life?"

Now this was an odd question, given that he had only been on this bender, for less than twenty-four hours.

"Look I know it's difficult right now."

Mel had now adopted a conciliatory and more sympathetic tone, which actually annoyed him more than her usual censorious manner. Mel feeling sorry for him was definitely not what he wanted right now. He wanted her to rage on at him.

"Really?."

Billy had sharpened his tone to cynical and sarcastic before looking up into Mel's eyes, but, when he finally did so, he couldn't see any sign of anger on her face, only compassion.

"Of course, I do. I spoke to Suzette this morning and she told me all about your run in at Finch and McEwan."

Billy wondered why those two had been chatting on the phone. Mel rarely ever called him at work. Personal phone calls to the studio were frowned upon, unless there was a personal crisis or emergency. So, what was this personal crisis that could involve the two currently most important women in his life? He was slow and drink befuddled, so he didn't immediately make the connection. Then the bolt of lightning from a clear sky it hit him. They had been gossiping about him! Behind his back.

"I quit. It's not my problem. It's theirs."

"So, then I rang Saskia..."

"Wait," Billy interrupted her,

"You rang Saskia? Why?"

Mel looked startled at Billy's sudden angry interruption. She stumbled over her answer, swallowing her words and then starting again.

"Well Suzette had just told me you quit your job, I got no answer when I rang you here, it was the next logical thing to do."

"How did you get her number?"

"She gave it to me a couple of months back at a party. Anyway, she told me you two had split up."

Mel's cheeks were starting to colour up. She didn't like to be on the defensive.

"I bet she didn't tell you that she has been fucking this other guy behind my back."

Mel to give her credit, at least had the good grace to look shocked.

"Well er, no."

She stuttered her voice fading slightly,

"She didn't go into detail."

"Well why does that not surprise me? She seemed way more upset that I discovered her shagging around, not over our break up. The other night, she left a message saying she had to work this weekend, but the lying bitch was really going away on a dirty weekend at some hotel with her lover boy"

Billy was trying not to sound bitter but failing miserably.

"Oh, Billy I am sorry."

Mel reached out for his arm. She wanted to lay a reassuring hand on his forearm, but Billy shook it off and pulled his arm away instead.

"But that doesn't mean you have to get shit-faced drunk for the rest of your life."
"Oh please spare me the 'plenty more fish in the sea' line."

Billy was getting angry now and his sharper tone showed it.

"I have been drunk for less than twenty-four hours. It's hardly a lifetime."
"You don't have to be like that."

Mel was getting angry too. She had tried sympathy and empathy and both had failed miserably. Now, to cap it all the whole conversation was in danger of descending into a full-scale shouting match, which neither of them wanted.

"Billy. Listen."

Mel's tone was once again conciliatory and calm,

"We are not in Israel anymore, this is London, not Tel Boker. There are different rules here."
"Oh great, now I get the 'Toto we are not in Kansas anymore' speech as well".
"You know, sometimes I want to kick your teeth in."

Mel was smiling now and in a moment, Billy cracked a smile too.

"What and spoil my boyish good looks?"

Billy grinned, showing off his teeth. He reached for another cigarette and lit it. He finished his coffee and tapped the cup back down on the table.

"Mel, what am I going to do? I have no job and no girlfriend."
"Well you still have money and a passport, so you are better off than the first time we met."
"Yes, but at least I had beer then. I have only got scotch right now."
"What? No beer in the fridge?"
"Nope. Sorry, fresh out. I think Mark took the last one the other evening."
"But you have money, right?"
"Yes, I have money."
"So, what are you sitting there for? The supermarket across the street is open until 10 isn't it?"

Billy pushed himself up from the sofa and went in search of his wallet. He located it and then stuck his feet into a pair of old trainers, before leaning his head around the living room door.

"Have you got to be anywhere tonight?"
"No, not really, why?"
"Shall I get some food while I am over there? I can rustle something up for us."

Mel considered this for a moment and then nodded her head.

"Yes, why not."


Billy collected a basket as he entered the supermarket. He had no idea what he was going to cook for them both, so he thought that he would let the owner of the shop have the final word. He would look in the fresh meat section first and see what they had left, then build the meal around that. He was not a bad cook. Despite the fact that his mother's job in the supermarket had meant a life largely living off microwaved ready meals, Billy was more than capable of holding his own in the kitchen and while his repertoire and ability would not see him donning chef's whites and opening his own restaurant any time soon, he could stitch together an edible meal, if needed.

He found some chicken breasts in the cooler cabinet and then shopped accordingly for the rest of the ingredients. His last stop was the booze section, where he raided the fridge for a cold six pack and a rather inexpensive, but nice looking bottle of white wine. He took all this stuff up to the checkout and chatted with the owner, while he was ringing and bagging them up for him. Billy took the precaution of adding another bottle of scotch and two packets of Marlboro, before collecting his bags and heading back across the road.

Bugger. He had forgotten his keys. He pressed the buzzer and then waited patiently as Mel figured out the phone entry system. Eventually the loud buzz told him she had worked it out and he shouldered his way inside. When he got up to his floor he booted the front door to let Mel know he was outside, so she opened the door, cautiously at first, before throwing it wide open. Billy hauled the two heavy carrier bags through to the kitchen and heaved them on to the worktop.

"Wow. Have you bought the whole store?"
Mel asked, peering inquisitively into the top of one of the bags.
"Oh goody! Beer!"
She pulled the whole six pack out of the bag, detached a single can, popped the ring pull and took a long slow mouthful before shoving the rest into the fridge.
"Oh that tastes sooooo good."
Billy was busy unpacking the rest of the groceries and laying them out on the worktop.
"So what are you cooking for us tonight?"
Mel had come up behind him and was looking over his shoulder at the goods he was laying out.
"Chicken and Bacon, with Lemon and Tarragon."
As he named the parts of the meal he pointed to the various ingredients.
"With a side of mashed potatoes and sweetheart cabbage."
"Are you alright with that?" Billy asked. His hand was obviously hovering over the packet of bacon. Mel pulled a funny face and stuck out her tongue. They had discussed her relationship with bacon many times in the past.
"Sounds delicious, oh, and when did you learn to cook?"
Mel stepped away smartly as Billy turned around to face her.
"Are you going to help or just chuck insults at me? Coz if it's the latter you can sod off into the living room and I will call you when it's ready."
Billy grinned, mimicking Mel,
"Oh, and there will definitely be no more beer."
Mel pulled a face and put her head on one side as if she was contemplating a very difficult or potentially life changing question.
"OK, I'll stay and help."
Billy tossed her an apron which she caught one handed.
"You're on veggies."
He pointed at the bag of potatoes and the cabbage. Mel chirped out a playful,
"Yes Chef."
They both settled into their tasks, Mel by the sink washing and cutting up the potatoes and then stripping the outer leaves off the cabbage. Billy gesturing towards the cabbage, from the other side of the cooker, where he had been chopping up the meat and the herbs, said
"If you can slice that really thin, it will cook much better."
An identical "Yes Chef." was swiftly repeated by Mel.
When everything was prepared, Billy began to cook. Mel sat up on the worktop, sipping her beer and watching him work. Their conversation was light. Mel did most of the talking. She talked about the events of the week in college, making a conscious effort to steer away from topics that might upset Billy, such as relationships or work. Billy, for his part, concentrated on cooking, then tasting the sauce and when the dish was nearly ready to eat, he sprinkled in a little salt, before stirring and tasting it again.
"That smells really good." Mel said from her perch.
Billy scooped a little of the rich golden sauce into a teaspoon.

"Come here and have a taste."

He offered the spoon to her. She slid down and took it, raising it towards her lips.

"Careful, it's hot."

Mel blew on the spoon gently and then popped it in her mouth.

"Mmmm, that is good."

Billy laid the small table and put out the wine glasses and cutlery. He served up straight onto the plates and they sat opposite each other at the small table in the kitchen. He poured them both a large glass of white wine and they ate almost in silence. They finished the meal and then cleared up the kitchen, two old friends working side by side, content in each other's company. When the last plate and pan was put away, they took the wine bottle and retired to the living room. Billy topped up their glasses and they sat back to watch the late evening news. After that had finished they carried on watching the telly until Mel suddenly stood up, slightly unsteady after all the beer and wine.

"I really should be going. It's getting rather late."

Billy's watch showed it was very close to midnight. Billy offered,

"Stay here the night."

"What? No."

Mel sounded shocked by Billy's proposal. Billy looked alarmed by the violence of Mel's reaction. Realisation dawned instantly.

"No, not in that way. It's late, you can stay here. I'll sleep on the sofa if you want."

Mel seemed mollified by Billy's reaction and the magnanimous, gentlemanly offer he had made and she visibly calmed down.

"Well it is a long trek back to the halls and it is late. As long as you promise not to try any funny stuff, I guess I could stay here for one night."

"Not worried about your reputation, the walk of shame in the morning?"

Mel hurled one of the sofa cushions at Billy.

"Not funny, but anyway I am going home tomorrow morning, so I won't have to go back to the halls, I can go straight there from here."

With the wine bottle empty and the beers all gone and with neither of them really wanting to get stuck into the whiskey they slowly drifted off to bed. Billy found Mel a large t-shirt to sleep in and then managed to find a spare, unused, toothbrush, still in its plastic packet, in the back of the bathroom cupboard. He was pleased he had the spare, because it avoided any awkward questions about what had happened to Saskia's toothbrush, which he had used to clean the rim of the toilet bowl before setting fire to it and chucking the flaming brush out of the window onto the rooftop behind his flat. He had sat and watched as the plastic mess had burned and twisted up on itself. It had been a cathartic experience at the time, symbolic of how he felt about the end of the relationship, but now it just seemed a trifle petty. He left her alone to get ready for bed and went to have a final smoke in the kitchen. When he heard her leave the bathroom he went and brushed his teeth and then went into the bedroom. There was just a single reading light on above the bed and Mel was snuggled in under the covers. Billy walked towards the bed and Mel lifted the side of the duvet.

"No funny stuff," she said in a serious voice.

Billy just crossed his heart and slid under the covers beside her.


It was strange waking up with Mel's buttocks pressed against his thigh. It had been a while since they had shared a bed and therefore a long time since he had woken up in such a position. He carefully slid out of bed, anxious not to wake her and padded through to the kitchen. He filled and switched on the kettle and began to prepare the mugs for coffee.

"Good morning."
The voice behind him startled him and it took a momentous effort not to scatter the contents of the teaspoon all over the worktop. He had become so use to being alone in the flat and even when Saskia stayed over she had usually left before he woke up. He turned around. Mel was stood in the doorway of the kitchen. She was still just wearing the t-shirt she had borrowed from Billy, which clung in all the right places and showed off her gorgeous figure. Billy felt a brief pang of lust, but turned quickly away to attend to the coffee in order to cover his arousal and hide his feelings.

"Good morning. Are you still taking two sugars?"
His voice was still slightly thick from sleep and he hoped that Mel would not hear or read anything into his tone of voice.

"Yes please."
Satisfied that Billy was focused on the coffee and not about to jump her, Mel ventured into the kitchen and took a seat at the table. She was conscious about her naked thighs and tried to pull the t-shirt down a little to cover them. Billy thought about complaining as she was stretching one of his favourite t-shirts, but he held his tongue, so as not to antagonise her or destroy the mood and ruin what had been, up until now, a very pleasant experience. As he handed Mel her coffee, he noticed that she had stopped pulling the t-shirt out of shape and was now sitting comfortably with her knees hidden under the table.

"Did you sleep okay?"
He asked wanting to keep the conversation light and non-committal.

"Like a baby, thanks."

"Me too."

"Strange dreams though. I had a repeat of the dream I had back on the beach in Eilat."
Billy looked puzzled, so Mel continued.

"The first night we were together I dreamt you made love to me, it was very vivid."

"Oh yeah I remember you asked me about it in the morning. Why I had taken the time to redress you?"

"Well I had the same dream again last night."
Billy held his hands up defensively.

"I never touched you."

"I know Billy, you behaved like the perfect gentleman."
Billy wasn't sure whether there was a note of disappointment in her voice. He decided that maybe that was just him being over optimistic. They carried on drinking their coffee talking about their respective plans for the day, which for Billy amounted to little more than cleaning up in the flat and trying to stay off the booze until a respectable hour.

"Are you coming to the pub later for the reunion?"
Mel asked after she had drained the last of her coffee.

"I was planning on stopping by. What about you?"

"Yes. I will be there from about nine. Got to do the Shabbat meal thing with the folks first."
She wrinkled her nose in distaste at the prospect.

Mel came from a Liberal Jewish family who, although they didn't keep strictly to the word of the law, often used the excuse of their religion to meet up as a family on Friday evenings. Billy had never warranted an invite to such a gathering as he and Mel had been over before he made it back to England, Mrs Bishop had made sure of that. She had other plans for her precious daughter and they did not include marrying an out of work film actor. She had set her sights more on a doctor or lawyer type. Billy wasn't sure he could see Mel as the wife of either, but then he had seen the free-spirited side of Mel's personality when they had lived together in Eilat. She had adopted certain heirs and graces, since returning to

London under the stricter influence of her family, but Billy sensed underneath this thin veneer there still beat the heart of a rebel.

Mel having finished her coffee now glanced at her watch. This was a delicate and elegant Cartier. It had been the main present from her family on her twenty-first birthday a few months back and as far as Billy was aware, it had not been off her wrist since. He often warned her about walking around with such an expensive item of jewellery particularly in his neighbourhood, but Mel had so far completely disregarded these warnings.

"Look at the time, I had better be getting on, I am supposed to be shopping with my mum this morning".

"If you want to take a shower before you go there are some clean towels in the cupboard in the bathroom."

"I might just do that."

Mel stood up and flicked the end of Billy's nose playfully. She took her mug over to the sink and then shimmied out of the room. Billy couldn't resist a quick glance at her departing rear. He went to the kettle and made himself another coffee then went through to the living room. As he passed the bathroom door he could hear the sound of the shower running at full pelt. In the living room he opened the curtains and then the window to let in some fresh air and clear away the last of the stale smell from last night. He perched on the window ledge and smoked a cigarette while he drank his coffee. He had the time to think and to plan what he would do with himself today. He had no job to go to and there was a danger that if he stayed in the flat for too long he would just hit the bottle again. He looked around him. The place could definitely benefit from a clean-up, so he would start there and then see what happened afterwards. He knew that to be idle today would prove fatal and would result in the usual afternoon drinking, meaning that by the time he arrived at the pub later on he would already be drunk and things would probably go downhill very rapidly from then onwards.

Mel came in a few moments later with her clothes on, but her wet hair was still wrapped in a hand towel.

"I don't suppose you have a hair-dryer?"

"Nope." Billy scrubbed his hand over his buzz-cut hair, "I don't need one these days."

"Bugger. Oh well it's towel drying for me today."

Mel sat down on the sofa and began to roughly towel her hair. Every time she removed the towel her hair looked wilder than before.

"You must have a brush I can borrow?"

"Somewhere." Billy stayed perched on the windowsill.

"Any chance you could help me out and go and find it?"

"Sure, you just have to ask nicely."

"Pretty please Billy darling will you go and find your hairbrush." Mel's voice was honey sweet but dripping with sarcasm.

"Before I come over there and rip your balls off."

This was delivered with a menacing movie villain voice, but finished off with another simpering smile. Billy stubbed out his cigarette and went in search of the hairbrush. It was an item he knew he possessed, but had not needed or used for several months, so it really could be anywhere. He began a slow but methodical search of possible locations starting with the obvious places, like the bedroom then the bathroom, but came up blank. Then he stood in the hallway and tried to visualise the last place he could recall seeing it? This proved to be a fruitless exercise and he was aware that time was running out and Mel was keen to be on her way. He then began to search randomly, pulling open drawers and cupboards in the kitchen, rifling through shelves in the living room, all to no avail. Just as he was about to give up and admit defeat he spotted the bright blue end of the hairbrush handle sticking out from behind the back of the stereo on the large shelf in the corner of the living room. It was almost hidden behind the pile of cassette boxes and loose tapes that were lying around. Billy blushed as the memory came back to him. He now remembered the last time he had used the hairbrush and it had not been for any grooming related task. One night while he was a little the worse for wear, he had chosen the hairbrush to double as a microphone, while he sang along at the top of his lungs to some of his favourite tunes. It had lain undisturbed, obviously abandoned there at the end of his performance. No way was he going to admit such a tale to Mel, so he kept schtum about the discovery and its location as he handed it to Mel.

"Maybe keep it in the bathroom from now on?"

She said with a sly wink. Billy hoped she hadn't realised the reason the brush had been nestling behind the stereo, but he had a strong suspicion she had sussed out the truth. Perhaps she was simply being kind or just keeping the revelation of Billy's performance, as ammunition for a later date?

Eventually, Mel had fixed her hair, so she gave Billy a chaste peck on the cheek and disappeared out the front door. Billy made himself another cup of coffee and then began to sort through his clean clothes, trying to decide what would be appropriate to wear for this evening's reunion. After he had settled on an outfit, he then decided that the flat would benefit from a good general tidy up, so he started by cleaning up in the kitchen. Although he and Mel had made a good start on it the previous evening, he still wanted to put everything away.

Then he went into the living room. In the short time that he was in there, tidying, he must have moved that half empty whiskey bottle several times. From the coffee table to the window ledge, then to the bookshelf, where he disturbed a box that contained a few photos of his time in Israel and they fluttered down on to the carpet. Billy looked at the collage of faces starring up at him, some smiling, some laughing, some kissing, all with drinks in hand. There were pictures from trips to historical sites, nature reserves and all of them showed, happy, tanned and healthy looking youngsters, all enjoying their lives to the full. A tearful Billy stared down at the chronical of his last two years and he could feel his resolve weaken a little. In the end he succumbed and unscrewed the lid, poured himself a measure, not a big one, just enough to take the edge off. He returned to his perch, with the photos on the windowsill, lit a cigarette and enjoyed the first flood of warmth from the scotch as it began to invade his blood stream, producing that delicious relaxing feeling of wellbeing that everything, however bad, would turn out alright in the end. As he drank the first mouthfuls of scotch, he made two promises. One: to finally put the photos in a proper album. Two: that he would only take the one drink and he was making that same promise to himself as he tipped the last few drops of the once half full bottle into the glass and swallowed them down in a single gulp. He was not disappointed with himself, as he still had two more completely full bottles in the kitchen, so he had not run out of whiskey and he didn't feel drunk. He therefore reasoned that he would be able to go out later in the day and enjoy himself together with his friends and that might well have been the case, if Billy had stopped there, but this was not something Billy was very practiced or indeed good at. So, inevitably, when by the middle of the afternoon, he was staring at another almost empty bottle of scotch, he knew he was in for another interesting evening.

Billy stumbled slightly as he stepped off the bus. It was still negotiating the junction from Islington Green onto Upper Street, but had slowed down enough to mean the dismount from the open platform at the rear, was not that dangerous. The conductor, however, seemed to disagree with Billy's assessment of the danger, as she yelled something incoherent and largely incomprehensible at Billy, as he dropped from the platform and walked to the curb.

He had alighted here, because he wanted to head north up Upper Street and the bus, now picking up speed, was heading rapidly in the other direction.

His destination was the Crusader's Arms, an antiquated establishment secreted away in a small courtyard behind Upper Street. It had none of the glitz or glamour of the wine bars and other assorted themed watering holes that lined Upper Street itself, but the landlord, aware of the shabby state of the place, ensured there was one big thing in its favour. He was quite happy to turn a blind eye to the licencing laws and allow the pub to stay open long after the normal eleven o'clock curfew. Its location in the narrow courtyard assisted with this deception, as there was an alternative exit from the rear of the premises, which could be used once the main doors were locked and bolted at eleven. The additional income generated by these weekend lock-ins was sufficient to encourage the owners at the brewery to keep the place open and the landlord in a job long after most of the adjoining properties had been sold and redeveloped. The crumbling stained brick facade of the building certainly made it stand out in amongst the shining glass and concrete structures that surrounded it. The Crusader Arms had one other, slightly more dubious and certainly less provable claim to fame. A wooden sign over the front door announced that this one of the 'oldest' pubs in England. Inside the pub there was a wall plaque that explained the premises had been one of the gathering points for Crusader knights before they set out on the long and dangerous journey to the Holy Land.

There were many pubs throughout the country, which claimed similar origins or links to the crusades and therefore vying for the title of England's Oldest Public House. Billy had even visited a few over the years. The building itself despite the state of the fabric was nowhere near old enough, but consultation of the placard inside and a little careful reading of the small print there, informed you that the original building had been damaged by a fire in the time of Queen Elizabeth I and that the pub had been partially pulled down and rebuilt.

It meant that only a few sections of the building fabric were from the original structure and one of those parts was, without doubt, the drains. At certain times of the year and in certain weather conditions the smell emanating from the gents' toilets at the rear of the main bar was overpowering, prompting one wag to quip that he thought one of the original crusaders had probably died and been entombed down there without a proper burial.

Billy doubted the hype about the age of the place, but this didn't stop the place being popular among a certain crowd and even the foul smell from the toilets, couldn't keep them away. The late-night lock ins, coupled with the historic link to the Holy Land, made it an ideal place to stage a reunion for people, who had made the, slightly less dangerous, modern day equivalent, of the Crusader pilgrimage.

Billy placed his hand on the brass plate and pushed the heavy wooden door. The frosted glass panel in the top half of the door made it impossible to see inside, but as soon as the door was half open Billy could sense that the space beyond was crowded. A warmish blast of air escaped, rich with the smell of booze, cigarette smoke and warm human bodies. The front bar was a smallish space or 'snug' by name and nature that appeared overcrowded once there were more than thirty souls in the space. The presence of a floor to ceiling mirror along one wall only added to the claustrophobic atmosphere, as it doubled the apparent size of the room without actually increasing the floor space.

This layout of the Crusaders was what made it ideal for the late-night lock ins. The snug only had a small bar in the corner, opposite the entrance, to serve customers. The rest of the back wall was made up of a long, dark, oak wood, floor to ceiling partition. This divided the pub and effectively sealed off the rear portion of the pub from the street. It also disguised the presence of the much larger, lounge bar. It sealed off the visibility of all light, sound or movement from people passing the pub after hours. So unless you were in the know, or much more importantly, inside, before the front doors were closed for the night, it was near impossible to tell there was anything going on in the pub. Consequently, the police were unable to see that the place was open long after closing time, although, Billy suspected that local law enforcement were well aware of the goings-on and merely chose to turn a blind eye to proceedings, provided things didn't get out of hand. This tacit arrangement was complimented by the fact that the landlord was totally non-selective as to who could remain behind, so no special clique or regulars existed as it did in most other pubs. This place was open to everyone if they abided by the rules. The most important of these rules was,

*'When you leave the pub you do so very quietly and through the rear exit'.*

A corridor connected the snug to the back bar. Billy knew this was where his group would have assembled and he had no problem spotting familiar faces, in amongst the crowd when he pushed his way through the swing door and into the room. The group of former volunteers from Tel Boker had effectively taken over two of the large booths on the left hand side of the room and were spread out in a large circle around that part of the pub.

Billy approached the bar conscious that the alcohol he had imbibed earlier was still running hot through his veins. When the barmaid came to serve him, he asked for a pint of lemonade and lime. Beer on top of all the whiskey he had drunk would be a step too far. He was also very thirsty, so this soft drink would help to quench his thirst. The presence of excessive alcohol in his blood stream always gave Billy an overwhelming, but slightly misplaced, sense of confidence. He somehow seemed to think that he was funnier, and of course much more appealing to the opposite sex. In reality he was neither. With the addition of his merciless teasing and his willingness to push the bounds of what was acceptable in terms of behaviour to newfound limits, he actually often found it had the opposite effect, particularly on people who didn't know him very well.

Billy, for his part, stuck in the midst of an alcoholic haze didn't register any of this and when pushed or reminded of events at a later date, would categorically deny they ever happened. At any of these gatherings it was usual that apart from the core of ex-Tel Boker volunteers, there would be friends invited along for the evening. Some of them would have experience of kibbutz life, whilst others, the vast majority in fact, would have none and would therefore rely on the accounts of events and personalities told to them by their friends. No matter what had passed between them on this subject nothing could quite prepare them for Billy at his best, or worst, depending on your particular point of view. And this evening he was going to be spectacularly badly behaved.

It all started off benignly enough as Billy slithered across the floor, pint glass in hand. He knew a large number of the people present in the group, all ex-volunteers from Tel Boker, but as usual there were a few others in the group who were strangers and whilst he nodded at those he knew, he made a show of bowing, hand over heart to those he didn't. It was a little theatrical and a bit over the top and elicited a few ribald comments from the group, as did the fact that Billy seemed to be sticking to soft drinks. He rolled with this the first couple of times, but eventually the barbs stuck and under pressure, he cracked and ordered a pint of lager. It was probably, with hindsight, not the smartest move.

A better option would have been for Billy to make his excuses and leave. Once the fresh wave of alcohol mixed with that already in his system, Billy succumbed quickly and his behaviour deteriorated as a result. He had forgotten that one of the main reasons for staying sober was the possibility of running into Greta and Tracey. There was a strong possibility that if those two were still in London, they would have been invited to this reunion. Billy had no idea what Greta's itinerary was. All he knew was he had managed to waste one half day of her stay, while she waited for him in the rain. Billy had therefore made himself a promise that he would offer his most sincere apology if they turned up.

When the pair eventually arrived it was clear from their attire that the "Crusaders" was probably only a starting point for a night out on the town. Both of them had forgone the usual casual attire of denim and had chosen instead to put on their best frocks. As they took off their top coats they revealed their choices for the night out. Tracey had a shimmering silvery blue cocktail dress, Greta's was an alarmingly bright 'fire-engine' red. Both had matching shoes and handbags. Greta had also added a shocking red lipstick, which really complemented her creamy skin, platinum hair and steely blue eyes. Billy admired her from across the room, she looked good enough to eat. It was inevitable that at some point their paths would cross, so Billy took the time to think carefully about what he was going to say. When the moment arrived and both Greta and Tracey were stood in front of him, Billy tried to read their mood from their expressions.

"Hello Billy".

Greta's German accent was rich and her voice was pitched low. Under any other circumstances it would have been as sexy as hell. But for Billy it struck him as comical and he tried to supress a smile by covering his mouth with his wrist. Midway into this manoeuvre he realised how it would look, so he changed his mind, raising the glass as if he was toasting the pair instead.

"To Greta and Tracey."

Billy took a swig from his lager.

"Well? Have you nothing to say?"

Greta had her arms folded and Billy was sure that if he took a moment to look down he was sure her foot would be tapping impatiently on the floor as she awaited his grovelling apology. He did have something to say. All the way here on the bus he had been rehearsing his apology, refining it over and again until the whole thing sounded plausible and sufficiently remorseful, without being overly repentant and therefore fake sounding. But at that precise moment all of those carefully prepared words evaporated into thin air and Billy's mind went a complete blank. Aware of the pregnant pause in the conversation and the void that was waiting for someone to say something, Billy uttered the first thing that entered his head,

"You look like a total tart in red."

As the words escaped his mouth Billy tried desperately to recover them, to swallow them, to call them back, but as he watched, the full impact of what he had said, hit home. The colour fled from her cheeks and her lip began to quiver with anger. Tracey who was stood next to her had not caught the exchange, but she looked alarmed at the instant change in her friend's expression and she immediately identified the source and cause.

"Billy Randell, what did you just say?"

Tracey was indignant.

"Er nothing,"

Billy hoped that in the general hubbub in the room his words would have escaped general notice and he was frantically thinking what to say next. Tracey had turned to Greta and laid a hand on her arm to reassure her. She waited for Greta to calm down and fill her in with the details of the exchange. In the meantime she launched a vicious verbal attack on Billy, haranguing him for his behaviour earlier in the week. It was sufficiently strident to silence most of the other conversations in the bar as all eyes turned on Tracey and the object of her verbal assault. Billy was aware that many eyes in the room were now focused on him and people seemed to be straining to catch every word of Tracey's denunciation. Whilst Billy liked to be the centre of attention he drew the line when it involved a woman howling at him and bad mouthing him, because of his behaviour. He listened in stony silence, his arms held loosely at his side, as Tracey's reprimand ground slowly to a halt. In the absolute silence, Greta's voice was easily heard, her accent made a little thicker by her emotion.

"He said, I looked like a total tart in red."

There was an audible intake of breath among the assembled audience.

"I didn't. I said you looked really smart in red."

Billy was quick to counter. Now it was a case of 'he said, she said' or at least that was Billy's hope. Unfortunately too many people knew Billy and knew him for what he was capable of doing and saying, so there were very few in the assembled group who believed him. Billy's words were treated therefore with the degree of scepticism that they deserved and his pronouncement was met with active jeers of disbelief and Billy felt sure he heard one or two people yelling apologise in amongst the general uproar. Billy was not about to admit his misdemeanour, so he simply turned on his heels and sought refuge in the only place he knew the two women wouldn't follow him. The gents. The smell was excruciatingly bad and left Billy gagging and retching. He endured the smell for about a quarter of an hour and then made his way back to the bar.

Although things seemed to have returned to normal they didn't improve, if anything they got worse as Billy began to interrupt people, while they were speaking, convinced that his opinion or point of view was far more important than that of the person speaking, or his particular anecdote was much funnier or more relevant, than the one being told. Coupled with this was his predilection for making physical contact with members of the opposite sex, as he spoke to them. An arm around the shoulders or around the waist was his preferred method, but he lacked the awareness to see when this close connexion was unwelcome. This resulted in one or two further heated exchanges and harsh words. When he was finally accused by one of the ex-volunteers of leering down his girlfriend's cleavage it was the final straw for most of them and Billy was effectively ostracised and wandered off to the bar alone and in a foul mood. He chose to studiously ignore anyone of the party who approached the bar and this general truce seemed to suit both sides. He was sitting alone at one end of the bar, when Mark arrived and tapped him on the shoulder. Since that night at the Students Union, Mark seemed to have become a regular attendee at any pub nights or parties that Billy had been invited to. They had struck up a rather casual friendship where, although they would always spend time together at these type of events, they didn't seem to be on each other's speed dials. Best of all, seen from Billy's point of view, was that Mark seemed to be the non-judgemental sort, who could and would accept all of Billy's excesses with nothing more condemning than a wry smile. He slid onto a vacant stool beside Billy.

"What are you doing here all alone?"

He asked casting a look across the room and spotting the assembled throng from Tel Boker.

"The usual,"

Billy nodded at his drink. He had given up with the pints and was now back onto large scotch and cokes.

"Getting drunk and trying to keep my nose clean."

Billy concluded with a half-smile.

"I guess the fact that you are sitting here alone means you have succeeded with one and failed with the other?"

It was as close to a criticism as Billy would ever get from Mark and he looked over and grinned at his mate.

"Absolutely right there."

Mark broke off to order a drink from the barmaid and then waved in Billy's direction,

"and whatever this young man is drinking, oh and get one for yourself."

This last comment elicited a beaming smile from the young lady as she scurried away to service Mark's order. When they both had drinks in hand, Mark's money had been deposited in the 'tips' glass behind the bar and Mark had taken a long swig from his pint, they began the ritual catch up conversation. Mark started off by filling Billy in on the highlights of his life since the last time they had met. He had finished his studies, passed his final exams and was now working part time as a researcher for a media company. He asked Billy how his job was going and Billy told him how he had parted company with his former employers. Billy didn't go into details and Mark was too polite to ask. Instead he turned to other matters.

"How's Saskia, she not with you tonight?"

Billy's reply was automatic.

"No she is working tonight."

He had delivered the same answer every time he had been asked the question so far this evening, but it suddenly dawned on him that this was Mark he was talking to, not some casual acquaintance from the kibbutz days.

"Actually, that's not strictly true. She is together with a work colleague and as far as I know they are shacked up in some country hotel, fucking each other's brains out."

Mark winced at the venom in Billy's voice.

"Really?"

"Yeah really. I caught her and lover boy together the other day when I dropped over to see her. Seems like they had been working up an appetite in the bedroom and were just waiting for a pizza to be delivered."

"Ouch, that's brutal."

Billy just nodded his head in agreement.

"She had left me a message on the answerphone saying she was working this weekend when all along she and lover boy were planning their weekend escape."

"So you're a free agent again? No job, no girlfriend. What are you gonna do?"

"To tell you the truth I have no idea. I am just getting drunk at the moment."

"I can see that Billy, but there is no need to push the boat out every night. You need to give it a rest once in a while."

"The wounds are still fresh I will take a timeout when the pain fades a little."

"Look mate, I don't want to rain on your parade or anything, but you need to think seriously about what you are doing. I sense you have pissed off more than a few people tonight".

Billy began to object, but Mark raised a hand to silence him, so Billy shut up and listened

"Now I don't care, you can say what you like to me, I know the real Billy, but some of these others are less forgiving."

Billy nodded his head in agreement.

"I guess you get to realise who your friends are."

It was Mark's turn to remain quiet. He merely sipped his beer. Billy took a mouthful of his drink swallowed and then wiped his mouth on the back of his hand.

"There is a delicious irony to all this," he began.

"I don't understand." Mark looked at him over the rim of his glass.

"Just look around you."

Billy waved his arm in a circle that encompassed an arc including most of the erstwhile volunteers from Tel Boker and their friends.

"All these people, well most of them, have spent time in the kibbutz community. I could tell you stories of excess and bad behaviour about almost all of them. Yet look at them all now."

Billy took another, smaller, sip. He was warming to his theme.

"All I have heard tonight is reheated stories of the 'good old days'".

How much fun we all had, and how they can't wait to get back and do it all again. How they are jealous of the people who stayed behind, but not one of them would drop everything and leave tomorrow. They are all too comfortable back living their boring, buttoned up lives."

"Would you?"

"Would I what?"

"Would you drop everything and go back to Israel tomorrow?"

"Being honest? Yes. I would. I have been thinking about nothing else. I have nothing to hold me here anymore."

"That is interesting."

Mark swallowed the last of his beer and placed the glass on the beer towel in front of him.

"Part of the reason I showed up tonight was to pick your brains. You see I have been toying with the idea of making a trip to Israel myself. Signing on the dotted line, taking the shekel, whatever you call it. I want to go and experience this whole kibbutz thing and I figured you were probably one of the people I could talk to about it."

"Why me? Almost everyone you can see in this room has been a volunteer at some point."

"Yeah, but for me you will always be the embodiment of the volunteer spirit."

"Should I take that as a compliment or what?"

"A compliment of course you idiot," Mark grinned "are you going to get the next round in?"

Billy nodded and reached for his wallet. The barmaid was standing in front of them as Billy slapped his wallet down on the bar top.

"Same again?" She asked with a smile.

Billy nodded and when the drinks arrived he handed over a ten pound note.

"Oh and have one yourself."

He added as an afterthought and was greeted with another more beaming smile.

"She likes you," Mark said with a sly elbow in Billy's ribs.

"She's just doing her job."

"Bet she'd do a job on you."

Billy was keen to change the subject before the barmaid returned to their end of the bar and caught wind of what they were discussing. Getting barred for insulting the bar staff, now, would be the final straw, the icing on the cake, the mouldy cherry on the ice cream sundae.

"So why have you suddenly decided to head off to Israel now?"

"Is there a better time? I am twenty three years old, I have no real job, no commitments, no mortgage, no debts and no girlfriend worth speaking of. I think the timing is perfect."

Billy couldn't fault the logic behind his friend's argument. He had spent the first part of the evening surrounded by people who were reminiscing about the time they had spent out on a kibbutz, recalling all the highlights of their experiences, whilst at the same time bemoaning their present commitments to work, relationships or education and how this prevented them from dropping everything and returning there. There was a near evangelical zeal in their eyes and an intensity in their voices that Billy found himself almost believing them until he arrived at the conclusion that if any one of them really did feel that tangible pull to return, they would simply drop everything and make it happen. Having reached the conclusion that the evangelism was a false emotion Billy was pleased to be able to discuss Mark's forthcoming adventure. They were deep into discussing his options when Mel arrived.

Finally released from the suffocating and restrictive embrace of her family's Friday night arrangement she had made a quick change into some more comfortable clothes and rushed across town in a cab. Even with such apparent haste it was still almost closing time when she arrived. Mel had left it until the last minute to announce at the table that she was planning to head out to meet friends. Her mother had looked stonily across the table at her daughter. She was not being very cooperative in this search for a husband and ducking out of family gatherings to go off gallivanting around with her wild friends was certainly not the way to land a husband of any quality.

"What did I miss?"

She asked as she drained half a pint of lager and wiped her mouth on the back of her hand.

"Not much," Mark answered, "just Billy upsetting people again as usual."
Mel turned on Billy to reprimand him, but could see from his expression that anything she said of this nature was likely to lead to an argument, so she dropped the idea.

"So why are you two so deep in conversation?"

"Mark wants to travel to Israel and go to a kibbutz. We were just discussing the options."

"While Billy was laying out the options, I was just listening and taking mental notes."

"So what pearls of wisdom have you harvested tonight?"

Mel's tone was slightly sarcastic as if she couldn't imagine Billy, in his current state of inebriation, having anything useful to add to a conversation. Billy honed in on the sarcasm.

"Hey. Still here you know. Man with feelings."

Mel rested her hand on Billy's arm. She realised suddenly that Billy had been through a lot of personal upheaval just recently and was maybe entitled to blow off a little steam.

"Sorry Billy, that was uncalled for."

Billy looked up at his ex-girlfriend.

"Apology accepted."

"I need to go and talk to a few people, are you two going to come with me or stay here at the bar and sulk?"

Billy spoke over his shoulder without turning to face Mel.

"We would like to finish our conversation, but we will join you in a bit."

"And Billy will be on his best behaviour, I will make sure of that," Mark added.

Mel disappeared off into the crowd, intent on her one woman charm offensive, to rehabilitate Billy. It seemed to work because when Billy looked up a few moments later he noticed one or two people were glancing in his direction and their gaze was no longer hostile. Mel's PR job followed a simple and direct approach, which consisted of pointing out to people that Billy had recently quit his job and found out his girlfriend was having an affair with another man. These two events, taken together could more than explain his behaviour. This approach obviously worked because when Mark and Billy re-joined the group later they were welcomed back like returning prodigal sons. It seemed that even the "total tart in red" had decided she must have misheard Billy because, Greta, even if she was a little drunk by now, took a moment to hug Billy, plant a kiss on his cheek and thank him for the compliment. Tracey was also waiting anxiously to add her slightly sloppy kiss to his other cheek. Billy caught a whiff of beer on her breath and turned his head just in time to avoid an embarrassing lip to lip kiss.

Billy for his part and now under Mel's watchful eyes, tried his hardest to be charming and to behave himself and he largely succeeded. In fact, his rehabilitation went so well that one of the newcomers, a guy he had never met before tonight, someone he felt sure he remembered insulting at some point earlier in the evening, even extended an invitation to Billy, Mark and Mel to attend a party he was holding the following evening at his flat in Camden Town and even went as far as ensuring his address and telephone number were written down and handed to them on the back of three beermats, one for each of them to keep. Billy stuffed his in the back pocket of his jeans after thanking the host for the invitation. He was not sure if he would attend as he got a feeling from the host that the party would be another gathering of ex-volunteers and kibbutz groupies, all dewy-eyed over their love for Israel and life on the kibbutz.

Billy wasn't sure he could hack another night like this, not two nights on the bounce anyway. It wasn't that he found the company irritating it was the effort that some of these people put into the evenings. As well as the reminiscing there was the over the top use of the small amount of Hebrew that they had learnt during their stay in Israel, as if in some way using the Hebrew word for thank you or pass me the ashtray somehow kept the whole experience more alive for them?

When Billy entered the pub at the beginning of the evening he had been inundated with 'Shabbat Shalom's' from almost every other person. He had come very close to chinning someone after about the fifteenth time. It was annoying but Billy had to accept it. Part of the effort of the kibbutz, at integration was teaching the volunteers snippets of the Hebrew language, simple phrases, like greetings and minor pleasantries, 'Hello, how are you?' and such like. It was simple dialog designed to give the volunteers a sense of belonging and maybe it served some other purpose for the older kibbutz members who seemed to take this education as part of their responsibilities. Billy wasn't sure what anyone else felt about learning a half a dozen phrases 'parrot fashion' and what it did for either volunteers or members.

This was because Billy had set himself the task of learning to speak Hebrew and had sought help from the young members with the task. It had not been easy but Billy had mastered the language in a relatively short space of time. What Billy did object to was the way that time had clearly faded some people's memories over correct pronunciation and now some of the garbled attempts at phrases in Hebrew sounded like some people had a whole roasted potato firmly wedged in their windpipe. Billy had given up trying to correct people as it only seemed to add another layer of antagonism. He just cursed the kibbutz and all that it stood for. It was just another thing to add to the negative column on his list.

It wasn't that Billy hadn't enjoyed his time on kibbutz. He had, in fact, thrived in that environment and grown dramatically as a person. It was simply that by the end he had begun to see the flaws in the whole kibbutz experience and the potential challenges the movement and the occupants of the kibbutzim themselves would have to face in the not too distant future. So whilst the dream was still alive he could see it turning into a nightmare and he was not sure that the whole concept would survive. He was not always sure that people who visited for short periods of time, six months or less, got the chance to see this alternative side of the kibbutz experience.

Billy with an overall stay that ran to nearly two years, although not all of it had been as a kibbutz volunteer, had been exposed to the softer underbelly of the kibbutz. Having friends among the young Israeli members had also opened his eyes to the challenges that they, as individuals, faced.

Yara, Mike's girlfriend had often told them both about how she couldn't wait to finish her studies and get the hell out of the kibbutz. She had done just that by leaving to go travelling with Mike almost as soon as she was allowed to leave. Mike, and the access to money that he had provided had made Yara's dream a reality much faster than maybe she had ever hoped for. Others, among her friends and former army buddies, would not have been so lucky and may have had to work in one of the big cities to earn the money they needed to travel for a couple of years. It was one of the possible futures awaiting the young adults when they finished their national service. The other was to enrol in further education, which would be funded by the government, but if they remained as residents on the kibbutz they would be expected to offer themselves for work at every available opportunity.

It was well into the early hours of the morning before the crowd in the pub began to thin out and people started to head home. Billy, who had eased up on the alcohol intake, was sitting together with Mark and two French girls who were nothing to do with the kibbutz group. They were just tourists who were staying at a local hotel and had happened upon the Crusaders totally by accident. Not being among the misty-eyed volunteers had improved Billy's mood enormously and he felt that things were progressing nicely with Nicoline and Chantelle. Both the girls hailed from Paris and were over in London for an extended holiday. Coming from the city of light they both exuded that innate Parisian sense of style and sophistication. They were impeccably dressed in casual fashionable clothes, their hair and makeup perfectly coiffured and applied. Their English was passable, just as well, as French was not a language that either Billy or Mark had any knowledge of beyond a basic schoolboy level. It was certainly not sufficient to be able to woo these two sophisticated young ladies. The other thing was that the two girls' accents when they spoke English were rich and sexy. When the girls excused themselves to use the bathroom the two friends both looked at each other incredulously.

"Do you think we could?" asked Mark.

"Do you think we should?" countered Billy.

"I think it would be rude and very unpatriotic not to give it a try."

"Which one do you want to hit on? You can have first choice."

"That's very noble of you Billy, I think I would like to try my luck with Chantelle. I think you seem to be getting along fine with her friend."

The two friends shook on their decision and then waited patiently for the girls to return. When the two girls returned it appeared that they had just had a similar conversation in the ladies bathroom. Luckily they seemed to have reached the same decision as the boys had, as when they returned, it was with special focus on their chosen partners. That their decision matched the boys prevented any embarrassing moments and the four settled down to some serious flirting with each other.

Billy could see that glasses were nearly empty so he offered to go and get in another round of drinks. The girls had been sipping from glasses of wine but when Billy offered to buy, they both ordered double vodkas and coke. Billy scooted off to the bar and within a few moments had the four glasses lined up on the bar. He had two pints, one for him and one for Mark and two short glasses with large vodkas and a splash of coke in. He put his hands around the glasses and realised that whilst two pints and a short glass was within his grasp, the fourth and final glass was impossible to carry. He assessed the situation before hitting on a solution. He took the fourth glass and slipped it into his shirt pocket. It nestled their nicely, although the glass was a little cold on his left nipple through the fabric. He collected the other three glasses and returned to the table.

Up until now everything had seemed to be going well, and Billy and Mark were ready to make the next move by inviting the girls back to Billy's flat. Mark had even gone so far as to float the idea with the Parisian pair and had not been totally rebuffed. He gave Billy the wink as he returned clutching the drinks. It was just enough to distract Billy who forgot completely about the glass in his shirt pocket. He bent over at the waist to place the glasses he was carrying on the table and in doing so successfully tipped the contents of the fourth glass out of his shirt pocket and onto the table. No one escaped a dousing as vodka and coke splashed across the table top. Mark and the two French girls leapt to their feet to avoid the worst of it. Billy's shirt front was the main casualty and he returned to the bar to ask for a cloth to remove the worst of the damage and to dry off his shirt. This was a source of amusement to the cutie behind the bar who found Billy a stack of paper towels.

By the time he returned to the table the mood had changed, and not for the better. The girls were both talking heatedly in French and it was going above Mark's head. Billy was none the wiser. Eventually the two young ladies reached an agreement and informed the two boys of their decision. They thanked Billy and Mark sincerely for a wonderful evening but pointed out that they both needed to return to their hotel room as they were both very tired and were expecting a very busy day of sightseeing the next day. Billy toyed with the idea of offering to walk them back to the hotel in the vain hope of being invited up to their room, but Mark had seen the move for what it really was, a subtle blow out. As Billy went to open his mouth to offer to accompany the girls as far as their hotel Mark simply shook his head once. It was enough and Billy's mouth snapped shut like a trap. The two boys were rewarded with light pecks on both cheeks, in the continental fashion and the girls were gone leaving behind a faint whiff of expensive perfume.

"I thought we were on a promise there."

"Yeah Billy, so did I. Oh well nothing ventured."

Mark didn't seem in the least annoyed that Billy's clumsy act had probably been the cause of their sudden rejection.

Billy cast his eyes around the room assessing who was still left and if there were any single women among them. It was pretty poor fare and most of the single women were single for obvious reasons, and then there was Mel.

Mark was more philosophical.

"Best not to get too involved if I am leaving the UK soon."

"You are probably right there."

Mel seeing the two lads sitting alone came over to join them.

"Blown out?" she said with a cheeky grin. "Oh Billy."

She noticed the dark stain on Billy's shirt front,

"really losing your touch there. Did one of them chuck a drink at you?"

Billy snarled and then smiled at Mel.

"No Billy managed that all by himself." Mark offered.

Billy, who could never be mad at Mel for too long, particularly when she was telling the truth, like she was right now, just nodded and pulled a hurt face.

"And with you two being two of the cutest guys in here. It's just not fair."

"Don't push it Bishop," Billy growled under his breath.

"I am serious." Mel said this with a convincing degree of seriousness in her voice,

"Those two just don't know what they are missing out on."

"Thanks for the confidence vote Mel. Well I am going to try and find a taxi."

Mark stood up and shrugged on his jacket.

"Will I see you two guys tomorrow night?"

Mel made a play of consulting her expensive wrist watch.

"Don't you mean tonight?"

"Yeah whatever," Mark was nonplussed by Mel's correction, "just proves how much I need my bed. See you guys later then."

He made his way towards the rear exit of the pub and disappeared from view

"What time are you two guys meeting?"

"I have no idea I will call Mark later and arrange a time and a place. I am not sure I even really want to go."

"Why not?"

"You know, more of the same as tonight, misty-eyed reminiscences about what a wonderful time we all had in kibbutz, me walking around on eggshells on my best behaviour, trying desperately not to upset anyone."

"Well I did have a good time Billy, both on and off the kibbutz. I met you for starters."

Mel had placed a warm hand on Billy's forearm and he did nothing to shake it off. Her hand felt good, almost reassuring, there. Billy studied Mel's face looking for tell-tale signs of drunkenness. He couldn't see any so he assumed that this was a genuine feeling from Mel. She hadn't finished yet.

"And I really enjoyed myself last night. It was the first time I have felt safe in ages."

"You weren't scared of food poisoning?"

"Not during the meal silly, it was later when we were in bed. That was where I felt safe."

Billy caught his breath sharply and released it slowly. He couldn't quite believe what he was hearing and at the same time he didn't want to probe any further. There was a chance he had got the wrong end of the stick and misread too much into her comments. He didn't want to risk scaring Mel away. He knew he would have to be patient and see how things developed. He had to admit to himself, even though it was a little reluctantly at times, that he still fancied the pants off Mel and he regretted the fact that they had broken up in the way that they had. He didn't blame her for the breakup he knew that once she returned to the influence of her family then their relationship was doomed, Mel's mother had made that much clear when she had visited the pair on Tel Boker. Mel's hand remained in place on his arm.

"What are you going to do now?"

Billy considered the question carefully. Did Mel mean in the immediate future, like the next couple of hours or was the question more general, like,

'What are your plans for the next few months?'

He decided to play things straight with Mel.

"Right now I am thinking of getting a cab home, in the longer term I have no idea."

Mel nodded her head in understanding. She removed her hand from his arm which Billy took as a bad sign. He weighed up his next question for only the briefest of moments before he blurted out.

"Do you want to share a cab back to mine?"

There it was said. It was out there in the world, the question that maybe he shouldn't have asked. He braced himself for the fallout, the pouring out of scorn on his head, the comments about missing the point of her earlier comments.

"I would like that very much Billy."

Billy was left speechless and breathless for the second time in as many minutes. In all his wildest dreams he hadn't expected Mel to agree to his suggestion, but he was secretly pleased that she had. He realised that he had only got her to agree to accompany him home, nothing else. The rest would have to be taken slowly but it was a step in the right direction.

"Will you go and ask the bar staff to ring us a cab, please Billy?"

"On my way."

Billy stood up and in his haste almost tipped the stool over. He caught it with his knee and righted it before crossing the room to the bar. The barmaid who had been giving Billy big smiles all night was now standing leaning against the rear shelf of the bar. She looked tired, bored, and distracted as if she wished that everyone would just drink up and go home. She probably had a dozen better places to be on a Friday night, a hundred better offers but she was stood serving drinks to an increasingly inebriated crowd. It was no surprise she looked thoroughly pissed off with her lot. Even so, she still managed to summon a smile for Billy. She nodded at the pump.

"Another one?"

"No thanks I was wondering if you could ring me a cab, please?"

"Yes sure, where are you going?"

Billy gave her the address and then waited for her to place the call. While she was speaking on the phone she was writing something on a message pad beside the phone. When she returned she handed the folded paper to Billy.

"You just gave me your address so there's mine. I put my phone number on there too. I am free on Monday and Tuesday nights if you want to meet up."

Billy hurriedly shoved the paper in his back pocket alongside the beermat invitation. He looked over to see if Mel was watching him. She was oblivious to the exchange that was taking place at the bar. She was engrossed in another conversation. Billy turned back to the barmaid who was standing patiently waiting for a response.

"I might very well call you."

"Look forward to it."

She gave Billy another winning smile and then turned and walked away. Over her shoulder she called back
"The name is Natasha and your taxi will be about ten minutes."
Billy thanked the empty space where Natasha had been standing and returned to find Mel who was busy saying goodbye to those hardy souls from the group who were still there.
"Taxi will be here in ten minutes."
He reported to Mel and then joined in the round of farewell hugs, kisses and promises to keep in touch. Even though there was a strong chance that he would be seeing many of the same faces later on that same evening at the party, it was a ritual that had to be observed and failure to do so would be seen as rude or boorish behaviour. Worthy of note and strangest of all the farewells that evening was when he came around to the two young ladies, still dressed up to the hilt for their night on the town. Greta and Tracey had not made it out of the Crusaders and the whole night of drinking had left the pair of them in a fairly inebriated state. Gone now, completely, was all trace of hostility towards Billy, for any slight, real or imagined. In its place there was instead almost pure unconditional carnal lust. Greta was the first, making an excessive show of affection for Billy. Her farewell kiss was far from chaste and Billy felt that if it had gone on any longer than it did, it would have developed into a tongue down the throat snog. When he broke away from her she clung onto his arm. He turned next to Tracey, who seemed slightly more sober but maybe looks defied the reality as she moved in for a kiss she whispered, rather too loudly for Billy's comfort.
"Do you want to come back with Greta and me and fuck our brains out?"
The look that passed between the two ladies made it clear that this was something they had been planning for a while. The look of expectation on Greta's face told Billy that she was equally compliant in the conspiracy. Billy glanced over his shoulder looking around to see where Mel was positioned, not because he was thinking of blowing her out and taking the two up on their offer, but because he was afraid that Mel might have overheard Tracey's offer and it would cause problems for him. Mel was outwardly at least, oblivious to the exchange. Billy turned back to the expectant Tracey.
" Tracey, I would love to take you up on the offer, maybe another time."
"But Greta's only here in London until next Wednesday."
"I'll call you." He promised, "I have your number."
Billy wasn't sure if the offer would still be good in the morning when their hangovers kicked in, so a cooling off period for all concerned might be a good idea. Although as he extracted his arm from Greta's firm grip, he did wonder whether this had been the plan from the outset and was, in fact, the real reason Greta had been so aggrieved that he had failed to show up for their meeting. Had Tracey been conveniently waiting back at her flat for Billy and Greta to show up? He closed the gap and resolved to stay close to Mel as they said the final round of goodbyes.

When they were finally ensconced in the back of the minicab and on their way back to Billy's flat, Mel shuffled across the seat and pulled Billy's arm around her shoulder. This enabled her to rest her head on Billy's chest. It felt normal to Billy, if a little strange. It was the first time he had felt close to Mel since their breakup. The taxi driver only spoke once to break the mood and the silence. He made some mention about roadworks and would they mind if he went an alternative route. Billy mumbled his assent. It would probably end up costing them a few pounds more on the fare but he was enjoying the mood in the back of the cab so it would be money well spent. Mel was so still that Billy thought she had fallen asleep but she sat up with no prompting as the taxi arrived outside Billy's apartment block. She was waiting patiently, by the street door to the flat while Billy collected his change from the taxi driver. Billy fished his keys out of his jacket pocket and opened the door, standing back to let Mel pass him. She punched the light switch and started to climb the stairs.

Because they ran on a timer which only gave you enough time to climb the stairs before plunging you back into an impenetrable inky blackness, Mel punched the light switch again when she reached the top. This gave Billy enough time and light to find the keyhole to the flat's front door. Billy stood back again to let Mel go first. He was expecting her to turn to the left and head into the lounge or right and head towards the kitchen. Instead she went straight ahead and into Billy's bedroom. Billy shut the door and double locked it before shrugging off his jacket and hanging it up. He flicked off the hall light and went into the bedroom. Mel had already taken off her jacket and she was sitting on the edge of the bed kicking off her boots. They hit the floor and she stood up, popped the button on her jeans and shimmied out of them. In the light from the bedside lamp, which Mel had turned on and dimmed Billy got a look at her glorious legs, for the briefest of moments before she pulled up the duvet and dived inside the bed.

"Come on lover boy, don't keep me waiting. It's freezing in here."

Billy didn't need a second invitation. He joined Mel under the covers a few moments later. They made love with all the familiarity of old lovers. The physical side of their relationship had never been a problem for either of them and there was none of the shyness of new lovers between them. Afterwards they lay in each-others arms as heart and pulse rates returned to normal. Mel was lying with her head on Billy's chest, one arm lazily draped across his stomach. Billy's arm was around Mel's shoulders and he was enjoying the warmth from her naked body which was pressed close to his.

"I suppose I owe you an explanation," Mel murmured.

"Would be nice. I am a little confused right now."

Billy was talking to the top of her head. Mel looked up at him through the gloom and as the lamplight caught her face in sharp profile, Billy could see she was smiling.

"You know that if I had a choice in matters, we would still be together."

Billy had never heard this admission from Mel before. In private he had suspected that the rapid demise of their relationship was due to external forces but Mel had never been forthcoming on the subject and had sited other reasons for their breakup. Now in the first light of dawn, and for the first time, Billy was on the verge of getting to the truth. He remained silent hoping that Mel would continue her confession. She didn't disappoint him.

"I think you may have known from the outset that a relationship with me was doomed to failure, but you went ahead with it anyway."

Billy mumbled a denial under his breath and kissed the top of her head.

"Even if you didn't, I should have said something to warn you."

"About what?"

Billy's voice was barely a whisper. He felt Mel move away from him and sit up. He opened his eyes and saw she had half turned around and was propped on one elbow, her naked torso was now caught in the lamplight.

"About having a relationship with a girl like me, from my background."

Mel could see the confusion on Billy's face.

"A Jewish girl, from a good Jewish family. It was never going to work out. There were too many expectations from my family, and you are not Jewish. You would never be acceptable in my family's eyes."

Mel could see that her last words had stung Billy and she reached out to stroke his cheek.

"I think you are a wonderful man, Billy Randell, but you would never be good enough for my parents."

"Because I am not Jewish?"

"Precisely."

"Is that really such a problem in today's world?"

"That's exactly why it would never work. You just don't understand what goes on inside my parents' heads. The way they think."

"So educate me."

Billy had pushed himself up into a semi sitting position, placed an ashtray on his chest and lit a cigarette. He inhaled deeply and blew a cloud of smoke towards the ceiling.

"Well take this evening for an example."

Mel extracted the cigarette from Billy's fingers and took a long lungful of smoke. She handed the cigarette back to him and exhaled.

"I thought it was going to be a normal Friday night Shabbat meal and turned up dressed accordingly. My mother was flapping around like a headless turkey and I thought she was going to have a seizure when she saw what I had on".

"What were you wearing?"

"What I am wearing now."

"Well I can understand her." Billy's grin was lascivious in the extreme.

Mel realised what she had just said and burst out in a fit of giggles.

"I meant what I was wearing, you know, earlier."

"Oh good," Billy smiled, "You turning up for the Shabbat meal in your birthday suit would have ruffled more than a few turkey feathers I imagine."

"Well even my best jeans and boots was not presentable enough. Luckily I still have a couple of acceptable outfits at my parents' house, so I was dispatched upstairs to find something more suitable."

"More suitable for what?"

"Entertaining important guests."

"Oh, so you had guests?"

"Yes, and the worst part was my parents had neglected to tell me in advance."

"Would that have made a difference?"

"Yeah. Particularly as then I would have asked who was coming to dinner."

"And would that foreknowledge have influenced your decision?"

"Most definitely."

Mel pinched the cigarette again and took another long pull.

"And who were these important guests?"

"Isaac and Esther Fischer."

"I am still not following you, do you have a particular problem with these two?"

"Nope, but I do have a real problem with their son, Jacob."

It suddenly all became clear to Billy.

"Oh and Jacob Fischer just happens to be a doctor,"

"Solicitor actually, and about to be called to the Bar."

"So Mama Bishop was doing a little matchmaking for her baby girl."

Mel pulled a sour face.

"I do wish she wouldn't do such things, it's embarrassing."

"I don't," Billy had that lustful look in his eye again,

"Particularly if this is the result of her efforts."

Mel smiled at the thought.

"Yes she would probably stop, if she knew what the outcome was."

Billy stubbed out the cigarette and looked over at Mel. She was still half turned towards him her upper body naked. Billy could see goose bumps forming on her skin where the cool air touched it.

"Want to come back under the covers and warm up?" he asked hopefully.

Mel let her arm slide down and lowered her body back towards the mattress pulling the covers up as she did. Billy placed the ashtray back on the night stand and stretched out his arm towards her. She slid into the circle he created and placed her head back on his chest.

"What about you?" Mel mumbled into his chest.

"Me, oh I am quite happy to make love with you, whenever and where ever you want me to."

Mel dug him in the ribs.

"No I meant what are you going to do now?"

"Me? I think I am either going to make love with you one more time or I am going to fall asleep and I will leave the choice up to you."

This time the dig was a little harder and Billy flinched at the pain.

"Not now, next week. In case it has escaped your notice in your drunken haze, you don't have a job anymore."

"Oh that,"

Billy sounded disappointed. He really did want to either go another round with Mel or get some sleep, he would have been happy with either. What he didn't want to get into right now was a deep and meaningful conversation about his future, but he knew there was no easy way to stop this particular discussion thread until it had been played out and a suitable resolution had been reached. And then it dawned on him.

"I am thinking of heading back to Israel."

Billy felt Mel stiffen next to him and she drew away slightly.

"Really, would you seriously consider going back?"

"Thinking about it, why?"

"To Tel Boker?"

"Maybe, I haven't decided yet."

Billy could sense a rift opening up between him and Mel. This had clearly been caused by his words. Spoken to try and resolve the impasse and get things back onto a more pleasant footing, they had clearly had the opposite effect.

"I am only considering it as one possible option."

This hasty retraction seemed to have a positive effect and Billy felt Mel draw closer to him again.

"Maybe you just need persuading that there is more for you here in London than Israel."

Billy felt Mel's hand slither under the covers and touch his manhood. Their lips met in the semi-darkness and all talk of Israel was forgotten for a while.

## Chapter Four

Billy placed the paper napkin on his lap exclaiming,
"I'm starving."
Billy was having difficulty keeping the smile off his face. He was deliriously happy and he wanted to share his new found happiness with the world. He looked up from his plate across the small table to where Mel was sat. She was focused on her own breakfast.
"So, tell me more about Jacob Fischer."
"Really? Do I have to?"
Mel pulled a sour face
"Well I need to know about the competition."
Billy picked up his orange juice and studied Mel over the rim of the glass. She placed the knife back on her plate and took a small bite from the croissant she had just been buttering. She chewed it slowly with a thoughtful expression on her face. The croissant was hot, fresh from the baker's oven, so the butter now started to melt all over her fingers and some trickled down her chin. She picked up a napkin, wiped her hands and then her chin.
"He is a nice enough guy, wet as a windy weekend in Blackpool, if you ask me. Always very conscientious as a child."
"So you have known the family a long time?"
"Yeah, we were in the same class at primary school and both families attend the same Synagogue."
"Childhood sweethearts, how touching".
Billy pulled a moon face and clasped his hands together across his heart.
"Zip it Randell or I will stab you with your fork."
Billy hurriedly snatched the fork up, moving it out of her reach and returned his attention to the plate of bacon and eggs in front of him.

They had woken after ten and decided on a leisurely start to their Saturday with a stroll down to the Towpath Café by the canal which always served brunch at the weekends. They decided to sit outside in the sunshine and read the papers, whilst their food was being prepared. It had arrived a few moments ago, so they now both focused on eating and their conversation went on hold, until they had both finished. Billy then ordered two coffees and lit up a cigarette.
"Anyway, Randell, about last night?"
"What about last night? You are not going to tell me you regret what happened?"
"Billy, don't be a pratt. No, I mean about you going back to Tel Boker?"
Mel had her serious face on again.
"Are you really thinking about it?"
Now that they were no longer naked in bed, but now sat on opposite sides of a table and as Billy saw it, 'in the cold light of day', even though the sun was heading towards midday, becoming increasingly stronger and the air getting warmer, he sensed a degree of candour was required, simply, because their friendship deserved it.
"Last night, before you arrived, Mark and I were talking about it in the pub. He was asking my advice about travelling to Israel and it was his idea that I should go with him."
Mel had stopped fiddling around with her cutlery while Billy spoke as she was now studying him from the other side of the table, hanging on his every word, whilst trying to fathom out his real intentions.
"I don't care what Mark thinks. What do you think? Mel was earnest now.
"Well, this is pretty much like last time, as I have no ties to here. No job and no ..."

Billy tailed off into silence. He had managed to stop himself before he said 'girlfriend'. Whatever the circumstances of their new arrangement, he didn't want to spoil it before it even got started. Billy had noticed a flash of pain cross Mel's face, when he said that there was nothing to bind him to England. Billy briefly considered clarifying his explanation to include his feelings about their current situation, but something held him back. He had suffered badly when Mel had announced their separation and he didn't see how one night of passion could possibly make up for the hurt she had caused him back then. He still loved Mel, but Billy knew that there would always be the spectre of her family lurking in the background of any relationship they might form. He had accepted the truth back then and it might be fairer on Mel to accept the same truth now.

There were several eerie similarities between now and the last time he had left for Israel. Back then he had just been fired, this time he had quit, but the result was the same, no job. Further more there were no emotional ties to hold him in England. Last time, his best friend was leaving and Billy felt it was right that he should go with him. The only difference was that last time he had been totally skint and while today, he was not exactly flush, at least he would not have to embark on the suicidal course of action he had followed last time by borrowing the money from a psychopathic loan shark. He had a bit of cash put by and then there was his final pay-check, should that ever turn up. So, he had about enough to afford the ticket with a bit of spending money left over. It was not ideal, but what was the alternative?

"Are you seriously thinking about it?"

Mel seemed determined to pin him down. Billy had other ideas. He didn't want to spoil what had up until now, had been a rather promising weekend.

"I haven't really decided one way or another. I just need some time to really think it through."

"But on the balance of probability?"

Mel could be a terrier when she wanted an answer.

"Well, when you put it like that"

Billy grinned at her,

"I think, I will, just order another cappuccino, do you want one?"

Mel snorted with frustration, but she knew Billy well enough to realise when he was being evasive like this. She wanted to make one more attempt to get him to see her point of view.

"Billy you know I care about you."

"I guessed that, you were very caring last night." Billy's lecherous grin was back.

"Billy Randell I swear I will come over there and slap you. I am trying to be serious."

Billy wiped the grin off his face, placed his elbow on the table and rested his chin on his hands. He tried to pull a serious face.

"Billy, you have to realise that you need more in life than a pocketful of charm."

Billy absorbed her words but despite he could see what Mel was getting at he still wanted another coffee.

"Cappuccino or not?"

Mel realised that at this point in time, in the sunshine this was the best she was going to get from Billy.

"Oh go on then."

She had obviously admitted defeat, because she dropped the subject now and they moved on to talk about other things.

Billy had been amazed at how quickly they could fall back into being 'a couple', with all the shared jokes and silly stories. The fact that they had lived so closely during their time in Israel, obviously made a difference. The intensity of a twenty-four by seven relationship was almost akin to a marriage. There was no real downtime from each other except when they slept and this intensity had forged a very close bond between them. After they had finished brunch they went off in search of a pub that was showing a football game and settled down there for an afternoon's entertainment. Mel disappeared at half time saying she wanted to go back to her digs and have a bath and change her clothes. They agreed to meet back at Billy's flat later and then go to the party together. The plan was for the party guests to assemble, later, in a pub at Camden Lock, so there was no urgency to be anywhere on time.

After the game Billy had left the pub with a crowd of disgruntled supporters. Their team had been leading until the final ten minutes, but two goals from the visiting team had snatched their victory away. Both goals had been due to terrible defensive mistakes, so there were loud groans each time the ball crossed the line, followed by expletive laden outbursts about the quality of the defenders and the legitimacy of their birth and parents. At the final whistle the collective groan was probably heard all the way to the ground where the match was being played. Rather vocal and personal comments about the ability of the manager to continue in the job were also now being made. Billy tried to match the mood among the supporters but to be truthful he couldn't give a rat's arse either way, but to reveal such feelings amongst such a staunch group of supporters would have been life threatening so Billy put on his best poker face, hunched his shoulders and walked with the crowds to the nearby tube station.


A live band were playing on the stage when Billy and Mel entered the pub later that night and Billy was struck by how talented the group were. He was more accustomed to amateur provincial bands, so to see a group of musicians who were on the cusp of a flourishing musical career was very refreshing. He made a mental note of the name of the band, just so that in a few years time, when and more importantly if, they had hit the big time, he could brag about how he had seen them, when they were still unknown and playing in a small pub in Camden Town. He knew it was a fruitless exercise, as he wouldn't remember the band's name the following morning, but he secretly envied those people who claimed, genuinely or otherwise, to have been present at the first public outings for superstar bands like Dire Straits, the Clash and Duran Duran.

The band came to the end of their set causing ragged and sporadic applause from the audience. They left the stage and made a beeline for the bar where several aloof looking geezers were congregated in a group. Billy guessed they were the power-brokers, the men that held the fate of this band of hopefuls in the palms of their hands. These were the A&R men from the record companies, invited here by the band's management, in the hope that they would be sufficiently impressed to offer the band a lucrative recording contract. Billy spent a while watching the elaborate posturing and power-plays, before losing interest and going off in search of Mark and the rest of his friends.

Mel had left Billy almost as soon as they entered the pub. Billy wondered if she was keeping her distance to prevent the usual chin-wagging and scuttlebutt. Most of the people who had been invited tonight, knew that they had been an item in the past, had now split up, but remained friends. To arrive together, as friends, would be natural enough, but to spend too much time in each other's company would start tongues wagging. As neither of them knew what exactly was going on or seemed particularly keen on confronting their feelings, it was probably better that way. Billy was happy enough to give Mel that freedom without causing an unnecessary scene and Billy was still trying to decipher Mel's strange comment from earlier. What exactly was a pocketful of charm. He had heard several stories from volunteers returning from Egypt with pockets crammed full of lapis lazuli scarabs, given to them by hawkers and conmen alike who seemed to infest every public monument. Maybe they were the ones with real pockets full of charms. Billy couldn't see what Mel was going on about. Maybe he could ask her later if they had a moment alone.

Right now Mel's absence meant that he was free to flirt with whomever he chose without fear of repercussions from the sisterhood. Spending the day with Mel also meant that he was not as pissed as he might have been, if he had spent the whole day alone. This partial sobriety made Billy a more amenable person and therefore not as obnoxious as when he was drunk.

He was standing among a group of friends, when the guy who Billy eventually recognised as the party's host, broke into the middle of the group and said that people would be moving on shortly to where the party was taking place. Billy was in no particular hurry to leave the pub as there was the prospect of another band taking to the stage in a short while. Their roadies were swarming all over the small stage setting up mic-stands and guitar amps with what looked like practiced efficiency. If this crew were anything to go by then the band would probably be quite professional too. Billy glanced over at the bar and noticed there was still the posse of music business fixers still milling around, so this next act had already done enough to pique their interest.

Mel found Billy and told him she was going on to the party. Billy said he was going to stick around for the last band, so Mel gave him a rather chaste peck on the cheek and took off with a couple of other people in tow. The band had just started their opening number, when Billy felt a tug on his arm. He looked up and saw Mark smiling at him. Mark leaned close and yelled in Billy's ear.

"They're good aren't they?"

Billy didn't bother to answer but just nodded his head. Mark raised his glass and looked enquiringly at Billy. Billy nodded in agreement and Mark headed off to the bar, returning a few minutes later with two pints and two large whiskeys on the rocks. Mark had done the same as Billy and tucked one of the whisky's into his shirt pocket. Billy winced as he remembered last night's incident. He reached over and extracted the glass to prevent a repeat accident. Mark grinned at Billy as they both raised their glasses and downed the contents in one. Billy then began to sip slowly from his pint.

Forty five minutes later and after the statutory two encores the band were gone and the roadies were packing away their gear. In the quiet after the band's departure Mark and Billy had begun to talk again.

"Should we go on to the party when we've finished these?" Billy asked.

"Yeah, probably a good idea, before the flat gets too crowded and they start turning people away. I have heard most people in here talking about this party, even if they don't know where it is or who is holding it."

"Is there an offy round here? I need to get something to take."

Mark, who was a local to the district, thought for a moment and then consulted his wristwatch.

"Too late for an off-licence mate."

Billy tried to hide his disappointment. It would be a dry old party without any booze.

"But, now I come to think of it, there is an Asian mini-market that still is open that will sell you a bottle, even after hours".

Billy's face now beamed.

"Excellent, lead the way."

The two friends left the pub and headed off into the night.


The flat where the party was being held, like so many of the apartments in this part of the world, was situated above a row of shops. To gain access to the flats it was necessary to go to the end of the row and then take a side alley that smelt of cat piss and dog shit that led around the side of the shops. A metal staircase scaled the side of the building, before turning into a concrete walkway that led you past the front doors of the individual flats. The walkway was dimly lit and also stank of excrement, but not of the animal kind. Underneath the walkway, were the stockrooms and offices for the shops and along the length of the row, there were glass skylights into the premises below. These were lit from within, so the walkway itself was largely in deep shadows. There was an access road running behind the shops and the street lights along one stretch, seemed to be permanently out. In the pitch blackness two cats were howling at each other in a rowdy and raucous argument over territory. As Billy and Mark walked along, their caterwauling rose slowly until it exploded, as one of the animals made a lunge at the other. In the struggle a dustbin was overturned with a loud metallic crash and the lid careened off along the lane, sounding like a noisy cymbal crescendo at the end of a rock song.

"Lovely." Billy commented to no one in particular.

As he gazed out across this wasteland, a tube train thundered past with the sparks flying along the live rail, like camera flashguns at a press call, illuminating the decay. In the flickering strobe light, Billy caught brief flashes of the landscape. The lane behind the flats was choked with weeds, overgrown grass and cluttered with an old fridge, cooker, a couple of mouldy mattresses and a rusting bike frame.

"Yeah nice place."

This brief glimpse had confirmed Billy's initial evaluation.

It was not difficult to find the flat where the party was being held. There were two or three people standing outside leaning on the metal railings and the front door was open, the sound of loud music spilling out along with the light from the hallway. Billy nodded at the guys propping up the railing as he and Mark went inside. The hallway light had been shrouded with a red plastic bag to dim it and there were a couple taking advantage of the gloom to get much better acquainted. Billy swivelled sideways to avoid disturbing them and then moved further inside the flat. The layout was similar to Billy's, but larger, with three bedrooms as opposed to his one. This meant with the living room and kitchen, there were five different spaces and five distinctly different vibes to the party. In the living room someone had cranked up the stereo and installed a couple of disco lights. A few couples were dancing in there. In one of the bedrooms the smell of cannabis was overwhelming and there were about ten people all sat around in various states of intoxication. A couple of people were diligently rolling joints on the obligatory album cover, ensuring there was a non-stop supply of reefers. Billy had never been a big fan of drugs. Growing up on a council estate, he had seen, from a very early age, the unhappiness and chaos that drugs could cause. He, therefore, gave the dope heads room a wide berth.

In the next room there was a very intense political discussion going on. As some of the party guest were students at Mel's University it was inevitable that some highbrow discussion about politics, religion or philosophy would break out. It was impossible to mix alcohol with intellect and not avoid it, although the absence of common sense and restraint caused by the former usually meant that these things ended up in screaming matches and tears, or even physical blows being exchanged. Billy passed on that room too.

The last bedroom was the box room and it was where people had dumped their coats, it also seemed to be occupied at the moment, as the door was firmly locked from the inside and two girls were hammering on the door trying to get the attention of whoever was inside, because they wanted to collect their coats and leave. Billy being the helpful person that he was, stopped beside the two girls.

"Problem?" he addressed both of them.

"The door is locked and our coats are inside."
One of the girls answered for the pair.
"Are they passed out or awake?"
"Awake, I think. We just heard voices from in there."
The girl's cheeks flushed slightly with embarrassment. Billy immediately grasped the essence of the problem. Someone had locked themselves in the room for that additional level of privacy required for intimacy and hadn't realised that the place was doubling as a cloakroom or had been too out of it to realise. The girls had probably heard them in the advance throes of passion, hence their red faces. Billy pounded violently on the door nearly taking it off its hinges. He yelled something suitably rude and then pounded on the door once more to enforce his point. There was no reaction from inside the room, so he turned apologetically to the girls.
"Short of kicking the door down, I don't know what else to suggest. Maybe the hosts can help, they might have a spare key?"
The two girls smiled at Billy and thanked him for his help. They set off to try and track down one of the hosts of the party to see if there was possibly a spare key. Billy followed Mark down the corridor towards the kitchen.

As with most student parties, the kitchen along with the stoners' room were always going to be the most popular. This kitchen, despite its surprisingly large size, was no exception, it was rammed. The hosts, in a vain attempt to be just that, had taken the trouble to lay on some snacks, but they seemed to have been largely ignored, with the exception of one large bowl of crisps that had been spilt on to the floor adding a slightly crunchy texture underfoot. The food, spread out on the kitchen counter, was being diligently ignored by everyone and the main focus of attention was the kitchen table, which had been pushed up against the wall and was serving as the bar. Billy was carrying a green plastic bag containing eight cans of lager, which he unpacked and dropped on the table, but not before first freeing one from the plastic and handing it to Mark and then taking one for himself and popping the ring-pull. As the beer had been taken from the cooler cabinet at the mini-market it was still cold enough to be pleasant. Standing in front of the table he surveyed the contents of the bar. There were several bottles of wine, a litre of beer and another of cider, along with several bottles of spirits. Billy was drawn to the three-quarters full bottle of Bells scotch towards the back of the table, so he hooked it off and tucked it under his arm. He took a couple of plastic cups from the stack and then turned away from the table.

He glanced around the room checking out the noisy throng, looking for signs of Mel. She didn't seem to be in the kitchen. He leaned in close to Mark who was also surveying the room, although probably searching for single females to charm the pants off, literally.
"I am going to try and find Mel."
"Okay I will be with you in a moment."
Mark clearly wanted to be thorough in his investigations. Billy left the kitchen with his beer in one hand, the plastic cups in the other and the whiskey bottle still tucked under his arm. He seriously doubted that Mel would be ensconced in the stoners' room, that wasn't really her scene either. That left the debating chamber or the dance floor. He chose the debating chamber first, as it was closest. A body in search of a place to sit had wedged itself directly behind the door, so Billy met with some resistance when he tried to push his way inside. The body relented and the door opened just enough for Billy to squeeze inside. The room was dimly lit by only the single bedside light and a couple of large blocky candles burning on a dressing table. Most of the occupants were sat on the floor, as the bed was fully occupied. As Billy swung the door open he heard voices raised in acrimonious argument, but they fell silent when Billy appeared. All the faces in the room were turned in his direction. Billy waved his hand holding the beer.

"Carry on, don't let me stop you," he addressed the assembled group in general. "You can't supress freedom of speech."

Billy was about to open his mouth to reply that he had absolutely no intention of supressing anything when he realised that the comment had not been directed at him. The number of heads nodding their agreement told Billy that this was just a continuation of the discussion that had been taking place when Billy had barged in. Billy looked over at the speaker, a typical right-on student type, with the right mixture of post-punk hair, smart suit jacket and jeans, intense face enclosed by John Lennon glasses. He, in his turn, was examining Billy and clearly didn't like what he saw, because he sniffed at Billy before launching back into his diatribe against the evil Tory government and their fascist policies. Billy, satisfied that Mel was not in the room, backed hastily out into the hallway and pulled the door shut behind him, just as another voice took over from the first, adding their viewpoint to the general argument. Billy took another mouthful from the beer can and set off for the living room, drawn by the deep throbbing bass of the music.

To add that extra kick to the house stereo one of the hosts of the party had borrowed an amplifier and a couple of column speakers. The owner of the sound rig, probably a part time DJ had also loaned them some disco lights and a projector, so the room was bathed in intermittent shades of red, blue and green, while one wall was a kaleidoscope of dripping and coagulating colours as the wheel containing oil based paint spun inside the projector. From time to time shadows passed across the coloured wall, as bodies danced through the projector's beam of light.

As Billy worked his way around the edge of the room, the music changed, shifting from some pounding reggae beat to a more laid back funk style. Billy looked over at the posse who had captured the stereo and effected the sea change in the music. They were in a tight group with their heads close together as they nodded in time with the beat. Billy always found it amusing that the music at house parties was constantly changing. No sooner had one group commandeered the stereo and put on whatever they wanted to hear, or dance to, only to be unable to actually enjoy themselves and dance, because as soon as they moved away from the stereo, someone would move in and replace the song playing with whatever they wanted to hear. There never seemed to be a consensus, even with popular songs at the top of the music charts. It was a total catch 22 situation and could often become a serious flashpoint later in the night after alcohol had drowned common sense and tempers started to fray. The funksters, currently in control of the stereo, were obviously wise to the game, so they stayed close, maintaining an over-watch as their music played. The funk, proved less popular with the rest of the audience who had been dancing, so they left to replenish their drinks or visit the bathroom. As the space cleared, Billy spotted Mel. She was on the far side of the room sat on one of a set of beany bags talking with a girl and a guy who were cuddled up close on another of the bags. Mel looked up as Billy approached and smiled. She said something to the couple and they both smiled up at Billy too. Billy crouched down close to Mel, so he could speak to her over the noise of the music.

"Have you got room for one more on your bag?"

Mel scooted around making room for Billy. He handed her the two plastic cups and then used his free hand to remove the bottle from under his arm, before turning around and sitting down heavily. Mel held up the two cups while Billy poured out a measure of the scotch into each then they touched cups and drank. Without ice and neat, the scotch was pretty raw on the tongue and Mel winced a little. Billy chased his with a mouthful of beer. Mel produced a can of her own and did the same.

The funk track came to an end and there seemed to be an extended debate among the group of DJ's on which song to follow it with. Mel took the advantage of the quiet to introduce Billy to her two friends. Kev and Simone were fellow students from Mel's course.

The topic of conversation was light, mostly about gigs and pubs the two had visited since their arrival in London from rural Hampshire and the difference between the two places in terms of nightlife and general excitement. The pair did most of the talking in that cute couples finishing each other's sentences way, that Billy found slightly nauseating. There was plenty of hand touching and public shows of fondness between the two.

Billy did his best to remain polite and attentive to their conversation, but was intermittently interrupted as the music cut in, but trying to provide music by committee is never a good idea, as the decision process seemed to be reversed after a few bars of the song and the debate around the stereo became more heated with disagreements clearly taking place over which direction the music should take. The crowd in the room was definitely thinning out as people wandered off looking for alternative entertainment.

Billy had placed the scotch bottle on the floor, beside his cushion and Mel waved her cup in front of him signifying she needed a refill. Billy obliged, topped up his own glass and then replaced the cap placing the bottle down by his side again. The bottle did the rounds once more when the music again ground to a halt. It had just started up, a different beat from a different group. The funksters had retired to a corner to plan a new strategy. In the silence a new DJ took over but he had a trick or two up his sleeve. His mixtape was firmly grounded in the party tunes, floor fillers from the seventies and within a few bars the room was packed with sweaty posturing men and simpering women as the full force of glam rock took control.

Billy had to turn sideways on his cushion to avoid being trampled under stamping feet and he considered moving from the beany bags to a safer place, when the lights in the room came on and a new crowd strode into the room. Billy recognised the guy that invited him among the newcomers. One of them went straight for the stereo and turned the music off eliciting a loud groan from the dancers, who had just got back into their swing again. Voices were raised and arms waved, red faces fuelled by booze and sweaty from their recent exertions, turned on the gang, who had surrounded the stereo, demanding an explanation. Billy, who with the cessation of all the jigging around had decided it was safe enough to remain seated wondered what the problem could be? Usually this sort of behaviour was reserved for ejecting gate crashers or when some form of damage had been done to the property and the hosts were keen to identify and eject the perpetrators, after extracting as much compensation as they could. Payment was usually demanded with menaces, verbal at first and then with a rising scale of violence. The problem was that by this time on a Saturday night people, particularly students, were lucky if they had more than their bus fare home on them. Hardly enough to replace a broken light fitting or repair any substantial damage to the fabric of the property. On one occasion, Billy had heard, the offenders were frog marched down to the local branch of Barclays Bank and threatened with actual bodily harm if they didn't withdraw the necessary compensation from the cashpoint. Whatever the reason for the interruption, the host had turned up with a sizeable backup team, a number of whom looked suitably boozed up and aggressive. Billy thought it might be a good moment to charge his glass. If there was going to be a scene, he wanted to have a front row seat with a drink in his hand, so he could enjoy the show. He had just replaced the bottle down on the floor and looked up when he realised that the crowd had surrounded him. He was looking, at knee height, into a jungle of denim clad legs. He strained his neck to look upwards at the faces of the group. The host, the one who had personally invited Billy to the party, was stood in the centre at the front of the group.

"Is this the guy?"

He pointed an accusatory finger in Billy's direction. A voice behind him uttered a single word.

"Yes".

From the group backing up the host, one broke ranks, bent down and made a grab for the whisky bottle that was stood on the floor beside Billy, handing it to the host. Billy made no attempt to stop him, he had a full cup, so he didn't care. The host held the bottle aloft and towards the overhead light, examining the remaining contents of the bottle.

"You fucking thief."

The rest of the group echoed the single word "thief", like it was some ritualistic chant. Billy noticed that Kev and Simone were sidling away, attempting to put distance between him and them. Staying close to the wall and trying to remain inconspicuous, they were moving slowly away from Billy and Mel. Billy struggled to his feet and met the host eye to eye. The guy was red in the face, maybe from too much drink, or maybe he was just naturally florid in his complexion. Billy sized up his opponent. He was not muscled in the way an athlete might be, but he was still bigger than Billy and he had an ugly bunch at his back. Billy, however was not afraid and he was not about to back down and go quietly.

"What the fuck did you just call me?"

"Thief,"

The guy was unrepentant and unflinching and certainly not about to withdraw his accusation. The rest of his backers again repeated the word for him like some ghostly, sibilant echo.

"Thief, thief, thief."

"You stole this bottle of whiskey," he added helpfully, just in case there was any question about what Billy was guilty of stealing. He held up the bottle as he spoke, like Exhibit A, so that everyone around him was left in no doubt as to the severity of the crime. Billy snatched at the bottle as it was waved in front of him and his reflexes were just a little faster than that of the host. Billy held the bottle with his hand covering the label and pointed the metal cap in the direction of his principal accuser.

"This bottle was sat on the table along with all the others. There was no sign on it to say 'don't touch'."

He prodded the bottle in the direction of the host with every other word the metal cap was getting closer to the host's breastbone. Before the end of the sentence Billy had forced him into taking a humiliating step backwards to avoid being thumped in the chest. Billy was getting angry now and his voice was starting to rise along with his temper.

"You just don't do that sort of thing. Take a bottle. That was why there were cups beside it."

"Oh I thought the cups were for drinking out of."

Billy's voice dripped with sarcasm which was wasted on the group.

"You want your bottle," Billy waved it close to the ringleaders face,

"Come on then, take it."

He jabbed the bottle forward aggressively, this time it was as if he was going to drive the metal lid into the soft skin of his cheek.

"Billy! Stop it, now!"

Mel's voice was loud in Billy's ear. He was temporarily caught off guard by her intervention and took his eyes of the group as he glanced at Mel. Two things then happened at once. One of the other group members, spotting Billy's momentary distraction, made a grab for the bottle and snatched it free and the ringleader, fearing that the diplomatic dialog had broken down, decided that he would try and launch a physical attack on Billy. He was obviously not familiar with the brawling game because he began his punch a long way back, telegraphing his intention for all the world to see. Billy caught sight of the movement out of the corner of his eye and responded instantly. Billy had experienced his fair share of bar-room brawls while growing up and knew the importance of the first strike. He also knew that a long wind up, left the attacker horribly exposed. Billy took advantage of that exposure and deployed a simple straight jab from the shoulder. It was faster, more accurate and with Billy still retaining most of the musculature he had built up during his time in Israel, deadlier. His fist connected with the ringleader's nose, snapping his head backwards and breaking the nose in the process. Although, the ringleader's knees now had given out and he had toppled backwards in a faint, he was still being held upright by the press of his supporters who let out a collective animal howl, as they moved in on Billy. Fists were raised and Billy got ready to defend himself. He was not going down without a fight. This wasn't necessary though.

At that exact moment Mark chose to enter the fray. Billy's attackers were clearly not expecting involvement and certainly not from the rear and they fell aside as Mark forced his way through the pack.

"Alright, alright, alright." He bellowed.

His voice was strident and authoritative enough to freeze everyone in place. He smothered Billy in a huge bear hug, pinioning his arms and preventing any further violence from his friend. He pressed Billy up against the wall. Billy struggled briefly, but then sensing Mark's superior strength, he relaxed. Mark sensing that Billy had calmed down now turned back to face the group. The ringleader was sobbing and holding his shattered nose, as blood flowed freely through his clenched fingers and stained his shirt. Someone yelled out to call the police and there was a general hubbub of raised angry voices.

"It's okay, we are leaving."

Mark announced to the group and then looked back over his shoulder at Billy who just nodded his head. Mark looked at Mel who also nodded. Billy who was still clutching his plastic cup of whiskey drained the remnants and then tossed the empty cup onto the floor in defiance. The three left the room accompanied by a stony silence, broken only by the host who was whimpering over his shattered nose.

"Someone better get him some ice." growled Billy to no one and everyone.

Outside the flat they made their way back down to street level and began the search for a taxi.

"These fucking people. These fucking people."

Billy kept repeating under his breath. He was both angry and disappointed at the same time. For good measure he then yelled it out a couple of times at the top of his voice and was rewarded with a couple of bedroom lights going on along the street.

"Hush, Billy be quiet," Mel said in an angry voice, "or somebody will end up calling the police."

Billy turned around and walked backwards facing Mel.

"But they just don't get it, just don't get it at all."

Billy had dropped his voice to a more conversational level.

"Don't get what?"

Mel was prepared to talk sensibly with Billy, if he was prepared to maintain an even tone and not annoy the sleeping neighbours.

"The whole meaning of life. The way it should be lived. All this over a six quid bottle of whisky. It's not really worth it, is it?"

"It's somebody's hard earned money. Not everyone wants to share."

"They are bloody students, and it's somebody else's hard earned money."

Mel flashed an angry look at Billy. They had been down this particular route before over student grants.

"That's not the point, Billy, it's a different set of values, different priorities."

"I don't see why? Half the people in that flat tonight, at least half of them were in Israel and yet none of them, yeah none of them, found what happened in the least bit upsetting? Have they all forgotten the way we lived out there?"

Mel got the point Billy was trying to make, but she countered it with logic.

"Billy this is North London not Tel Boker. We are in England and not Israel."

"So, you keep reminding me."

Billy's voice had lost its edge now and was normal, if tinged with a little disappointment.
"Well there is no escaping the ugly truth."
"That's where you are wrong Mel. It's easy to escape this horrible truth. I can hop on a plane tomorrow and be back in Israel by the end of the day."
"And what are you going to do? Just go back to Tel Boker and hope they need a lifeguard again?"
Mel's voice had taken on a lightly mocking tone now.
Billy, who had not really thought through the plan, had no answer. What he was certain of was that he felt a pressing need, a visceral hunger to return to Israel and that he was uncertain that he would have any inner peace or contentment until he had achieved this goal.

Mark had drifted off across the road. He wanted to give them some space to argue in private and he also wanted to try and get a taxi, so that they didn't end up walking all the way home. Mark yelled out and Billy looked up. Mark was standing next to a black cab with its light on and waving them over. Mel waited for a break in the traffic and then began to cross the road. She paused, on the traffic island in the middle of the road and then she realised that Billy wasn't following her. She looked back at him.
"Are you coming?"
Right up until that exact moment there had been no discussion on a repeat of last night. Billy had spent some time trying to figure out whether it was a one-off, or whether it meant that things were back on between him and Mel. He had reached no satisfactory conclusion. And now Mel was stood in the middle of the road yelling at Billy to join her. Billy's legs were refusing to move.
"I'm heading in the other direction to you two. You go ahead, I'll catch another cab or a night bus."
Mel hesitated, indecisive. She wanted to come back and at least give Billy a hug, but the lights had changed again and there was a fresh stream of traffic racing towards her. If she waited, crossed and then had to wait to return she knew the cab driver wouldn't wait for her and it might be ages, before they found another free one. She raised her arm in a farewell gesture and then crossed to where Mark was holding the door of the taxi open for her.

As the black cab disappeared off down the road, Billy turned and carried on walking in the direction of the bus stop. His timing was impeccable as usual. There was a monstrous clap of thunder, the heavens opened and the rain came teeming down. Billy shrugged his jacket closed and thrust his hands deep in his pockets. Rain was dripping off his collar and trickling down the inside of his shirt, his feet in his sneakers were wet through in minutes and his hair was beginning to cling to his head. Great, fucking great. As he stood shivering at the bus stop he thought about the weather in Israel right now. Even at this time of the morning there would still be a warm breeze and instead of standing here drenched, he might even be raising a slight sweat. He knew in that moment that he would make the trip. Right now he just had to figure out the logistics.

## Chapter Five

Billy woke next morning, to find the rain had stopped sometime during the night, as the sky now had that washed out grey colour to it. Before crawling into bed, Billy had taken the time to stuff all of his dirty washing into a massive sports holdall, as he intended to make use of the brand new washing machine and drier that his mum had purchased after Billy had left home. They had started to sell bargain-price white goods in the supermarket where she worked and with her staff discount these two items were now affordable. Finding space for them in her flat though had proved to be more of a challenge. Eventually, Billy's mum had made the tough decision to remove the bath tub from the bathroom and install a shower cabin, as the extra space this created was then perfect for stacking her washer and dryer. This decision was only possible, because Susie Randell had taken the bold step of buying her flat from the local council, under the 'Right to Buy' legislation that had been enacted by the National Government. Her former landlords, the local borough council would never have approved such a fundamental change to the layout of one of their properties, but as the owner, she could do almost whatever she wanted.

So Billy was lugging a full holdall of dirty laundry as he made his way across town that morning towards the main terminus at Kings Cross. The sky was overcast and there was a slight breeze blowing, so Billy zipped up his jacket as he got off the bus and crossed the road. He then had to negotiate the large paved area in front of the main station building. Crossing to the main entrance he was accosted three times by scrawny, ill-fed and dishevelled looking women in various states of undress, asking if he wanted "any business?" These were the street walkers, the prostitutes, the chancers and the con-artists who plied their trade in front of the station. They could be found in larger numbers after dark and in most of the side streets of the surrounding area. Some were genuine prostitutes, others were con-artists, who would take your money and run.

Billy had witnessed his fair share of ugly scenes when men, often drunk, had been ripped off and then challenged the woman concerned only for her pimp or handler to step in and throw his weight around. It was easy money. Who, in their right mind, is going to complain to a police officer that they have been denied sexual favours in return for money? Admitting to soliciting for sexual services, whether a transaction had taken place or not, was an offence in itself and as a result the pimps and their girls often got away with it and their success in this practice merely encouraged others to join in. It was a growth industry and had made a negative impact on the 'red-light' scene in the whole area as people started to look elsewhere for girls who were less drug-addled and also more honest. Billy couldn't blame the girls. Who, given the choice would want to endure a drunken fumble when you can take the money and run? Literally.

Billy rejected all three offers and ignored the two down and outs who begged him for money for a cup of tea. He knew they were collecting money, but the object of their desire was not a refreshing cup of tea, but rather their next can of Tennents super strength lager. The soliciting and begging stopped as soon as Billy pushed his way through the doors and entered the station building. The uniformed British Railways employees kept a close eye on the comings and goings of these night-denizens and beggars and were quick to intervene and eject any who strayed onto station property. This meant Billy was able to stroll over to the ticket machine and buy his train ticket without constant harassment. Ticket in hand, he joined the large throng of people on the main concourse, in front of the departures board detailing today's train traffic.

Being a Sunday, there was a reduced service, so there were trains only twice every hour to Billy's destination, but he had timed his arrival perfectly and there was a train due to leave in about ten minutes, but the station controllers had not put the platform number up just yet. The announcer's voice cut through the general buzz of people talking to inform passengers that 'The next train to Leeds was ready for boarding from platform 6 stopping at ...' and a number of people, who had clearly been waiting for this snippet of information picked up their belongings and started to move like a small army in the direction of that platform. Billy could feel that the shot of coffee he had consumed in his kitchen before leaving was starting to wear off and the first signs of an encroaching hangover were beginning to make themselves felt. He looked around to assess his options. There were a couple of places he could purchase a coffee to go or there was the station shop where he could purchase something a little stronger and take away the craving that he knew would begin to bite really soon. He dug deep in his jeans pocket for some cash and began to walk in the direction of the shop. He had just pulled out a handful of coins and crumpled notes, when he felt a hand tug at his elbow. Billy turned around and caught a full blast in the face.

There was the overwhelming smell of stale alcohol, rotting teeth, un-washed body and underlying it all, there was a faint whiff of urine. One of the local 'personalities' seemed to have evaded the ever watchful eyes of the station staff and was now plying his trade, aggressively, amongst the passengers waiting in front of the departures board. Probably realising his time was short and that at any moment he would feel the unwelcome hands of the station staff on his person and be forcibly, if necessary, removed from the concourse and slung out in the street, this particular chap had no time for the usual pleasantries and preamble.

"Have you got a quid for a beer?"
He looked shiftily over his own shoulders to left and right, looking for possible inbound station staff, before doing the same over both of Billy's. Billy was struck immediately by the fellow's honesty. Not for this chap the usual baloney about a 'cup of tea' or 'something to eat'. No, this guy was not going to disguise his ultimate aim, which was to secure himself enough money to purchase his next can of premium strength lager. This honesty had a remarkable effect on Billy who took one look at the filthy, dirt encrusted, hand, outstretched towards him, palm upwards. The whole soiled extremity was quivering with anticipation or the DT's. Billy looked down at his own hand. It was cleaner and the finger nails were neatly manicured. The gold of his money shone from the centre of his scrubbed palm, but as he watched the hand it trembled slightly. He snatched two pound coins from his own palm and dropped them into the centre of the tramp's. The vagrant stared at his hand until his brain registered what had happened and the coins were whipped away somewhere inside the rags. He snapped a half salute at Billy accompanied by a drunken,

"Sah. Thank you Sah"
before this forgotten hero, turned on his heels and marched back into the crowd.

Billy walked across the station forecourt, trying to rid himself of the foul smell that had invaded his nasal passages and now seemed reluctant to leave, as it hung around long after its previous owner had departed. In the station shop he was fidgety as he queued up, consciously aware that his train was departing imminently. When it was his turn to be served he didn't even think twice before ordering a half bottle of Bells scotch whiskey. He dropped the exact money in coins on the counter and swept out of the shop. He checked the departures board and saw his train was leaving from one of the suburban platforms away from the main concourse. He started to trot in that direction, pausing only for a moment to crack the seal and twist the metal cap off the bottle before taking a long swig. On the platform he lit a cigarette, puffing hard to finish it in time. Hearing the doors closing warning bleeps, he flicked the lit dog end into the gap, between the platform and the train and then hauled the heavy holdall into the carriage, just as the doors thumped shut.

Being an early Sunday morning the train was deserted, so Billy found an empty group of seats, pushed his holdall under the seat opposite and collapsed backwards, shuffling across to gaze out the window. The train began its slow progress through the tunnels and cuttings as it headed out of the heart of the city and into the northern suburbs. As the train began to pick up speed, the scenery began to flash by so he picked up an abandoned newspaper from the seat opposite him and while scanning through the headlines, he occasionally took a nip from the neck of the bottle. The train made its way through the Hertfordshire countryside stopping at almost every station to let passengers disembark as was the way with the Sunday service.

An older woman sitting on the opposite side of the carriage, kept looking over at him and tutting loudly. Billy wasn't sure whether it was a reaction to the rather well-endowed woman, whose semi-naked torso was sprawled across the page of the newspaper that was facing her, or the fact that he was openly and continually drinking. Whichever was causing offence, Billy didn't give a shit, because the scotch was beginning to weave its highland magic, arming him with that subtle feeling of invincibility and banishing the last shreds of his hangover. No prudish, church-going, dolled up old biddy in her Sunday best twinset and pearls was going to spoil his day.

Two stops before Billy's, where the house prices started in the hundreds of thousands and most of the properties came equipped with backyard swimming pools or horse paddocks, she let out one final rather explosive and pointed tut, as she stood up. Then sniffed disapprovingly at Billy, almost intimating that his very presence was an unacceptable blot on the landscape. She tutted loudly once more as she passed Billy on her way to the exit. As the train rolled to a stop and the driver released the doors with a hydraulic hiss, she and Billy made eye contact. She sniffed one more time, shook her head and was gone. The doors closed and the train began to move. She remained, standing stock still on the platform, starring daggers at Billy. It was definitely an art-form, perfected by ladies of a certain age and breeding. She had been able to convey her absolute disgust and thorough disapproval of Billy and his actions, without uttering a single word. Even Billy had to acknowledge the success of her actions, he had truly been in the presence of a master of the art. He raised his forefinger to his temple in a mock salute then joined it with his middle finger as he lowered his hand slightly flicking a V sign in her direction. As he watched her eyes widened in shock and her mouth formed a perfect O.

The effect on Billy was minimal, as he continued devouring both his paper and the half bottle of scotch with such relish that both were finished as the train pulled into his station. He consigned both the paper and the empty bottle to the plastic bin by the doors as he waited for them to open. Eventually they slid back and Billy joined the crowd slowly tramping up the stairs to the ticket hall. Unusually for a Sunday, there was a full complement of ticket inspectors, waiting at the barrier, ready to ambush the unwary traveller who had boarded the train without a ticket. Those guilty were herded to one side for a talking to and a penalty fine. Billy handed over his ticket and sailed through the barrier unhindered. He swung the holdall over his shoulder and began to cross the bridge that led from the station to the town centre. Only the fast food restaurants were open at this time on a Sunday, all the other shops were shut. Billy waded through the drifting garbage of burger wrappers and empty plastic cups, chip papers and old beer cans. He navigated a course through the proliferation of pavement pizzas and discarded food, the left overs from last nights revelries, looking down occasionally, always being careful to check where he put his feet. Eyes cast down in this fashion he barely registered the pushchair that was approaching him, but he automatically stood sideways to allow both chair and mother to pass him by safely.

"Billy? Billy Randell?"

Billy looked up at the sound of his name. The woman, correction, young lady wheeling the pushchair had stopped and was looking at Billy in a strange way. Nothing new there? Billy's face was obviously blank although he felt that he should know this woman.

"Billy, it's me, Jo."

Memories came flooding back to him of a couple of stolen nights of passion, just before he left England for Israel. Joanna, he never did get her surname, had sold him his plane ticket for the trip and then kept him company for the next couple of days. She had confessed after their first night of passion that she actually had a boyfriend, but fortunately for both of them the boyfriend would not be returning home until long after Billy had left the country. They had enjoyed a couple of nights of good sex and then each gone their separate ways.

"My God, Jo, how are you? I must confess I didn't recognise you."

"I am lucky these days if anyone so much as looks at me, let alone recognises me."

She sounded bitter and resentful.

"Pushing one of those around usually does that for you." Billy nodded at the pushchair. He couldn't resist a little peek at the sleeping toddler. All he could see was a head enclosed in a woolly hat.

"Cute kiddie though, how old is it?"

Billy suddenly had a horrible thought and began to count forwards from his original departure date. This thought was clear on his face, because Jo threw back her head and laughed. It was a rich and strangely sexy laugh.

"Don't worry, it's not yours. Unlike some of the kids in this town this one was conceived and born inside wedlock."

She held up her left hand to show Billy her wedding band.

"Oh wow, you tied the knot."

"Yes. I did, with Allan."

"Was he?"

"Yes, he was the guy I was seeing when I met you."

Billy listened carefully to the tone of Jo's voice, searching for any indication that their past fling had left any favourable impression on her. Her voice was flat and Billy took that as a No. He was expecting to hear stories of a fairy-tale wedding and blissful married life. What came next completely floored him.

"It was the biggest mistake I ever made."

Seeing Billy's astonishment Jo felt she had to explain herself.

"Allan is a lovely guy, very kind and he is good with Simon. When he is here, which isn't very often."

"How come?"

"He works away on the oil rigs, so he is gone for months at a time and then only home on shore leave for a couple of days. Oh don't get me wrong the money is excellent, but I sometimes get really lonely."

She pulled a sad face.

"But enough about me, how are things with you?"

Jo clearly brightened at the prospect of changing the subject and moving the conversation away from her own woes.

"You never did come back and tell me about your adventures like you promised?"

Jo folded her arms across her chest and looked disapprovingly at Billy, before cracking a smile. In that smile Billy saw a flash of the old Jo.

"Oh you know, went away did my bit, starred in a film, met lots of women, got drunk a few times and came home. That's the highlights."

"And the details?"

"Would take too long. I am sure you have places to be. My mum is waiting with a roast in the oven."

"Well why don't you take me out for a drink this evening and then we will have time and you can fill in all the gory details."

"What about the little one?"

"My mum will have him. She loves her quality time with Simon. I'll give you my number and you can call me later?"

"Err OK. Do you have a piece of paper?"

"No. Do you?"

Billy made a show of patting his pockets, but he already knew he didn't possess a single scrap of paper and he certainly lacked a pen. Jo grabbed the changing bag and hunted through the various pockets. She also came up blank. She patted her jacket pocket and found a stump of eyeliner pencil. She pulled one of the disposable nappies out of the changing bag and scrawled her number on it before passing it over to Billy.

"Don't worry, it's clean," she said with a cheeky grin.

Billy took the nappy and shoe horned it into the top of his bag.

"I will call you later on," he said.

"Looking forward to it."

Jo kicked the break off the pushchair and headed off. Billy stood for a moment and watched her depart before picking up his bag and heading off in the opposite direction.


Billy swung the holdall across his back, hooking his arms through the handles, crossed the town centre and entered the small estate where his mum had her flat, located on the seventeenth floor of a tower block. This block was one of three on the estate built, towards the end of the sixties, to provide affordable accommodation for a growing industrial workforce. They were the concrete utilitarian nightmares, popular with town and city planners at the time, but now several decades later they were the equivalent of human rabbit hutches. The local council, in line with National Government policy had decided to make the flats in one of the blocks available for private purchase by sitting tenants. As Billy approached he could easily identify which one it was. The outer facia of the tower had been cleaned and the metal shields over the balconies painted in a jaunty green. This was in contrast to the other two, which remained in council control, where the balconies were a drab gun-metal grey. This dingy colour and the dirty facia gave these two an institutional or asylum like look.

As Billy drew closer still, it was possible to see other cosmetic distinctions that could be easily missed from a distance. In the council buildings there were a number of missing windows, which had simply been boarded up with plywood. One flat had suffered a fire and the facia above the main window, to what would have been the living room, still bore the blackened signs of fire damage. The council engineers hadn't got around to boarding up the missing window so it stared out at the world like a dark malevolent eye surrounded with exaggerated kohl eye makeup. The footpath led between the two council owned properties past the shared car park which was blighted with rubbish and waste. A burnt out car had been abandoned astride the curb, the rubber of the tyres destroyed in the blaze, so the vehicle now stood on the metal wheel rims. This was flanked by some discarded sofas, dirty stained mattresses and a number of abandoned and broken kitchen appliances. The main entrance doors at the bottom of the complex had been smashed at some time in the past and the remnants of one of the glass panels was hanging drunkenly from a single remaining hinge.

In contrast, the privately owned block, now managed by the tenants association was clean, the grass of the lawns were billiard table smooth and the beds alive with flowers and colourful shrubs. The door and entry phone were intact and in perfect working order. Billy knew the six digit passcode, so he entered it on the keypad and was rewarded by a loud click and buzz as the door released. He pulled on the door and entered the lobby. It smelt of fresh pine rather than rancid piss, like it had in the past. Billy looked across at the other tower blocks. Those blocks were the gangsta's paradise, where Delchie Matthews had plied his trade. He shook his head in disbelief that the place had fallen into such a shit state, so quickly. He let the door swing closed. His Converse sneakers squeaked on the shiny tiles as he crossed the brightly lit lobby to the lift.

Billy reached through the letter box to retrieve the front door key to his mum's flat. It always hung on a string and was just long enough that when it was fished out it could just reach the Yale lock on the front door. It wasn't there. But it was always there. This was obviously a recent development from his mum. He wondered whether there had been a mini crime wave in the tower block, which had forced residents to reconsider their personal security arrangements. Billy knew at least a dozen key string residents. Had they all removed them? Why?

Billy straightened up and rang the door-bell instead. Almost instantly, from within the flat, he heard a door open and footsteps in the hall. There was the rattle of a security chain being put in place and then the clicks of several locks being opened. Finally, the door opened and his mum's face appeared around the side peering over the heavy security chain. Seeing who was waiting outside, she closed the door, undid the chain and opened it to its full extent.

"Hello Billy Love"

She stood to one side and allowed Billy to enter the hallway. Billy dropped his holdall in the hall and shrugged off his coat, tossing it on an empty hook. There was an awkward moment, while the two of them who had never been particularly physical or demonstrative with each other, hugged. It was only the briefest of clinches and they stepped apart quickly, both parties clearly embarrassed by the encounter. He then unzipped his bag and handed her the bottle of white wine he had just purchased at the local minimarket.

"There was no need for that Billy, but Thank You, I will just pop it in the fridge." She then hurried off into the kitchen. Billy called after her.

"Is it alright if I make a start on this lot?"

"Of course it is silly. You know where everything is."

Billy set about dragging the large holdall into the bathroom, sorting out the laundry into piles and firing up the washing machine. Once the water was running on the first load he went into the living room.

There were two other people already sitting in there. Ensconced at one end of the sofa was Billy's 'Aunty Joyce'. She was no blood relation to either Billy or his mother but instead a long-time friend of Susie's who as seemed to be the tradition among the working classes had been gifted with the moniker 'Aunty', way back when Billy was still a small child. There had been an endless stream of both Aunties and Uncles back then. Billy was certain that his mother was, like him, an only child, but as compensation for this lack of siblings, she had promoted various friends along the way to the honorary position of Aunt. If Billy remembered correctly, Joyce had been a school friend of his mum's.

Now, like his mother, in her late forties, she had the general appearance that kind people called bubbly, while those of crueller disposition might term brassy. Her hair was bleached blonde and piled high in a Doris Day beehive and her clothes and overdone makeup would not have looked out of place in the stage show Grease. Her pendulous looped earrings waggled excitedly as she greeted Billy.

"Well, you're a sight for sore eyes. You're a handsome lad, just like your dad." Joyce gushed at him. Billy glanced in the mirror that hung on the wall over the sideboard, looking at the person gazing back at him. Billy had never known his father. He had left while Billy was still an infant and his mother never mentioned him and as far as he knew didn't possess a single photograph of the man. But 'Aunty' Joyce had known him, naturally enough and she said he resembled his father. He looked once more in the mirror before he turned away.

The other character, much more sullen and dour in nature was introduced as Ted. He was Joyce's latest boyfriend. He seemed a joyless individual who looked uncomfortable to be closeted for an afternoon with two chattering women and would probably have been more comfortable down at the local Trades and Labour club with his mates, a few pints, and scampi in a basket to look forward to. His mood brightened a little when he realised he was not going to have to endure Susie and Joyce alone. He merely nodded a greeting to Billy and then refocused his attention on his pint glass, occasionally sniffing loudly as if he was suffering greatly from the early onset of a cold.

The two women bustled off into the kitchen to carry on preparations for lunch. Billy uncomfortable with the silence suggested they put the telly on and watch the Big Match. It removed the awkward silence as Brian Moore took over the role of communicator. All Billy had to do was ensure that Ted's glass, the washing machine and tumble dryer were all filled when necessary to keep things very cordial between them. The final whistle coincided nicely with the arrival of their meal and the four sat at the table and ate the roast chicken and all the trimmings. Billy suddenly remembered the beef that was promised? Chicken, I had a bucket load of this in Israel. Might as well be back on the bloody kibbutz then, he mused, somewhat ungratefully.

After helping to clear the table and do the washing up Joyce and Ted departed. As she was leaving Joyce enclosed Billy in a perfumed, boozy hug and planted a wet kiss on his cheek. She was a little tipsy, so Billy was surprised when he heard her arranging to meet his mum later at a local pub.

Then Billy remembered his encounter on the way home and went to retrieve the nappy from the bathroom. He walked back into the lounge trying to decipher the number Jo had scrawled with the eyeliner pencil. He held it up for his mum to see.

"Is that a seven or a nine?"

"Is that a nappy!" Susie sounded shocked.

"Yes, but it's unused. Anyway it's a long story, now nine or seven?"

"Seven."

Billy hooked the phone off its cradle and dialled the number, it rang once before it was answered. Billy recognised Jo's voice as she recited the number. He identified himself.

"You called. I didn't think you would."

"But you were sitting by the phone in case I did."

There was an embarrassed laugh from the other end of the phone.

"Not really, I 'm just back from dropping Simon at my mum's."

"Okay, good. So where do you want to go? To be honest I don't really fancy the old town tonight."

Billy knew that if he ventured into any of the pubs in the old town, even on a Sunday evening, there would be a strong chance he might run into old friends. Whilst catching up with them was good every once in a while, he didn't want to spend the whole evening fielding questions about Saskia's absence and Jo's presence and besides repeatedly explaining why he and Saskia were no longer together would put the mockers on the whole evening.

"They have refurbished the Five Moons recently, I haven't been inside but the reports are good."

"Not surprised, it was a shit hole"

Billy knew the place, but like Jo he had not ventured inside for many years. 'The Moons', like so many of the pubs scattered around the town's periphery was placed in the middle of one of the neighbourhood shopping precincts and served one of the local communities. Whilst the mainstay of their clientele were mainly ageing locals, these places did, from time to time, find favour with groups of the town's young, and for a brief period they became the 'in' place to hangout. After their moment in the spotlight, after the last youngster had moved on, the establishment heaved a sigh of relief and returned to its former role as a place where pensioners could sit and play dominoes or darts while enjoying a few pints.

"Well then let's give that a go then. Shall I meet you at your place?"

Jo hesitated for a moment.

"No, best not. I will meet you outside. Seven thirty, alright?"

Billy checked his Timex. He had about half an hour to get there. It was plenty of time.

"See you there." He replaced the phone on the cradle.

"So are you going out tonight?"

Susie Randell had a slightly disappointed note in her voice.

"Aren't you?"

Billy was not going to take any of his mum's crap, not anymore. He had heard her making plans to meet Joyce later, so staying in would mean an hour or two of rather stilted and distracted conversation in front of the telly, before she left.

"But we haven't had chance to talk yet."

Susie sounded hurt at Billy's quick comeback.

"Honestly? What is there to talk about? I quit my shitty job. My girlfriend, ex-girlfriend, is fucking some dickhead from work and I am probably going to fly back to Israel as soon as I have the money for the ticket."

Billy had tried desperately to keep any trace of anger out of his voice. He didn't want this exchange to descend into a slanging match. He had failed. All the bitterness and resentment he felt, showed itself in his choice of words and his method of delivery. Susie Randell gathered herself and Billy waited for the onslaught. His mother had raised him alone and had battled hard her whole life. She was a warrior and quite prepared to stand her ground and fight if that was what was required. Billy was now expecting to be verbally torn to shreds. Instead something very strange happened. A peaceful look crossed Susie's face and her eyes were filled with love and compassion. In that moment she became his mother again. Then to top it all she smiled.

"Good. I think that is what you need more than anything else right now. I have watched you struggle since you got back. You don't belong here anymore. I am not sure if running back to Israel is the answer, but I know you don't belong here."

If her words caught Billy slightly off guard, then what she did next nearly floored him. In two strides she had closed the gap between them and enfolded Billy in her arms, holding him close and burying her head in his chest. It was an embrace filled with a mother's love. It was all the protection of a mother for one of her young, everything Billy had never experienced before in his life. Not trusting his voice he stood in silence for several moments as he was welling up. Billy couldn't hear her words clearly, as his mother was mumbling something into his sweatshirt. He didn't want to break the mood. Patiently, he just held her, until his mother pushed away slightly and looked up at him.

" … that's why I think you should take this chance."

She wiped her hand across her eyes to remove the last of her tears and at the same time smudged her eye makeup. She noticed the grey-silver stain on the back of her hand.

"There you go," she said with a wry smile, "bet I look a right state now?"

She pushed him away, then walked past him and out of the room, no doubt, on her way to the bathroom, to fix her face. Billy watched her leave the room. He would probably never know what his mother had been thinking or the words she had uttered, while her face was buried. One thing Billy knew for sure, he would never ask his mother to repeat them.

There was no sign of that emotion when his mother returned from fixing her makeup in the bathroom. The old Susie Randell, the fighter, was back. She went straight to her faithful handbag and rooted around in its depths, eventually she emerged again and held out one hand. Dangling from her fingers was a Yale key on a small ring.

"You'll be needing this."

Billy took the key without needing to ask what it was and fished in his pocket for his own keys.

"I have stopped leaving the key on the string. There have been too many burglaries happening around here recently. The place has gone downhill since Delchie Matthews went to prison. At least when he was here, he kept an eye on the place".

Billy thought it was ironic that not only had a career criminal succeeded in keeping the estate largely crime free, a task the local constabulary seemed singularly incapable of doing, but that his mother had played her own small part in sending Delchie Matthews to jail, and was now mourning his departure. Billy had wound the door key onto his own keyring then patted his mother on the shoulder and left the flat to head to the bus stop

## Chapter Six

His mother's words and actions were still troubling him as he hopped off the bus outside the Five Moons. Her bombshell acknowledgement that she realised that Billy had not been able to settle down since his return had been surprising enough, but her close and intense show of emotion had caught Billy completely off guard. Jo was waiting outside the front door of the pub. The two of them exchanged a brief hug, before they went inside. The pub, like so many establishments on a Sunday night, was largely empty, with a few diehard locals congregated along the bar on stools and a few more over by the dart board and pool table. They had no problem getting drinks or finding somewhere quiet to sit.

"So Billy Randell, back home and in the flesh. Judging by the lack of a tan I guess you have been back a while. What have you been up to? No wait, you promised to tell me all about your trip that day I sold you the ticket. You owe it to me and it's time for me to collect."

"Really? You want to hear all about my adventures?"

"Every last detail. I am not likely to be having any of my own, any time soon, so I will have to get my kicks from hearing about other people's adventures."

Jo picked up her glass and took a sip, her eyes were filled with an expectant longing. Billy thought for a moment, trying to decide where to start, what to include and what to leave out.

"I don't know where to start," he said, honestly struggling for the best place to begin his story.

"Start at the beginning, leave nothing out, not even the more juicy details." Jo winked.

"That's not fair. I have never been one to kiss and tell."

"Then it's about time you started. My life at the moment consists of nappies, baby food, mother's groups and infant swimming. I need a little adult entertainment in my life. So go ahead, shoot. The whole uncensored truth."

So Billy began at the beginning with his arrival at Tel Aviv airport, and his first impressions of the country on the drive down to the kibbutz, before continuing with his first impressions of the kibbutz itself, the room, the food, the other volunteers, the first night party. He tried, and failed, to skate over the events of his first night but Jo was clearly paying close attention because she stopped him dead.

"Did you just say you ended up in bed with two Swedish girls?"

Billy reddened. "Er yeah."

Jo's mouth formed a perfect O and her eyes went wide with shock and as Billy watched a strange change came over her. She leaned forward on her seat slightly, arched her back and wiggled her backside as if her buttocks were itching. A faint trace of red flushed at the base of her throat and her breathing deepened slightly. Billy was no expert, but he could have sworn that the mere thought of his first night exploits had left Jo a little aroused. She tried to cover it up by taking a large swig from her beer, not the smartest of moves as she choked and coughed on it, dribbling some of the contents out of the corner of her mouth, so it splashed on her blouse. She grabbed her handbag for a packet of tissues and dabbed the worst of the damage away.

"That's gonna stain." Billy said trying to be helpful.

Jo, still furiously dabbing her breast with tissue looked up.

"It's alright, I'll just soak it in some cold water as soon as I get home. Having young kids teaches you a lot about stain removing."

Realising this was the best she could do for now Jo dumped the soggy tissues on the table.

"Now where were we?"

The incident had passed and Jo seemed to have regained some internal sense of equilibrium.

"Oh yes, in bed with two Swedish hotties", she exclaimed, making the whole thing sound matter-of-fact, like it happened to everyone everyday, and was of no more importance than their recent discussion about stain removal techniques.

"How did that work out? What was it like?"

"Terrifying." Billy was trying to be honest.

"Oh come on Billy it's every guys' wildest dream."

"Dream maybe, but in reality it is a frightening experience. Suddenly there are two of everything, four of some things."

Billy grinned at his own lewd joke. Jo threw her head back and laughed out loud attracting strange looks from some of the other patrons in the bar.

"Ah, yes, I can see the problem there."

"Exactly. Now can we move on?"

"Yep. Now tell me about life in the kibbutz. What was the work like?"

Billy, much relieved to have moved away from reliving his sexual encounters, spent the next half an hour explaining the basics of the work regimes on the kibbutz. The physical nature of some of the outdoor jobs, the monotony of the indoor jobs and the occasional 'peach' of a job. Billy's 'peach' had been landing the gig as the lifeguard at the kibbutz swimming pool.

"And all this time, you were together with your Swedish girlfriend?"

"Katarina. Yes. We were together until she left to go home."

"And then what happened. I would think the job at the pool made you a target for every girls' affections."

Jo seemed keen on getting back to Billy's love life. Billy not so much. At the time it had all appeared so normal, so natural. But now on a dark evening in a pub back in England it seemed anything but. The non-stop procession of women through his life, the constant stream of sexual encounters seemed slightly sordid and even sleazy, when viewed from afar. To have no experience of the transient nature of the kibbutz volunteer experience would put the casual observer at a disadvantage and lead to unjust condemnation. Billy decided to bluff his way out of this one by using humour.

"I was a bit like a kid in a candy shop."

"I bet you were." Jo rolled her eyes in mocking disapproval.

"So was the lifeguard job all year round?"

"Dunno, wasn't there in the winter."

"Why where did you go? Did you take a holiday?"

Billy hesitated for a moment, unsure of how much he wanted to tell Jo. He weighed up the pros and cons of honesty. At this point he could have invented something, picked a random adventure out of the air. Jo would be in no position to prove or disprove it. He decided to tell her the truth and let the cards fall as they may. So he went with,

"No. They kicked me off."

Now, some two years later, he could be sanguine and even a little upbeat about the whole incident. After all, the wounds had been given time to heal, mistakes had been admitted, hatchets had been well and truly buried and everyone had been exonerated. The incident would never be forgotten, but for now all parties had at least been forgiven. This meant that he could recount the whole incident with icy cool detachment.

Jo listened intently as Billy recounted the next phase of his Israel adventure, her eyes widening in shock at some of the horrible events and her nose wrinkling in distaste as Billy described some of the ignominious and odoriferous tasks he had been forced to perform. He could see a certain look of disbelief creeping into Jo's eyes, as if she couldn't comprehend the depths to which people would stoop to be fed and keep themselves in booze and fags. He suddenly realised, that for the first time since his return, he was describing these events to someone who had no prior involvement or experience of volunteer life which made all this sound totally incredible.

If ordinary volunteer life had appeared scandalous, then aspects of his time in the Eilat Trap would be downright shocking. Billy gave Jo credit, because as she listened with increasing horror to events being described, she grasped the predicament he faced and asked a very probing and pertinent question.

"So how on earth did you ever escape?"

"Well, I got lucky. Kismet" Billy said with a wry and slightly enigmatic smile.

He then went on to tell Jo about his chance meeting with Christian and how this ultimately led to the film, which would never see the light of day now, the fees and the opportunities which ultimately meant he had escaped the clutches of the Eilat Trap and was able to return to normal volunteer life.

Billy had paused his story twice to refresh their drinks and now he had reached a natural break, both their glasses were empty, so he made another trip to the bar for refills. He glanced at the clock behind the bar and realised that closing time was fast approaching. He wondered where this evening was going? With this in mind Billy tried to steer the conversation away from him and his exploits and attempt to learn more about Jo's life. He had got the distinct impression that everything was not exactly rosy right now, but he wasn't sure. As he placed the drinks on the table and sat back down he looked across the table at Jo.

"Enough about me. Your turn. What have you been up to?"

Jo paled, alarmed at being suddenly put on the spot and sipped her drink to cover her discomfort.

"Well, "She said after a moment "What would you like to know?"

"Don't mind really, not all the gory details, just the highlights, will do"

"No gory details, except for the childbirth of course. Trust me, Motherhood soon put paid to any of that."

At least Jo had the good sense to look embarrassed by her revelation.

"What can I say? Allan proposed. I accepted. Did the big white wedding thing. Honeymoon. Got pregnant, everyone was pleased, 'cept us. Eighth months in, he suddenly announces he's off on his new job on the rigs. Better money, security, buy the house, blah, blah, blah. Perfect."

Jo pulled a sour face, but then morphed it into a sarcastic smile.

"Hmm, getting the feeling, not so perfect."

"No shit Billy. It's far from bloody perfect. I spend weeks all on my own, alone, when he's on that rig. When he's home, he's just pissed all the time, down the pub, with his mates. No time for his wife. Don't get me wrong, he's great with Simon, spoils him rotten. But I get nothing. Selfish prick"

Jo looked at Billy who had adopted a sympathetic expression. Seeing that look she laughed out loud, although it was more of a bark, than a genuine chuckle.

"Don't pity me. Sure, I get the occasional consolation fuck, he's usually drunk, back from the pub, bit horny and that's it."

Now Billy looked shocked. He wasn't expecting the gory highlights, such a full and frank rendition of these finer details, which made him feel quite uncomfortable, now. Lines from Kirsty McColl's New England were now bouncing around his head. He even began to question the wisdom of his agreement to meet Jo tonight. The first time they had met, Billy had been slightly flattered by her candour and the way she had sought him out in the pub that evening, leading him to believe she was genuinely interested. They had connected, then spent the night together and it was only in the morning, Jo had confessed about her steady boyfriend. She now had a child, with her husband, a family, however dysfunctional and Billy did not want to end up in the middle of it.

"Now I've shocked you, haven't I? Should, really keep my big mouth shut. Just leave it to you."

Jo was on the verge of bursting into tears. Billy scanned the pub, quickly, fearing this would be misinterpreted. He reached across the table, took Jo's hand, reluctantly, worried someone who knew Jo or her husband would leap to the wrong conclusion. That would make things more difficult than it already was, for Jo. The touch of his hand calmed her. She looked up and smiled.

The landlord behind the bar started to yell time and ring the bell. They both had nearly empty glasses so they quickly finished off the dregs and left the pub. Outside in the street a few people were passing by, some making their way over to the 'Chinese Chippy' for a late night feast. Others were on their way home or out walking their dogs before bedtime. As it was a Sunday night, most people had work in the morning, so the streets would be utterly deserted in the next half an hour. Once the last bus from the town pulled away and the Hong Kong Garden Takeaway closed its doors and the neon sampan on its marquee went dark.

Jo pulled the sleeves of her cardigan down. It was not exactly freezing, but there was a bit of a nip in the night air.

"Do you want to come back to mine for a coffee? I only live round the corner."

Billy considered the offer for a moment, weighing up what had passed through his mind not ten minutes ago.

"What about your son? Aren't you picking him up from your mum's?"

"No, he will be asleep by now. Mum wanted to keep him, until tomorrow."

"Ah. Right."

"Come on Billy? Please? Keep me company. I don't want to be alone."

There was a small hint of desperation in Jo's voice, weakening Billy's resolve. Keeping Jo company was something Billy could handle, so the two of them walked the short distance to Jo's house. It was a terrace with a small front garden. Jo walked through the gate, up the path and opened her front door. Billy followed her inside and waited while Jo put on a couple of lamps. Once he could see, Billy picked his way through the obstacle course of toys that littered the floor of the living room.

"Sorry about the mess" Jo said, as she zig zagged across the floor making a token effort to chuck a few of them into a large plastic box.

"I was in a bit of a rush, earlier".

Jo had taken herself into the kitchen and returned a few moments later with a bottle of wine and a couple of glasses.

"Want to help me finish this?"

She held up the bottle. It appeared to be almost full, as if Jo had, perhaps, had a glass earlier, maybe for Dutch courage.

"Yeah okay."

Billy waited while Jo poured him a glass and then clinked it against hers.

"Make yourself at home." Jo pointed toward the sofa.

Billy picked up a couple more stuffed toys and tossed them into the box, as Jo placed her glass on the coffee table and left the room, Billy guessed, to use the bathroom. He took off his coat and laid it over the back of one of the armchairs, then sat down on the sofa making himself, comfortable. He picked up his wine glass and took a sip. It wasn't bad, chilled and crisp, the glass, just starting to dew up was cool beneath his fingertips.. He rolled the wine over his tongue, before swallowing. Jo hadn't skimped on her wine choice. He took another sip. Then the lounge door opened and Jo slid back in. She had exchanged her stained blouse for a baggy t-shirt, taken her shoes and socks off and loosened her hair, losing five years in the process, looking much more appealing, as she stood in the doorway.

"This is excellent," Billy said, holding his glass aloft.

Jo walked slowly across the room towards him, somewhat seductively. She didn't pop her hips, nothing quite so cheap or obvious, but as her whole body moved, it was kind of predatory, a panther-like stalk. She stopped in front of Billy, standing so that their knees were almost touching. Then she leaned over and took hold of Billy's wine glass. Snatching it from his hand, putting the glass to her lips, draining the remnants in one long swallow. She placed the glass behind her on the coffee table, before sliding herself slowly down on his lap. Instinctively Billy's hands went to her hips, he didn't know whether to pull her towards him, which he wanted to do, or ease her away, which he felt he should. He rested his hands there, for a moment. Jo, sensing his reluctance, leaned in, her face just inches from Billy's. He caught the scent of her perfume. She moved her face closer, their lips, almost touching. Her breath was hot on his face. He searched his feelings, but Jo seemed to have no such restraint. She just closed the last inch, their lips meeting, softly at first, a mere brush, but with a growing intensity and urgency, as the seconds passed. It didn't take long for Jo to discover Billy's heart was clearly not in to this. She pushed herself away and sat back, her weight was now all on Billy's knees.

"What's up? Don't you want this?"

"Well, err, Yes," Billy stuttered his response, not sure what he wanted.

"Well what's the matter then?"

"Well, it's just, well, you're ..." Billy's voice trailed off into silence.

"Married?"

"Mother with a small child?"

"Not sexy anymore?"

Jo spat the three questions in rapid-fire succession.

"Err, Yes, err, No" Billy wasn't sure which question he should answer first.

"Well, Billy which is it? What is so different from last time? You couldn't keep your hands off me then."

"Well last time you weren't with someone."

"Actually, I was. Just hadn't told you."

What Billy had said was only half true. On the first night they had spent together, Billy hadn't known of Allan's existence. Jo had only told him on the Sunday morning, over breakfast, so technically, when he spent the Sunday night with her, it was in the full knowledge that she was in a relationship.

"You weren't married, then, to Allan."

Jo held her left hand up in front of Billy's face.

"Is this what's bothering you?"

Jo pointed at her engagement and wedding rings on her finger.

"Is this the problem?"

Billy half nodded. Jo encircled her ring finger with the first finger and thumb of her right hand and slipped the rings off. She held them up for a moment, so Billy could see them and then tossed them over her shoulder.

"Better now?"

It wasn't really, but Billy was convinced enough by the gesture, so he nodded. Jo then slid down his thighs and landed in his lap. She put her hands round his shoulders, bent her head in and began to kiss him, ravenously. Billy now responded much more enthusiastically.

Afterwards, as they lay in each other's arms, naked under the bed covers, Jo went to some lengths to reassure Billy that he was the only man she had slept with since her and

Allan had started dating and wasn't in the habit of taking lovers to her marital bed. In fact, there were no others.

They had started making love on the couch then the lounge carpet before agreeing it was too uncomfortable. So, they moved upstairs, naked, to the bedroom. By then Billy was so aroused that he hadn't stopped to think that this was the matrimonial bed. Now, in the afterglow, this fact crashed into Billy's consciousness like a runaway freight train. Fortunately, in the dark, Jo couldn't see him blushing, but she must have sensed something else about Billy, because she suddenly rolled away and switched on the bedside lamp.

"Is everything OK?" she asked with a worried look on her face.

"Something wrong?"

Billy looked over at her, naked in the diffused light from the lamp.

"No, nothing's wrong. Nothing."

"I know my body's a bit different now. You don't go through pregnancy and childbirth without a few changes."

Billy's eyes swept up and down her body. There was no discernible outward difference to her body. After the pregnancy, she had shed any excess baby weight, looking just as slim and lithe, as Billy remembered her.

"No. You don't look any different to the way I remember you." Billy smiled

"But what about the?" Jo looked down at her groin region.

Billy got the gist of what she was asking.

"Never crossed my mind." he said.

It was Jo's turn to smile.

"Good. There are some things I just can't bring myself to ask Allan. I am frightened he might tell me the truth."

"Do you think I've lied to you?"

"Not sure Billy. Maybe? Or it's me just being stupid as it doesn't feel the same anymore. Different somehow?"

Billy was no shrink, so he felt that silence was the best answer to Jo's uncertainties.

"Well, if you want me to try again, I'm not going anywhere, for a while."

Jo was across the bed in a flash and on top of Billy.

"Yes. I want to try again."


Billy awoke in the first light of dawn to find the bed beside him was empty. He reached out of the bed for his shorts, then remembering they were lying with the rest of his clothes, on the lounge floor. He grabbed a pillow off the bed to cover himself and walked slowly, downstairs, into the living room. Luckily, as he approached the door he could see that the light was on, so he was not going to have to navigate his way through the minefield of discarded Lego bricks and other toys in the dark. He pushed the door open slowly and was rewarded by the sight of a pair of perfect, naked buttocks. Jo was bent over, slowly sifting through a pile of Lego Duplo bricks. She heard the door squeak, straightened up and turned around, using her hands to cover her nudity. She saw Billy in the doorway, clutching the pillow to cover himself and laughed out loud.

"We make quite a pair don't we?"

"What are you doing?"

"Looking for my wedding ring."

"Well let me put some shorts on and I will help you look."

Billy found his shorts, where he had dropped them and Jo, remembering she too had abandoned clothing on the lounge floor, located and donned her panties and t-shirt. Semi-clothed the two of them resumed the search for the missing wedding band. Billy surveyed the plethora of kiddie's toys, scattered all over the floor and knew it was going to be a herculean task, to find the ring in amongst all this mess. He went over to where they had both been on the couch and then tried to trace the trajectory the ring would have followed as it was cast over Jo's shoulder. He used this as the starting point for his search. Jo's approach was much more random, just moving things about and replacing them, if she drew a blank. In the end, they were both wrong, as the ring had taken a deflection off some object or other and then landed on its edge, rolling a fair distance on to the wooden floor of the dining room, where it had finally come to rest under the sideboard. It was purely by chance, that Billy caught a glimpse of gold, as it reflected the light and bothered to investigate.

"Got it!" he held the ring aloft, with both hands, like a football trophy.

Jo came over and snatched the ring from him, sliding it into place. As she did this, Billy saw that she had already retrieved her engagement ring and had put it back on. Being set with a stone, it had not rolled away like her wedding band. Jo looked at the back of her outstretched hand, admiring the two rings now safely back on her finger. This simply served to remind Billy that Jo was a married woman and caused a fresh wave of guilt to wash over him. Jo caught Billy's expression and instantly dropped her hand behind her back.

"Sorry." she looked sheepish, "Shouldn't have reminded you, I 'm married."

Billy was about to agree with her, when he had a sudden flashback, to the brief affair he had had, with another married woman, at Tel Boker. He really, couldn't claim the moral high ground, when it came to the sanctity of marriage vows, either. Could he? He sat down on the sofa and reached his hands out towards Jo.

"Come over here and sit down," he invited, patting the sofa beside him.

The restoration of her wedding band seemed to have had an adverse effect on Jo, as she brushed off Billy's advances.

"What are you doing? I don't have time for that. My mother will be here in a minute. She's dropping Simon off, on her way to work. You can't be here, when she arrives. My mum has a real soft spot for Allan and would take his side, if there were problems between us."

Billy got the message, so began to recover his clothes and got dressed. He felt hurt that things between them, had come to such an abrupt halt, but then that was the nature of illicit affairs and if Billy was honest with himself, he was not likely to be back here for a very long time, so it was better to take what had been freely given and move on. He was rewarded with one final passionate kiss, before being ejected out of her front door. He made his way slowly to the bus stop, glancing guiltily, at every woman wheeling a pushchair with a child. He might have passed Jo's mum with Simon, but he couldn't be sure.

When he got back to his mum's flat she was already long gone, as she started work early. She had left a note propped up by the kettle, which Billy read, as he made himself a coffee.

*Billy,*

*I guess I always knew that you would outgrow this town and move on. I just want you to know that I support you in whatever you decide to do and wherever you decide to live, is fine by me, as long as you let me know, from time to time, that you are okay.*

*I trust that this trip, wherever it takes you, will not be funded by money from a loan shark, so that you will be able to keep in touch.*
*Send me a postcard, please.*

*Love*

*Mum xx*

He placed the note back on the worktop and took a sip from his coffee cup. His mother had a point. She did deserve to know where he was and doing okay. The first time he had left, he did not contact her, to tell her where he was and that he had arrived safely. He had made this decision, to protect her from the clutches of Delchie Matthews and his crew. This time it would be different. He had his own money, earned through the sweat of his brow. It was not much, enough to buy him a ticket and a little bit of spending money for those little luxuries that would make kibbutz life a bit more bearable. He would not be leaving the country in secret, with no immediate prospect of a safe return.

Ironically and rather tunelessly whistling 'Whistle while you work' he folded and packed all his clean washing into the holdall and zipped it shut. He then scribbled a short note on the back of his mum's and left it and the key together on the worktop. He then let himself out of the flat and headed back to the station.

He had timed his arrival so he was eligible for a cheap ticket back to London. Despite the fact it was after the 'rush-hour' both the platform and the train were crowded. Billy was lucky, he managed to secure himself an aisle seat and then using his upturned holdall as a writing desk, and a pen and paper he had 'liberated' from his mum, he began to make a 'to-do' list. First on the list he wrote the word 'flat'. He needed to contact his landlord and tell him he was moving out. The flat was in a building that had been in the landlord's family since 1926, purchased straight off the architects' plan. Billy doubted there were any outstanding mortgages , so the rents were all pure profit, after tax of course. Informing Mr Giorgio, the landlord would start the departure clock counting down. Next on his list he wrote the words 'Ring Mark'.

He wanted to call his fellow traveller to confirm he was still committed to making the trip with him and to check if he had reached out to the Kibbutz Reps group to get himself registered, vetted and approved. He didn't think he needed a comprehensive packing list at this stage, as he had experience from last time, of the essentials, nice to have's and finally what just took up room and added weight. Items that never really saw the light of day. Thirdly, he needed to chase up his final wages from Finch and McEwan.

After the train had arrived back at Kings Cross, Billy rode on the top deck of a bus all the way back home. He much preferred the bus to the tube for two reasons. Firstly, in his part of East London the bus service was actually better, more direct, no changes needed, like there was with train or underground. Secondly, he could see the city, as it passed by, rather than being stuck down in the underground. It was strange that this was a working day, but for the first time in ages, he was out and about on the streets, but not working. Obviously, he was not earning, so the funds at his disposal were now limited. If he wanted to make the trip with enough money in his pocket, he would have to put a lid on the amount of money, he spent over the next couple of weeks. However, there were two factors that he could bank on, literally. First, at the end of the month, he was owed some pay, at least for the days, he had worked, before his spectacular exit. Second, the return of the deposit on his flat: two months' rent. It would take a superhuman effort, to clean the place up, in order to get all of that back, but he reckoned he could probably rope in a couple of mates to help, if he bribed them with dinner.

As he walked through his flat's front door, he could see that bloody answerphone red light was blinking again. He dropped the usual pile of junk-mail on the phone table and hit the replay button. The machine clicked, whirred and rewound. The first message, timed on

Sunday morning, was from Mel, asking him to call her when he had got back. Then there was another message from Mel, left the previous evening, where she sounded slightly stressed, desperate to speak to him and annoyed that he was not home yet. The last message was a bit of a surprise. It was from Suzette at Finch and McEwan, left a bit earlier, that morning. She was also annoyed to be speaking to a machine, but covered it well and asked Billy to call her back when he got this please? She gave no further indication as to why she needed to speak to Billy, which both piqued his interest, but also made him feel a bit uncertain.

Checking his watch, he decided he had a few moments grace, before making any calls. He chucked his holdall on the bed, ambled into the kitchen, then filled and flicked on the kettle. Before returning Suzette's call, he would make himself a coffee. As he waited for the kettle to boil he spied the half full whisky bottle, on the side. He switched off the kettle and poured himself a generous measure of scotch, instead. If this was bad news, at least the whisky might take the edge off it. He downed it in one, waiting for the alcohol to hit his bloodstream. He poured a second and returned to the phone. From memory, he dialled the general switchboard number, as this would be answered by Suzette. He was right. After three rings he heard her voice.

"Good Morning, Finch and McEwan, how may I direct your call?"

"Suzette, it's me. Billy Randell," he added, to avoid any misunderstanding.

"Billy, where have you been? I have been calling you, since last week."

Billy was puzzled. He had only left yesterday morning and was back in now. There had been no other messages left on the days between him quitting his job and yesterday? He might not have been keen to talk to anyone from Finch and McEwan, with Suzette probably being the only one, whose calls he would have returned. Then he remembered, she had absolutely no patience if the phone was not answered by the third ring then she would just hang up in disgust. Billy had set his answerphone to cut in after four rings. Suzette was not the dedicated, work at the weekend type, so any calls she had made to him, apart from this morning, would have been at the end of last week, when he was deep in his cups, passed out and missing the phone ringing. Nevertheless Billy felt it necessary to lie and therefore cover up the depths of depravity he had plummeted into since he had walked out.

"I went away for a few days, at the end of last week, home, to see family. Try and straighten my head out. Decide what to do next."

It was all bollocks. Sounded convincing enough, though, well it did to Billy.

"And did you come to any conclusions?"

Seems Suzette had bought it.

"Nothing concrete yet. Just a few ideas."

"Well before you get too wrapped up in any new projects, could you possibly drop by the office, please, as I have some paperwork to sort out with you?"

Billy really didn't want to face the crew at the office again.

"Can't you just drop it in the post?"

"Guessing you don't really want to see anyone here, right? Okay, fair enough. But, I must have your signature on a couple of things, admin. Look, if you don't want to come here, how about we meet in The Grapes, at lunchtime?"

Billy brightened at that suggestion. The Grapes, was close to the office, but was not popular with the staff. Chances were he would be able to slip in and out without meeting anyone.

"What time?"

"One-ish?"

"Ok, see you there."

He rang off and then thought he might as well ring Mark. He dialled Mark's work number and a stranger picked up.

"Mark's phone."

"Mark around?"
"No, he's not in the office today. Called in sick. Can I help?"
"No, it's fine. I will try him tomorrow."

He hung up quickly, as he didn't want to get Mark in any trouble. He reached for his phone book and found his home number and dialled it. Mark picked up after four rings. He did sound unwell.

"Morning mate, rough night?"
"Billy, do you have to shout?"
"Well that answers my question. What you up to later on?"
"Dying, just like now. I've got the flu."
"Well snap out of it. If you are serious about this kibbutz thing, we need to get the ball rolling."
"Already done it mate. Hand delivered the application last week. Told them I was keen to leave ASAP. They said they will contact me in a few days and there is an induction meeting this weekend.."
"Okay. Great."
"What about you?"
"Returning volunteer, so I have all the paperwork already and plus the reference letters from my old place."

That reminded Billy that he had to search through his papers and find the reference he had been given by the kibbutz, when he left. It was in Hebrew but there was a copy in English. They would be just as good, if not better, than any letter written by the organisers based in England in securing him a place on a new kibbutz. He guessed that the rest of his details would still be on file with the parent organisation in Tel Aviv. He found them surprisingly quickly and put them together with all the other documents he needed, in a plastic folder. With bugger all else to do for now, he settled down to watch daytime TV, until it was time to go and meet Suzette.


The bar of the Grapes was largely deserted, so it was a doddle to spot Suzette. She was sat alone at a table, about halfway down the room. Billy could see she already had her drink, so just ordered a pint for himself, before joining her at the table. Physically, The Grapes was just a few hundred yards from the offices of Finch and McEwan, so it could easily have become the company's favourite, except for one major drawback. The bar was located right opposite one of the indoor markets, so the majority of its clientele were market workers. This was reflected not only in the atmosphere, but also the decor. Probably, the building would have been a merchants' office. The single room, with its high ceiling and hardwood floors, would have rung with the bustle of commerce as goods were bought and sold over the long counter, now the main bar. The owners had done very little to the decor they had inherited with the building, so many of the original fixtures and fittings were still in place. It was easy to imagine Victorian gentlemen, in tall hats exchanging pleasantries, whilst haggling over the price of the latest load of coffee or tea, recently landed at the nearby riverside wharfs. Despite the best endeavours of the owners, the place was a 'spit and sawdust' pub as were its clientele. Only Billy and latterly Suzette, saw the regulars for what they were. Hardworking ordinary people. Salt of the earth. Diamond geezers.

Suzette stood up, when Billy approached and enclosed him in a close hug. She smelt strongly of her favourite perfume and the French Gitanes, she loved to smoke. One was alight in the ashtray, the smoke was powerful enough to make Billy's eyes water. To counter this noxious smell, Billy lit one of his own, but his American brand was no competition for its Gallic counterpart, in the toxicity stakes.

Suzette had a brown folder set to one side on the table, which she pulled in front of her and opened. Inside, were a couple of paper forms, one of which Billy recognised as a P45. This was a certificate of the income tax Billy had paid during the current tax year and was to be kept by him. He could then hand this to his next employer. As it was unlikely he would take another job in the near future, he would need to file this somewhere safe for when he returned to the UK. Suzette handed him the P45 and then asked him to sign a couple of other documents. These covered confidentiality and intellectual copyright. They were standard for anyone leaving the company to prevent them taking ideas, leads or clients to a competitor. Billy had no intention of doing this, but Suzette insisted, he must sign the forms, so he scrawled his name on the bottom of both documents.

Suzette counter signed both and then gave Billy his copies. Then she opened an envelope and handed him a cheque.

"This is your months' pay, up until last Friday."

Billy was astonished that the company had gifted him the extra couple of days, but if that was a shock then an even bigger one was about to hit him. Suzette then pulled out another cheque.

"This, my young friend, is your bonus."

Billy stared at the cheque in his hands, not believing the amount that was written on the cheque.

"Is this some kind of joke?"

"No Billy, we had a really good year, last year, and as you contributed to our success you get to profit from it. I might add, I had to fight with the partners to get them to cough up, but fight I did and they eventually, relented."

Billy noticed his hands were shaking slightly. The amount was close to three months' salary and really gave him a substantial financial cushion, with which to travel.

"I don't know what to say."

"Well you could start with a thank you, then follow that up with a 'would you like another drink'?"

"Sorry," Billy looked sheepish, "would you like another drink?"

"Yes. I will have a large vodka and tonic."

Billy went to the bar and did the honours. They sat and drank their drinks and talked about Billy's plans. When he announced, he was considering returning to a kibbutz, Suzette looked suitably surprised.

"I thought you did that already?"

"Yeah. I did. But I still miss the place, the people, the culture. I just don't fit in here."

"What makes you feel like you fit in over there, then? What's different?"

Put on the spot, Billy found it hard to articulate his feelings. He knew that there was something that was not right about him living and working in London, but what it was and how to put it into words, eluded him. Suzette was staring intently at him, her ringed fingers impatiently tapping on the side of her glass.

"Dunno. It's just a, feeling."

"Seems to me, if you can't express it. How do you know the kibbutz has all the answers?"

It was a valid point. Not one he really wanted to hear right now, but valid nevertheless. It was funny how out of these three women in his life, Suzette, Mel and his Mum, two of them, thought it was a bad idea for him to go and re-join a kibbutz. As he left the pub and headed for the nearest branch of his bank, to pay in the cheques, he wondered, which of these three women was the best qualified to assess whether he should stay or go, now?

## Chapter Seven

Billy and Mark emerged from Golders Green Tube station into yet another rain shower. They mirrored each other, pulling their coats tight around their bodies and hunching their shoulders. Neither of them had thought to bring an umbrella. Billy didn't own one and he was not sure whether Mark did either. The forecast had predicted a mixture of sunshine and showers, so Billy had taken the precaution of bringing a waterproof jacket and it was enough to keep the worst of the weather off while they trudged through the streets. Mark had the directions and a small photocopied hand drawn map on the second page of the invitation letter he had been sent, for today's introduction. Billy, like the last time, had no letter of invitation, instead, folded into a plastic wallet and stuck in an inside pocket of his jacket was the reference letter from Tel Boker and its English copy. He didn't know if he would have to use them, but he had brought them along anyway. Today, was in fact all about Mark. Billy was there just to back up his friend. Mark had shown him the invitation letter a few days earlier and Billy had read its contents. The only letter Billy had seen before was Mike's acceptance letter. His friend had never showed him the invitation to the introduction day, or if he had, then Billy had blanked it out. Having never been to one of these meetings, as his decision to travel last time had been last minute, he thought it would be a laugh to come along and see what was said and how much the introduction actually differed from the reality. He was certain that the official introduction would contain no details of the drinking and fornication that had formed the mainstay of volunteer life, or at least 'life' as it had been for Billy, last time. He expected to hear words like 'rich cultural heritage' and the like, not Arac, Noblesse, Gold Star and Vodka. Mark had sworn him to his best behaviour and Billy had only consumed a couple of lip looseners, before leaving home to meet Mark. As a result he was just slightly buzzed, rather than totally smashed. He felt he would be able to hold it together at any rate.

According to the map and the address printed next to it, their destination was the St. Barnabas Church Hall and as they walked along the street there was no missing the large grey stone building with the dark slate roof. The large imposing buttresses and the arched tracery windows, suggested the building might have been a church, at some point in the past century, but now had been abandoned in favour of a more modern and infinitely more comfortable, centrally heated and welcoming property, on the other side of the road. The old church building, with its draughty windows and leaky roof, was now the parish hall and doubled as the local community centre.

They were greeted at the door by an earnest and bespectacled man called Chaim. They both knew this was his name, it was written in marker pen on a white sticky label affixed to the breast of his shirt. Although just to make sure, he did take the time to introduce himself before directing the pair, inside to a table where sheets of sticky labels and marker pens were laid out, so all the delegates could make themselves an ID badge. Billy picked up a black marker pen and wrote B I L L Y in block capitals, likewise Mark wrote M A R K. Some artistic souls had bothered to use other colours and one, Muriel, had manage to draw a large red heart over the letter 'i' in her name. They all fixed these on to their shirts or blouses as their jackets were still wet from the rain. Billy took a moment to look around the room. The interior merely confirmed his earlier suspicions. The building was obviously a former church that had been converted into a community hall and it retained many of the features of its former function, not least the large plaster and wood crucifix that hung above the open space that must have been the original altar. A stone baptism font, too large and heavy to move out during the renovation, stood over to one side. Their hosts had erected a projector screen across the front of this open space and in an attempt to disguise some of the more obvious Christian elements of the building, they had stuck posters, liberated from the Israeli Tourist

Board, depicting some of the more scenic panoramic views of the country, on the walls and pillars. Strangely, despite the fact the place was known as the Holy Land and was famed as being the home to three major world religions, none of the posters showed any religious sites.

There were around thirty people milling around in the body of the hall. There was a refreshments table serving tea, coffee and watery orange squash in plastic cups. The tea looked weak and the coffee was indescribably bad. Billy took one sip and abandoned his cup on an adjacent table. He and Mark were among the last people to arrive, and shortly after entering, someone called for everyone's attention and asked them all to take a seat. The wooden chairs were the uncomfortable fold together sort, beloved of church halls the length and breadth of the land. Billy found a delicious paradox that a Jewish based organisation would hold a recruitment meeting in a Christian church hall. People filed into the seating area and waited patiently as the organisers had a quick last minute discussion amongst themselves.

Looking around among the assembled group Billy spied a few individuals sitting alone, but most of the rest were made up of small groups of two or more friends who were talking together and even though the conversations were in hushed or muted tones the combination gave the room an overall background hum. This faded as the first speaker walked to the front of the hall and raised his hands for quiet. He opened his speech by welcoming everyone to the hall and outlined the agenda for the afternoon. There was to be an introduction to the kibbutz experience from a former kibbutz member, who was now living and working in London. This would cover the background to the kibbutz movement, touch briefly on the history and the political reasons why kibbutzim came into existence in the first place. Next, the group would be shown a short film about volunteer life on a kibbutz. Finally, the session would conclude with questions and answers.

The first speaker introduced Chaim, who came to the front of the hall and began to speak. Billy had heard most of what was said before at one time or another, during his first stay in Israel, so there was little that was new to him. The first timers listened intently though, in silence, as Chaim said his piece. The way he spoke, merely confirmed Billy's first impressions that this guy was really intense. On the verge of tears, he described the early years, when the kibbutzim were on the frontline, in the fight to defend the newly founded State of Israel from extinction at the hands of the surrounding Arab armies. The struggle to tame the land and turn it into the fertile paradise that it had now become. After a brief pause, whilst they wrestled with a rather ancient and unwieldly film projector, the lights were dimmed and a grainy black and white film began flickering, Billy struggled throughout most of the film to supress his giggles. The film was very dated, as the haircuts and fashion choices of the main characters showed. At one point, Billy leaned over to Mark and whispered rather too loudly.

"That's complete bullshit! Not even the Germans, are wearing shorts that short anymore."

Mark, nodded and Billy, who had spoken rather more loudly than he thought, was surprised when the audience around him erupted with loud shushing noises. The film had been shot many years earlier, as the credits at the end showed. Billy felt it was a very poor reflection of the volunteer experience, as it was today; bordering almost on misrepresentation. After the film, there were some rather surprising questions from the audience, about living on a kibbutz and the volunteer life. One questioner wanted to know, if the volunteers were free to read after lights out? Billy burst out laughing after this question and wondered what particular horror stories the questioner had been told because if reading was not permitted, and 'lights out' was enforced, then why on earth were they sitting in this draughty hall, wanting to sign up for the trip? Another enquired, if they were free to come and go from the kibbutz and how long did they have to stay before they would be armed with a machine gun? The second questioner was sitting just behind Billy, so he naturally turned around when the guy spoke. If the question itself was a little strange, what made it stranger still was the person who asked it. His clothing and haircut were ordinary enough, ostensibly, he appeared to be a middle class university student with a sensible haircut, white button down shirt and jeans. Then Billy looked a little closer at him. His hands were twitching as he clenched and unclenched his fists. Billy saw a zealous fire burning deep in his eyes. What a nutter. As Billy watched, he half expected him to leap to his feet and start bouncing around the place yelling at the top of his lungs about how he just wanted to kill. He didn't. He remained seated and listened to the rather restrained answer from Chaim, who took some time to point out that security for the volunteers was provided by the kibbutz members and that he had never heard of any instance, where volunteers were trusted with firearms. A wave of disappointment passed briefly over the questioner's face before being swiftly replaced with one of resolve. Billy reckoned this psycho would try his hardest to get his hands on some kind of gun and hunt desperately for an excuse to use it. The rest of the questions were innocuous enough, covering the weather, the work and the finer points of the accommodation and the food. Billy already knew exactly what to expect, so he largely tuned out for most of these answers.

He and Mark were on their way to the door, when Chaim detached himself from the group and ambushed the pair. He addressed Billy directly.

"I couldn't help overhearing your comment during the film. Have you been to a kibbutz before?"

"Yeah," said Billy, "I was a volunteer on Tel Boker for a while, a year or so back."
"So why are you here? Returning volunteers don't usually bother to attend these meetings as they feel they know what it's all about?"

"I was more here to support Mark. He's a first timer."
Chaim nodded his head.

"So you didn't have any problems last time? I have to ask?"
"What sort of problems?" Billy didn't like the way this conversation was going.
"Like expulsion for example?"

Chaim folded his arms across his chest as if he was waiting for Billy to confess his sins. Billy thought for a moment about explaining the problems he had faced on Tel Boker, which had led to the curtailment of his first stay there, but decided that this might have an adverse effect on his chances of returning to Israel. Instead he focused on his second stint on the kibbutz, when he had left reluctantly and with praise ringing in his ears over a job well done and a valuable contribution made.

" ... and I do have a letter of reference from Tel Boker or you could always pick up the phone and call Yossi, there, who would back this up too. How come you are questioning my credentials? I would be way more worried about giving my approval to our mad machine gun toting friend over there."

Billy nodded in the direction of the guy who had asked about the weaponry, who still seemed a little twitchy. Chaim broke eye contact with Billy and glanced in that direction. Whether it was this break in his concentration or something else that attracted his attention, he just turned on his heels and walked away. Mark cleared his throat beside Billy.

"Was that good or bad?"
"What do you mean?"
"Well are we in or out? Are we going or not?"
"We are most definitely going and I will be heading to the travel agency on Monday to buy a plane ticket, are you free to meet around lunchtime?"
"I wouldn't miss it for the world." Mark beamed.

The difference between buying plane tickets in his home town compared to London was the presence of the Bucket Shops. Back home the only place to buy any kind of foreign holiday, or flights was through the limited number of Travel Agents with shops in the town. In the big city, you could take an afternoon and wander through the backstreets around Victoria train station, where literally hundreds of these independent travel offices existed.

With crudely hand-written signs in their windows offering cheap flights and holidays, the premises behind the signs were often little more than a single room, with a couple of desks, a computer terminal and a phone on each. Most had the word 'Fly' or 'Away' in the name of the business and as Billy and Mark progressed down Vauxhall Bridge Road, they were joking about the company names. How 'Fly by Night' sounded the most dodgy, while 'Good-Times Tours' probably specialised in sex tourism.

They were looking at the handwritten signs, most were offering single fares to Tel Aviv for about two hundred quid. As the prices were pretty much the same, it then fell to picking the place that looked the least dodgy. Eventually they made a decision and went in. As they entered the last customer was just finishing. The man behind the desk was handing over an airline ticket.

"Well Mr Smith, I hope you enjoy your trip to Mombasa."

The customer took the ticket, stood up and left the office without saying a word. If either Billy or Mark had paused to assess this customer, they might have noticed he had a certain look about him. They didn't. The guy behind the desk didn't look up straight away as he was still tapping at his keyboard. This continued for a minute or so before he paused to read what he had just typed. Satisfied he pressed the send key with a flourish and looked up. He looked mildly surprised that he had two more customers, so soon after serving the last one.

"What can I do for you guys? You look a little young to be in here?"

Billy was confused. He wasn't aware that there were age restrictions on travel.

"Mind you," the guy continued, "you could both have been boy soldiers and still served your five."

This statement did nothing to clear up the confusion for either of the two friends.

"So which unit were you in?"

"I am sorry," Billy managed to stumble out, "I have no idea what you are talking about?"

"Straight forward question man. Which army unit were you in?"

"I wasn't." Billy said flatly, "I did two years in the Scouts and hated every minute of it."

"So you have never served in the British Army?"

"Nope."

"So what are you doing in here?"

"Trying to buy a couple of plane tickets."

"Oh you want the travel agency, they are up on the first floor."

"So what do you sell in here? Package holidays?"

The guy behind the desk barked out a laugh.

"Not exactly, we place retired servicemen in military positions overseas."

"Wow, you mean mercenaries."

Mark seemed enthralled that he was in the presence of someone connected to such a supposedly glamourous occupation.

"I saw the Wild Geese that was about mercenaries starting a war in Africa."

Mark was clearly warming to his subject.

"Now who was it that played the main character?"

The guy behind the desk frowned.

"We prefer the terms Military Contractors or Military Consultants."

Billy was almost dragging Mark towards the exit door.

"Oh well sorry for wasting your time." He burbled.

They both took the stairs two at a time and stumbled and almost fell over the doorstep into the office on the first floor.

There was one other customer in the place and only a single desk occupied by a middle aged lady. She was busy hammering away at a keyboard. She finished and looked up at the customer.

"Right, so we have the ticket from London to Sidney, via Dubai, Business Class. That will be two thousand seven hundred pounds. How would you like to pay?"

The customer, another woman, this time in her late twenties dipped into a large designer handbag.

"With this," she said.

Perfectly manicured, if a little gaudy nails, fingers bedecked with gold rings handed over a gold credit card. The travel agent took the card and flipped it over to check the signature and then reached for the phone.

"What you doing?" the customer asked instantly looking a little uncomfortable.

"'I need to ring for authorisation on amounts over one hundred pounds."

She began to dial the number.

"Wait."

The customer leaned across the desk and pushed the cancel button on the phone cradle.

"Don't you just run it through the machine?"

She made a swiping motion left to right.

"Then I sign?"

"Well yes, that's what we do, but only after I get the authorisation code."

She started to dial the number again from memory. A little bit pointless since the customer's fingers were still on the cancel button.

"Why do you need to ring? You can check the signature on the back and that's enough."

She was getting agitated now.

"Normally, yes that is the case. But with this large amount I need the credit card company to authorise the transaction."

"Why? You just put it through the machine over there."

The woman pointed to the credit card machine that lay on a side table.

"You hand me the paper. I sign. That's it."

"Like I said, normally for purchases under one hundred pounds this is the case, but over a hundred pounds I need authorisation. So I need to ring your credit card company."

She pulled the phone base closer to her side of the desk and in the process freed the cancel button from the customer's finger. She listened to the handset and satisfied that she had a dial tone, she began to dial the number again. The woman now stood up, leaned across the desk and pressed the cancel buttons, quite forcefully. She was clearly not very happy about something.

"Just swipe the card with the paper."

She made the same swiping motion with her hand

"You give me the paper I sign it. You check and hand me the ticket. Why do you have to phone the credit card company?"

"For authorisation." the travel agent was obviously beginning to tire of this repetition.

"But I just sign the paper, you check the signature and that's it."

The customer now that she was on her feet was getting increasingly wound up and her voice was rising to a near hysterical shout.

"I have never had problems before, why do you need to involve the credit card company, are you stupid or something?"

Now it was getting personal it was taking a supreme effort from the travel agent to maintain her composure. She took a deep breath to gather herself to explain one last time, but before she could open her mouth the customer leaned across the desk and snatched her credit card back.

"You bloody stupid woman, you just lost my business. I'm gonna find another agency, where they know how to use the credit card machine, properly. I hope your manager finds out and sacks you."

She thrust the credit card into her handbag and flounced out of the room. The travel agent took a second to compose herself before she looked up and smiled at Billy and Mark. Both of them were stood there open mouthed at what they had just witnessed. The woman saw their looks and shook her head ruefully.

"Occupational hazard, either the credit card is stolen or maxed out, we usually get at least one of those in here every day. Now. How can I help you?"

## Chapter Eight

Billy reached for his small backpack, unzipped the front pocket and pulled out his sunglasses. The first rays of the morning sun were just appearing over the horizon and casting dazzling streams of light across the surface of the water. The reflection was hurting Billy's eyes and he felt that the glasses might help by taking the edge off the glare. Beside him Mark was softly snoring, his head resting on his pack. The two of them were killing time waiting for the Kibbutz Reps office across the road to open its doors. The proximity to the beach had been the deciding factor for them both, so instead of waiting outside the office, they had crossed the busy HaYarkon Street then the beach road itself and hit the sand to wait. Neither of them had slept much on the overnight flight down here. Billy had been unable to settle due to anxiety. Billy had never been afraid of flying until last night.

When they had both boarded the aircraft they had made their way to their assigned seats at the rear of the aircraft. At that point the majority of the boarded passengers were in the middle of the aircraft, so Billy and Mark were the only two this far back in the rear section of the plane. The curtain was drawn across the galley area, but as they approached their seats a flight attendant stuck her head around the curtain.

"Oh good, two strong lads. I wonder if you could help me, please?"

Billy looked up from his boarding card. He had been double checking the seat number.

"Of course, how can we help?"

The attendant gestured to them to join her in the galley. As they pushed through the curtain into the small space Billy could immediately see the problem. Two of the ceiling tiles in the galley had come loose and were hanging down exposing all the wires and ducting behind them.

"I need to tape these two tiles back in place."

She held up a role of white gaffa tape.

"I am just not tall or strong enough." She simpered.

The two friends leapt into action with Billy commandeering the role of tape dispenser and Mark, who was the taller of the two holding the tiles in place. Billy peeled off strips of tape and handed them to Mark who placed them across the drooping tiles. In no time at all the ceiling looked like new, except for the cross hatch of tape across the joins. The flight attendant was effusive with her thanks and praise was ringing in their ears as the two went and found their seats.

"That didn't look too clever." Mark said once they were seated.

Billy who was in the process of sliding his backpack under the seat, looked up at his friend.

"It's cosmetic, relax. I don't think we are going to come plummeting out of the sky."

He was forced to swallow his words a little later when they were again summoned out to the galley. The pilot had just called for the cabin crew to arm the slides and cross check. This meant that the crew had to secure the doors for take-off. Apparently one of the rear doors of the aircraft was not shutting properly, so Mark and Billy were again asked to lend a hand. The flight attendant explained what the problem was and the two lads set about the task. A strong heave on the door enabled them to swing the locking handle into place and a few seconds later the light in the centre of the door turned from red to green.

"That's done it guys. Thanks for your help. I will see you right as soon as we get in the air."

She gave a conspiratorial wink and made a drinking motion with her hand. Billy was still transfixed by the aircraft door that despite being closed and locked as the green light suggested still seemed to have a large gap all around the edge of the frame as if it was not seated properly. He said as much pointing out his concern.

"Oh don't worry about that love," the attendant was full of reassurance.

"If the green light is on then all the contacts are in place and the door is shut."
'Shut it maybe', Billy thought to himself as he returned to his seat, 'but is it airtight and could it burst open at any time sucking us all out of the fuselage in a split second?'
He tightened his seat belt even tighter than usual once he was sat down and resolved to keep it on and tight as long as the aircraft was in the air. The flight time to Tel Aviv was about five hours. This was on a good day when there were no delays and the flight got a direct routing through to Ben Gurion. It looked like today was not going to be one of those days. After three hours of flying and just as everyone was settling down to get some sleep, the captain came on the tannoy to announce that they were making an unscheduled stop to replenish their dwindling fuel supplies.

Billy wracked his brains to see if he had ever heard of an aircraft running out of fuel mid-flight. He hadn't, but the captain went ahead and made his pitstop to refuel before taking off again and continuing their journey. Running out of fuel and a dodgy door did little to help Billy settle down and rest, so he spent the dark of the night hours awake, often sitting staring into space. The flight attendant had kept her word, supplied both of them with free drinks from the bar throughout the flight, but even the alcohol in large quantities hadn't been enough to take the edge off Billy's apprehension. As a result he was now sat on the sand, rather hung over and tired to boot. He probably didn't look his best, but then he had seen the state that some other volunteers had got into and they had never had any problem getting assistance from the kibbutz office to find new placements. Billy, therefore, wasn't too concerned about his outward appearance, when they finally re-crossed the roads leading to the Volunteer office.


Tel Aviv central bus station was overwhelming in so many ways. It conducted a full on assault on all the five senses, simultaneously. When Billy and Mark disembarked from the local city bus an hour later they were assailed from all sides. Billy had experience of the bus stations of Israel from before, but even he was taken aback by the intensity of this onslaught. From all sides people streamed towards them, past them, as they stood gathering their stuff, their wits, and trying to figure out their next move. Uniforms of every colour circled around them, predominantly the olive green of the Army, although this came in a kaleidoscope of variants according to the age of the uniform. Mixed in were the uniforms of other service branches, tourists in a variety of colours, Hassidic Jews in their black and Arabs in their white or blue robes, all focused intently on getting somewhere. They were jostled by people, by large army kitbags slung on shoulders and even the odd buttstock of a weapon hanging in a sling.

The ambient noise with so many people talking, laughing and shouting at each other was deafening and then over this general background noise was the shouts of the Sherut drivers yelling out the names of their destinations. Aside from the pervading smell of diesel fumes, there was the lush smells of cooking meats and frying falafel balls from the many food stands. Blended with this was a mixture of other underlying smells, gun oil, cigarette and dope smoke, as well as alcohol. The sum of which clogged the nose and coated the back of the throat and the tongue. Billy grabbed Mark's elbow and guided them both across the road, narrowly avoiding a departing Egged Bus, which was zooming out of the place, like a formula one car on race day and a Sherut packed to the roof, which was heading off in hot pursuit.

Inside the ticket office Billy consulted the scrap of paper that they had been given by the girl in the kibbutz office. A bus number and destination was written in the scrawl of someone not used to writing in English, the letters badly formed, as if by the hand of a six year old child. Billy could just about decipher the handwriting enough to be able to ask for two tickets to the correct destination. This was the first time since their arrival that Billy had used Hebrew properly and the first time he had used the language for nearly a year, so he was surprised how quickly it all came back to him. He had resisted the urge to speak Hebrew with the two security officers at Gatwick Airport, when he and Mark had undergone the screening that all passengers were subject to, wanting to ensure that Mark had been able to follow everything that was said to them during the interview. This had been a wasted effort because as soon as Billy had admitted that unlike Mark, this was not his first trip to Israel the two friends had been separated and interviewed individually. Billy was therefore subjected to a much more rigorous interrogation, where the person concerned was asking detailed questions about Billy's movements during his previous visit. He wanted to know where Billy had stayed and for how long, why his passport was missing visa stamps for a long period of time. Billy reluctantly admitted to working in Eilat for several months, when his passport had been stolen and then returned to him at a later date. The matter of the theft and the circumstances of the return of his documents were all documented in the relevant police files, so Billy gave the names of the two officers who he had dealt with in Eilat. These were duly noted and no further action was taken on the matter. After what seemed like an hour of questioning and re-questioning, but was probably only about fifteen minutes, Billy was handed back his documents and sent to check in. The security officer wished him a good stay and as a parting shot, recommended that Billy be a little more careful with his passport this time. Billy discovered that he was drenched in sweat as he shouldered his bag and went to meet Mark, who had waited for him by the exit from the screening area.

Billy only made one small mistake when he asked for the bus tickets and the woman behind the sales counter had looked impressed that someone who was clearly not Israeli could speak her language. She sat behind the glass pane for eight hours everyday and had to field questions, requests from everyone, Israelis and tourists alike and while she had a reasonable command of the English language, it was a prerequisite for the job, the way that some non-native English speakers spoke the language was enough to give her a headache. When she looked up each time and saw a non-Israeli staring at her through the glass, she took a deep breath and prepared herself for the worst. On this occasion she had seen Billy and Mark looking back at her, two tourists, from Europe given their untanned faces, she had inhaled deeply and braced herself.

So when the dark haired guy on the left had asked for two bus tickets in nearly fluent Hebrew she was prepared to forgive him that he made a small mistake over the actual gender of the tickets. It was one of the idiosyncrasies of the Hebrew language that inanimate objects could switch gender according to proximity to either male or female persons. Therefore an ashtray on a table surrounded by women was female until a man sat down at the table at which point it switched to become male. As a test of the newcomers ability, she had asked for the money in Hebrew and Billy immediately began to count it out onto the counter. There was no hesitation, no pause while he translated the numbers back into his own language, did the math and then translated the result back into Hebrew. She spent all day doing this job and she knew the tell-tale signs. She handed the tickets through the glass and gave the young man a big smile.

"Enjoy your journey."
She said, a complete departure for her from her normal dour demeanour.
She was rewarded with a smile and a wink from Billy who was pleased with himself.
"Thank you very much." he said as he gathered up the tickets and the change.
This small interaction put her briefly in a really good mood. Two difficult customers later, and this mood was all but forgotten.

The interior of the Egged bus was a cool and a peaceful relief after the intense heat and deafening noise of the bus station. They had stowed their large bags in the belly of the bus and then climbed aboard, showing their tickets to the driver, before finding two seats together about halfway down the bus. This bus, was heading north, so there were plenty of seats occupied by uniformed soldiers, heading back to their bases or rotating home to settlements in the Golan and the Galilee. As the doors finally closed and the bus pulled away from the stand, Billy thought back to the last time he had ridden an Egged bus. It had been the day that he had accompanied Mel to Ben Gurion Airport, for her trip home to England. It had been a melancholy trip, one which Billy had been reluctant to take. Once it had become public knowledge, that Mel was leaving, there was a gloomy atmosphere around the kibbutz. In the short time she had been a volunteer on Tel Boker, Mel had definitely won her share of fans, both among the members and the volunteers. Her job in the children's house, put her in daily contact with many of the young members' families and she was forever receiving invitations to visit their homes, for the obligatory coffee and cake, or ice cream and sodas. Her departure meant, that every home had to be visited and proper leave taken of the families and their children. Billy had accompanied Mel on many of these visits, so he was used to the inevitable questions, about whether the two of them would pick up again when it was time for Billy to return home to England. The first few times this subject was raised, Billy dismissed the question with a shrug and a laugh, followed by a casual "maybe", but the question persisted and it seemed, in the end, like it was a conspiracy among the members to discover their intentions.

Billy, who was well aware of the deterioration of their relationship after Mrs Bishop had returned to England, was reluctant to raise this subject with Mel. He was afraid of exactly how she would answer, so instead Billy continued with his shrugs and evasive responses. There was no doubt their relationship was in trouble. Mel had taken to sleeping back in her own room more often than she did with Billy and their intimacy had become non-existent. It was true, that during her two week stay in Israel, Mel's mother had made it increasingly obvious to Billy, that Mel was destined to take another path in life and that he could not hope to be her partner. Whatever had passed between mother and daughter on their day trips around the country, or in their private moments together, it was abundantly clear to Billy that it had made an impression on Mel and the way she reacted to him had changed accordingly.

It really shouldn't have surprised him when her attitude changed, but it still left Billy feeling sad and lonely. Billy would have been quite within his rights to let Mel travel alone to Ben Gurion, but he had made a promise to escort her and he followed through with it, even if it meant an awkward couple of hours thrust together in the confined space of two adjacent seats on the bus. It was like they were in a halfway house between being lovers and just friends. It was also the first time that Billy had failed to fall asleep on an Egged bus journey. Normally he was asleep almost before the bus had reached its cruising speed. He secretly suspected that the drivers introduced some form of sleeping drug into the air-conditioning to help subdue their passengers. On this occasion, the journey to Tel Aviv was long, as he sat rigid, unwilling to even allow his arms or legs to make any contact with Mel, the whole way to the Airport.

The goodbyes at the departures gate in Ben Gurion had been stilted, unemotional and yet strangely painful for Billy. His bus journey home to Tel Boker was long and sorrowful. If their separation at Ben Gurion had been emotionless, their recent farewells in London, two days earlier, had been the complete opposite. Mel had refused point-blank to have anything to do with the airport departure or accompanying him there. They had a final enormous shouting match in the street, outside Mel's student hall and parted. That was it. As Billy stalked off into the night he had felt an enormous sense of relief. The last week had been a living hell of negativity every time he and Mel were together. From the moment Billy confirmed the trip back to Israel, she had been incensed, and had taken every opportunity to pour scorn on his plans.

When Mark and Billy had returned from the travel agent clutching their tickets the arguments had started. This hadn't been a sullen sulk by someone who had been left behind. Mel was absolutely incandescent with rage. Billy had been shocked by the violence of her reaction and had tried to defuse the situation with humour. A fatal mistake on his part. It was like pouring a bucket of petrol on a fire in the vain hope that the liquid might extinguish the blaze. What was most unusual was that she stuck around to fight. Normally with Mel she exploded and then at some point a self-control filter kicked in and she would leave the argument. If they were out somewhere then she would go home, if they were home then she would go out and if they were talking on the phone she would hang up. This time, however, she would not back down. It was more because of this clear determination to be heard, at any cost, that Billy actually listened to what she was saying and therefore learnt a few home truths.

The main thrust of Mel's argument was that Billy, by returning to Israel and life on a kibbutz, was in fact running away from reality. He was trying to escape from real life. Instead of facing up to his problems and dealing with them, he was taking the coward's way out. After that particular revelation, she then embarked on a total character deconstruction, pointing out all the flaws in Billy's personality. Billy let her speak her mind, more out of respect for her as a friend, than through any desire to hear what she had to say. All the time that she was speaking, Billy had been sat on his sofa, chain smoking cigarettes and guzzling scotch from a bottle. The whiskey was helping to numb the pain caused by Mel's words, but it also brought out one of Mel's final and most damning assessments.

"Let's face it Billy, you're an alcoholic."

Mel emphasised this by waggling her right index finger at Billy.

Billy paused the glass of scotch halfway to his lips.

"I beg your pardon?"

"You're an alcoholic and instead of running away back to Israel, you should stay here and fight your demons. You need treatment." Mel continued waggling.

Billy looked straight at Mel, intensely studying her face looking for tell-tale signs of a smile dancing at the corner of her mouth, a wicked glint of mischief in her eyes. He found nothing. Her mouth was a firm line, the lips pressed tight together. Her eyes were cold as black flint, and dark as the longest night. Billy forced himself to laugh, it was a hollow bark. Right now he needed something to break the intense atmosphere in the room.

"I like a drink, like any other guy, that much I'll admit, but alcoholic? That's a bit strong."

"Billy, take a long look. Since we have been sat here you have managed to polish off the best part of a whole bottle of whisky."

Billy looked at the bottle, which was perched on top of one of the cardboard moving boxes. The bottle was looking a little empty, Billy had to admit that much, but he didn't feel particularly drunk or out of control. He couldn't see the problem. He felt fine and he was prepared to say as much to Mel.

"Mel, I think you are exaggerating, I feel fine, absolutely normal."

"It's not normal to drink spirits in the quantity that you do. Billy you have a problem."

"I will only have a problem when the money runs out and I can't afford to buy more."

He grinned at Mel hoping to lighten the situation. He failed. She remained stone faced.

"Ah come on Mel lighten up will you?"

"Billy, I honestly can't. I am worried about you."

"Worried? Why?"
"Because you are out of control."
"And you never get drunk?"
"Of course I do, but I am not the one with the problem."

Mel's voice was beginning to climb in volume, pitch and intensity. Billy sensed she was about to explode into another one of her rants. He had been on the receiving end of one or two of those over the last couple of days. He wasn't sure how many more he would have to endure over the next few days, before he finally made it to the relative calm of the departures hall at the Airport.

The problem was that Mel had stepped in to offer Billy a place to stay in the intervening days, between him leaving the flat and then the country. She had also, rather grudgingly, offered him space in the garage at her parents' house to store the five cardboard moving boxes that contained his life up until now. These contained mostly books, cassette tapes, a few clothes, as well as some ornaments and household items that had not been provided, as part of the flat's inventory. The last of these boxes was now sitting in front of them, serving as a temporary table, the same table where the now almost empty scotch bottle was standing. The root cause of their current disagreement.

"I don't think I have a problem, I like a few drinks that's all."

Billy was trying to adopt a reasonable tone of voice in an attempt to diffuse the situation. He seemed to have succeeded because Mel fell silent, puffed out her cheeks and exhaled noisily then blew air out her nose. The snort made her sound like a horse and Billy smiled.

"I don't know why you are smiling, I think you are making a big mistake and it is going to cost you." Her finger was back again.
"What d'ya mean?"
"You're going to realise, that you don't fit in there either, anymore."

Billy obviously looked puzzled as Mel took his silence as an indication to continue.

"You came back here with high hopes and big plans to make a success of your life and you were on the right track."

Now Billy did the horse snort. Mel ignored his disagreement and continued.

"You had a good job, a circle of friends and then in forty-eight hours, you just threw it all away. Decide to run off and hide. Really, what would Mike say?"

That was a very low blow. It struck him, hard, right in the guts. It hurt worse because it had come from Mel.

"Mike! He's not fucking here anymore. Swanning around on the other side of the bloody world, with Yara, he's got no right to an opinion. None."
"Well, maybe if he was here, he could talk more sense into you. This is a huge mistake."
"You're just bloody jealous, because you can't drop everything and come too, can you?"

These were evil words but Billy had almost reached the end of his tether. He knew he had made a mistake before the words were even out of his mouth and as he watched Mel's face darken in anger, he wished there was some way he could unsay them. Mel was silent for a few moments as she gathered herself for her next verbal assault. Billy knew it was going to be a fierce and bloody character assassination. Words would be said that would be hard to forgive and impossible to forget.

Before this huge row, they had spent the whole day cleaning the flat from top to bottom and packing Billy's few possessions. He felt he had earned a drink after that effort. In a while, the Landlord was coming by to collect the keys and, hopefully, return some of the deposit Billy had paid him, when he had moved in. Billy had worked hard cleaning the flat. The place now looked considerably cleaner than it had been when Billy first moved in. The kitchen and bathroom were spotless, even the dark ring around the bath tub had been banished, by repeated scrubbing with a bath cream on a scouring pad. He didn't think for one moment, that he would get his full deposit back, these things really didn't work like that, but enough cash to be able to join up with his friends and helpers, later on, and reward them for their help, with a curry at the local Indian, would be nice.

Despite the fact he had keys to the apartment and the front door of the block, the landlord was old-school, at least with Billy, always was courteous enough to ring the bell. Billy took the interruption for what it was, the perfect excuse to draw a line under this current uncomfortable conversation. He knew this discussion was far from over, but like a field marshal whose troops have suffered a setback, he was pleased to call a truce, give the troops a breather and have time to regroup his forces before the next assault came. He sprung to his feet like a jack-in-the-box and rushed out when the entry phone warbled.

It was the landlord, Billy buzzed him upstairs and then waited by the front door to let him into the flat. Mr Giorgio was an elegantly turned out Italian gentlemen of indeterminate age. His grey hair and wrinkled skin put him in his twilight years, although fixing an exact decade was more of a challenge. He seemed sprightly enough, even after climbing the stairs, but the liver spots on the back of his hand as he shook Billy's implied an octogenarian or older. He was always impeccably dressed with suit, waistcoat and highly polished brogues, his grey hair always perfectly styled. He carried with him, at all times, a tan leather attaché case. The two of them began the inspection tour of the place. At some time during which Mel stuck her head around the door and told Billy she was going back to her parents' house.

"I will see you later."

She said rather coldly, before hoisting the last cardboard box into her arms and turning her back on Billy.

"You're not moving in together then?"

The landlord said as soon as they both heard the front door slam shut.

"No, she is just storing some of my stuff for a while."

"That's good. She doesn't look very happy with you."

"She isn't," Billy said with a wry smile.

"Girlfriend?"

"Ex, but it's complicated."

"Aren't they always?"

The whimsical smile on his face told Billy that this man had clearly had his share of upsets in his love life.

"So where are you moving to?"

"I am not. I am leaving the country next week and going back to Israel, to a kibbutz."

"I see."

The landlord's tone like his face was blank. He was clearly not familiar with the concept or the idea. Billy was not keen to go into details, so he let the matter drop and they continued their tour. It didn't take them long to visit all the rooms of the flat and at the end the landlord said he was very satisfied with the effort Billy had made and the care he had taken with the place.

"I wish all of my tenants were as careful."

Despite his ringing praise he had noticed and remarked on some small items that would need to be attended to or repaired, before the flat could be let again. Billy couldn't be sure but felt convinced that most of them had been in that same state of repair when he had moved in, but he didn't want to argue, so he just accepted the landlord's decision along with the wad of cash, which was the balance of his deposit. Mr Giorgio had made a show of counting out the crisp ten pound notes onto one of the gleaming white countertops in the kitchen. He made a note in his cashbook and then passed the book over to Billy for his signature. Billy signed and then Giorgio tore out the page and handed the pink copy and the pile of notes to Billy. The white copy he folded and tucked into the inside pocket of his jacket. The cash book went back into his leather attaché case along with an envelope containing all the keys for the flat bar one set which Billy hung on to. He had promised to drop in the mailbox on his way out of the building. Billy stuffed the wad of notes into his jeans pocket and then showed Mr Giorgio to the door. They shook hands and Billy closed the door, alone for the last time in the flat. He wandered through each of the rooms in turn with the excuse that he was doing a final 'idiot-check' for anything that he had left behind, but there was nothing left just his cigarettes and the scotch bottle on the living room windowsill. He slumped back down on the sofa, poured the last of the contents of the bottle into the glass and then lit one final cigarette. He would have to wash the glass up, place it back in the cupboard and then empty the ashtray into the bin. The bin bag would go downstairs into the large trash container behind the block and that would be it. His association with this place would be at an end. He picked up the glass and took a sip. Was he really an alcoholic? Could he really make a success of his next adventure in Israel? Only time would tell.

## Chapter Nine

Billy looked out of the window as the landscape unfolded before him. Tel Boker, his former kibbutz lay in the south of the country, close to the Negev desert. Their destination, new to Billy, was in the north. He had only made a couple of forays to the north of Israel, on supervised volunteer trips, so the new terrain and the sights were dramatically different from the dry desert conditions of the south.

Their interview in the kibbutz office had been intense and a little scary. After fierce questioning from one of the staff about their reasons for travelling to Israel and their intentions for coming to work as volunteers in the first place, they had both been given the standard chapter and verse about the rules, regulations governing the volunteer relationship to their host kibbutz, what would be expected of them in terms of work and also their general behaviour. It appeared to Billy that in the intervening months since his departure there had been questions asked about the general fitness of volunteers from certain countries, to be included in the programme, in the first place. Their UK passports along with the pair's dishevelled and hungover demeanour, had clearly put them firmly on the list of potential undesirables. Billy risked a glance around the office and tuned into some of the other conversations, with what appeared to be certainly fresher faced individuals. These people did not seem to be getting the third-degree on their intentions and their interviewers were all smiles, a massive difference from the rather sour-faced young woman sitting across the desk from them. Billy waited for a suitable break in the tirade, before he laid down his trump card. He placed the reference letter from Yossi, the volunteer leader on Tel Boker, face up on the table.

"I have this reference from my previous stay."

The woman sitting on the other side of the desk eyed the piece of paper as if it was a venomous snake. It was a little travel worn, stained, but the words and the contents were good, or at least Billy had to assume they were. She reached across the desk using the point of her pencil to flip the paper around, so she could read the text, without having to actually pick it up and risk contamination. Billy had never mastered the art of reading Hebrew, so he had to accept that the contents of the letter, at least the Hebrew version, bore some resemblance to the English version, which was still nestling in his pocket. Clearly the two contained some of the same sentiments, because there was a huge improvement in the attitude of their inquisitor. She even cracked a smile, as she reached the end of the letter, before she looked up.

"So you even speak our language." She smiled as she spoke Hebrew to Billy.

"I do, but he doesn't."

Billy answered her in English and nodded with his head towards Mark.

"I am sorry."

The interviewer said in Hebrew, before she switched back to her accented English.

"You should have said at the start, that you were a returning volunteer. I would not have wasted such a long time on the lecture. Do you want to return to Tel Boker?"

"No, I think it would be better for us both."

He indicated at Mark, sitting quietly beside him,

"If we started afresh. That way, we are both at the same starting point with people."

"That's a very sensible idea."

"Also, we would like to try out a kibbutz in the north of the country."

"That's also a wise choice. You will get to see more of the country that way."

After the production of the reference letter, the rest of the interview had been a mere formality and in no time at all, the two lads were back on the street and heading for the bus station, with the good wishes of the kibbutz office staff, still ringing in their ears.

"That was lucky." Mark said as they waited for the bus to whisk them down to the central bus station.

"What? The letter?"

"No, that I didn't puke up in the office."

With that Mark leaned over a nearby wall and vomited loudly into the flowerbed on the far side.

---

Billy looked across at Mark, who was dozing fitfully, in the seat beside him. He was curled up in what looked like a very uncomfortable manner, with one leg raised and wedged against the back of the seat in front. They had only known each other for just over nine months, but Billy felt that they had a good friendship. It was not as intense or as enduring as his relationship with Mike had been. That had been forged in the fires of their collective experiences, whilst growing up together.

Mel, in one of her further rants, during Billy's final days in England, had questioned Billy's friendship with Mark. She highlighted the fact that they had only met at the university Freshers Ball, the previous September. Billy had countered with the argument that many of Mel's current friends, were of the same vintage, so was she casting doubts on her own friends as well? She responded that she was not planning to travel with any of those friends to another country, at least not anytime soon. This spat had been symptomatic of their last days together. Silly arguments had flared up from time to time, some of them had resulted in quite heated exchanges. These occurred when Billy answered back or tried to defend himself. He quickly discovered that saying nothing and merely grunting in a neutral manner, resulted in the argument dying, before it even got started.

Billy certainly felt that he had the upper hand in his relationship with Mark. He spoke the local language, whilst also being familiar with the country and its people. Mark up until now, had been reliant on Billy for some guidance. Billy knew that this, would not last forever, as Mark was the kind of guy, who would find his feet in any social situation, which Billy would welcome; Billy would help his friend too. So, Billy trusted Mark, like he had Mike, to watch his back.

---

Billy and Mark climbed down the steps into the midday heat. The Egged bus had eventually reached their destination, the bus station in the northern city of Safed. They collected their bags and began to look around for the correct stop for the local bus, to take them on the final leg of the journey up to the kibbutz. They found the stop, where the timetable indicated that the next departure was not for a couple of hours.

"That's good," said Mark, "my stomach's rumbling. I need food."

Billy cast an eye over the fast food stands at the Bus Station and decided, that although any one of them would fit the bill, with time on their hands, they could venture a little further to find something better. They made their way out of the bus station complex onto the road and turned right.

"Where are we going?" Mark asked.

"No idea. I have never been here before."

Mark didn't seem too pleased with the answer, he was hungry but on top of that he was tired and still a little hungover after the drinking at Gatwick and on the flight here, but before he had any chance to complain, Billy found exactly what he was looking for. Lounging by the side of the road, feet up on the railings, body nestled comfortably on his kit bag and with his automatic rifle cradled across his lap was a soldier. He was puffing languidly on a cigarette and watching the world go by. Billy greeted him in his own language, which coming from someone who so clearly looked like a volunteer, was enough to cause the guy to drop his feet off the railings and sit up straight.

"That's a pretty good accent you have there, where'd you learn to speak Hebrew?"

"Eilat, Tel Aviv, around."

Billy had adopted the same languid and louche attitude as the soldier, leaning on the railings, his cigarette dangling from the corner of his mouth.

"Well you are good man."

"Thanks. Look do you know, where to get the best falafel round here?"

"Yeah sure, there's a place just up here on the left."

"What about a wine shop or supermarket?"

The soldier grinned mischievously.

"You want Arac or are you more a Vodka person?"

"Either, they both work." Billy grinned back.

"Just a little bit further up then, same side of the road. There is a wine shop there."

"Thanks my friend." Billy said.

"No problem." The soldier extended his arm the palm of the hand open.

Billy knew this was not a formal hand shake, so he just slapped the outstretched palm in a casual goodbye. The soldier returned to his cigarette and his people watching, replacing his feet on the railings.

"What was all that about?" Mark said as Billy led them away.

"Simple really. If you want to know the best place to eat in any town ask a local, and if you can, a local soldier. They will always know the best and cheapest places to eat. It's how they stay alive."

"So you just stroll up to a complete stranger armed with a machine gun and strike up a conversation?"

"Yeah, I guess so."

"Cool." Mark was clearly impressed with Billy's courage.

"Well, what did he suggest?"

"There's a place just up the street a bit, best falafels in the whole of Safed."

"Lead on."

Mark shouldered his pack and the two headed off up the road. They found the place exactly where the soldier had said it would be. It was easy to recognise from the long counter at the front piled high with every variety of salad, all protected by a curved glass screen. The rich smell of deep fried falafel balls, emanated from the open store front, which then engulfed passers-by, on the pavement. There was a small service area off the street, which was crowded with hungry people. The two lads manning the counter were working like Trojans, keeping up a free and healthy banter with the customers. When it was their turn Billy ordered for both of them, but stood back and allowed Mark to dress his sandwich, when it was his turn. The server poised over the sauce bowls and looked up enquiringly.

"What's the red one?" Mark asked, "is that chilli sauce?"

"Yeah sort of," Billy replied his mouth still full with food.

Mark signalled to the server that he would like some on his food. When the server drizzled a little of the sauce over the meal Mark waved his hands around. The server looked puzzled. In heavily accented English he asked,

"You want more?"

Mark nodded his head. The server rolled his eyes to the heavens and then shrugged his shoulders with resignation before adding two more large drizzles of the sauce. He handed the meal over to Mark and turned his attention to the next customer. The two friends exited onto the street and stood to one side, so as not to block the path for pedestrians heading up and down the street, or customers trying to get inside the shop. The tables out front, were all taken, but there was enough space for them to stand without causing a major obstruction. Billy was already tearing into his meal. Mark eyed his from various angles trying to decide the best way to attack.

Billy swallowed and cleared his mouth.

"You dive in. There is no right way or wrong way to eat one of these."

Mark took Billy's advice and took a large bite, before chewing and savouring his first taste of the national Israeli fast food. Whether it was by sheer luck or careful planning, Mark was a couple of mouthfuls into his falafel before he encountered the chilli sauce. Billy noticed that suddenly Mark almost stopped breathing then his face went a deathly white and a sheen of sweat broke out on his forehead. He swallowed and then made a lunge for one of the two water bottles that Billy had bought and placed on the shelf beside them. He tore the top off one, the lid spinning away across the sidewalk and into the gutter and downed almost half the contents in one long gulp.

"Shit! That's really fucking hot!"

Billy smiled.

"Yeah, not like the chilli sauce back home."

"I know that. Nau."

Mark sounded like his tongue had swollen up to twice its normal size.

"What is that stuff."

"It's called Harif. The word means sharp in Hebrew. It's called Harissa in Arabic, means the same thing."

Mark had downed the rest of the water bottle and was now back eating his falafel, but exercising a little more caution with each mouthful. Billy had polished off his own sandwich and drunk a little of the other bottle of water, before Mark finished his and greedily guzzled the rest of the water.

"God, my mouth's on bloody fire. It's like I just licked a volcano. Can we get some more water, please?"

"Yes, the next stop is just up the road and we will get a couple of large bottles of water there."

They covered the short distance to their next stop in next to no time. The interior of the shop was cool with the air-con going at full blast. Mark made straight for the cooler cabinet, liberated a litre bottle of water, screwed off the cap and drank deeply.

"You will have to pay for that."

A voice boomed menacingly from the shadows at the back of the shop.

"It's okay we have money."

Billy spoke to the shadows, holding up a ten shekel note to prove his point. The shop's owner came forward into the light. Billy had to struggle to stifle a giggle. Such an authoritative voice had led him to picture a more imposing figure. The person who stepped out of the shadows was diminutive in stature and shrew like in appearance. He blinked myopically from behind bottle top glasses as he moved forward to take the banknote from Billy's hand.

"I can't always trust you volunteer types."

There was no mistaking the voice or the owner. The two just seemed at odds with each other. He eyed up the two new customers taking in their rucksacks and the duty free carrier bags they were both carrying.

"Newcomers?"

"Yes we just arrived on the bus."

Billy was quite prepared to be friendly with the shop keeper. He might turn out to be a regular in this shop and there was no point getting off to a bad start.

"Kibbutz?"

"Yes."

"Which one are you going to?"

The man's English was good, although he, like many of his generation, spoke slowly as if they were uncertain of the words to use and as always with a rather thick accent.

"We are volunteering on kibbutz, Sde Avram,"

Billy said, hoping that it was not one of the settlements on the shop owner's blacklist.

"So, you are new to this volunteer life?"

Billy considered mentioning that he was an 'old hand' at the volunteer game, but a quick look over at Mark and an almost imperceptible shake of the head and Billy was away with his cover story. They had discussed whether or not to mention Billy's previous stay in the country and had reached an agreement that they would assess each opportunity as it arose. Billy had made a snap decision that right now he wanted to be a 'newbie'. In the same conversation the subject of the Hebrew language had come up. Billy had explained to Mark that he didn't think it was a good idea to reveal to their new hosts that they both spoke Hebrew.

"You do, I don't. My Hebrew is terrible."

Billy passed on commenting on Mark's ability, not wanting to encourage or offend. He merely pointed out that they would not, as newcomers, be expected to speak a word of the language and that it might be useful to be able to eavesdrop on conversations. Billy knew, from experience, that people often spoke the truth when they thought no one around them could understand what they were saying.

"Yes we just arrived in the country this morning and we heard there were some good kibbutzim up here in the north and we didn't much fancy life in the desert, which seemed to be the only other alternative, so we opted to come up here."

"Well there are plenty of kibbutzim up here along the Lebanese border. Sde Avram is one of the better ones."

"Well that's good to know."

"So what will you be wanting, Arac or Vodka?"

"I think we had better have some of both".

"Well with the Arac, I have three types, the difference is in the strength. The most popular is the medium strength Elite Arac, that's the one with the green top."

He waved his hand in the direction of a shelf, where there were bottles with green tops lined up like a phalanx of troops, dressed in rows as if they were ready for inspection by the commander in chief.

"The red top stuff, Emir, is not quite so strong, blue is the top of the range, the Alouf."

The blue and red topped bottles were lined up, in lesser quantities on either side of the green, like auxiliary troops to the main battle formation. Billy considered his options, before eventually selecting a couple of bottles of Elite and one Alouf. He placed these on the counter. The shop owner had been digging around under the counter and he straightened up when Billy placed the bottles down on the counter top. He was holding two bottles in his hands.

"These are the last two. You might know the brand, Stolichnaya, from Russia. They are on special offer, which is why I have almost sold out."

Billy wondered how many more cases of the stuff were lying out in the stockroom, just waiting to be the 'last two', but at least he had heard of the name, so he agreed to add those to his purchases. Billy pulled out a wedge of local currency and started counting off the notes, laying them down on the glass top of the counter next to the bottles. The shopkeeper scooped up the notes when the tally was complete and rang the sale up on an old fashioned till. Billy was amused to see that the currency indicator that popped up on the left hand side was a pound sign, which meant that the till had probably been in use since before Israel existed as a country, when the British had ruled the Mandate of Palestine as it was then known.

Billy didn't say anything though, not sure how any such comment would be received and really unwilling to get into the shopkeeper's bad books. Instead he collected his purchases off the counter top and began, together with Mark, to try and place the bottles inside their rucksacks. Billy didn't think it was the smartest move to turn up on the kibbutz for the first time with masses of bottles of alcohol clinking in carrier bags. The two bottles of whisky in the duty free bags, would be expected and would be enough for starters. Packing the bottles in amongst the t-shirts and shorts the two were able to cut out the tell-tale clink of glass on glass and they left the shop and walked slowly back to the bus station. Mark was still nursing the bottle of cold water.

The meal break and the shopping trip had cut into their waiting time, so when they arrived back at the bus station and had purchased their tickets for the last leg of their journey, there was only about thirty minutes to go before the bus departed for Sde Avram. They sat in the relevant bus stop, whilst Billy puffed on a cigarette and Mark was taking sips from the water bottle.

"Was it like this last time?" Mark asked, "All this hanging around for buses?"

"No, not at all. Last time we were collected from Tel Aviv and driven in a minibus straight to the gates of the kibbutz, as we were part of a group then."

"I think I might have preferred that."

"It does have advantages, but I think this is more of an adventure. And besides you would not have eaten that first class falafel if you had been on a minibus."

Mark, who was clearly still suffering some discomfort in his mouth and whose voice was still a little husky as a result, could not agree with Billy's observation.

"That's kinda what I was getting at."

Billy slapped Mark on the back.

"Cheer up mate, what doesn't kill you makes you stronger."

"That fuckin' chilli sauce very nearly did kill me."

Billy burst out laughing at Mark's gloomy comment and slowly Mark began to see the funny side of things and joined in.


The bus that wheezed to a stop in front of them had clearly seen better days. This one looked like it had been in service almost as long as the cash register in the wine shop. The engine belched out a good thick cloud of diesel smoke as the driver revved the engine. In the time the two friends had been waiting a sizeable queue had developed and now these people began to file onto the bus showing their tickets and passes to the rather disinterested driver. Billy hung around until it became clear that the driver was not budging from his perch behind the wheel and would not be opening the luggage compartment, before he and Mark struggled onto the bus with their heavy bags. They found the last two seats together and sat on top of their bags.

The bus was completely full and there was no extra space to stash the bags inside. Rucksacks became footstools, daypacks became armrests and they clasped their duty free carriers close to their chests like armour. The heat inside was overwhelming and the people sat around waiting for departure were preoccupied with frenzied fanning, using whatever they had that would create even the smallest breeze. The small sliding windows along the top of the bus were all pushed fully open promising some distribution of air once the vehicle was in motion. Both Billy and Mark had large maps of Israel that they had been given in the kibbutz office that morning and they were now put to good use as temporary fans. Eventually the driver checked his watch and when he was satisfied that there were no late comers he started the engine and reversed the bus out of its parking bay. The noise from the engine and from the wind coming in the windows made conversation almost impossible, so Billy just sat back and stared out the window at the passing scenery.

There were substantial differences, between the higher country in the north and the barren deserts in the south that Billy was used to. The land was green, cultivated and the steeper slopes set over to plantations of trees; mostly pine or fir trees. The whole place had a less desolate look to it, even at this time of year. There were patches of dead grass, where pastureland had been left to its own devices and was not irrigated, but the areas that were under cultivation, were lush and green. As they drove higher into the hill country, they were afforded a remarkably beautiful view of the source of water that was used to make this place, so green and fertile. The huge expanse of the Sea of Galilee opened up behind and below them through gaps in the hillsides. The surface of the lake caught the sunlight in places and flashed it back in a focused beam of light that hurt the naked eye. The surrounding water was a deep turquoise, like a huge life-giving precious jewel set amidst the rock and grass.

The bus struggled up some of the steeper inclines, with the driver grinding down through the gears, when the engine lost power. Progress was torturously slow and there was worse to come. Finally, when they made it to the first settlement, Billy discovered that the security on this northern border was considerably tighter than that down in the Negev. As the bus approached the gates of the first settlement, Billy noticed that the defences around the entrance were noticeably more impressive than the single wire fence that had surrounded Tel Boker. Here, there was a much more complex arrangement with rolls of razor wire and double height and width fences. The gate setup was also much more imposing.

On Tel Boker the gate had been a single span and although it was sturdy enough to stop a speeding car, it was only a single gate. This first settlement had two gates and between them a fenced off area with more high screens of razor wire, overlooked by a sandbagged enclosure manned by armed soldiers. Once the bus had passed through the first set of gates, these were closed behind the bus and several armed soldiers appeared. Some examined the outside of the bus with mirrors on poles, searching the underside of the vehicle, whilst two climbed on board the bus. One made his way down the bus examining the passengers individually, whilst the other remained close to the driver, his finger resting alongside the trigger guard of his weapon. The weapon's barrel faced the ground, but you had the feeling that the young man was more than capable of bringing the weapon to bear, if the need arose. He was vigilant, despite the constant squawking from the tactical radios they were all wearing. Billy tried to tune into the Hebrew, but it was too distorted to hear exactly what was being said.

When the soldiers had satisfied themselves that no one on the bus was a threat to either them or the members of the settlement they were protecting, the second gate was opened and the bus was allowed to proceed. Sensibly, in Billy's eyes, the exit procedure was less time-consuming although they still operated the two gate system, with the inner gate being completely closed, before the outer one was opened and the bus could leave.

This heightened security protocol was the procedure at each settlement along the route, so although it was no great distance, it was a time consuming journey. It all made practical sense, as this border here, was active and there had been countless penetrations through the border fence by armed terrorists. Billy was beginning to doubt the wisdom of his decision to swap the relative peace of the south, for the uncertainty of life on what looked to be a very dangerous border. He comforted himself with the thought that if the defence and security was this tight, then there was a strong chance that the residents within the communities, including the Volunteers would be safe from harm.

At each of the respective settlements some of the passengers left the bus, but strangely no one climbed on-board. Billy speculated over this with Mark and a soldier sitting behind overheard him. He leaned forward between the seats to offer an explanation.

"This is the last bus of the day, so when it gets to the end of the line, it stops, the driver stays overnight and then drives the first bus back to Safed in the morning. It would be dangerous and a little stupid to drive along the border after dark, the lights would make the bus a target."

'A very slow moving one.'

Billy thought to himself as the driver ground the gears again and the bus wheezed its weary way up another incline. Billy thanked the soldier for the information and he returned to doing what soldiers do on buses. At the last but one settlement, the driver yelled out that the next stop would be the last stop and that the bus was terminating there. Billy was delighted to hear that the next stop was to be Sde Avram, because it meant that the end of their journey was in sight.

Billy was hot, thirsty and really in need of a shower, a change of clothes and a cold drink. He knew that it might be a while, before he could have the first two but there was a strong chance that he could ask someone on Sde Avram to point out the way to the dining room and there he would be able to at least get a glass of cold water. When the bus set off for the last leg of the journey up to Sde Avram, there were only a few passengers left on the bus.

Billy looked around at the remaining passengers. About three rows behind him there was a young soldier. His uniform beret marked him as a member of the Golani brigade. Like many soldiers he looked incredibly young and like most of his fellow conscripts he was taking every opportunity that was presented to catch up on some sleep. He was sleeping heavily using a rolled up sweater as a pillow and with his arms tightly clutching his weapon. Elsewhere there were another young couple. These two were not in uniform and looked slightly older. Billy guessed they were students, who were using the kibbutz as a dormitory or they were children of member families, who had chosen to study after completing their military service. These two were deep in conversation about something.

The only other group were six lads, who had occupied the seats at the rear of the bus. Billy had noticed them at the Bus station in Safed and knew immediately that they were all volunteers. They were all being noisy, laughing and joking with each other. They looked to be slightly drunk and as Billy watched he saw cans of beer being passed around. The big bags they were all sitting on or that took up the extra seating places around them were clearly stuffed with all sorts of bottles and cans. They had just been on a 'booze-cruise' to Safed. Billy was more than familiar with the concept. He had made many such trips himself from his old kibbutz.

The reality was that the kibbutz members, in a vain attempt to control the occurrence of drunkenness and the fallout that such behaviour could cause in terms of violence and loss of productivity, had decreed that the kibbutz shops should limit the availability of strong drink like spirits and in some cases ration the beer that was available to the volunteers to buy. It was a hopeless and largely pointless exercise because the volunteers, being the masters of enterprise and invention, just pooled their resources and then elected a representative or representatives to make a trip to the supermarket in the nearest town. It might be a once a week event or take place more frequently depending on consumption but the one thing that always seemed in plentiful supply in the volunteer quarters was alcohol.

For the most part the members had resigned themselves to the heavy drinking lifestyle of the volunteers and provided that ultimately it didn't result in violence or in volunteers not turning up for work then, they mostly turned a blind eye to the practice. It was only where volunteers did get violent or destructive or where a volunteer repeatedly missed work due to drinking that they stepped in and intervened. The result was usually expulsion for the people concerned and that was the end of the matter.

Drugs, on the other hand, were a different story. The presence of illegal narcotics in the volunteer community was one thing that the authorities and the members did not want. Their reasoning went that if the volunteers possessed narcotics then it was only a short jump to all their precious children becoming rabid junkies. There had been television programmes and newspaper articles on the subject. The fact that many of those same children would, in the fullness of time, like any other young people anywhere in the world, acquire and want to experiment with narcotics was a fact that might have been missed.

That ultimately it was the young members themselves who often turned out to be the source of these very same narcotics was also ignored. It was easier to blame outside influences for their problems, rather than looking too deeply within their own communities. It was, simply put, the fact that anyone caught in possession of illegal narcotics, would be removed from the kibbutz. In some cases the local police might become involved and if that happened, then there was a strong chance that the volunteers concerned would end up being deported from the country.

As the bus wound its way towards Sde Avram the ringleader of the volunteer group, Billy guessed he had to be the group's defacto leader, as he was sat in the middle of the backseat, decided to come and introduce himself. He had probably been waiting to ensure that Billy and Mark were bound for Sde Avram, before he bothered to make his move. No point in showing out to a couple of newbies, who were bound for another settlement. Convinced that the newcomers were heading for the same destination, he decided to make an introduction. He rose from his seat and allowing for the rolling motion of the bus as it wove its way through the bends, in the road, made his way towards where Mark and Billy were seated. Two of his compatriots followed behind him like shadows or bodyguards.

They were all three clad in familiar volunteer dress, made up of a mixture of kibbutz work clothes and items from their own wardrobe. The leader had on a kibbutz grey work shirt that might have at one time been blue, but had been now washed out to a dull grey colour. Over that time it had also lost the sleeves, so his suntanned and well-muscled arms were on display. All three had longish hair, with the leader's hair the longest and caught up in a pony-tail. Their hair showed signs of sun bleaching, a strong indicator that all three worked outdoors every day. One of the lads had a bandana around his head, but his long hair was still visible at the back. Their dress, their tanned limbs and their swagger convinced Billy that these three were 'old hands' at the volunteer game. He watched as they made their way towards him and Mark. Although none of them were smiling, Billy didn't feel threatened, as there didn't seem to be any air of menace about them.

Billy, as soon as space had become available, had taken up one of the vacant double seats, so he was now sitting with his back to the window, one leg raised and the other hanging over the edge of the second seat. Mark was in the row in front, sitting in a similar pose. The newcomer took a seat across the aisle from Billy and leaned forward to make himself heard over the rumble of the engine and the grinding of the gearbox.

"New volunteers?"

"Yes," Billy answered for the two of them.

"First time on a kibbutz?"

"Yes," Billy answered again.

He had again shot a quick look at Mark and given the same almost imperceptible shake of his head that he had used in the liquor store. Once more he chose to be a newbie, he wanted to see how this conversation was going to pan out.

"Well it's all right, this kibbutz life. Plenty of sunshine and booze. Work is okay, although it gets in the way of having fun, sometimes."

This was all delivered in one rapid-fire sentence, in a broad Scottish brogue.

"I am Adam, by the way, but everybody calls me Jock."

"How original."

The words were out of Billy's mouth before he had time to stop them. He glanced anxiously at the young man sitting over the aisle, but he either chose to ignore them or was so wrapped up in his discourse he had failed to notice them.

"These two reprobates are Davey and Paul."

The other two nodded and smiled. Then there was a small pause, until Billy realised it was his turn to speak. The three were waiting for him to introduce himself and his friend.

"I'm Billy and this is Mark."

"You both sound like Cockneys."

It was Davey who spoke in a lilting Welsh voice.

"Yep that's because we're both from dear old London Town." Mark had finally found his voice and joined in the conversation. Adam nodded at the

Duty Free bags which were lying on the seat beside Billy.

"You got any British fags in there?"

"Yep four hundred B&H."

"Well you'll be a hit tonight. The local fags aren't up to much."

Billy was about to say he quite liked the Israeli cigarettes, but then remembered he was supposed to be a new arrival.

"You got any booze?"

"Couple of bottles of Scotch."

"Ah well you'll be all right then. See, they don't sell strong spirits on the kibbutz."

"That's why we've been down to Safed this afternoon. Stocking up, like." This came from Davey.

"The local vodka is pretty raw but it does the trick."

"And don't forget Arac." This was the first time Paul had spoken.

"Arac, what's that then?"

Mark knew the answer he had bottles of the stuff in his rucksack. He was playing along with the plot nicely. Paul took a moment to fill them in on the king of all spirits, even taking a moment to explain the ways in which it was consumed and dwelling, all but briefly, on the side effects that drinking too much could cause.

"That sounds scary."

Mark sounded genuinely concerned. Either he was acting the part brilliantly or he had just learned something about Arac that made him a little uneasy.

"So is there gonna be a party tonight? What's the reason for the celebration?"

Billy tried to inject a curious tone into the question, although he very much suspected the standard volunteer answer.

"There's a party every night. We don't need a special reason."

'Bingo'. Billy thought to himself. No prizes for guessing that might be the answer.

"Oh good." Now Billy was struggling to make himself sound amazed.

Mark on the other hand was having no such difficulties asking non-stop questions about everything relating to volunteer life on Sde Avram with particular focus on the social life among the volunteers. At some point the remaining volunteers from the back of the bus ventured down to join them and someone handed around cold tins of lager. Billy noticed it wasn't from one of the local Israeli breweries, but was a premium Dutch lager. One of the others saw Billy studying the label and interjected.

"They were on special at the supermarket so we bought a couple of cases."

Billy was not complaining and the cold beer was definitely doing the trick with his thirst.

The bus finally made it through the security gates at Sde Avram and deposited the last remaining passengers at the bus stop, which luckily enough, was right next to the dining room. Billy recognised the building for what it was as soon as his feet hit the pavement. It was almost identical to the structure that served as the dining room on Tel Boker, even down to the ornamental flower beds, the curved lines of the structure and the thin, floor to ceiling windows that admitted just enough light but did not allow the room to bake in the summer sun. It was as if the dining room from Tel Boker had been picked up from the Negev and dropped down here on the Lebanese border. Maybe, Billy thought to himself, the dining rooms on kibbutzim throughout Israel were ordered from some sort of Kibbutz R Us? He was about to saddle up and climb up the short flight of steps when he suddenly remembered he was supposed to be a newcomer to all things kibbutz. He stopped himself and turned around. The five lads were sorting out who was carrying what from among their small mountain of bags and boxes. All of them were tinkling and clanking merrily with the glass and metal contents inside them.

## Chapter Ten

The bus having deposited the last of its passengers from Safed, wheezed across the car park like an old man with emphysema and into an especially reserved parking bay. The engine gave a hiccup and a cough as it expired for the final time. Billy didn't trust his ears, but it sounded exactly like some ancient person finally collapsing on the sofa after some extended period of exertion. There was probably a perfectly reasonable mechanical explanation for it, but he distinctly heard the bus emitting what sounded like a gentle fart. He shook his head. He was tired, hot and in need of a shower and some sleep.

"Adam, sorry Jock, before you go charging off. We were supposed to meet the volunteer leader in the dining room. Where's that?"

Adam did just that. With an elaborate wind milling action of his arms, like some baseball pitcher winding up for a fast ball, he thrust his arm forward as he pointed at the building that was directly, behind them.

"Thanks. I hope we can catch up later." Billy picked up his pack.

"You just have to follow the noise. We'll be there."

Adam and the others set off in what Billy presumed was the direction of the volunteer quarters. Mark and Billy shouldered their packs and climbed the stairs to the dining room, pushing the doors open and entering the cool quiet within.

This late in the day, the team that were responsible for the kitchen and dining rooms had already finished their shift, so the place was completely deserted. It was quiet enough inside that they could hear the slow drip from the cold water tap somewhere in the back.

"Magic, fucking magic."

Mark had dumped his bags on the floor by the door, pulled out a chair from one of the tables and slumped down in it.

"I'm hot, tired, need a shower and a change of clothes."

Billy, who was slightly less despondent, had started to scan the notice board by the door. There was a phone hanging on the wall just inside the main door and he guessed that it would probably be on the internal kibbutz exchange, so all he needed to find was the right number for the volunteer leader, call them up and let them know the two of them had arrived. He had the name of the person scrawled on a piece of paper. There was only one problem. All the lists of internal numbers by the phone were printed in Hebrew and Billy couldn't read a single word.

He gazed intently at the name on the small piece of paper and then scanned the list hoping that something would trigger in his mind. Unfortunately it didn't, but then mercifully their wait was cut short when two young people came in to the dining room. They had the usual, slightly hippy, look of kibbutz kids, their long hair not yet fallen victim to the first cut by the army barber. These two lads looked old enough to be on the cusp of starting their military service.

"Hi guys," Billy addressed them in English, "We are new volunteers, I was hoping you could help me. I need the number for Orin Levy. Unfortunately this is all in Hebrew."

He pointed at the telephone list. One of the boys, obviously not trusting his spoken English, merely traced his finger down the list and then stopped at the correct name. He tapped the name three times with his index finger. Billy read the number off.

"Thanks."

He said to the backs of the two lads as they set off across the dining hall without uttering a single word.

"Friendly bunch." Mark said to their backs in a hushed voice.

"Careful. They probably understand English perfectly well, they are just too shy to speak out loud."

"They wouldn't be able to hear me under those birds nests."

Billy decided that Mark was definitely a bit of a grump when he was tired. Although Billy didn't really hold this against him. He knew, himself, he was running on the last dregs of energy and adrenalin. He picked up the phone and dialled the number he had memorised. The phone rang a couple of times and then was answered by a voice that was thick with sleep.

"Ken."

It was not a name but the Hebrew word for Yes and used to answer the phone, or to admit someone when they knocked on your door.

"Hi is that Orin?"

"Who is this?" The voice had lost its sleepy edge and now just sounded annoyed.

"My name's Billy Randell, I am a new volunteer. We just arrived on the bus from Safed."

"What the hell are you ringing me for?" Now the voice sounded really annoyed.

"The kibbutz office gave us your name as a contact. They said we should contact you when we arrived."

The person on the other end of the phone must have placed their hand over the receiver as their voice became muffled. To Billy's ears, the bits he could make out sounded like a long stream of curses in a variety of languages. Whatever was said it had a positive effect, because when he came back on the line, the person Billy was speaking to, sounded a little more awak and composed.

"Okay, I guess it's not your fault. You need to call Rachel, she is on extension 271. She is responsible for getting you settled in."

"Thank you," Billy said trying to sound contrite, "Sorry for waking you."

He had a feeling that if it was Orin who had answered the phone then he had missed this last part because the dial tone cut in straight away indicating that the connection had been broken at the other end. Billy dialled the new number and waited a few moments while Rachel came to the phone. When she answered Billy again explained that he and Mark had just arrived and that they were waiting in the dining room. Rachel asked for their names again and then said she would come straight over to meet them. Billy sat down opposite Mark and lit a cigarette.

"Just a word of warning. We might end up on the shit-jobs list."

"Why's that?" Mark looked up alarmed.

"I get the feeling there are two people running the volunteers here. The guy I woke up probably does the job allocations and the woman who is on her way over looks after the domestic side. The fact I woke up the work supervisor from his afternoon siesta might mean we end up on the list for the shittiest jobs. It's just a warning though. He might not be the vindictive type."

Billy's assessment of the division of duties was confirmed when Rachel arrived ten minutes later, although they would have to wait a further twenty-four hours to confirm if the second part of his prediction would come true. Rachel arrived in a cloud of purple cheesecloth, strong perfume and billowing red curls. She was clutching a stack of paperwork under her left arm and puffing continuously on a Noblesse cigarette. Billy stood up to meet her, offered his hand and quickly withdrew it as he realised Rachel had both hands full. She was explosively effusive with her apologies for not having been here to meet them in person, citing family duties as the reason. Billy took a moment to study the newcomer. She was not very tall, reaching only as high as Billy's shoulder. She was wearing a hippy ensemble of purple cheesecloth skirt and blouse set off with bangles and bracelets at the wrists and an impressive number of bead and shell necklaces around her neck. Her feet were clad in the traditional open toed sandals favoured by kibbutzniks, but Rachel's most striking feature was her cascade of natural red hair. It fell in billowing curly waves well past her shoulders. Her other striking feature was her broad West Country accent.

She saw both the lads do a double take as she spoke and was clearly used to this type of reaction from volunteers.

"Yes I'm British by birth. I came here as a volunteer ten years ago and met the man of my dreams. We got married and I have been living here ever since. My home town is Bristol, I support Rovers not City and I have no plans to return to the UK anytime soon. That usually takes care of most questions. Anything I missed?"

Both boys were a little startled by the tirade all delivered in that friendly West Country burr, but they both managed to shake their heads indicating they had no further questions.

"Good, right, let's get down to business. I have some forms I need you to fill in, so I can get your insurance papers drawn up, then I will show you to your rooms. Everything you need, like sheets and blankets are already in the room, work clothes and the rest we can sort out in the morning".

With her little spiel delivered she dished out the papers to the two lads and then left them to fill them out. She wandered around the room occasionally drifting by the table to check on their progress. Billy and Mark worked quickly and after a few minutes had passed, they both put down their pens and collected the papers together. Rachel gathered them up and then slid them back into a clear plastic cover.

"I'll get those processed in the morning."

She had not even bothered to check them for mistakes.

"Right if you collect your bags I will show you where you are sleeping. I have put you two in a room together. We are quite full at the moment but there was one room empty so it will be just you two sharing. Just a word of warning, though. The rooms are designed to take four volunteers each, so if we get many more volunteers it might be necessary to move people in with, you."

Rachel watched as they slung backpacks over shoulders and picked up their Duty Free bags. She pulled a funny face when she heard the bottles inside clink together.

"What did you bring?"

"Scotch whisky," said Billy. Mark nodded indicating he had purchased the same.

"That won't last long around here. Have you got any British fags?"

"Yes, why? Do you want a pack?" Billy moved to open the carrier.

"No, you are all right. I got used to smoking these many years ago."

She waved the green packet of Noblesse under their noses.

"But with British fags you will be highly popular with certain people, until they run out."

She turned on her heels and led the way out of the dining room with Mark and Billy in her wake.

"I was hoping my personal popularity might last longer than these damn cigarettes." Mark sounded a little discouraged by Rachel's prediction. He was, after all, a non-smoker, but Billy had insisted that they both bring two hundred B&H with them.

"Don't worry mate. I am sure you will be a hit with all the ladies."

Billy grinned and had to duck as Mark took a swipe at his head. Rachel was waiting by the door holding it open. Her sandaled foot tapping impatiently on the tiled floor.

"Have you two stopped clowning around?"

"Yes," they said in unison sounding both like naughty schoolboys.

"Good. Yalla, let's go."

The path to the volunteer area of Sde Avram led through a small forest of local pine trees. They probably served to screen the place off from the rest of the kibbutz and maybe even acted as a sound baffle. This seemed to be the case, because it was only when they were halfway through the plantation that the sounds from the volunteer quarters, became audible. With dub reggae music playing from one sound system and then almost as a counterpoint, in some horrible discordant musical battle, pop music was blaring out from a rival stereo. The two when blended together, made one unholy racket.

As they emerged into the clearing in front of the volunteer quarters, Rachel came to a very abrupt stop, surprising Billy. He was gazing at the sight in front of him, so he swerved left, cannoning into Mark barely managing to avoid, throwing the two of them to the ground in an undignified heap. Rachel seemed oblivious to the chaos and collisions that were taking place behind her. She was stood stock still. Just like a bloodhound dog on point, she sniffed the air, dramatically inhaling a huge lungful of air. Billy and Mark waited behind the stationary volunteer leader.

"Right. That's enough time."

Rachel said to no one in particular and then set off again crossing the parched grass and mud patch that bordered the volunteer area.

"I have to give them enough time,"

Rachel said over her shoulder,

"time to put out their spliffs and hide their stash. If I don't see it then it doesn't happen."

Billy knew exactly what Rachel was referring to. Drugs. It appeared that the policy on Sde Avram was 'no see, no problem'. If the volunteers didn't take drugs openly and in sight then there was no real drugs problem among the volunteers. This was different to the policy that Billy had encountered on Tel Boker on his last visit to Israel. He was wondering how this policy squared itself with both the members and the young members, when Rachel conveniently filled in the missing piece of the puzzle.

"The volunteers are pretty much left to their own devices down here. We actively discourage the mingling between volunteers, young members and children under the age of sixteen are expressly forbidden from coming within two hundred yards of this place."

Billy considered this setup for a moment and decided it was probably not the best solution. An important part of his time on Tel Boker had been the interaction with the young Israelis and their presence, in considerable numbers amongst the volunteers, whilst it had led to the occasional problem, had given an extra dimension to the whole experience. But rules were rules and each kibbutz had them, so it was best to get a handle on them as quickly as possible in order to avoid falling foul of the kibbutz authorities.

It certainly looked like Sde Avram looked after its volunteers, if the accommodation available was anything to go by. When Billy had emerged from the pine forest he had expected to see rows of concrete structures similar to the ones that had housed the volunteers on Tel Boker. In place of these concrete boxes were what looked like a couple of modern accommodation blocks, similar to those you would find on University campuses up and down the UK. Two storeys in height and with rows of windows down each side, the place even had air-conditioning units bolted on the side of the buildings. Whether they were actually connected was one thing, if they were effective was another. The two units closest to them both seemed to be humming away happily and the lack of open windows indicated they were probably doing a passable job of keeping the interior cool. Entering the first of the buildings, denoted by a huge letter A on the side as, funnily enough, A block, Billy was hit by a refreshing wave of cool air. Well at least in the atrium area the air was cooled down. Inside the entrance and directly opposite them was the door that led to the ground floor rooms. This was a fire door and a sign just visible on the facia read, 'Fire Door Please Keep Closed'. The sign was difficult to read though due to the fact that the door was propped open with a wooden wedge driven under the door and as an extra precaution someone had thoughtfully removed the fire extinguisher from its hook on the wall and used it as an additional door stop. Rachel ignored this potential life threatening breach of fire safety regulations and led the way up the stone staircase.

On the top floor there was a landing and another fire door, also propped open by the same method as its twin downstairs. Again Rachel made no comment, but passed through the door and into the corridor beyond. There were rows of doors on either side of the corridor, some fully open, others closed and a few left ajar. The corridor was deserted, but it was possible to hear music and raised voices emanating from some of the open doors. Rachel stopped by the second door on the left hand side and unlocked it, pushing it open she walked inside. Billy and Mark followed hot on her heels.

Unlike the exterior of the building and the communal hallways the interior of the room was more of a return to familiarity for Billy. Whilst the quality of the accommodation had thrown him, inside the individual rooms things were more as he had expected. There were four beds, standard kibbutz volunteer issue, with steel frames, wooden tops and the thinnest of foam mattresses. On top of two of the beds lay a pile of bed linen, two sheets and a blanket. The rest of the furniture consisted of four identical metal lockers. Each of these was placed at the bottom of one of the beds, against the wall, door facing outwards into the room. It was institutionalised to the max. The floor was stone, marble tiles and there was a single metal ashtray lying on the windowsill, with a single stubbed out dog-end in it.

"You are expected to keep your room clean. There are mops and buckets in a cupboard in the bathroom at the end of the corridor."

"The evening meal is served in the dining room at six thirty, breakfast starts at seven. You will not be working tomorrow, but someone will stop by to pick you up at eleven to take you on a quick tour of the place and show you the key features. Orin will find you during the day tomorrow to give you your work assignments."

She paused as if she was mentally going through a well-rehearsed and often repeated checklist. Satisfied she hadn't missed anything she moved to the doorway, before turning around to face back into the room to deliver her parting comment.

"Make yourselves comfortable, I am sure other volunteers will be by in a while to introduce themselves; they're a nosey bunch here. I hope you enjoy your stay with us." With that she walked out of the room closing the door behind her.

Mark had tossed his rucksack on one of the beds, Billy took the other bed that was under the window and tossed his own pack on it. He unzipped the side pocket and extracted two glasses.

"Where did you get those from?" Mark looked surprised at their appearance.

"I pinched them from the dining room. We can't drink scotch out of the bottle."

Billy set the two glasses on the window sill and proceeded to pour two measures from his bottle of duty free scotch. The whisky was warm but the powerful spirit hit the back of Billy's throat like a velvet boxing glove. He winced slightly and noticed Mark pull a similar face.

"It's okay, but it would be better with a couple of ice cubes in it."

"Did someone mention ice?"

A voice thick with a familiar Scottish drawl came from the doorway and Adam waltzed into the room.

"Greetings fellow travellers and welcome to the House of Fun."

Billy and Mark greeted the Scotsman.

"Now in return for a wee dram, I might be able to secure some ice for your drinks. We just happen to have a fridge on this floor that works and is kept well stocked with cold beers and other chilled refreshments. There is an ice tray in the freezer box and it is full."

"I'll swap you a shot for a couple of cubes." said Billy without hesitation.

"I'll be right back."

Adam disappeared and returned in no time at all with a bowl of ice and an empty glass. The drinks were poured and the ice shared out and then the cigarettes did the rounds and everyone sat on the beds enjoying a smoke and a cold drink.

"So you got to meet the lovely Rachel."

Adam said as they all settled, backs against the walls and feet stretched out in front of them.

"Yeah," said Mark,

"It was a bit of a shock when she opened her mouth and started talking with that Wurzel's accent". He added.

Adam nodded his head because he had a mouth full of scotch. He swallowed it.

"Yeah it took me by surprise too. But she's a good sort. Gives us plenty of rope anyway."

"I noticed that," said Billy, "the whole count to ten palaver outside."

"Oh that's for the benefit of the stoners on the ground floor. I am surprised, she did it. As you are with us up here. Maybe it was just for effect?"

"I think she was probably doing it to make a point. Is there loads of dope smoking here?" Billy replied.

"Nah, not really, just a few of them down the end of the downstairs corridor. The kibbutz aren't too happy about it, but as long as they stay here in the block and in their rooms then they seem to turn a blind eye."

"Isn't that unusual?" Billy asked.

He purposefully made it a question rather than a statement. On his previous trip to Israel, he had met dozens of volunteers, during his time working in Eilat, who had been expelled from different kibbutzim, for possession of drugs, like he was. Adam considered his answer whilst savouring another mouthful of scotch.

"To be honest, I dunno. I have only had experience here on Sde Avram, you would have to ask some of the others who have been elsewhere or have been here longer than me."

Billy filed that question away for later and concentrated on what Adam was saying. He began to explain about life on the corridor, how the toilet and shower facilities at the end of the corridor were divided up with girls on the left and boys on the right. He said, with the arrival of Mark and Billy, the rooms were now all full.

"These two beds are the last ones empty on the block."

"So how many are we in total?" Mark asked.

"There are four rooms on each side so that makes a total of thirty in all." Adam seemed pleased with his mental arithmetic.

"Gonna be long queues for just 8 showers then."

"Actually it's worse for the girls as there are five rooms of girls and only three rooms with guys in them and anyway there is always plenty of hot water to go around. The showers do get busy at times. After work is one time and then again when people come back from the pool or wake up before supper, so it is best to allow plenty of time then."

Adam then started naming and describing some of the other volunteers who lived on their floor. Billy's ears pricked up when he mentioned that there were two rooms that were occupied by Swedish girls. Billy had fond memories of a certain Swedish girl he had met on Tel Boker when he had first arrived there. He liked the Swedes, particularly the girls, as they were rather liberal in their attitudes. In fact this was the case for most of the Scandinavian countries. A couple of those other volunteers duly appeared, although thankfully, Billy noticed, they had brought their own drinks. The room was beginning to fill up slowly as people stopped by to say hello. Some, merely stopping by to cadge a British cigarette and departing soon after the thing had been smoked, whilst others were genuinely interested in sussing out the newcomers. It was a process that Billy had witnessed a hundred times before and had even been part of it, himself. For Mark it was something new, so he was sitting proud in the middle of the room and lapping up the attention. The beds were filling up and people had started to sit on the floor. Someone had brought in a couple of bottles of Arac and a jug of water. This was starting to do the rounds among those who were drinking.

"What's that?" asked Mark.

He had never seen what happened when you mixed the clear Arac spirit with water. The resulting cloudy milky liquid was a potent drink. The thicker the cloudiness, the stronger the drink was. Billy noticed some people were only taking a small amount of the Arac before filling the glass up with water. Others were braver, or more reckless, depending on which viewpoint you adopted, and were drinking much stronger mixtures. Adam had moved onto the bed beside Mark and was demonstrating how to mix the two elements together. Billy watched as Mark took his first experimental sip of Arac and water. He pulled a face. The same face Billy had seen pulled by a hundred different volunteers. Arac and water was not to everyone's taste.

"You are supposed to drink it down in one."

Adam was explaining and he mixed himself a shot and demonstrated how the drink should be consumed. When he had got his voice back he waved the bottle in Billy's direction.

"You wanna try a shot?"

"Go on then".

Billy drained the last dregs of his scotch and then took the bottle from Adam. He poured a hefty measure into the glass.

"Easy tiger," Adam's voice had a warning tone in it.

Billy ignored the warning and added a mere splash of water, he knew what to expect. He had been introduced to Arac and water as a mixture by some 'old hands' on his last kibbutz; they favoured it as an alternative to breakfast. After a couple of large glasses the two friends had departed for a shift in the Refet, leaving Billy to crawl away and collapse into his bed and sleep it off. He had thereafter, acquired a taste for Arac and had built up a general tolerance for drinking it. This did not mean that he never got drunk on the stuff. He had suffered some of his worst set-backs as a result of overindulgence with Arac. Sitting here in this room he was not worried that he was going to make a fool of himself. He had seen enough first timers make fools of themselves trying to drink Arac down in one to know that those paying attention to him were just waiting to see whether he was about to choke or vomit. He raised the glass to his lips and caught a whiff of the strong aniseed smell of the spirit. He touched the glass to his lips and drank. He did not take the whole thing down in one, but drank it slowly as he would a glass of water, swallowing steadily. He actually enjoyed the taste of the stuff. He finished off the last drops and set the glass down smacking his lips. He looked around the room. Those who had been paying attention to the interplay that was going on between Adam and the new volunteer were all sitting wide-eyed, mouths open in silence. Adam was one of them, disbelief written across his face.

He quickly recovered his composure.

"Now if I didn't know better I would say you have done that before."

Billy shook his head. "Nope, first time", Billy lied.

"Well I take my hat off to you there man."

Adam raised his hand palm flat and the two high-fived each other. Billy shook his head to clear it one more time. That stuff was stronger than he remembered. He should really take it steady and get something to eat before long or he might lose his self-control and once his guard was down he might inadvertently blurt out something about his earlier visit and time as a volunteer.

The rest of the room, now the moment had passed uneventfully, returned to what they had been doing before and the volume of chatter in the room rose again. Billy took a moment to assess the visitors in his room. Mark was sat on one bed engaged in a deep and meaningful conversation with a guy whose head was shaved almost bald. He had the closest of crop cuts, a white vest top and white sweatpants shorts on. He looked like a real thug, but he seemed to be conversing in perfectly civil tones with Mark. There was a girl sitting beside him, saying little, but hanging on his every word. Billy watched her for any tell-tale signs that there was more than just mutual fascination between these two, but after a few moments he decided the body language between them made any assessment of a romantic relationship, impossible.

On the spare two beds there were groups of both girls and boys, all dressed in volunteer standard dress, the hybrid of kibbutz work clothes and their own t-shirts, shorts and vest tops. Limbs were suntanned and hair touched by the sun and little else in the way of haircare products, brushes or combs. Jewellery was minimal, the odd earring, nose stud, ear cuff or toe ring glinted in the light, along with an eclectic mix of ethnic bead and shell necklaces. By far the most common element was woven friendship bracelets that adorned both wrists and ankles in a variety of colours and weaving styles. All of those gathered in the room looked healthy and vitally alive, the product of the good diet and the long hours of work out in the orchards, fields and gardens.

Although they hadn't been given specifics in the kibbutz office in Tel Aviv, Billy knew that the kibbutzim up here in the north of the country largely favoured apple or grape production, although some of them did own or rent field systems in the lowlands of the Hula Valley, where they had crops growing or fishponds. Billy had heard about fish farming during his last visit and he wondered what it would be like to work in the fishponds. He had a mental image of a line of people sitting on foldout stools with fishing rods and a bucket at their feet, pulling out the fish one at a time. He would be in for a real shock, if he was rostered on to work in the Sde Avram fishponds. This speculation, about work assignments was definitely tomorrow's problem.

For now, Billy poured himself another Arac and water and turned to meet the latest crop of volunteers, who had arrived through the door. This happened to be three girls and they were all clutching cans of lager. Their hair was wet, either from a recent shower or from the swimming pool. All three were blonde and had blue eyes and Billy took in their general appearance and decided, before any of them had opened their mouths, that these three were Scandinavians. He was not sure if they were Swedes or Danes, but he was absolutely certain they hailed from one or other country. The three stood in the middle of the room, looking around for somewhere to sit down. Space was currently at a premium as most of the beds were occupied. Billy had stood up from his own bed to take the Arac challenge, so there was space beside him. He caught the attention of one of the girls and pointed to the open space. There was enough room there for at least two of the three to sit down comfortably, although all three would be a squeeze. Billy looked behind him and realised that he could sit on the windowsill. It would be precarious, but as long as he was careful he could probably pull it off.

The three came over and sat down on the bed. They introduced themselves as Annabelle, Connie and Kirsten. Billy was right, the three were from Sweden. They all shook hands, rather formally and Billy made sure that he introduced the three of them to Mark who was still deep in conversation with the two people sitting on his bed. They all waved madly at each other and then returned to their respective conversations. Billy looked around the room and saw that most people were engaged in conversations, either speaking or listening. Then it hit him. This demonstrated, essentially, the difference between life, here on the kibbutz in

Israel and his life in London. These people, sitting around in his room, showed so clearly, that there was a world of difference between the two. To have this many people in a single room, even in a public place, like a pub, would be impossible without some form of drama, conflict or animosity. That these people came from about a dozen different countries was also a marvel. Tribalism in the UK, rivalry between football team supporters, even in the same city, could quickly escalate into all-out war. If you took things on a national scale then there were often conflicts between the various countries that made up the United Kingdom. When things shifted to an International level then there were further rivalries and disagreements, often the product of ancient historical disputes.

Here in this room all these problems, seemed to evaporate into thin air. The fact that he and Adam had already developed a mutual respect, a Scotsman and an Englishman was further proof of the magic. Back home they would be at daggers drawn in minutes simply because of their respective birth places in relation to an imaginary line drawn on a map. Out here they could be best mates. The air in the room was blue with cigarette smoke. It seemed that almost everyone in the room was smoking and cigarettes were freely being passed around. Likewise the drinks were flowing and if a bottle was finished then it was quickly replaced by another full one. Billy cast his mind back to the recent incident at the party where there had been a colossal scene made over a single bottle of whisky. Half in disgust, half in despair, he shook his head at the memory. Yes, he decided to himself, this was why he preferred Israel over England.

He turned his attention to the three Swedish girls and began chatting with them. It had been increasingly difficult concealing his previous experience on kibbutz. Every new encounter had to be evaluated on merit. Is this something he might have heard about or read about before arriving in Israel or is this something unique that only an established volunteer could know about.

As the events of the first few days unfolded and Billy experienced the life on Sde Avram, there were certain things that were the same as before, but many that were different. It was his desire to comment on these similarities and differences that made life a real challenge for Billy. A clear example was when Billy stepped into the dining room that evening for supper. Although from the outside the room had appeared similar to the dining room on Tel Boker, inside and in use it was clearly set up differently. Both rooms were L shaped, on Tel Boker the smaller part of the L had been used as the serving area and seating had been laid out in the larger section.

On Sde Avram the serving area was laid out at the point where the two sections met and there were seating areas on either side. The seating in the smaller section was for the volunteers and in the larger section for the members and their families. This segregation was not something that Billy had seen before, but, of course, there was no way he could make comments about the arrangement. He merely collected a tray of food and then turned to the right and followed the other volunteers, whilst members and their families turned left. Even if there had been an informal separation between volunteers and members on Tel Boker, often caused by barriers of language there was no strict segregation and it was often the case that members and volunteers, who worked together would often dine together at breakfast or lunch and even occasionally in the evenings. This apparently wasn't the case on Sde Avram and the majority of volunteers, knowing no different merely accepted this.

The food was the usual kibbutz fare, but Billy felt that as a newcomer from the UK he should at least voice his concerns over the quality. He wasted no time in doing this by disappointedly spooning away at the thin gruel that they had been served at the evening meal. One of the Swedish girls was sitting across the table saw him.

"It's chicken soup," she said hoping to help.

Billy filled a spoon up and let the contents trickle slowly back into the bowl. Left on the spoon was a single green leaf of indeterminate origin.

"This looks like water that they might have once let a chicken swim in." Billy said to no one in particular.

"We call it 'Ghost-Chicken soup'," another wag added from further down the table.

"At least its hot," someone else added.

"Which is of course just what we need when the temperature is still above 25 at six-thirty in the evening."

This was from a person sitting down the table from Billy. He could not see the speaker as Mark was sitting between him and them. Billy pushed the soup bowl away untouched. He actually quite liked the taste of the soup, but he was playing the part of a new arrival, so he had to be suitably underwhelmed by the standard of the food. His ruse continued the next morning when he showed up for breakfast. Kirsten and Connie, two of the Swedish girls who, incidentally, occupied the room across the hallway from Mark and Billy, were both serving in the dining room, when the two friends arrived. Mark went straight for the fried eggs and bread. He was slightly hungover, so he needed the grease. Billy took slightly longer, enquiring at some length about all the various cheeses and yoghurts that were on offer in the dairy section. It all added to his little cover story, because as he finally made his selection and placed the small bowls on his tray, Connie leaned across the counter giving him a brief, unintentional flash of flesh down the front of her vest top.

"When I finish work would you like me to take you on a tour of the kibbutz?"

She flashed him a beaming smile.

"That would be kind of you. I think we have some kind of tour after breakfast, but it would be nice to get the volunteers view of things as well."

"I will pick you up about two thirty."

"I'll be ready and waiting."

Mark looked up as Billy sat down.

"What was all that about?"

"I was getting a guided tour of the buffet options, having them explained to me."

"Come on Billy," Mark said under his breath, so no one could overhear him.

"Stop playing the innocent newcomer".

"Oh and I forgot to mention, I was also sorting out a date for this afternoon."

"Lucky you." Mark tried not to sound envious.

"There is a method to my madness. A little vulnerability and they all rush to offer protection. You should try it."

"Right now the only thing vulnerable about me is my head. That Arac stuff, is bloody poison."

Mark had certainly indulged in a fair few glasses of the stuff after they had returned to the volunteer block from supper. Billy had carried him to bed around midnight, had to kick him out of his pit this morning and throw him in the shower in order to get him here for breakfast. They returned to their room after breakfast and watched while the majority of other volunteers struggled off to work in the various places around the kibbutz. They had no firm idea when they would be collected, so Mark took advantage of the free time and crawled back into his bed. Billy sat on his own bed and used the time to write letters.

At some point during the previous evening's festivities, Billy had taken a moment to think about Mike, his long-time friend. It had been Mike, who had inspired Billy to make his first trip to Israel. Mike and Yara had embarked on their trip, before Billy had left to return to the UK. The last that Billy had heard they were staying in Sydney. Since that card, there had been no communication between them, so he suddenly realised that Mike would be unaware that he was back in Israel. He had an address for Mike in Sydney, but given the transient nature of their travel, there was a strong chance that Mike and Yara would already have moved on. Billy knew there was one way he could get a message to Mike and that was to write to Mike's parents in the UK. They were more likely to have up to date contact information for Mike and Yara. He also knew, Mike called them at least once a month on the phone to let them know he was alright and Billy suspected, to ask them to wire him more money. Mike's parents were both successful professional people; they could afford it.

In the letter he informed them that he had returned to Israel and that he had decided to volunteer on a new kibbutz at the other end of the country. He hoped that they were both well and would pass on his new address to Mike the next time he made contact. It was a short letter, less than a page in length, but he folded the paper and placed it in one of the airmail envelopes he had brought with him. He knew that at some point he would be given a handful of aerogrammes, but these he wanted to keep for longer letters to friends like Mel. For now, he addressed the envelope and sealed it, placing it on the windowsill, where he would see it and remember to buy a stamp at the first opportunity.

He then pulled another sheet of paper from the pad and wrote his second letter. He took his time with this one, choosing simple words and writing in block letters rather than script. He was writing a letter to his old friend and former volunteer leader, Yossi. In this letter, he explained his reasons for returning to Israel, whilst justifying his choice not to return to Tel Boker. He was aware how his former friend might view this decision, particularly in the light of their final conversation, before Billy had left. He read the letter back at the end and then screwed the paper up in a ball, before launching it across the room. It was no good, any reasons he gave just sounded hollow.

He knew that however he dressed it up, Yossi would have trouble believing him, and would probably read more into the fact that Billy had chosen to write him a note, rather than meet him face to face. There was really only one solution, he would have to summon up the courage and go and face him. Although nothing had been mentioned during their brief introduction the previous afternoon, Billy knew that all volunteers earned holiday days for every completed month they worked and that in a few months he would have saved enough time off to take a trip south to the Negev, to visit his old stamping ground. In some way he was grateful that it would be a couple of months, because by then he would, hopefully, be established here on Sde Avram and therefore able to resist the temptation to return to Tel Boker. The only real motivation for returning there would be if Mike and Yara had returned from their world tour; Mike had always vowed that he could never return to live full time as a member, on the kibbutz. Ultimately, if they decided to return to live in Israel, then it would be in one of the big cities. However, time in the big wide world could mellow a person and Billy knew that Yara could be very persuasive. So, he knew it would be better for him and for all concerned, if he had settled, into life on Sde Avram, before he ventured back to Tel Boker.

Billy also knew that part of that settling in process would involve what type of job he was allocated. The previous evening, in an effort to maintain his cover story and therefore, just like any newcomer would, Billy had asked about the jobs that were available for volunteers. He sat and listened as the group had collectively explained the various jobs, along with the pitfalls and horror stories used to scare new arrivals. Billy had shown the good grace to be shocked and appalled as necessary. It seemed that along with the usual jobs offered to 'virgin' volunteers like the dining room duties or kitchen, there was a high demand for volunteers in the main agricultural area of the kibbutz, which focused on apple orchards. Sde Avram had large orchards lining the slopes around the kibbutz and this was the main heart of the agricultural side of the settlement. Alongside this, they also had a factory that specialised in making moulded plastic pieces. Billy had prior experience with plastics factories. Tel Boker had manufactured sheet plastic and he therefore knew what a hell on earth the factory could become with the heat from the machines needed to melt the plastics, particularly during the summer months. He knew that avoiding the factory was one important objective, but with the two main areas of volunteer employment being the orchards or the factory, there was a strong chance he would eventually end up in one or other. He quite liked the sound of the apple orchards, where they were still in the pre-harvest time and were thinning out the crop, to enhance and encourage a better harvest. Again one of the volunteers had been happy to provide an insight into this process.

He guessed that like most kibbutzim they would probably end up in either the dining room, the dishwasher or the kitchen. None of those would trouble Billy too much, in fact the lowest of those jobs, considered to be the dishwasher, was actually one of the places that Billy had enjoyed working on Tel Boker. So, if it came to it that this was to be his fate tomorrow, he would not whinge about it. He knew that getting his head down and putting in a few good shifts would also raise his stock with the work managers. In most cases having one less volunteer who did not have to be turfed out of bed in the mornings or sent home halfway through a shift because of a monster hangover, was a relief for them and your personal stock rose accordingly.

Also, when they were looking around among the volunteers for people to take prime jobs, those that required effort and commitment, having a reputation for being reliable made you a more obvious candidate. The other thing that Billy had come to realise was that there was a pecking order in volunteer jobs with some of the more responsible jobs, like dairy workers being able to command a higher wage, if they eventually left the kibbutz and sought work in one of the privately owned Moshav farms. He knew that there was a Refet or Dairy, on Sde Avram, as he had met one of the volunteers that worked there the previous evening. He also knew that getting placed in that kind of job from day one was almost impossible and that very few people achieved this. He didn't however rule out asking to be transferred to the Refet at some point in the future. It could be useful to be able to earn extra money if he did decide to move to a Moshav in the future.

They had been promised the guided tour by the work manager, but in the end it was Rachel who showed up to collect them. Orin, the aforementioned tour guide, was apparently engaged in resolving some issues between volunteers and their work supervisors. The details of the exact issues were sketchy and Rachel was clearly not in the loop when it came to the finer details. All that she knew was that she had been asked to deputise as tour guide and she was determined to give the two newcomers her undivided attention, from now until lunchtime. She was obviously a little flustered that this task had been thrust upon her at the last possible moment and had as a result, interrupted her own daily schedule, which as far as Billy could see consisted of a thorough inspection of the volunteer quarters, room by room.

This intelligence, gathered in the morning after breakfast, was then used later, at the lunchbreak, to call out the owners of the rooms that did not match her exacting standards of cleanliness. She delivered a stinging rebuke to both Billy and Mark when she entered their room to collect them. Since their room had been the venue for last night's impromptu gathering and had seen a non-stop parade of volunteers coming through the door from before suppertime until the early hours of the morning. The room looked as if someone had opened the door and hurled several trash bags of bottles, cans and cigarette stubs inside. Billy had already determined that a period of the afternoon would have to be set aside to tidy the place up. He would have started first thing, but he took pity on Mark who was suffering the after effects of his first night among volunteers, and after returning from breakfast had swallowed a handful of painkillers and taken himself back to bed with a cold cloth on his forehead.

It appeared that sickness or disability, even self-inflicted, was no excuse in Rachel's eyes and she took the two lads to task about the mess as soon as she came through the door. Billy promised that the room would be cleaned at the first opportunity. Thankfully Rachel left the matter there, although she took a moment to remind the two of them of the location of the

cleaning materials and as they were leaving the volunteer building she waved her arm in the direction of the two green plastic dumpsters that stood on the far side of the road.
"That's where you can dump all the empty bottles, cans and bin bags."
Billy nodded his head vehemently to show he had understood. Mark just let out a faint croak. To have moved his head in any violent manner at this point might have brought on a massive cranial haemorrhage, or at least that was what he was afraid of.

## Chapter Eleven

Outside the volunteer block Rachel went over to the driver's side of one of the small jeeps that the kibbutz owned.

"It's open."

She waved her hand in the direction of the passenger door. Billy pulled the handle and opened the door. He climbed in first and took the middle seat. Mark, if he was going to throw up, which was still a distinct possibility, would be better situated by the open window or with easy access to the door. The inside of the jeep was littered with the usual detritus that could be found in any kibbutz vehicle. There were bits of various farm machines, irrigation pipe fittings and naturally the ever present water cooler. There was a radio attached to the dashboard emitting a constant burble of chatter. Billy listened for a moment and picked up that this was the security channel and the chatter was the guards at the various checkpoints, in the vicinity, keeping up a running commentary on their observations of activity along the border. Billy tuned the voice out. It would blow his cover instantly if he reacted to one or other of the messages.

Instead he focused on what Rachel had to say as they began their tour of the kibbutz. It became clear almost immediately to Billy that Sde Avram was a completely different operation to Tel Boker. As they drove out from the volunteer quarters through the small wooded area and into the kibbutz proper, Billy saw straight away that this kibbutz was much bigger and from the look of things much better off financially than his former place of residence. They set off in a counter clockwise direction around the perimeter fence. Adjacent to the volunteer area was the large factory zone. Whereas Tel Boker had a small scale operation producing sheet plastics, Sde Avram had a much larger factory building where they manufactured finished plastic pieces used in medical systems like catheters and other intravenous equipment.

Rachel pulled the jeep to a stop in the car park and together the three of them entered the building. Inside it was a far cry from the biblical hell of the factory on Tel Boker where the heat inside the factory was often in the mid-forties. Here the whole place was a white walled and efficient air conditioned paradise. The machines were all spotless and the filtered air had the sweetness of a pine forest in spring. All the staff wore white overalls and the whole place was as sterile as the isolation ward in a major hospital. This need for sterile working conditions severely restricted the areas that could be shown to visitors, but Billy got the overall impression of a slickly run and rather profitable enterprise that didn't lack for investment. This was a huge departure from the rat infested hellhole on his old kibbutz.

On the same area of land and lying adjacent to the plastics factory was the 'jewel' in Sde Avram's crown. This was not quite how Billy saw the plain and rather non-descript concrete edifice that lay across the car park from the plastics factory. The 'jewel' was the description that Rachel employed as she swept them across the car park towards the entrance. As she was about to enter the building she paused and rather theatrically gathered the two lads together as if she was about to impart some earth-shattering secret.

"Of course the place is not at full production yet. This place will really start to fly in about a month or two when the main harvest starts. Then it becomes a thing of beauty."

She winked at them and then led them inside. Billy was intrigued and felt like holding his breath as they went inside. Like the other factory it was necessary to put on white coats and silly paper hats before pulling on some overshoes, but unlike the medical facility they were allowed full access to the factory floor. Once they had passed through the section that housed the offices, break room and changing facilities the three emerged into the cavernous, cathedral like space that formed the main part of the factory. It was completely deserted. All the machines and production lines stood silent. The sunlight beat down through the clear parts of the roof forming pools of intense white light and, Billy thought, probably searing heat at the hottest part of the day. Water could be heard dripping off in the distance from a tap that had not been turned off properly. A bird, disturbed by their presence, fluttered away into the higher part of the roof, looking for an alternative place to roost. It was caught briefly in one of the columns of light, its wings turning to flashing silver as they transitioned through the sunlight.

Rachel seemed disappointed that there was not more life or action in the place. She walked several paces into the open space and looked around to see if there were any members of staff, maybe hiding behind one of the conveyor systems. Unable to locate anyone she returned to where she had left Mark and Billy standing together.

"I guess you will have to take my word for it."

Rachel sounded a little sullen, as they disrobed and she led the two back out to the car park and they climbed back into the jeep.

Their next port of call was the opposite of the apple factory. The Refet, or Dairy was in full swing when the three showed up. Although the main job of the morning, the first milk was long over, you do not keep a herd of close to five hundred milking cows and have nothing to do. Hence the place was a hive of activity. The jeep narrowly missed a large tractor and trailer combination that was weaving in and out of the various cattle pens distributing food. Another tractor was moving bales of hay or straw from one barn to another. There were members of staff in their blue work clothes herding a bunch of cows from one of the holding pens back towards their main enclosure.

Billy was familiar with the workings of the Refet from his time on Tel Boker, but once again he had to play the wide-eyed newcomer and ask the dumb questions as they were taken on a guided tour of the place by one of the kibbutzniks.

At the end of the tour, as they were returning to the jeep, Mark asked about the chances of working in the Refet. Rachel, who had said from the outset that she had no influence over where the two eventually ended up working, said that she didn't think it would be possible to be assigned there as they were fully staffed but she added a hopeful note, that as was the case with all volunteer jobs, vacancies did arise as volunteers left the community and either returned home or continued on their travels to other destinations.

Adjacent to the site of the Refet were several low wooden structures. They didn't bother to drive the jeep there, the nearest of the buildings was close enough to walk to and close enough for Billy to catch a whiff of the tell-tale stench. One breath and his nostrils were assaulted by the unmistakeable odour of stale, sun-dried, chicken shit. The rank ammonia smell was enough to make the eyes water, even in the open air.

Billy was all to familiar with how much worse the stink would be inside the small enclosed sheds. He shuddered at the memory of the nights he had spent, in the company of other sleep deprived volunteers harvesting the young chickens and placing them in cages. Bending down almost to eye level to scoop up the birds by their legs before turning them upside down and carrying the whole squawking shitting mess to an open cage. Respite came only when a crate was full and the forklift removed it and replaced it instantly with a fresh empty cage, or the shed was finally cleared of the last chickens. The job had been a dirty, dusty, smelly, eye-watering experience. Billy shuddered again at the thought of having to endure the job again.

"You have worked the chicken sheds before?" Rachel had caught sight of Billy's involuntary reaction.

"What? No."

Billy realised his unconscious reflex had betrayed him. He thought quickly for a plausible excuse. Mark inadvertently helped him out.

"That smell is enough to make you lose your breakfast".

"I was just thinking the same thing. What is that awful smell, it's not the cows is it?" Billy watched Rachel's face carefully. She had looked suspicious for a moment, but the look vanished as Billy asked the question.

"These are the chicken sheds. They were emptied three nights ago so it will be a while before the next batch are ready. If you are lucky you might escape the dreaded 'chicken-picking'".

"Sounds like a gas," Mark said with absolutely no conviction in his voice.

"I think gas masks would be necessary," Billy retorted with a slightly ironic tone. As if to confirm his statement two volunteers emerged from one of the sheds pushing wheel barrows piled high with chicken shit. They were both wearing masks that covered both nose and mouth. The thin cotton masks, similar to those worn by health professionals, probably did nothing to cancel out the smell, but were more for protection from any airborne germs or dust caused by their labours. Billy studied the two from a distance, making a mental note to try and avoid sitting anywhere near them at lunchtime. Actual facial recognition would probably prove unnecessary as the pungent smell emanating from their clothing would give the game away from across the room, that and the fact that they would most likely be sat at a table on their own. Fortunately Rachel didn't feel the need to take them any closer to the chicken sheds themselves and the three beat a hasty retreat to the comparatively sweet smelling Refet, where they climbed back into the jeep and set off for their next destination.

Timed to almost perfection, the kibbutz shop had just opened its doors as the Jeep pulled to a stop in front of the main entrance. Amid the arriving tractors, jeeps and golf buggies, Billy and Mark climbed out. The shop building itself was like most things on Sde Avram, newer, shinier and considerably larger than its counterpart on Tel Boker. This one even had automatic sliding doors like a proper supermarket and a section by the side, where there was a line of shopping wagons, ready to be wheeled inside. The three waited their turn and then entered the building.

"I will have a word with Gilad, the shop manager and get your shop cards sorted out, you two go ahead and have a look around."

Rachel headed off in the direction of the till leaving the two friends standing at the entrance to the aisles. The first thing that struck Billy was the difference in size. If the shop on Tel Boker had been the size of a corner shop back home, Sde Avram's emporium was the size of a small supermarket. The breadth of stock and the available choices were light years away from what Billy was used to in a kibbutz store. The two set off up the first aisle of the shop glancing both left and right at the range of goods. The back wall was dominated by a line of chest and cupboard freezers. Tel Boker had offered a single chest freezer containing ice cream. Sde Avram had frozen meals, frozen vegetables, cold drinks, milk and dairy products and a huge section with ice cream and frozen cakes.

In the domestic products aisle there were a range of shampoos and shower gels. Some were marked with orange tickets others with green.

"I wonder what the difference is?" Billy asked no one in particular.

"The orange ticket items are free." A helpful soul explained as she reached past the pair and collected a bottle of shower gel from the shelf.

Billy picked up one of the orange ticket items from the same shelf and popped the lid, taking a sniff.

"Hey this doesn't smell too bad." He wafted the open bottle under Mark's nostrils.

He took one each of the shampoo and shower gel and then continued on. His eyes were now more focused on the orange ticket items, the free stuff. Billy was amazed at how much stuff there was available for free.

"You had to pay for most of this stuff on Tel Boker."

He confided quietly to Mark as they approached the checkout. Billy was in for one more surprise. There were two checkouts open and available to customers, but Billy and Mark joined the line for the one, where they could see Rachel waiting patiently at the far end. Next to her stood an elderly and distinguished gentleman with a balding head and a pair of horn-rimmed spectacles balanced on his shining forehead. He was dressed in the usual kibbutz blue but wore a thin knitted cardigan over his shirt to counter the air-conditioned coolness of the shop.

As Billy and Mark made it to the front of the queue he left Rachel's side and came over to the till handing the two pink shop cards to his assistant. She placed the cards in the reader on the till and turned to the items on the belt that the boys had just finished stacking there. When the assistant had rung up the items and bagged them she asked in heavily accented English, which cigarettes they wanted? Billy knew exactly which brand but under Rachel's watchful and suspicious gaze he made a big play of asking about the relative strength of the various brands, eventually settling for Time. The woman grabbed a handful of packets and dropped them in the bag before turning to Mark and asking the same question.

"Oh I don't smoke,"

Mark said raising his hands defensively. The shop assistant looked at Billy with a puzzled look on her face as if to say 'do you want to answer for him?'

"He'll have Time as well."

The assistant took another handful of cigarette packets and dropped them in the paper carrier, before handing the whole lot over to Billy. He picked it up carefully trying not to spill out the mountain of Time cigarette packets that were balanced precariously on the top of the bag. Mark had collected the two large bottles of coke they had purchased. Billy was counting the packets of cigarettes, while trying to arrange them in a fashion, so they would not spill out of the mouth of the paper bag. He counted fourteen packets of Time, seven each. That was three more each than they had been given on Tel Boker and it was hard for Billy to hide his astonishment. Some of his reaction must have been visible, because Rachel commented on it.

"I know, we give you more cigarettes and free stuff than most other kibbutzim, it's our worst kept secret. Try not to brag about it in Tel Aviv we don't want to be overrun with volunteers."

"I have no idea what is a good deal or not. I know most kibbutzim give free ciggies, they said as much to us back in London at the introduction meeting. But they certainly didn't mention all this other free stuff."

Billy waved his hand over the top of the bag. He turned to Mark who had bagged the large soda bottles in a carrier bag and was guzzling a cold tin of Cola.

"How much did this lot cost us?"

Mark shook his head, his mouth still full of cold Coke. Billy hoped his vagueness might help to cover up his astonishment. It seemed to work as Rachel once again let the matter drop. Billy mentally kicked himself. He was going to have to be more focused and less easily amazed if he was going to carry off this whole 'new to kibbutz' deception with any degree of success.

"So where to next?" Billy wanted to make sure the matter was dead and buried.

"Well over the road is the Members Club and over there is the Admin Offices."

There were two low slung modern looking buildings across an open plaza. The fourth side of the plaza was the glass wall on the backside of the dining room. Billy could see from this side that those large windows could be slid open allowing tables and chairs to be brought out and set up in the plaza if the kibbutz wanted to have an al-fresco dining event. The plaza was largely empty right now, but Billy could conjure up an image of the place filled with tables and peoples at one of the Jewish holiday festivals. He had witnessed the scene plenty of times on Tel Boker. There was a real feeling of togetherness at those festivals. The food was a level above the normal Friday night Shabbat meal as if everybody, the kitchen staff included had made an extra effort. Billy was not getting the same vibe from Sde Avram so he decided to test his theory.

"What's further up the hill beyond the Members club?"

"That's the area of the kibbutz where the members live".

"Do we get to see how the other half live?" Billy said with a wry smile on his face.

"Not today."

There was a finality in Rachel's statement that seemed more like 'Not ever', and maybe she realised sub-consciously what she had just said because she immediately qualified the statement.

"There isn't time today. It's lunchtime in a short while and I really wanted to show you the Orchards before we eat. There is a strong chance you will be joining the volunteers there tomorrow."

They drove out of the main gate and then circumnavigated the kibbutz until they were on the slopes below the kibbutz. Here there was row after row of apple trees. They seemed to extend almost as far as the eye could see in every direction. Even though it wasn't yet the harvest season the place was hive of activity with people zipping around in yellow cherry picker machines. These nimble machines consisted of a four wheeled drive system and an extendable arm with a basket at one end. The basket was big enough to hold a single person and they drove the machine from a control panel in the front of the basket where they had various knobs and levers to manoeuvre and extend the lift arm and move it around. They looked like fun things to drive and the more experienced operators were able to perform quite complex movements that looked almost balletic.

Up amongst the trees the workers were thinning out the trees giving space and light to the apples as they embarked on the final stage of their growth. The more mundane job and one that Billy feared newcomers would be tasked with, was to move along the rows and collect all the cuttings dropped from the trees. These were being piled up for later collection and then removal. They didn't stay long in the orchards, just enough time to get a flavour of what was occurring and soon they were entering back through the security gate. Rachel dropped them where the bus had deposited them the previous day.

Mark seemed enthusiastic about the new surroundings and talked non-stop about the place as they made the brief trip down to their room to drop off their purchases. Billy was quiet as he took in what he had seen of the place from the morning's tour. He had begun to form an opinion of Sde Avram and was now comparing it to Tel Boker. It appeared that Sde Avram was a reasonably wealthy kibbutz. They had some bright shiny factories and the facilities were all top notch. The volunteer accommodation was streets ahead of the shacks that they had lived in on Tel Boker. There the air-conditioning was an open window and the rooms were like ovens in the summer and freezers in the winter. Clearly the kibbutz here gave more to the volunteers in terms of free items from the shops. Shampoo and shower gel had to be purchased on Tel Boker, here you got it for free. Also a quick glance at the shop card showed that they paid more to the volunteers in a monthly allowance. It was not much more, Billy guessed there were probably rules governing the amount that could be paid, but it was still more.

All this left Billy with one nagging question. If Sde Avram did so much for the volunteers then what were they not giving them? Billy thought he had the answer and that was they gave nothing of themselves. On Tel Boker there had been plenty of involvement and interaction between the volunteers and the members. Volunteers were asked to visit members in their homes. He got the feeling that this might happen here too but it would be the exception rather than the norm. He knew he was building this hypothesis on scant data, so he would have to reserve judgement until he could accumulate more evidence.

"Earth to Billy," Mark's voice cut into his contemplation, "Are we going to have some lunch?"

"Yeah, sorry." Billy gathered himself and the two left the room and walked back in the direction of the dining room.

Billy continued his investigations over the next few days as he discovered more about life on Sde Avram. He knew that he couldn't ask direct questions or make direct comparisons, for obvious reasons, but he did manage to devise some questions that were sufficiently vague in detail that gleaned him the information he needed without giving the game away. In general conversation with the volunteers in the afternoons he managed to discover that there wasn't a single volunteer who had been invited to visit with a kibbutz member in their house, even among those who seemed to be close to the members they worked with during the day. He did consider testing his theory by trying to sit among the members in the dining room at one lunch sitting, but when it came to it, no one would come and sit with him and he was reluctant to draw attention and possible censure to himself by doing it on his own.

There were one or two other marked differences between life on Sde Avram and life as it had been on Tel Boker. The first was the way that the children were cared for. On Tel Boker all the children from the youngest right up to the oldest had lived in their parents houses. Some of the older children on Tel Boker had been allocated rooms which they either occupied in small groups or shared with another child of the same age.

On Sde Avram all the children lived in children's houses. They were released from these houses for a few hours in the afternoon and early evening to spend time with their parents, but afterwards returned and slept within the confines of the children's houses. There had been children's houses on Tel Boker, Mel had worked there. The major difference was that on Tel Boker they were more akin to the kindergartens and playgroups back home in the UK, where the children were merely supervised, while their parents were working and released to the same parents at the end of the working day.

But here they were returned to the houses at night. Billy had this confirmed by one of the female volunteers who worked with the children. She said that alongside her work during the day, where she was responsible for a group of toddlers, every few nights she had to spend the whole night watching over the children overnight. The job was an easy call, because they usually put the young children to bed around eight and then sat watching TV or chatting in the staff room until they went to bed. Of course with a house full of kids there were sometimes issues during the night when the children had to be cared for, but the majority of the time they went to bed and slept through until dawn. An overnight shift in the children's house automatically guaranteed you a free day the next day so it was a sought after job on the kibbutz.

Billy who had not had the benefit of a normal family life at home, his mother worked all hours of the day and night, could therefore sympathise with kids who only saw their parents for a brief period of time every day. The girl had, however, pointed out the added security that came from having all the children safe in one place if there were problems with incursions by terrorists from outside the kibbutz. If one group of adults were responsible for safeguarding the wellbeing of the children it left the other parents free to deal with any threats to security. Billy could see the sense with this on an active border like the one adjacent to Sde Avram.

Another direct difference on Sde Avram and again a direct consequence of the heightened need for security were the kibbutz guard dogs. These ferocious beasts were positioned at intervals along the perimeter fence. Each dog had its own shelter or kennel and then a running wire that stretched almost to the next kennel along the fence. Each dog could therefore patrol and defend the area between its kennel and the next. These dogs were kept almost on the edge of starvation to keep them alert and were trained to respond and attack anyone who came close to them who they didn't recognise. Volunteers were warned that these animals were not pets and to stay away from them. This message was largely accepted and understood although there were one or two volunteers who strayed to close and did get a nasty nip from the canine guards.

Billy was rapidly coming to the conclusion that volunteer life on Sde Avram would be a totally different experience to Tel Boker with less connection to the Israeli members and their children, the members of the IDF who were tasked with protecting the settlement and any other young Israelis who lived and worked inside the kibbutz. He got the feeling that the Members, as a group, felt their responsibilities to the volunteers started with giving them a pleasant and comfortable existence, and ended with a minimum of involvement on their part. Personally he felt that was a shame, but he knew that he would have to go with the flow, at least for the time being.

When Mark and Billy finally got to meet the volunteer work manager it was late afternoon on the second day of their stay. They had eaten lunch and then returned to their room until the first volunteers had returned from work and announced that they were all going to the swimming pool. Mark and Billy had grabbed towels, sun screen and joined the exodus in the direction of the pool. Again there was the unofficial segregation with members claiming sunbeds and tables on one side of the pool, while volunteers took up positions on the other. Although there was no hostility between the two groups there also seemed to be a distinct lack of involvement or even interest. This was quite amusing for Billy who merely sat and watched as the dramas around the pool unfolded. He had a critical eye for the details, gleaned from hours working as a life guard, so he was able to read the people and their actions.

He noticed that one particular group of kibbutz girls seemed interested in the volunteer lads but were restrained, probably by group pressure from talking to them. Instead they behaved in an aloof and uncaring manner, but all of their actions and words pointed to a high degree of interest. If one of them stood up and re-arranged her towel, it was done with much exaggerated movements of her body and a fair degree of noise, hoping, Billy felt, to attract maximum attention from the crowd of admirers on the other side of the water. It was pure comedy and Billy was enjoying it. It seemed silly and eventually it began to bore him, so he picked up his towel and headed back to the room for a rest. Mark appeared about an hour later slightly pink around the shoulders. He was just applying some after sun when Orin walked in unannounced. He hadn't even bothered to knock. He just opened the door and came in.

He was tall and very dark skinned, his hair cut razor short. A pair of aviator shades rested on top of his head. He had strong features and a large nose. His clothes were the usual mixture of kibbutz blue shorts and a checked short sleeved shirt. His feet were enclosed in a pair of sandals. He stood in the middle of the room and glanced briefly at the clipboard he was holding.

"Billy Randell?"

Billy raised his hand. It seemed the best thing to do under the circumstances.

"Dishwasher 7:00 am start."

"Mark Sampson."

"That's me." Mark said earning him a brief harsh scowl from Orin.

"Dining room 7:00 am start. Both of you try and be there on time I don't want to have to come and find you."

And with that he was gone. No explanation, no small talk and no chance to appeal their sentences. Orin was judge, jury and executioner all rolled into one.

"I guess he doesn't do small talk." Mark said wiping the excess after sun cream off his hands on his bed sheets.

"I think we are both lucky we weren't having a wee drinkie. That would have been an instant black mark against our name and a trip to the naughty step."

"Well I think I am going to try and find some ice right now and remedy that fact. You in?"

"Yeah I'm in."

Mark disappeared off and returned presently with some ice in a bowl. He did the honours and handed the scotch over to Billy who hadn't moved from his place on the bed. Mark slumped down on his own cot.

"So what is involved in this dining room job?"

"I can only tell you what was involved on Tel Boker. It might be different here."

"I'd be happy for any clues. I am not going to get them from our lord and master."

Billy started to fill Mark in on what his job tomorrow would entail. He was cut short by the arrival of some other volunteers returning from the pool.

Billy flicked the tee-towel off his shoulder and crumpled it into a ball aiming it at the linen basket that stood in the corner of the room. The towel performed a perfect arc and disappeared inside deep into the basket. Billy turned away performing his ritual NBA winning athlete celebratory dance in the space in the middle of the room. Mid dance he stopped and looked up. Abigail, one of the volunteers was leaning on the wall by the entrance to the dishwasher, her arms folded watching Billy closely. She had a vague expression of amusement on her face. She was smiling slightly. She had intruded on what was a private moment for Billy. She would refrain from comment for now but the potential for a little merciless teasing later on was there. Billy could not deny his actions.

"Rachel is looking for you and she seems really pissed off."

Billy tore off the plastic apron he was wearing and ditched it in the bin.

"Where is she?"

Billy asked as he pushed past heading in the direction of the dining room.

"When I saw her she was out the front puffing furiously on a ciggie."

"Thanks." Billy said, without turning his head.

"You're welcome." Abigail's tone was sugary sweet.

The dining room was almost completely deserted as Billy crossed the space weaving between the tables. The volunteers who worked on the dining room crew were long gone. There was probably only a skeleton crew left in the kitchen. Most people had either returned to their rooms for siesta or headed back to finish the last of their tasks before knocking off for the day. The place was winding down towards the afternoon rest period when everyone took a little time for themselves. Billy wracked his brain searching for reasons that Rachel would be pissed off at him. He was well into his third week on Sde Avram and as far as he was concerned everything was going well. In the first week there had been a couple of incidents, where he and Mark had been singled out for attention from Rachel over the state of their room. They weren't the only ones to be sure, but it seemed that their room had become a 'focal point' for volunteers wanting to pass an evening away enjoying a few drinks and smokes.

Rachel had continued her regime of morning inspections and although it wasn't necessary to have all the beds made, hospital corners and all, she didn't accept the detritus of the previous evening's debauchery, empty bottles, overfilled ashtrays and dirty drink stained floors to be present when she made her rounds. Billy, as he had done before on Tel Boker, always made a point of tidying his room and washing the floor when he returned from work in the afternoon, but he soon realised that in the scheme of things this was a waste of time as

Rachel would never make an appearance at that time of day and by the time she set foot in the corridor the next morning the place would be a shit tip again.

Billy had been faced with two alternatives. Either spend time cleaning up before he finally went to sleep or ensure that the party took place elsewhere. He favoured the second option and therefore had been instrumental in instigating the setting up of a party area outside the volunteer block. It had been easy enough to source some old sofas and armchairs from where they had been abandoned in one of the bomb shelters and transport these down to the volunteer area. With the creation of a fire pit and the construction of a small outside bar from discarded pallets the place was complete and it had been in non-stop use ever since.

While it had solved the problem of individuals being targeted for special mention at lunch over the state of their rooms it had moved the problem to a more collective responsibility although with such a large number of volunteers the impact of Racel's attention was distributed and therefore possible to ignore. Of course it was in their own interests to make sure the place did get a tidy up once in a while, but the urgency to do so, and personal responsibility was largely removed. One of the fastest ways to tidy the place had been suggested by one of the volunteers who worked in the Refet. After work, about once a week, he arrived outside the volunteer block with the yellow JCB tractor used in food preparation and as a general workhorse around the place. By setting the bucket at a certain angle it was possible to drag it across the open area of the party area, removing a thin layer of dirt and at the same time gathering all the cigarette dog-ends that had been scattered there along with any other rubbish. This gave the area a totally fresh and new look. The dirt they had scraped away could be collected in the JCB bucket and dumped elsewhere.

Billy had merely suggested the creation of the outdoor area and had taken no part in sourcing or creating any part of it. This meant that the part he had played in the project had remained unknown and others had taken the credit and ultimately the heat from Rachel for the idea. Billy was therefore at a total loss as to what he could have done, personally to invite Rachel's ire. He emerged into the afternoon heat and shielded his eyes against the sharp sunlight as he scanned the open ground between the dining room and the member's club. Sure enough Rachel was there sucking on a Noblesse and striding back and forth. Even from this distance it was easy to see, from her body language and facial expression that she was in a rage. Her halo of red hair seemed to crackle with some form of internal electrical energy as Billy slowly crossed the square. He had taken a moment to light a Time and blew out a cloud of smoke. Rachel looked up and caught sight of him. She made a beeline straight for him and Billy thought for a moment that she was about to physically assault him: she was pissed off and wasted no time in telling Billy exactly why.

"You lied to me, you lied to all of us."

Her words were spat out at him, the finger jabbed threateningly at the centre of his chest. Billy raised his hands. It was a reflex to defend his body. But the raised hands caused Rachel to pause. She stood her ground and her words were no less harsh.

"Why did you lie? What are you hiding from us?"

Billy having arrested the physical side of the assault now sought to calm the situation, which was beginning to attract attention from others who were within earshot.

"Rachel, I don't know what you are talking about?"

"You lied. When I asked you if you had been on a kibbutz before, you said no. You lied."

Billy dropped his hands to his side. She was right he had denied having previous volunteer experience when he was asked. He guessed he was going to have to confess now and try and explain his reasons. However it looked like it was not going to be that easy to get a word in as Rachel was in full flood.

"I thought I smelled a rat that first day when we went on the tour. One or two of the things I said you just accepted without question. That made me suspicious. The way you reacted in the chicken houses was another indicator. And then today I ask around and find out you have fixed the dishwasher three times already. You must know what you are doing."

"It's true I was a volunteer before on kibbutz Tel Boker in the south."

"I know, I found out today when I went to register you with the office in Tel Aviv. You wouldn't believe my surprise when I gave them your name and they said they already had a file on you."

"So you know the full story?"

"I want to hear it from you. In my experience the only reason for a volunteer to lie about a previous stay is if they have been expelled from their earlier kibbutz."

Rachel was still angry and she was waving her free hand around while dragging viciously on her newly lit cigarette.

"That is partially true." Billy said his voice low and containing a slight tone of regret.

"I knew it. They didn't have the details, the full file was not available. I don't know the full story. But it's enough for me. I can't let you stay, not if you have been expelled from another kibbutz."

"But I was reinstated there."

"You what?" It was Rachel's turn to look puzzled.

"Yes after a while away from the kibbutz I was asked to return."

"Why?"

"Because my expulsion was unjustified. I stayed for several more months and if you want to come with me back to the room while I pack my stuff I will show the letter of reference I was given by the Volunteer leader the day I left Tel Boker."

Rachel was now struggling to retain a degree of her dignity.

"I will need to see that letter," she said rather stuffily.

"By all means. Now?"

Rachel cast her eyes around the open space. A few interested persons were still observing the heated exchange from a distance. She made a snap decision.

"Now would be just fine."

She led the way, heading for the volunteer buildings.

"I have copies in both English and Hebrew," Billy added hoping he was being helpful.

Rachel didn't even turn around to acknowledge him, she ploughed on and the only indication Billy got that she had heard him was a brief wave of her hand over her head. This time she didn't wait the customary few minutes, but stormed into the building and up the stairs. She stood back while Billy entered the room and went to his locker. He pulled out the folder containing all his papers and handed over the letter from Yossi, his former volunteer leader.

Rachel took the paper and unfolded it as she walked over to the window. She used the additional light streaming in from outside to read the text printed on the page. As Billy watched her facial expression changed. She started with a fierce look of anger which slowly morphed into a look of approval before ending as one of admiration as she read the concluding statement. Billy couldn't remember the exact text of the letter, but knew that the final paragraph really sang his praises to the heights. Rachel looked up and saw Billy was watching her. Her face dissolved into a look of neutrality.

She indicated the letter with her free hand.

"Nice letter, I will have to verify its authenticity."

"Ring the kibbutz and ask to speak to Yossi, I am sure he will back me up."

"You are sure he will not mind that you didn't choose to return to Tel Boker?"

"You can tell him hello from me and that I will be back for a visit really soon."
Billy hadn't considered that fact when he had blithely suggested Rachel make the call. He wasn't sure how Yossi or any of the others on Tel Boker would react to news that he had settled on another kibbutz. The subject had never come up during any of their long conversations. He guessed that all concerned assumed that a return to Israel would mean a return to Tel Boker. He would have to ring Yossi separately and explain his reasons for choosing a fresh start. Rachel, as if she was able to read his mind now asked that very question.

"Why did you do it Billy? Why did you choose to make a fresh start?"
Billy slumped down on his bed and now he pulled his pack of Time from his pocket, shook one out and lit it. He puffed on it for a few moments, taking long drags, inhaling, holding it before exhaling. He was trying to arrange his thoughts into some cognisant order. He wanted his reasons to make sense to him before he shared them with anyone else. Rachel remained standing, but leaned back propping herself on the windowsill. She too lit another Noblesse while she waited for Billy's explanation. Billy took his time while he considered his answer. There was an immediate response that sprung to mind about giving Mark and himself a level playing field. His main fear had been announcing the fact that he was an 'old-hand' might have resulted in different treatment and he had wanted them to experience the same treatment whether it be from the volunteers or from the kibbutz members. But for Billy there had been something more.

A deeper sense that what had happened on Tel Boker should remain there and all the experiences he had endured in Eilat, should also not be brought into the equation. That this particular episode in his life had ended so well was probably more through luck than anything else. Being in the right place at the right time, and all that had come to pass because of that. It could all have ended so differently as it had for countless other volunteers, both before him and probably would for others in the future. They might not be so lucky. He started to try and explain these ideas to Rachel who, to give her credit, remained silent while he rambled on.

"And I thought it might have been because you wanted to give Mark a fair start to the kibbutz experience."
She leaned over and stubbed her cigarette out in the ashtray.
"Mark did play a part in my decision yes."
"Did I hear my name mentioned?" Mark pushed open the door and walked in. He was clad only in a towel wrapped around his waist and his hair was still wet from the shower. He was carrying his green toilet bag under his arm. He stopped as he saw who was with Billy.
"Oh hello Rachel. To what do we owe this honour?"
"It's OK I was just leaving."
She handed the letter back to Billy.
"I will ring and speak to Yossi soon. For now this remains between the two of us."
She left the room and pulled the door to behind her.
"What was all that about?" Mark sat down on his bed.
"My dirty secret is out."
"Which dirty secret is that?"
"That I was a volunteer before on another kibbutz."
"Oh that secret. Is that a problem?"
"Not now that Rachel has seen my reference from Tel Boker. But it got a little bit heated earlier."
"So now it's out in the open are you going to make it public knowledge?"
"Who me? No. I am going to keep it to myself as long as possible. I hope Rachel will do the same as well."
"Only time will tell mate, only time will tell."

Rachel did keep her word and kept the details to herself. She obviously did make the phone call as she sidled up to Billy a few days later and pulled him aside.

"Yossi says hello and asked me to tell you that Mike and Yara will be back in a few weeks."

Billy had been sceptical about Rachel actually calling the kibbutz but this additional piece of information meant she had actually gone ahead and placed the call. There was no other possible way she could know the details of Billy's best friend and his Israeli girlfriend. That the two would be returning to the kibbutz, so soon, came as a bit of surprise to Billy. He felt certain they would not have returned there, not yet at least. It did mean he would have to call Yossi himself in the next week or so and face the music. Then it would be a matter of arranging to take a few days off to travel south to Tel Boker to see his old friends.

## Chapter Twelve

"Instant Sobriety."
This was how Billy described the effect later, when he was asked for his reaction. It was if all the alcohol flowing through his veins had disappeared in an instant. And what was it that had this profound and miraculous effect on him? Billy was together with a large group of the volunteers. It was late in the evening and the party was in full swing. The music was turned up to eleven or so it seemed and the fire pit was ablaze. The bar, on its precarious construction of several pallets was doing a roaring trade, although the two volunteers who had been manning it earlier in the evening, had gone AWOL and were now among the revellers. The bar had reverted to self-service, so a steady stream of bodies were flowing past the large plastic buckets that contained tonight's 'cocktails', refilling their glasses and beakers, themselves.

On the hard packed mud, in the area in front of the bar, two dozen or so were engaged in a loose-limbed dance, their feet slapping the dirt in time to the beat. In the dark around the periphery of the party site, couples were engaged in various acts of intimacy. Closer in, within the ring of fire light, couples were being less flagrant. Passionate kisses and intimate caresses were being exchanged, but nothing blatant was taking place. Billy had been sitting on one of the sofas with his latest girlfriend, a cute blonde Dane called Anne-Mette, on his lap. She had just stood up and was moving through the tight packed dancers, en-route to the bar. She was carrying both their plastic beakers and was in search of more refreshments. Billy watched her cute butt, in her tight denim shorts as it wiggled through the crowd. Suddenly, it was if she and all the other dancers surrounding her leapt a foot in the air in unison. Billy felt as if the ground leapt under his feet and instantaneously a pressure wave pushed him firmly back in his seat. A nanosecond later the flat boom of an explosion reached their ears. As Billy watched the scene in slow motion, he saw confusion replaced on faces with abject fear as realisation dawned on the assembled group. A second explosion a moment later caused many of the group to fall flat on the ground. People were shouting, some were crying, others screaming, one or two were laughing hysterically. An experienced head among the group started yelling for people to head for the nearby bomb shelter.

Unlike the bomb shelters on Tel Boker, which were used for other purposes, the ones here on Sde Avram were used as intended. Although attacks on the kibbutz were sporadic. Occasionally someone on the other side of the border took it upon themselves to point a missile or two at the settlements to the south, so the shelters were by far the safest place, to be in the event of any prolonged attack. Some of the volunteers began to run for the adjacent shelter, whilst others remained rooted to the spot. Billy stood up and moved to where Anne Mette was stood. The two empty cups still in her hands. Billy took hold of her wrist and led her in the direction of the shelter. She didn't resist him and followed meekly in his wake.

Billy noticed two brave volunteers were manhandling one of the punch buckets off the table and were beginning to carry it in the direction of the shelter. There they could be safe and still carry on with the party. They were struggling to get the heavy bucket and its liquid contents to the bunker as quickly as possible and with a minimum of spillage. He secretly tipped his hat to those two for their forethought. Billy had his own Arac and water in a bottle and he had remained calm enough to pick this up from beside the armchair before he made his move. The shelter doors had been thrown wide open, so people were beginning to descend the narrow staircase that led down into the bowels of the earth. The entrance was crowded and there was a bit of pushing going on as people were in a hurry to get to safety. Billy stood a little to one side. He had a sense that the attack was over. Together, he and Anne Mette waited to take their turn to descend as they were not risking breaking limbs by being shoved down the concrete steps.

Two IDF command cars arrived. The soldiers dismounted and headed to the perimeter fence. It was clear from the rising column of smoke that the two projectiles had landed outside the fence on the wooded slopes below. On the outer side of the coiled razor wire fence there was a large field, which in turn gave way to light scrub and then pine forests. Below the fence, where the field slope flattened out, the orchards started. These formed a ring around the settlement heading away from the border area and back around the southern side of the kibbutz. The soldiers were there to confirm the nature of the strikes and moments later, they were all deafened as the IDF response team swung into action. Two attack choppers swooped low over their heads, heading in the approximate direction of the source of the two rockets. Billy doubted they would meet with any success. It was highly unlikely that the rocketeers had stuck around after the missiles had landed. Even from some distance away, it would have been obvious that they had fallen short, missing their target. If Billy had been in their position, he would have made a run for cover as soon as he had fired, knowing that the swift, devastating and deadly IDF response was imminent. Only stupid, soon dead terrorists, would have stood at the launch site yelling Allah Akbar, waving PLO or Hezbollah flags. That, would have been somewhat ironically, suicidal. No, the most likely scenario would be that the perpetrators would have already blended back in among the local population.

On this side of the battlefield, they faced a more immediate problem. Billy could hear the tell-tale roar and crackle of a growing conflagration. The missiles had missed their intended target by about one hundred meters, landing in the forest below the kibbutz perimeter fence. Amongst the pine trees, the bed of needles and undergrowth, was as dry as dust and had burst into flames. Any resulting bushfire would spread down the slope, given the prevailing winds and threaten the apple orchards. A fire in those orchards would have a devastating long term effect on Sde Avram's economy. The kibbutz executed its contingency plans and it was only a matter of minutes, before an army truck pulled up on the road past the volunteer blocks. By now, the sleeping volunteers or those engaged in closed doors activities, were hurriedly dressing and emerged into the confusion, looking for answers.

Through the midst of the confusion came the distinctive shape of Orin the volunteer work manager. He stopped amid the melee of bodies and yelled at the top of his voice.

"I am looking for volunteers?"

"Well you've come to the right place," one wag called out from the darkness.

Orin ignored the smart remark and repeated his call.

"I need volunteers to come with me into the forest to fight the fire?"

After this clarification of his needs came a fresh wave of shouts. These ranged from the moderate 'You've got to be joking', to the more explicit, 'No fucking way!'

"Anyone helping out now will have the day off tomorrow."

Orin offered trying to sweeten the deal. This did have the effect of at least turning a couple of heads. Billy was already heading toward the volunteer leader even before he had offered the sweetener. The double missile strike had really sobered him up, so he was able to rationalise the situation. The fire would offer a clear beacon to any would-be terrorists waiting on the other side of the border and a second chance to wreak carnage among the kibbutz population engaged in fire-fighting. Billy doubted that any further attacks would be likely. The two circling attack helicopters would ensure their safety. He felt certain that as well as the two choppers every eye along the border for a few miles in each direction would be trained to the north and anything suspicious would call down a rain of fire. This didn't prevent one last wisecrack from out of the darkness.

"If you are looking for volunteers, most of them are in the shelter."

With the arrival of the Israeli troops first and now the volunteer leader, the frantic flow towards the bomb shelter had slowed. The fact that no further missiles had been fired at them may also have played a part. Billy went up to Orin.

"I'm in." He said.
Orin smiled.
"Go get in the truck."

He waved his hand in the general direction of the road. Billy was not the first at the truck. Some lads and a couple of girls, who were closer held that honour. In the end they were about twenty in number, who were driven off towards the scene of the fire. There was an air of silent anticipation in the back of the truck. No one knew exactly what they were heading towards. Obviously the same fears had all crossed their minds. Even in the half-light, cast every time they passed one of the street lamps on the perimeter road, Billy could see fear written clearly on the other faces around him. Orin was engaged in a radio conversation. Billy listened in, while trying not to make it too obvious, that he understood what was being said. The voice on the other end of the radio said there was a large area that was ablaze, though for the moment the fire was mostly limited to the undergrowth and had not managed to spread to the orchard trees. The Fire Marshall, who was coordinating the response, was confident that they could control the blaze, which cheered Billy up no end.

They arrived in the vicinity of the fire and jumped down from the truck. They were handed a smoke mask and a beater and then sent to join the line. The beater was like a yard broom, but instead of a brush at the head there was a large flappy piece of rubber. This was used to beat out the flames. Once the line was formed up, they began to work their way forward, beating out the fire to left and right. Billy watched one of the kibbutzniks off to his right, to check that he was using the most effective method and found that it seemed to be instinctive.

It was hot work, as the extinguished brush behind them was still giving off heat and Billy found that in a matter of moments he was sweating profusely, the droplets running over his forehead and stinging his eyes. He brought a wrist up to his face and saw his arms were black with soot, almost as far as his elbows. He knew that he would smear black dust on his face, but he did so anyway. The time for worrying about his appearance was long gone. It took them the best part of two hours to fully extinguish the brush fire. Their primary objective to keep the fire under control and away from the orchards was fulfilled and the Members among the fire crew, were effusive in their praise for the volunteers who had come to help. As a reward, instead of being returned directly to the volunteer blocks, the truck made a detour via the dining room, where the staff had prepared a feast of fried eggs and chips. These were served up and for once both members and volunteers all sat down at the same tables. One of the members even raided the fridges and returned with several crates of beer, which were offered around to members and volunteers, alike and toasts were drunk to each-other's health. Tonight, at least they were all equal.

Later as Billy stood in the shower and let the water cascade down and wash the soot in a swirl of dark water away down the drain, he wondered if this sense of camaraderie would last. For that brief moment, it had felt like the old days on Tel Boker, where they were all working together for a common purpose. He supposed that only time would tell. It was close to three in the morning, when he eventually slid into bed. Anne Mette raised her head off the pillow, opened one bleary eye to see who was joining her, but when she saw it was Billy, she just turned over, thrust an arm across his chest and was back asleep in moments. Billy lay in the dark puffing on a cigarette reflecting on the last few hours. Inevitably, with these comparisons, his thoughts turned to Tel Boker and his impending trip south. Anne Mette had said she would like to accompany him on the trip. Mark had seemed strangely reluctant to take the time off for the trip. His argument was that if he was taking time off, he would rather use it for proper sightseeing, a trip to Jerusalem or the like, rather than just going to another kibbutz. Billy could see his point, so had not pressured him further. Right now it looked like it would just be the two of them, who would be making the trip, if Anne Mette could get the time off from her job in the kitchen.

When Billy awoke later, she had already left and he looked across to see that Mark's bed was also empty. He focused on his Timex to see it was close to eight and he panicked and leapt out of bed, looking around for his clothes. The faint smell of soot that emanated from the pile of clothes at the foot of his bed, reminded him that he was excused work today. He collapsed back onto the pillow with relief. He could get dressed in a relaxed fashion, before taking a leisurely stroll up to the dining room for some breakfast. The whole dining room was alive with chatter about the events of the previous evening.

Whilst queuing, Billy eavesdropped on what the members were saying about the attack, as he pretended to study the available tray of fried eggs and assorted salads. It seemed that everyone had a different theory or explanation for the source of the missiles and ultimately the suspected targets. Everyone had an opinion, because they all had been affected, even the heaviest sleepers. The kibbutz authorities and the army had seen to that. By the main entrance to the dining room, where diners collected their trays, a couple of tables had been set up. On these tables lay the twisted and mangled remains of the two projectiles that had been launched at Sde Avram. Billy was shocked at how small and slender the two actually looked even in their partially destroyed condition, given the noise of their impact and the devastation they had caused.

At the volunteer tables, the predominant subject was safety, with questions being asked by all and sundry, over the frequency of these missile strikes and whether the attack last night was an isolated incident or the precursor of an escalation in cross border incidents. One or two of the longer serving volunteers, tried to calm everyone's fears by stating that this was the first attack of its kind in many months and was unlikely to lead to anymore incidents. Others who had done their research, were able to point to times in the past, when these attacks had been more frequent and settlements in the area, had also suffered from cross border incursions by armed fighters. They were quick to mention, that all of these attacks, had been neutralised by the Israeli armed forces or armed settlers; there had been no casualties on the Israeli side. Billy knew this to be untrue, as not half a mile from the gates of the kibbutz, lay a memorial to one of the local school buses that was ambushed and the occupants assassinated by terrorists. The loss of a whole school year's worth of children, had hit the local communities hard as all of the settlements had suffered losses. Billy, however maintained his silence and carried on eating his breakfast.

The only real impact of the attack for the volunteers, was the decision that the outdoor parties must come to an end. With hindsight, it was felt that the light from the bonfire was the target that the terrorists had been aiming at. The fact that both missiles had fallen short of their target was more to do with poor or hurried aiming by the rocketeers, rather than any failure of the weapons themselves. A blanket ban was therefore imposed on outdoor fires. Without the fires as a focal point and the return of a chill to the evening air, the parties moved back inside the volunteer blocks. However, in a slight relaxation of the strict segregation, between members and volunteers, it was also proposed that a Friday night party would be allowed to take place for all of the younger population in the main bomb shelter, under the dining room. This was to be a disco with music and some soft drinks provided by the kibbutz itself. Billy asked if harder liquor would be allowed and was told that anyone wishing to provide their own drinks would be allowed to do so, but that public drunkenness would be frowned upon. The disco ran from nine in the evening until one in the morning, at which point the party usually shifted to the volunteer quarters where the diehards could continue until dawn, as long as they did so inside the volunteer block.

Also, now, the occasional autumn rainy weather, along with a growing chill in the air, even in the early evenings, made outside parties a thing of the past. As Billy had spent his last stay in the desert at Tel Boker was not used to this. Even on Tel Boker it could become cold at night, but here on Sde Avram he could sense that the winter would not be the mixed bag of weather that it was further south, it was going to get cold and stay cold for several months.

The oncoming winter cold and the threat of further attacks had dampened Billy's spirits, so it was with some relief that a few days after the attack, he boarded the morning bus together with Anne Mette and they headed off towards Safed. They had been able to wangle a whole week of leave by both putting in extra shifts at their respective jobs. It had meant that they had seen very little of each other for the past week, passing occasionally in the dining room or the corridors of the volunteer block. Now they both settled down on a double seat and got comfortable for the day long trip south. It was Anne Mette's first trip on public transport. She had been part of a large group that arrived at Ben Gurion and were met by a minibus and driven straight to Sde Avram. Since her arrival she had participated in several volunteer trips, but again these had been on kibbutz supplied transport. She was clearly excited by the prospect of a new experience. This, for her, was the beginning of her 'real travelling' experience. Privately, Billy had been forced to admit to Anne Mette that he had a connection to another kibbutz, although he had been rather vague on the details and she hadn't really pressed him. She was just happy to be included in his plans. His revelations didn't end there. As they left the kibbutz gates behind them Billy turned to her.

"Honey I have something important to tell you."

Anne Mette looked out and up at him from under her blonde curls. There was a look of confusion and even a little fear in her eyes. Billy smiled trying to reassure her.

"It's okay. I am not about to dump your ass."

She processed his declaration, but found she could not accurately translate Billy's words. Her face lost none of its emotion. Billy realised what had happened and moved to correct himself.

"It's ok, I am not breaking up with you."

This helpful translation at least brought a smile to her lips, but there was still a trace of fear in her eyes.

"I want to tell you a secret and I need you to promise me that you will keep it to yourself. Will you promise?"

Anne Mette nodded slowly, the apprehension was still visible in her eyes.

"I can speak Hebrew, fluently."

Apprehension was instantly replaced by confusion and then relief. Whatever had been the source of Anne Mette's deepest fear, it had clearly not been realised, so she was relieved, but also a little confused by Billy's declaration. Billy's explanation of how the whole thing had started out as a silly game, but as time had gone by, it had become more and more difficult to confess to his hidden ability, didn't really explain the deception, but Anne Mette was prepared to skip over this, so she smiled sweetly and asked him to say something in Hebrew. Billy opted for the old favourite of saying "I love you." It sounded, so much more romantic in Hebrew. Anne Mette asked him what he had said. When he translated it first into English and then as an after-thought into Danish, she leaned across the space between them and placed a slow lingering kiss on his lips.

"I should say that more often." Billy said when their lips parted.

"You looked so worried for a moment there. What did you think I was going to say?"

"I don't know. Maybe you were going to confess to having a girlfriend on your old kibbutz or some unfinished business down there."

Billy shook his head in denial. There was nothing like that waiting for him down there, although he had heard that Daphna, a married member with whom he had a brief affair, was now divorced from her husband, he didn't think there was anything left between them.

"It's okay, just so you know. I would be happy to share you with another woman. I never before have a triangle."

It was now Billy's turn to look shocked. His mouth dropped open and his chin hit his chest. When he eventually recovered the power of speech he looked over at the elven features of the woman sitting beside him, her blue eyes shining brightly and the two dimples on her cheeks when she smiled. She looked the picture of innocence personified. But clearly under that innocent exterior lurked a much darker and depraved creature.

"Let me make no mistake here, this triangle you mentioned."

"Yes, you, me and your other girlfriend. It has to be two women, not two men, I am not interested in other men. So you and me and another woman."

She held up her hands and made the triangle shape with her fingers and thumbs, just in case there was any misunderstanding on Billy's part.

"Unfortunately there is no other woman waiting on Tel Boker. Just so you know."

Anne Mette shrugged her shoulders accepting Billy's assertion.

"Okay, so we wait until we come back to Sde Avram. Is there any other volunteer girl you are interested in?"

This was definitely a leading question and one Billy didn't really want to answer, truthfully or otherwise. It could lead to a whole load of trouble. So he decided to fluff the answer and was suitably non-committal. He shrugged his shoulders after a moment's thought.

"No one I can think of, off the top of my head."

The answer seemed to both please and annoy Anne Mette.

"So, maybe I have to choose, someone for us." She said with a degree of finality.

Billy decided it was probably better to change the subject, totally.

Among the possessions he had brought with him from England was a small photo album. Until today, it had remained firmly buried in the bottom of his bag, hidden from casual inspection, under the cardboard bottom. As they now settled into their journey, putting the gates and the people of Sde Avram, behind them, Billy fished the book out from his daypack. Billy had made a comprehensive job of documenting his first trip to Israel. He had bought a new camera for just that purpose and had the films developed regularly through the shop on Tel Boker. He had the usual panoramic views taken around the kibbutz, plenty of photos of personalities, some of whom Billy could remember, others whose names eluded him. Most of the volunteer photos were taken in party settings with people glassy eyed, clutching drinks, cigarettes and smiling manically at the camera, or caught in overdone embraces with other fellow volunteers of both the same and the opposite sex. There were sets of photographs taken on volunteer trips to key places in the south of the country. These were of particular interest to Anne Mette, who had been on two one day trips since her arrival but given the location of Sde Avram these had both been to places in the north of Israel. To therefore gain an insight into places at the other end of the country was of great interest to her. She knew that soon after their return, the volunteers from Sde Avram would set off on their three day trip and the destination of Jerusalem, Masada and the Dead Sea, was one of the worst kept secrets on the kibbutz. Billy's photos though were of other places, more off the beaten track than the usual tourist destinations. He had filled about half the album with his own photos. The rest he had cobbled together from copies of photos taken by friends. This was because he had sold his camera to avoid it being stolen and only replaced it with a new one towards the end of his stay in Israel. The purchase, made possible with the money he got paid as an extra on the film set, had allowed him to document some of the filming, which brought endless questions from Anne Mette, who wanted to know the full story.

Billy was forced to tell her all about his life in Eilat and the alternative lifestyle being lived there and other cities around the country, by expelled volunteers. She was fascinated, and wanted to know all about Billy's adventures there and wanted to hear all the stories about life on the Wall and the hand to mouth existence of the people that lived that way. She shuddered theatrically at some of the worst stories and laughed along with Billy at some of the more outrageously funny stories. By the time Billy had finished the bus had taken them to Safed and then after a short delay on to Tel Aviv. They were just arriving in the Central Bus Station as they closed the album for the last time. Billy stuck the book back in his pack and closed the clasp. When it was his turn he stood up and stepped back to allow Anne Mette to disembark first. He leaned over her shoulder as they walked down the aisle of the bus.

"When we get off stay close to me. It will be complete chaos outside and we do not want to get separated."

Anne Mette took suitable precautions and clung tight to Billy's arm as they made their way through the crowds to the ticket office. Billy advanced to the ticket window and purchased two tickets to Tel Boker. The bus was leaving in an hour, so he suggested they go over the road and grab something to eat from one of the fast food stands. Anne Mette was a complete virgin when it came to Israeli street food, so Billy took some time explaining what all the various dishes were and what they contained. Anne Mette quite like the sound of a falafel, so Billy picked the vendor that in his limited experience, served not only the best, but was also the best value. Money was not as tight for Billy as it had been last time around, but he didn't see any point in wasting it. The stall holder was doing a roaring trade amongst the soldiers who were transiting through the bus station. This was another good sign that the place was worth frequenting. Billy joined the back of the line and waited patiently to be served. When he made it to the front of the queue the man stood ready to serve him. He looked Billy up and down and saw before him a volunteer. He spoke to Billy in English whilst at the same time he swapped the piece of pita bread he had been holding in his hand for one that was considerably smaller. Billy fixed the guy with a steely gaze before asking in fluent Hebrew.

"What was wrong with the other piece of bread?"

The server's eyes bulged open with surprise and he hastily reversed his choice of pita bread before giving Billy a wan smile of apology. Billy had been counting the number of falafel balls that they were placing in the bread and he noticed that the server went some way to apologising by cramming an extra two into the bread. Billy acknowledged the tacit apology with a warm smile. He accepted the finished sandwich and handed it over to Anne Mette pointing her toward the counter where the dishes of salad were set out. He turned back and collected the second falafel before handing over a bank note and collecting his change. He went to the salad bar and began to fill his pita with salad. He checked the mirror in front of him and noticed all the staff were involved with either frying or serving other customers. He took a moment and hoovered the first load of salad off the top of his falafel and began to chew steadily, whilst he dipped into the bowls and refilled his sandwich a second time. Anne Mette caught sight of what he was doing and copied his actions, before reaching for the spoon and refilling her falafel. She looked at Billy as he lifted the sandwich to her mouth the second time. Billy saw the look in her eye and he shook his head once. She gave him a puzzled look and then followed him as he led the way outside.

"You wouldn't have got away with it a second time. You were being watched. There would have been a nasty scene, trust me I know the guys in there".

Anne Mette nodded her head, her mouth was still full of salad. When she had finished and was able to speak she turned to Billy.

"What did you say to that guy? I guess it was Hebrew?"

"Yeah, he switched bread on me. Gave me a smaller bit. I guess he thought we were tourists and he could get away with it."

"So what did you say? It sounded harsh, like you were swearing at him?"

Billy barked a laugh.

"No, I guess some of it does sound a lot like swearing. It's the guttural, back of the throat stuff that sounds like you are about to cough your lungs up. All I said to him and in a rather polite way, I might add, was what was wrong with the other piece of bread. Mind you, he did give us an extra falafel ball or two by way of an apology."

Anne Mette looked back at the stall and said in a rather loud voice.

"Thank you Mr Falafel man."

She waved her hand, still clutching the last of her falafel. If anyone in the store even noticed her actions, nobody responded by waving back. This didn't seem to bother Anne Mette who just shrugged her shoulders and carried on following Billy.

They wandered through the dense crowds while they munched on their meals. Anne Mette was wide eyed at the sights, sounds and smells of the place. Everywhere you looked there were soldiers in various configurations of uniforms, predominantly the olive green of the Army, but there were also people in Airforce and even a few in Navy uniforms. Amongst the army green it was possible to make out new recruits with shiny boots and neat uniforms as well as those who were older and probably either going to or coming from their time in the reserves. Their uniforms were a little more scruffy and ill-fitting, missing buttons or with vests or t-shirt sleeves visible, their boots where they were wearing them, a little more scuffed and unpolished. Berets of various colours were folded and stuck through epaulettes, the shoulder flashes indicating which units the troops belonged to. Everyone almost without exception was armed with some kind of deadly weapon: rifle, machine gun or assault rifle. Everywhere you looked there was death dangling casually from a shoulder strap. Even some of the girls, had Uzi machine pistols slung from the same shoulder as their handbags, the brass casings from the 9mm bullets in the unloaded magazines, dazzling when they caught the sunlight. Those not eating were smoking or drinking from soda cans and everyone seemed to be speaking at once. The background buzz of voices faded in and out as they passed through the crowd. Billy with his understanding of the language could tune in and out of the passing conversations, picking up snippets of what was being said. He realised that for Anne Mette with no understanding of Hebrew it must all seem like so much white noise. Above this general backdrop the speaker systems outside some of the bazaars were pumping out the exotic intricate Arabic melodies which wove their way in layers into the tapestry of noise.

Punctuating this were the shouts from the Sherut owners. Their vehicles were drawn up in a line on the open area across from the main Bus station. The owners calling out the destinations, while the drivers packed the customers and their luggage inside. They were heading for most major and many minor destinations, throughout the country, although one driver seemed to be having problems filling a minibus to the southern port city of Ashdod and his voice was becoming increasingly strident as Billy and Anne Mette approached. Other voices called out the other destinations, Eilat, Beersheba, Tiberius, Sderot, Ashkelon, Jerusalem. Billy knew that once one vehicle was full it would depart and another take its place until it in turn was full. They seemed to be doing good business, with the exception of the Sherut bound for Ashdod. There now seemed to be an argument going on between the passengers and the driver with shouting and arm waving taking place. It seemed the passengers were anxious to be on their way and were trying to negotiate with another driver in a smaller vehicle to take them. This enraged the original driver and Billy half expected the whole thing to dissolve into a physical fight. He took Anne Mette by the elbow and steered her across the street, pausing to let one bus drive past before negotiating their way around another bus that had stopped to let a group of soldiers ahead cross the road. Every so often, they were engulfed in a cloud of diesel fumes or clouds of cigarette smoke.

The heat was another factor and with the sun nearly directly overhead Billy quickly sought out some shade in amongst the bus stops. They found their stop with the bus already on the stand, but the doors were firmly shut and there was no sign of a driver anywhere. They still had ten minutes until they were due to depart. Billy squatted down in the shade and offered his pack to Anne Mette to sit on. She sank down beside him, opened up her large bottle of water and took a long cool draft. Billy did likewise from his own bottle, wiping his mouth with the back of his hand. People were starting to arrive to join their bus and the queue was lengthening. The passengers were the usual mixture of soldiers, kibbutzniks, men and women in business attire, tourists, students and volunteers. The bus was the express bus for Eilat, but on its route it passed along the main highway through the Negev and past the end of the road that led to Tel Boker. It avoided most of the major towns along the way, so the people not bound for one of the settlements would be heading for Eilat. Avoiding the major towns also made it the fastest and most direct route to Tel Boker, although it meant that on arrival the two of them would face a long walk along the access road from the highway to the kibbutz gates. When they reached their destination there would be a strong chance of picking up a lift from a passing truck or car heading into the kibbutz. Even if they were unlucky and no one stopped to offer them a ride, they were both reasonably fit. They would become hot and sweaty, but they would eventually arrive.

The driver finally showed up and opened the sides of the bus to allow people to stow any larger pieces of luggage, before fighting his way through the press of people waiting around the bus door. They reluctantly surrendered their space to allow him to pass. He performed the usual sleight of hand behind the secret panel that released the door and it hissed open. People immediately surged forward to try and get on board. The driver held out his hand to stop them and the door hissed closed behind him. He was not ready for passengers just yet and there was still a few minutes, before the bus was scheduled to leave.

Billy took a step away and fished a cigarette out of the packet and lit it. He inhaled the smoke deeply. There would be at least an hour or maybe more until the bus made it first scheduled stop and he could enjoy another one. He guessed that this bus like all the others would probably pull in at one of the service stations after Ashkelon, most likely the big one that was attached to kibbutz Yad Mordechai.

"Got a spare cigarette Billy boy?"

Billy span round in shock. The voice had been right next to his ear and startled him. That the voice had spoken English had also surprised him. That the accent was Liverpudlian had amazed him. That the speaker had used his given name didn't actually register with Billy at first until he had turned fully around and was confronted with a familiar face.

"Scouser you thieving scally. How are you doing? Still bumming cigarettes I see."

"Billy Randell, so you dragged your sorry butt back here after all."

Billy didn't even have to offer the cigarette packet to Scouser. As soon as he had access the lad had reached into Billy's shirt pocket and taken the pack, extracted two cigarettes, put one behind his ear and the second in his mouth, and replaced the pack in Billy's shirt before patting the pockets of his shorts and fishing out his lighter. He inhaled the smoke and blew it out again in a long stream.

"Still smoking Time I see," Scouser examined the white tip of the filter, "Not grown up enough for Noblesse?"

"You know I think those things taste like shit, we have had this discussion before."

Billy had first met Scouser in the Peace Cafe in the city of Eilat. When Billy had been down on his luck Scouser had been the guy who had given Billy his first break by inviting him to join his work gang. A while later Billy had been able to return the favour and invited Scouser to join him as an extra. When filming had finished, Billy had returned to his former kibbutz. Scouser along with many of the other extras had returned to Eilat to enjoy their earnings, but that money would have run out long ago.

"So man, what are you doing now? Are you back working the Wall?"

"No fear, I got a real job."

Billy looked a little closer and noticed that there were some small, but subtle changes, in Scouser's appearance. His hair was a little shorter and cut more neatly than before. The clothing he was wearing was not the usual eclectic mix of beachwear and cast off kibbutz work clothes, the scuffed and battered steel toe-capped boots seem to have been confined to a trashcan somewhere and replaced by a neat pair of leather loafers.

"What you doing? You working the hotels?"

It was a natural enough progression. After the work on the Wall, the next step up was to move into the Hotel or Catering business, where the hours were more fixed and a regular pay-packet was forthcoming, provided you could stand turning up for work every day, which was not everyone's cup of tea. Scouser shook his head at Billy's question and pointed at the logo on the breast pocket of his t-shirt. Billy had to lean forward to read the text, which was in a stylised script and faded from a few tours through the washing machine.

"Dive Tribe," Billy read the text aloud, "What's that then some bar?"

"Yeah 50 of them we hope." Scouser replied with a smile.

Billy clearly didn't get the joke, a confused expression spread across his face. Scouser left the joke hanging and moved on to explain his latest job.

"Dive Tribe is one of the diving clubs out on the Coral Beach. They teach people to scuba dive and take experienced divers on guided dives."

"So what has that got to do with bar work?" Billy was now totally confused.

"Nothing," Scouser breathed out long and slow. "Well they have a bar on the beach but I don't work there, just the occasional shift when they are short of staff."

Billy had completely lost the thread of this conversation and that fact was visible on his face. He held up a hand to stop Scouser talking.

"What exactly do you do at this place?"

"I am one of the Dive Masters. I take people who have qualified on guided dives."

The look of disbelief must have shown on Billy's face. When Billy had last seen Scouser he was almost horizontal on his back outside the Peace Café, after a night of heavy drinking. After that Billy had assumed that Scouser would simply return to his old ways of picking up work from the Wall and drinking his wages in the evening. Instead it seemed that Scouser had actually made a fundamental change in his lifestyle.

"How did that come about?"

"Well it was strange. After you left we were sitting in the Peace Cafe when a guy walked in and said he was looking for extras for another film. I was between jobs and remembered we had a blast and the money was good, so I jumped at the chance. Anyway while I was filming there was another English guy on the crew who told me that when they finished filming he was heading to Eilat to go diving. We got talking and one thing led to another. After the wrap I followed him down and we went to the Dive Tribe. They signed me up for a try dive. One half hour and I was hooked. After that I did all my training and then when I qualified they offered me a job. I have been there ever since."

Billy had managed to close his mouth while Scouser had been talking.

"Does it pay well?"

"As a guide not as well as Instructors. They get the top whack, but I do okay. It puts food on the table and I have a roof over my head these days. There are five of us who share an apartment."

"Wow! That sounds like a big change?"

"Listen mate, I need to ask a favour. Can you lend me 20 sheks for the bus fare? I had my wallet stolen last night with all my cash in it. I will pay you back when we get to Eilat."

"We're not going to Eilat. We're getting off at Tel Boker."

"Well next time you are in Eilat drop by the club and I will pay you back. Come on man I need to get back to Eilat tonight or I will lose my job."

Billy fished out his wallet and extracted the notes. He handed them over to his old friend.

"Cheers mate, you're a life saver. I owe you big time. Better get my skates on or I will miss the bus."

Scouser turned on his heels and headed off in the direction of the ticket office. Anne Mette who had remained with their bags while Billy was smoking now joined him and handed him his bag.

"The driver has opened the door should we get on the bus?"

Billy who had been watching Scouser's disappearing back now turned his attention to his travel companion. She was right. The driver had opened the doors to the bus and people were slowly climbing aboard and finding seats. Billy joined the crush and climbed the steps. He presented the two tickets to the driver who clipped them and handed them back to him. Billy led Anne Mette to the rear of the bus. If Scouser was about to join them then it would be easier if they had three seats together at the back of the bus.

Slowly, the bus filled up and still there was no sign of his friend. He had taken a moment or two to explain who Scouser was and also to apologise to Anne Mette that he might join them on this last leg of their trip. She seemed, grudgingly, to accept the fact she would have to share Billy for the duration of the journey to Tel Boker. Billy kept one eye out of the window, scanning the crowds swirling around the bus station and flowing from the direction of the ticket office, but there was no sign of Scouser. Finally the doors at the front of the bus hissed closed and the bus pulled away from the stand.

"Looks like your friend missed the bus."

Anne Mette, if she felt any satisfaction at the no-show, did an excellent job at concealing it. At least she would now have Billy's full attention, for the remainder of the journey and she could take some small satisfaction from that. Billy for his part was slightly peeved. He knew there could be a dozen reasons why Scouser had failed to re-join him on the bus, but right now there was only one that was howling in his mind. Billy felt he had just been conned. Scouser had just spun him a story and Billy like the trusting fool he was, had fallen for it completely.

He began to see the holes in Scouser's story. How would he have found the money to go through the expense of training as a scuba diver? Billy had no idea how much it would cost, but he didn't think it would be cheap. Scuba diving was a rich man's past time, not for the likes of Scouser or him. He could have bought or even stolen the t-shirt and then used it as part of his cover story. It was perfect. He could approach anyone, friend or stranger and spin the story of having his wallet stolen and how he needed to borrow money to get back to Eilat or risk losing his job. And the beautiful part to the story was that the person who has lent him the money has somewhere physical, somewhere they can actually go and collect their cash back. Billy reckoned that the Dive Tribe had never even heard of Scouser, except, maybe, as someone who was claiming to be a member of staff and who had ripped off a large number of people who all turned up expecting to receive twenty shekels back.

As the bus made its way towards the city limits Billy sat and did the maths. If there were 10 bus departures to Eilat every day and Scouser got lucky with half of them then he would be pulling down a hundred shekels a day with little or no overheads. Okay, he might not be lucky with every bus departure, but the story was feasible and Scouser was an excellent actor. Billy wasn't angry with his old friend really, he was just annoyed that he had been taken in by the scam. That was his fault not Scouser's. He guessed that one day, in some other place, their paths might cross again and he would get the money back. With interest.

With that decision made, he sat back and watched as the now familiar landscape from Tel Aviv southwards to Tel Boker unfolded before them. For Anne Mette, who had spent her entire time, so far, in the north of the country, this was a new experience. She asked to sit by the window, so she could stare out at the barren landscape, as they headed south.

## Chapter Thirteen

"Billy boy!"
Billy was able to turn around just in time to be engulfed and crushed by a strong pair of arms in a powerful chest-crushing bear hug. Released after a few moments and held at arm's length Billy set eyes on his oldest friend for the first time in well over a year. Mike and Yara had left Tel Boker to travel, but now they were both back. They had arrived back a week earlier and had just managed to settle back in to life on Tel Boker. Billy looked for signs of a change in Mike, but nothing was outwardly visible. It was the same smiling face looking at him. Yara was standing a few feet behind Mike, so when Mike released him Billy crossed to her and took her in a close embrace.

"Welcome back Billy," she said in her deeply accented English.
"It's good to see you again sweetie."
Billy said in fluent Hebrew, causing Yara to grin at him.
"You haven't forgotten," she said still smiling showing off her perfect white teeth.
"No I am a little out of practice, that's all."
"But you have been back here for a while." Yara showed a little confusion at Billy's comments.
"It's a long story, it can wait till later. Both of you, I want you to meet a friend of mine."
Billy took a step back and put his arm out towards Anne Mette, taking hold of her hand and bringing her in close to his two old friends.
"Anne Mette, this is Mike Spencer and Yara Sigal."
Anne Mette shook hands with both of them.
"I have heard so much about you two from Billy. I feel like I know you already."
Mike feigned a shocked look.
"I hope he hasn't told you all our dirty secrets?"
Anne Mette adopted a coy look raising one hand to her chin, the finger pointing up the side of her cheek, towards her ear.
"Now," she said slowly, "let me think for a minute."
Everybody laughed at that. Mike put his arm around Anne Mette in a friendly gesture.
"I like her. She has a sense of humour."
"You need one when dating Billy Randell." Anne Mette added quickly and there was another explosion of laughter.
"What's so funny, can anyone share the joke?"
A deep voice boomed from behind them. All four turned around to greet the newcomer. Yossi had changed very little since Billy had last seen him nearly two years ago. Maybe there was a few extra flecks of grey in his bushy beard and a few more lines around his eyes. Billy would have expected that as Yossi was solely responsible for the health and well-being of upwards of a hundred volunteers. That should be enough to make any man grey and add to the worry lines around his eyes. Whatever had changed about him, his fashion sense hadn't. He was still wearing kibbutz blue work clothes and leather sandals.
"So my two least favourite volunteers are back together." He grinned.
Billy knew he was only joking.
"Hello Yossi, how are you?"
"I am fine Mr Randell, all the better for seeing you again. And who is this then?"
He looked very pointedly at Anne Mette.
"Anne Mette Hansen."
Anne Mette extended her hand towards Yossi.
"I am with Billy."

"Oh that's a shame I thought you were maybe a new volunteer. We could do with a few more pretty faces around here."

"Yossi you old goat charmer." Billy burst out.

"Careful Billy or you'll be sleeping in the sheep stalls tonight, while the lovely Miss Hansen enjoys the relative luxury of one of the guest rooms."

"You wouldn't dare?"

"Try me, just try me?"

Yossi let the threat dangle in the air, but there was no real malice in it.

"Anyway I didn't think you had sheep stalls here. You don't keep sheep."

"Not anymore, but there are some derelict buildings over on the south side that used to be for sheep. I am sure we could put you there."

Billy knew he was going to lose this argument, so he held up his hands.

"Okay. I surrender. I promise I will be nice to you from now on."

"Good," Yossi smiled, "then if you would care to follow me I will show you to your accommodation."

Yossi led the way across the grass to a nearby row of rooms. Billy had passed them countless times before on his way to and from the dining room, but had never really paid them any notice. They were simply a row of rooms like those set aside for single unmarried members. They consisted of a small veranda and then a door, which led into a living room. To the left was a small bathroom and toilet, on the right behind a small arch was a kitchenette and behind this was a bedroom. The room they had been allocated was sparsely furnished with a small sofa and a coffee table. The bedroom was dominated by a double bed. The room had already been prepared for their arrival and the bed was already made with sheets and blankets. It all looked very comfortable. Billy and Anne Mette dropped their bags in the bedroom and then followed Mike and Yara outside again.

Yossi having shown the guests to their room and presented them with the keys, had already departed, but Mike and Yara were waiting for them. Billy and Mike had been talking on the way down to the guest rooms and Mike had suggested that they should head for his room to relax with a few drinks. With this in mind, Billy had retrieved a bottle of Arac from his luggage and he was carrying it, when he and Anne Mette, came outside. He automatically turned left and started down the path in the direction of the volunteer quarters.

"Where are you off to?"

Mike said, his arms folded across his chest, feet firmly planted on the grass.

"I thought we were going back to yours." Billy had stopped dead in his tracks.

Mike inclined his head in the opposite direction.

"This way, I am living up here now."

Billy gave a low whistle.

"Since when?"

"Since we got back. Yara and I have a room together."

"Next you'll be telling me you are a member candidate?"

Mike smiled,

"No not yet. We haven't decided, where we are going to live yet, so I haven't applied. It has been suggested, but we haven't made a final decision."

Billy shook his head and started back in the other direction.

"All right then, let's go and check out your new digs."

Billy found everything he needed in the small kitchen and came out with the glasses, a pitcher of cold water and some ice on a tray. He placed it all on the small table and began to prepare drinks for everyone. He passed them out. Mike held his up inspecting the milky white contents of the glass.

"I haven't touched this stuff for months."

He sniffed at the contents of the glass and wrinkled his nose a little.

"Drink up man it will put lead in your pencil."

Billy had already downed half of his glass and was licking his lips. He polished off the second half of the drink and let out a satisfied sigh.

"That's cleaned the travel dust out of the pipes."

He began to prepare himself another draught, which he again made short work of. Billy was on his way into his fourth Arac and water, while the others were still drinking their first and the powerful spirit was beginning to have an effect on him. There were concerned looks passing between Mike and Yara. At one point Yara looked long and hard at Mike and nodded in Billy's direction. Mike shook his head once. His message was clear enough. He had noticed that Billy was caning it a bit, but he didn't want to say anything. Mike for his part didn't want to ruin the mood or start an argument with his friend. The two were powerless, but to do anything and it was left to Anne Mette to notice the looks passing back and forth and it was she who chose to intervene.

"Billy before we get too settled down, you did promise to show me around the place. I would love to go and see the volunteer blocks. You told me they are very different from Sde Avram."

Billy looked up for a moment and then looked down at his drink. He had a half a glass left, which he polished off in one gulp and then stood up, a little unsteadily. Mike leapt to his feet and Yara followed his lead. Her drink lay virtually untouched on the table.

"I think that's a great idea. The fresh air will do us all good and help us to work up an appetite. Yossi is getting the stuff ready for a barbecue, so we could go down the volunteers first and then swing around by his place afterwards."

Everyone was on their feet and out the door in double quick time, separating Billy from the Arac bottle, at least for a little while. Billy wasn't too worried by the separation. He had fond memories of the free flowing booze from his time on Tel Boker and figured he would be able to wangle a drink from someone, when they arrived at the volunteer block. It was highly likely that there would be some kind of party going on down there, amongst the volunteers.

Unfortunately Billy didn't know the current crop of volunteers at all. On the way down through the kibbutz Mike told Billy that the number of volunteers had shrunk, since Billy had left. Now there were only about twenty five of them on Tel Boker. Two of the sections of the volunteers' accommodation were standing empty as Billy and the others passed them. There was a lack of life about the place. Some of the doors were left open like wide cavernous mouths, some of the window frames were damaged with the net coverings torn and missing, the orange curtains flapping through the raggedy holes. Rubbish had built up on the verandas in front of the rooms.

They hurried by these rooms heading towards the inhabited blocks. Billy stopped in his tracks and listened. He could hear a cow bellowing over in the Refet, obviously in some distress, but apart from that discordant bawling the place was quiet. This puzzled Billy. He would have at least expected to hear music of some form playing from a stereo in one or other of the rooms. Maybe, laughter, merriment or the sound of voices raised in excited discussion or argument. But, the whole place was eerily silent, almost like a graveyard or a church. Billy checked his watch. Could it be that everyone was up in the kibbutz dining room? It was too early for the evening meal. He shook his head and hurried to catch up with the others, who had made it to the end of the first block. Billy rounded the corner and was confronted with a familiar sight. The swing set that had stood outside his room throughout the duration of his stay was still around, albeit now more browned with rust than it had been when he had last sat on it. The cushions looked a little thinner, the covers replaced by colourful blankets. No one was sitting on it. Nor were there any bodies occupying any of the other armchairs or sofas that were scattered around the place. The whole place was a ghost town. All that was missing was the tumbleweed. The four of them walked slowly along the front of the block. All of the blue metal doors were shut tight. There was absolutely no noise emanating from any of the rooms. Nothing.

"This place is completely dead."

Billy voiced what all of them were thinking and there was a hint of sadness, a note of loss in his voice. Whatever he had been expecting, this was definitely not it. Billy had been a volunteer here, on and off, for nearly two years. He had seen the total volunteer population rise and fall as it did every season. There was usually a jump in volunteer numbers at the end of the school year, as people opted to take a gap year out and travel. There were also kibbutzim who ramped up their volunteer numbers at particular times of the year, utilising the extra manpower at crucial harvest times. And yet, even at its lowest ebb, the volunteer blocks on Tel Boker, had never been so deserted and devoid of atmosphere.

"This place is like a morgue." He reiterated his disappointment.

"And of course you are an expert on morgues," Mike said,

"You've never visited one."

Billy was about to fire back at his friend that he hadn't either, when he remembered that was not actually true. Mike had had occasion to visit the morgue in Eilat, when he had been asked to identify a dead body that the authorities thought, might be Billy. Mike therefore considered himself the expert on all things morgue-related and this place didn't even come close.

Just as they reached the end of the block and were about to turn around and head for home, one of the blue doors opened and a head popped around the corner.

"Hello?" there was a smile and friendly greeting, "are you lost?"

The girl asked. Billy took a moment to weigh her up. Just her head and shoulders were visible around the door and the head was topped by a frizzy cap of long dark brown hair. The face framed by this hairy curtain, was slightly chubby with full lips and an over large nose, pierced on one side with a diamond stud. The eyes were kind, the voice had been soft, as if afraid of waking anybody who slept within the room. The accent was English. Billy moved towards the disembodied head.

"Hi. We were wondering where everyone was?"

"In our rooms."

The answer was delivered deadpan and with a slight tone of underlying incredulity. It was almost as if Billy had asked her if she could count up to three. Seeing the vague, lost expression on Billy's face, prompted some further explanation from their newfound friend.

"We usually sleep from when we finish work until tea time."

'Tea-time', Billy thought. What a quintessentially English concept. Not totally alien for them to grasp. At some time or another all of them had taken advantage of the quiet around the kibbutz in the afternoons to catch up on some lost sleep. It gave you the extra energy you needed to power on and party through the night. Billy couldn't help himself.

"Is it tea-time now?" he asked slightly tongue in cheek.

Their new friend had a slightly puzzled expression on her face.

"Err, I don't know.

The head and shoulders disappeared from view temporarily as it sought guidance from those hidden within the room. The answer came through actions not words as a split second later the head reappeared accompanied now by a body. In one hand there was an old fashioned metal electric kettle.

"I will just go and fill this. Will you stay for some tea?"

Billy had a massive deja-vu attack. He appeared to now have become a bit part player in some Agatha Christie Miss Marple episode, with afternoon tea and crumpets on offer. He hesitated looking at the others for backup. They were all studiously looking elsewhere and avoiding his gaze. It was up to him to answer.

"Some tea?"

He said copying the best 'crusty vicar's voice' that he could summon up at such short notice.

"That would be splendid."

Of all of them at least Mike had the good grace to splutter with laughter. The joke was obviously lost on the two other girls, being foreigners. Their new friend had obviously also missed out on the irony, as she nodded and set off to fill the kettle, a slightly concerned expression on her face. When she returned, she glanced briefly inside the room, before pushing the door wide open and inviting the four of them in. Inside, the room had that eerie dark orange colour from the sunlight passing through the drawn curtains. There were three other people inside the room. All were now up and about, but the unmade beds and clothes scattered around, led Billy to believe this was a relatively recent occurrence and probably done purely for their benefit. The occupants moved around to make room for people to at least sit down, while their host attended to the job of making the tea.

"We have some real English tea bags. Becca's mum just sent out a care package."

Becca who had the good nature to blush, was a mousy blonde who stared myopically at the world through a pair of thick lensed glasses. She looked to be in her early twenties and her tan told Billy that she had probably been on Tel Boker for a few months. Just long enough to run out of the initial supplies, brought with her from home and then for the exchange of aerogrammes and letters to ensure a timely resupply. It was not that the Israeli tea bags were bad, but there was always a certain kudos, among the Brits, if they could offer a cup of PG or Tetley tea to guests. That and the presence of Marmite, to spread on the morning toast, was considered to be living in the lap of luxury. Billy wasn't a big fan of the dark yeasty spread; for him it was not that important. He did, however, know people for whom life started and ended, inside the dark glass jar with the yellow lid. The only thing marmite was good for, in Billy's eyes, was to wind up the Aussies, who swore blind that their own variety of the product, Vegemite, was superior in every way. Offering a proud Aussie Marmite was almost all the provocation one needed to start a very ugly scene.

When they had all been introduced and the teas had been handed around, Billy was secretly disappointed that there were no crumpets, scones, not even a packet of Israeli biscuits. He kept that disappointment to himself. Their hosts were keen to discover why Billy and his friends were lurking around the volunteer quarters in the middle of the afternoon. One of the hosts obviously recognised Mike as a familiar face, but Billy and Anne Mette were strangers. Billy decided to introduce himself and explained that he was a former volunteer who was back visiting the old haunts. That Billy and Mike were both ex-volunteers seemed to pique the interests of the current occupants and they were keen to swap stories about life as a volunteer then and now.

Billy was secretly amazed that these four current Tel Boker volunteers saw and treated the previous years, as if they had happened in another decade or century. Billy had to point out that it had not even been two years since he had actually been a volunteer here on Tel Boker, although when it came to the current occupants describing their lifestyle, Billy wondered not in terms of time, but whether the current incumbents were actually from another planet. Their idea of having a good time was so diametrically opposite to the life that Billy and the other volunteers had led back in the day that he did wonder where and when things had changed. Had this been a slow evolution or was their some cataclysmic shift that had given birth to this more sedentary lifestyle. There really was no other word to describe it. As Becca and her friends described their ideal way to spend an evening, chatting quietly with friends whilst sharing a bottle of beer, Billy saw his chances of getting another real drink, before he made it back to Mike's or to his own room, rapidly slipping away. Billy could see how a group of volunteers, who lived this almost monk-like existence, would be a dream come true for volunteer leaders like Yossi. Volunteers who never got drunk, never got sick, never got into fights and certainly never turned up late for work. Billy wondered what Yossi felt about the current situation with this particular group and he was determined to question his friend about it later. In the end it turned out that far from being ideal Yossi was struggling to find something, anything to do with his time. He had not realised how much of his time, up until now, had been occupied with dealing with the fallout from volunteers bad behaviour.

Their hosts could see that their guests, and especially Billy, seemed bemused at their way of life. They began to question the two former Tel Boker volunteers about how things had been when they had been volunteers. Again Billy got the feeling that he was describing life in another decade, not a mere year and a half ago. 'If a week is a long time in politics, a year on a kibbutz is a lifetime', Billy thought to himself. He was longing for another alcoholic drink and whilst he was happy to relate some of the stories about what life had been like in the 'good old days', he really did want to get as far away as possible from these people and get back to where there was some serious grain alcohol in a bottle. The new volunteers didn't seem overly impressed with some of the antics of their former counterparts and merely listened in polite silence as Billy recounted some of the stories of drunken stupidity. Mike chipped in the occasional anecdote, but the other two remained largely silent merely listening. Billy realising that the stories were not inspiring any desire to emulation eventually fell silent and when no offer of beer or other drinks were forthcoming suggested that his party move on and leave these good people alone. Yara who hadn't uttered a single word, since they entered the room backed up Billy's suggestion, so the four made their excuses and left.

Back outside and on the way back up through the kibbutz Billy was rather vocal about what he had seen.

"I can't believe these people are living the dream. They all seem bloody miserable."

Mike tried to mollify Billy by suggesting that maybe not everyone's idea of 'living the dream', was the same as Billy's. Billy was on the point of hitting back with a stinging retort, but at the last minute he just bit his tongue, hunched his shoulders and stopped talking. They went via the guest room allocated to Billy and Anne Mette, so Billy could acquire a fresh bottle of Arac from his luggage and then headed in the direction of Yossi's house.

Yossi's house was up at the top end of the kibbutz. As you moved up through the kibbutz it was possible to follow the development of the settlement through the years from the age and the quality of the buildings. Nearer the centre of the community there were smaller and older single person rooms. These were among some of the first structures built. Further out in the outer rings were the modern family dwellings. These were of various sizes to match the different sized families. It was not one size fits all. There were smaller family homes with just two bedrooms up to the larger properties with four and even five bedrooms.

Yossi's house was among one of the newest properties and consisted of the usual kitchen, dining and living rooms, but it also had four bedrooms and two bathrooms. Yossi still had three of his five children living with him on the kibbutz and as the children on Tel Boker lived with their parents and not in separate accommodation, he needed the large number of bedrooms. His eldest daughter was in her first year of service with the army, so she still came home at weekends. His eldest son, Dov, had joined the Israeli Air Force and trained as a helicopter pilot. Billy had met Dov when the IAF had assigned him to work on the film shoot in the Negev. Dov had been the pilot who took some of the crew and others on a flying tour around Israel after filming wrapped. He had also played a substantial part in what had happened to Billy after the trip finished.

Outside the house Yossi had a large area covered by an arbour made of split pine logs. The whole thing was overgrown with vines, wild jasmine and bougainvillea. In the shady interior, there was a comfortable seating area with a fire pit and a dining area with a brick built barbecue and outdoor kitchen. When they arrived Yossi, his wife and the eldest two of the children were hard at work preparing the meat and salads. They were being helped by a couple of their neighbours. The whole kitchen area was alive with industry and friendly banter. It was clear from the amount of food being prepared that this was not going to be a quiet or intimate family affair. If the food was anything to go by, then it looked as if Yossi had invited half of the kibbutz members to join them. Yossi turned to greet the new arrivals.

"Mike, Billy. Welcome to my house. Please make yourselves at home."

Yossi made a sweeping gesture to encompass the whole of the outdoor area. Billy took a moment to introduce Anne Mette to Yossi's wife. Yossi asked what everyone wanted to drink. Mike asked for a beer, so did Anne Mette so Yossi went to the fridge and pulled out two cold one's. Billy looked around expectantly, slightly pissed off that he had been ignored. Yossi opened the two beer bottles and then reached inside for a bowl of ice. He returned to the table and passed out the beers. Yara had grabbed herself a glass of coke from one of the large two-litre bottles that were stood in the centre of the table. Yossi laid the bowl of ice down next to Billy's glass and then with a flourish produced a bottle of Elite Arac which he stood beside the ice bowl. Billy cracked a smile, then the seal of the bottle and poured himself a large one.

Yossi proposed a toast and they all drank each-other's health.

"What have you been doing since you arrived?"

"We went on a tour around and checked out the volunteer quarters. It's a bit quiet down there these days."

Yossi's wife came across to place small bowls of olives and nuts on the table.

"And I see much more of him these days because it is so quiet."

"See my wife likes the new arrangements."

Yossi's wife, out of his sight behind his back began shaking her head violently, suggesting she felt the exact opposite. Billy stifled a smirk by covering his mouth with his hand.

"Maybe Mike and I should move back in and show them how it's done."

Billy grinned mischievously.

"Don't you dare Billy Randell!"

Yossi's wife was fierce when she wanted to be and she fell completely for Billy's outrageous suggestion. Yossi laughed out loud and Billy joined him.

"Nice idea Billy. To be honest life is very boring with these new volunteers. No drunkenness, no fighting, no one late for work, it's no fun at all."

"It's lovely."

Now he had called her out she was ready to tell the truth.

"He comes home early, doesn't get called out in the middle of the night to go and collect volunteers from the police station or the border post. He is much nicer to live with."

She was standing directly behind Yossi and as Billy watched she leaned forward and placed her hands on his shoulders, in a soft but firm and slightly proprietorial fashion.

"And besides Billy, I don't think you alone, even with Mike's help could change a thing. I think it would take an earthquake to get any movement going".

Billy shook his head. He wasn't disagreeing with his host or his wife. He was merely shocked and a little saddened that things had changed, so dramatically in such a short time. It was almost as if the spark that ignited the flame had been stolen from among them.

People soon started arriving and Billy was secretly amazed at just how many of them remembered him, even though there must have been hundreds of volunteers, who had passed through the settlement in the last ten years. Billy couldn't believe that they remembered every single one of them, but maybe a few of them had left a passing impression. Billy, who was now getting suitably buzzed from the alcohol began to wonder why these members, all of whom seemed to know his name and were anxious to know what he had been doing since he had left the kibbutz. Why did they remember him over all the other volunteers, who must have crossed their paths? Exactly what made him so special, why did he stand out? Maybe it was the alcohol or just his guilty conscience for not returning here when he had arrived back in the country, but Billy began to get paranoid.

Was he remembered for his brief affair with a married member? He had no doubt that their relationship had been a scandal at the time and probably the worst kept secret in a place where secrets were almost impossible to keep. She had been married at the time he had been involved with her. She was divorced now, but still living on Tel Boker despite her protestations about wanting to leave. If it was not for his indiscretion with a married member, there was also the matter of his unjustified expulsion for drug possession. He had been innocent, but still made to take the long walk up the exit road.

Yossi had welcomed him back, relieved to have a chance to undo the wrong. Billy now wondered how many members simply remembered about the drugs and not his exoneration. As he slowly became more obsessed with the attention he was getting, his temper began to fray and his attitude became more hostile. None of his anxiety was helped by the large amount of Arac he had consumed. Yossi's bottle was over half empty and Bill was the only one drinking from it.

Mike was the one who finally bore the brunt of his paranoia. An off the cuff comment about easing up on the booze prompted Billy to completely lose it. He stood up and yelled at Mike to mind his own business and keep his nose out before tossing his empty glass on to the floor where it shattered into a thousand pieces. He stormed off and away into the dark. Behind him he left a silent and startled group of people, who all stood mute as they watched him disappearing into the shadows cast by the surrounding trees. Anne Mette had made a move to follow Billy, but Mike had grabbed her arm and held her back. Anne Mette had struggled for a moment to free her arm. Then one look at the expression on Mike's face told her it was a battle she couldn't win. She went limp and slumped back into her chair, offering no further resistance.

"Leave him alone, he is being a cunt and he doesn't deserve you. Right now it's better to let him stew in his own juice."

Anne Mette didn't agree with Mike, but she acknowledged the fact that Mike had known Billy for much longer than she had. Nevertheless, she began to worry when an hour had passed and he had not returned to the party. She felt lonely and abandoned after Billy's departure. Although no one shunned her, she didn't feel part of this community, as she did on Sde Avram. All of the guests, with the exception of Mike and Yara, were strangers to her. The fact that most of the conversation was in Hebrew just added to her feelings of isolation. It was also difficult for her as a volunteer from Sde Avram with its strict segregation between members and volunteers, not to feel a little uncomfortable socialising with kibbutzniks. Despite their best efforts to make her feel welcome, the feeling of isolation just grew stronger.

At one point Yossi stood up to make a speech. He was switching between Hebrew, for the benefit of the older members of the audience and English for Mike, who even after his extended stay in the kibbutz seemed to only have a very rudimentary command of the Hebrew language. He was clearly making a number of jokes, if the response to his words was anything to go by. Yara and Mike still spoke together in English and Mike's excuse was that if they were to return to live in the UK, US or Australia then having an excellent command of English, would serve her well. She merely teased him that he was lazy. The English part of Yossi's speech, which Anne Mette could understand, welcomed Mike and Yara back to the kibbutz. He also made passing mention of their return bringing Billy back for a visit. Although he didn't say anything directly it appeared that Yossi was a little disappointed that Billy had chosen another kibbutz and not returned to Tel Boker. He didn't mention this directly, but rather made an oblique comment to the effect that

"Billy,"

and at the mention of the name, taking a moment to look around the assembled throng before he continued,

"seems to have chosen to leave us, spiritually as well as physically. Maybe never to return."

The joke delivered in Hebrew got a polite laugh and the same was the case, when it was repeated in English, although neither Mike nor Anne Mette joined in with the merriment. A short time after the speech Yossi sidled up to Anne Mette.

"Did Billy say anything to you before he left?" he asked.

"No not a word. I know he had an argument with Mike, maybe you should ask him?"

"This is rather awkward. Having a party, where one of the guests of honour has gone missing."

Anne Mette felt a flash of anger rise up inside her, but as she hardly knew her host she managed to supress it before it burst forth. Instead through gritted teeth and a fixed jaw she repeated her advice that he should ask Mike. But Yossi was not to be deterred.

"It must be lonely for you being here alone, not knowing anyone. Maybe you could go and see if you could find him?"

In some ways this was an answer to Anne Mette's problem. Yossi was right. She didn't know anybody at the party and it might be better, if she embarked on a fool's mission to try and find Billy in the vastness of the kibbutz, somewhere out there in the dark. Although, even an organised search party, probably could not locate Billy, particularly if he didn't want to be found. At least it gave her an excuse to leave the gathering.

"I could go look in our room and see if he is there, but I don't have the key. Billy does."

Yossi was prepared for this eventuality and produced a key from his shorts.

"This is an extra key for your room."

He handed it over to Anne Mette, who took it from him, stood up and without another word left.

As she walked through the kibbutz, she considered what had occurred. Yossi was clearly annoyed by Billy's childish tantrum. She couldn't help feeling that her continued presence at the gathering had been a gentle reminder to everyone there that one of the main guests was missing and had in fact made a scene and stormed off. By shuffling her off on this pointless search, he was removing the final reminder of Billy's presence. This fact really annoyed her. She began to consider what she could say to Billy to entice him to return to the party, if, of course, she could find him? The most logical place to start the search would be the guest room they were sharing. If Billy was not there, at least she could sit down, use the toilet in peace and quiet then decide where to look next?

As darkness had fallen, the street lighting throughout the kibbutz had come on. Light was also escaping through curtains and blinds casting a myriad band of coloured patches on pathways and lawns, from the members' rooms and houses. There was no light coming from their guest room. Anne Mette took this as a sign that Billy was not inside. She approached the door and tried the handle. It opened? There was just enough light shining from a nearby lamp post in through one of the windows to avoid walking into any large objects. She paused in the doorway, letting her eyes adjust to the gloom within. A slight movement attracted her attention. She was not alone in the room? On turning her head she saw there was a figure curled up on the floor. She reached for the light switch and flooded the room with harsh white light.

Billy was curled up on the far side of the room just by the archway that led to the bathroom. He was in the foetal position with his head pulled down, so his face was partially hidden by his upper arms. His legs were drawn up to his chest. He had stopped moving now, but there was a slow moan escaping from him. He sounded like a wounded animal in pain. Anne Mette crossed the floor in an instant and knelt beside him. She ran her hand over his head looking for signs of injury, then continued the search of all the visible parts of his body.

When she found nothing, she tried to encourage him to relax, so she could complete her examination of his torso and legs. Satisfied that there was no serious injuries she urged Billy to try and sit up and was partially successful. She stood behind him and supported his shoulders as his head lolled from side to side like his neck was broken. In the short time he had been away from the festivities Billy had managed to finish off the rest of the bottle of Arac that he had opened earlier. The empty bottle was discarded on the floor with just the last dregs still lying in the bottom. A glass half filled with Arac and water was sitting on the table top. Billy was almost unconscious from the drink.

Anne Mette struggled to get him closer to the bed, so she could stand him up and push him onto the mattress. The cool stone floor was flat and shiny, so it was easy to drag Billy across the floor. She could feel the cold stone through her shorts against her buttocks as she slid backwards dragging Billy's lifeless body behind her. The room was cool but she could feel sweat starting to break out on her skin. She made it to the bed and hauled Billy upright. It was a supreme effort and left her breathless and sweating afterwards.

She slid out from under his deadweight and crossed to where her bag was sat on a shelf. She unzipped the top, removed her toilet bag and headed to the bathroom, where she stripped and stepped into the shower. The flow was steady and the water was still warm. She stood under the stream for five long minutes, before she soaped up and then rinsed off. Whilst she was shampooing her hair and rinsing the suds out, the bathroom door suddenly burst open. She screamed and instinctively grabbed a towel, expecting to have to cover her modesty and confront a stranger. After wiping her eyes, her vision cleared, showing Billy standing in the doorway, swaying backwards and forwards.

"I'm gonna ..." he got no further, just bent over the toilet and vomited, very powerfully.

After finishing tying off her towel, she stepped over to help support Billy. She held him as he alternately shivered, shook and vomited for the next ten minutes. With each wracking wave, he sank lower and lower, down on to his knees, on to the ground, supporting his weight on his hands, palms flat and fingers splayed, his head now inside the porcelain toilet bowl. He said nothing. There was no remorse, no apologies, no promises never to do such a thing again. Just repeated silences, retching, spluttering, occasional coughing. Once Anne Mette was sure, he was not going to sink further down, she left him where he was, then pulled on a clean pair of knickers and a t-shirt. She found a clean glass and filled it with some cold water from the fridge. After waiting for the toilet to flush, she returned to the bathroom and handed it to Billy. He drank some of it, then rinsed the vomit from his mouth, spitting the dregs down the toilet.

He was still pretty woozy and needed help to stand up. Once he was up, Anne Mette closed the toilet seat and sat him down on it. She pulled off the vomit stained t-shirt and shorts and tossed them in the shower, before taking a wash cloth and sponging Billy clean. She used her own towel to dry him and then half walked, half carried him back into the bedroom and lay him down on the bed. She set another full glass of water on the night stand before, cleaning up the last of the mess, rinsing out Billy's clothes in the shower and hanging them outside to dry in the warm breeze. Next, she turned off all the lights, except the one outside the bathroom, before locking the front door and finally climbing into bed. The air-con unit made the room cool, so she covered herself with a sheet and pushed the blanket aside.

Billy was snoring softly beside her, lying on his back with both arms extended in a crucifix shape. She pushed one arm down to his side to make room for herself. This caused Billy to stir slightly and he rolled over onto his side and sensing her body beside him snuggled in close to her. She lay in the semi-dark and tried to will herself to sleep; it proved elusive. She knew that Billy had a problem. She wasn't strong enough to deal with it. Not on her own.

Having rid his body of most of the excess alcohol the previous evening, Billy was surprisingly chipper, when he woke up the next morning. Anne Mette, who had remained awake for a long time, agonising over her next move, was a little more subdued. Billy hopped naked out of bed and busied himself making them both coffee. The room had a kettle, coffee powder and sugar. As Anne Mette liked her coffee black, the absence of milk was not a problem. He carried the two steaming cups back over to the bed and handed one to her. The air-con, set on a timer, had switched off during the night and the room was a little stuffy. She sat upright, with small pin-prick eyes, her hair still messed up, so it fell around her face and was plastered to her skin with a little sweat. She pushed it away and took a careful sip of the dark liquid. Billy had made a very strong brew and the caffeine had an instant effect, banishing the last vestiges of sleep from her brain. Billy, still making no attempt to cover himself up, perched on the side of the bed.

"What happened last night?"

He didn't seem overly concerned about the recent events; more curious for her to fill in the blanks.

"What do you remember?"

"Going to Yossi's, having food, a few drinks, then it all gets a bit hazy?"

"So you don't remember having that row with Mike?"

"No?"

For the first time a little look of uncertainty crept onto Billy's face.

"How bad was it?"

Anne Mette had no idea about the severity of any past arguments there might have been between Mike and Billy, so a comparison was not really possible. She could just offer an opinion on how the argument appeared relative to normal interaction between two adults.

"Not pretty."

Billy did a manual check of his limbs, inspecting his knuckles and then feeling his arms, legs and torso for any signs of tenderness. Finding nothing reassured him a little.

"At least we didn't end up coming to blows."

"No. You just stormed off. Like some prima-donna."

"Ouch."

"Well that was how you behaved."

"By ouch, I mean that you even knowing that English phrase, means I must have been really bad. A total tosser."

"Don't get me started on what I found when I got back here last night."

For a moment Anne Mette caught a flash of real fear in Billy's eyes. The slightly cocky smile that had been slowly returning to his lips now vanished. The colour had drained from his cheeks. Billy was now genuinely scared.

"Why?"

He hesitated, not really wanting to hear any account of his behaviour from the dark zone of his blackout. He had no actual recollection of anything. He was ever fearful of what he might have done or said. Rationally, his brain was telling him that Anne Mette was still here, alive, unharmed, so he hadn't become aggressive or physical with her. Irrationally, it kept throwing up damning images. Anne Mette was still slowly sipping her coffee. In no hurry to put Billy out of his misery. In fact she was enjoying his discomfort, trying not to smile.

"Come on? Well, what did I do?"
"Okay. Maybe, I should apologise unreservedly for whatever I did?
"Then we can both move on? What do you think?"

The fear was making Billy gabble now, so Anne Mette took pity on him. She decided to end his torment.

"When I got back here last night."

She paused, enjoying the fact that Billy, had both tensed up and screwed his eyes shut.
"You were passed out on the floor over there."

She indicated a patch of floor on the far side of the room from the bed where they were both now sitting.

"I dragged you bodily to here."

She patted the bed beside her.

"Heaved you up onto the bed. Went to take a shower."

Billy was now looking puzzled as he tried to analyse, what he was being told and match that to his worst fears. On each point he was coming up with no comparisons.

"While I was in the shower," again Anne Mette paused and this time took a large gulp from her now cooling coffee.

"You staggered into the bathroom."

Now Billy's brain went into overdrive. He registered two things simultaneously. First, he was stark bollock naked. Second, his clothes were nowhere to be seen. Therefore, he must have leapt into the shower with Anne Mette and got a soaking. Whilst this was not so terrible in the scheme of things, being sexually assaulted by a drunken boyfriend in the shower was probably not particularly high on Anne Mette's wish list.

"What happened? I don't remember."
"Well to put it mildly, you threw up, rather spectacularly and very noisily."

The relief flooded over Billy's face and his body relaxed. His shoulders dropped down from their defensive position and some colour returned to his face.

"Is the bathroom in a state? I'll clean it up."
"No. Fortunately, your aim was pretty good. To be honest, I was impressed given the state you were in."

Anne Mette gave him a cheeky grin and stuck her tongue out a little between her teeth to show she was teasing him. Billy returned the smile.

"You spewed up a bit on your clothes. I stripped you and washed them. They are hanging outside."
"So, you were naked and wet. You took off all my clothes, but I was so drunk, I missed it? Bummer."
"Well you are still naked. I only have this t-shirt on. We can make up for lost time now."

The cheeky grin had turned into a lascivious one now. Billy didn't need a second invitation. The coffee cup was discarded and he threw back the bedsheet and then leapt onto the bed and into Anne Mette's open arms.

A while later as they both lay back exhausted with both their heartbeats returning to normal after their exertion, Anne Mette related the circumstances and details of the argument between Billy and Mike. She felt it was the only way to broach the subject of Billy's drunken behaviour without approaching it head on. She was using the indirect approach to try and gauge how Billy would react to criticism of his drinking. If he would not see that his behaviour had been unacceptable then she would have to find another way to tackle this. If, however, Billy was ready to admit fault then that would be the first step to getting him to acknowledge that he had a problem.

Anne Mette was an expert on alcoholics and alcohol abuse. She had grown up in a family environment where both her father and elder brother were addicts and she knew that the battle with addiction was a long, bloody and often frustrating one, but the first small victory was to get the person to actually admit that they had a problem and that they needed help with it. Personally, she had managed to get her brother to address his personal demons and get himself into a recovery program. She was not so fortunate with her father and his untimely death, had been one of the triggers to her setting out on her travels.

Whilst she would freely acknowledge that her feelings for her father and her growing feelings for Billy were on two completely different scales, she was unwilling to see another soul she cared, for lost to alcohol. Treading carefully to not overstate what was said between the two friends, despite a burning temptation to put words into both of their mouths and make the exchange much more intense. That would understandably ease the way into a more frank discussion, but ran the risk that Mike and Billy might replay the conversation and then the exaggerations would only serve to undermine any progress that had been made. Although Billy would have no recollection of the exchange with Mike, he would try to play it down or even deny what he had said then the whole thing would die a death. By sticking exactly to the words Mike had used then Anne Mette knew she was on solid ground. She therefore related it word for word and what Mike had said to her after Billy had left, exceptionally, even saying ' being a cunt', which never normally passed her lips, in any language.

Billy looked suitably sheepish when she finished her account.

"Sounds like I was a real prick last night."

Anne Mette remained silent and non-committal. This was the vital point in the conversation for her, the tipping point. At this juncture it could go either way. Either Billy would admit that his conduct was unacceptable and pledge to make changes or he would just laugh the whole thing off as errant behaviour and carry on as before. Billy was silent for a long time as he thought about what had happened. He was struggling to even recapture one shred of a memory of the exchange that had just been described to him. His whole memory was a blank. That the incidents of the latter part of the previous evening were a total blank was worrying for Billy. He had suffered from memory loss in the past as a result of alcohol and on one occasion it had resulted in a potentially life threatening experience. Possibly on that occasion, the fact that he was virtually unconscious and unable to fight back might have been what saved his life. This was probably his most dangerous encounter, but on reflection there had been plenty of other embarrassing incidents. Most of these had also happened after he had been drinking Arac in large quantities, but the unavailability of Arac in the UK had not stopped these occurring. They just occurred less frequently.

Billy's first thought was maybe he should cut down on his Arac consumption. Switch to another drink of choice like vodka; all the time in the back of his mind he could hear Mel's accusations and they were becoming louder and louder. He tried shutting them out, but they wouldn't go away. For a while, they faded, only to return and each time, louder than the last. Did he really have a problem with alcohol? If he did then he was not about to admit it to anyone, especially not someone like Anne Mette, who he had only known for a few short weeks. He resolved to try and keep an eye on what he was drinking, try and control his intake. Billy didn't realise what an impossible and thankless task that would be. Maybe if he had spoken to Anne Mette she, with her close personal experience, would have been able to set him right, but instead Billy shrugged his shoulders and got up out of bed.

"I think we need to go and find some breakfast."

As he spoke he was facing away from the bed, so he didn't see the expression pass across Anne Mette's face or the way her shoulders suddenly dropped in despair. If he had caught sight of that, he might have returned to the bed, had a serious talk about his problem, but instead he looked around the room for his clothes.

"I do hope you are going to put some clothes on before you head for the dining room."

Behind him Anne Mette, having recovered from her momentary disappointment, was now trying to put a brave face on things. She was up and out of bed now as well and hunting around for her underwear among the sheets.

"I hung your shorts and shirt outside the door last night. They should be dry now." She said over her naked shoulder.

Billy didn't seem too concerned about his nakedness as he walked over to the door and threw it open and stepped out onto the veranda to collect his shorts. No one was waiting outside the room and Billy collected his clothes and came back inside.

In a few moments they were both dressed and heading off in the direction of the dining room. In the dining room the breakfast meal was in full swing. Billy collected his tray and went straight for the hot eggs. Piling the plate high with several scoopfuls of scrambled eggs, before adding slices of bread and a finishing off with a topping of mixed cucumber and tomatoes. Anne Mette followed his lead and they both took a seat at a table together. There was no sign of Mike or Yara and Yossi was not in the room either. There were a couple of volunteers, sat at one table drinking coffee and smoking, but none of them were the ones that they had met the previous afternoon. Billy munched slowly through his food, grateful that it was slowly filling the gaping void left by last night's vomiting, but he was not really tasting or particularly enjoying the meal.

He was distracted. Mentally he was making a list of the people he should seek out today and apologise to. Obviously, Mike was top of the list, but Yossi as the host for last night was a close second. He knew that if he waited here in the dining room there was as strong chance that both of them would turn up, but he was not sure that he wanted his apology to be a public one; he began to think about where he could find the two people concerned. He knew that this early in the morning Yossi would normally be doing his rounds of the various work places, mostly checking up that his volunteers had shown up on time and in a fit state for work. One thing he had remembered from last night, was that Yossi had said in this current crop of volunteers, the no-shows were almost non-existent. Billy guessed that Mike, if he was working, would have re-joined the irrigation team. They sometimes came in for breakfast, if they were working in one of the nearby field systems. If they were further away, they ate breakfast in the field kitchen. This was a basic camp style breakfast cooked over an open fire, but usually the eggs were fresh, hot and straight from the pan, not left under a heater to congeal, like here in the dining room. Billy didn't want to hang around the dining room on the off chance that Mike would turn up. He wanted, above all, to locate and apologise to Yossi.

He took a chance and while he was up at the counter making himself a fresh cup of coffee, he passed by the volunteer table. There were a half dozen volunteers sitting there now drinking hot drinks and smoking cigarettes. Occasionally one or other would make a comment and someone else would respond, but on the whole they looked like a soulless bunch. Billy placed his coffee on the table and leaned over it.

"Anyone here know where I can find Yossi?"

A couple of the volunteers looked up at the interruption, a mixture of annoyance and intrigue on their faces. No one said anything at first then one exhaled his cigarette smoke.

"You a new volunteer?"

Billy toyed briefly with the idea of saying yes, just to see what was said. He decided that this current crew didn't look the sort that could take a joke, so he decided to play it straight.

"Ex-volunteer actually, I was here a few years back."

The speaker considered his answer for a moment before responding.

"Well he might be here in a few minutes as a couple of us don't have a work assignment for today, but I couldn't say for definite."

Billy guessed that vague promise was the best he was going to get, so he smiled and thanked them for their help, scooped up his coffee and returned to where Anne Mette was sitting alone.

A few people coming in for breakfast, mostly those who had not been at the party last night, but recognised Billy from before, stopped at his table to say hello. Most wanted to know if he was back and staying for a while, others wanted to know what he had been doing since his departure, but all seemed pleased to see him. Anne Mette made some comment about how many of the people, the members, knew and recognised Billy. She found this a little strange after her time on Sde Avram as she didn't know a single member personally. She was probably totally unknown, as an individual, to all but maybe three members. She was certainly not on first name terms with a single member of the Sde Avram community. Billy was trying to explain the difference in the relationship between the members and the volunteers on Tel Boker, how it was not unusual to be invited to their homes and to be made to feel part of the family, when he was engulfed from behind in a pair of slender, tanned and muscular arms.

A familiar perfume filled his nostrils and a warm cheek was pressed close to his. Billy knew who it was before she opened her mouth to speak. He turned slightly and started to stand and the arms stayed around his neck and a lithe body was pressed against his in an intimate embrace.

"Hello Dafna."

Billy tried to get his arms around her waist in order to move her away to arms-length, but she clung tight to him for a few moments more, before she released him and took a step back of her own accord. She still clung to his upper arms as she looked at him with shining eyes.

"My god you are still such a handsome lad", she said, not caring who overheard her comments.

Billy had the good grace to blush red and he stammered a little as he tried to introduce Anne Mette to his ex-lover. On the bus trip down he had skirted around the nature of his relationship with Dafna. There had been a couple of pictures of her in his collection, but he had not felt comfortable elaborating on his illicit affair. He had been honest with Anne Mette about all the other girlfriends, whose pictures were in the photo album, but for some reason he had omitted any details about Dafna. She had broken her embrace to greet Anne Mette and then as quickly as she had arrived, so she was gone leaving Billy and Anne Mette both looking at each other.

"She seemed more than pleased to see you. I think if I wasn't here she would have had you over the table. Want to tell me about her?"

Billy sank back into his seat after looking around to see who had witnessed the scene. Thankfully most people seemed to have either missed or ignored Dafna's little outburst.

"No, not really."

He looked across the table and saw a look of disappointment pass across Anne Mette's face.

"Oh, all right. But trust me I am not proud of myself."

"Why not? She is a stunning looking woman. Did you sleep with her?"

Billy nodded his head.

"Yes a couple of times. That wasn't the problem."

A look of realisation replaced the sad look on her face.

"Oh, don't tell me. She is married."

"Was married, she's divorced."

"But she 'was' married when you had your little affair?"

Anne Mette had made the little quote marks in the air when she had said the word 'was'. Billy thought it was better to tell Anne Mette the whole story, so he went into it in some detail. Anne Mette had listened to what Billy had to say and at the end she had merely looked up at Billy and without any trace of jealousy had simply stated.

"I think she has still got feelings for you."

Billy was about to open his mouth to reassure her that the feelings were not mutual when Yossi appeared by their table.

"You were looking for me?"

Billy stood up and faced his old friend. The two of them had been through plenty of things together over the years and Billy liked to think that their friendship had endured its fair share of ups and downs, but right now standing there Billy was unsure what to say.

"Look, Yossi, about last night. I am really sorry I acted the way I did. I was drunk and I know that was no excuse for my behaviour, but please ..."

"It's okay Randell, relax. I am not mad at you."

Yossi cracked a smile and reached out to clasp Billy by the upper arm. He gave the limb a powerful squeeze. Billy felt relief flood through his body and his knees weakened forcing his to make a grab for the table to support himself.

"But next time you storm off from a party and leave a young lady alone," he nodded his head in the direction of Anne Mette across the table, "I will personally hunt you down and put a bullet in each of your kneecaps."

He patted the service issue pistol that was holstered at his hip as if to emphasise the point. Billy smiled weakly and sat down.

"What have you two got planned for the day? Sightseeing tour?"

Billy nodded.

"Well if you want to use one of the jeeps to get around then drop by the office and I will tell them to give you the keys. I have gotta run, need to get some volunteers out to the avocado orchards. See you later."

He waved over his shoulder as he strode off across the dining room. Anne Mette spoke first.

"He's a remarkable man and he seems to have a soft spot for you. I would have been furious with you if I had been the host last night".

Billy looked up and smiled.

"I think someone else has made an impression".

Billy looked long at hard at her, a big smile on his face.

"After all it was me he was threatening to shoot in the kneecaps."

Anne Mette smiled as she blushed.

"Quite right too."

## Chapter Fourteen

After a whirlwind tour around the kibbutz in an open jeep, Billy and Anne Mette arrived back at the dining room in time for lunch. Billy opted to join the large group of volunteers at their communal table and they made space to allow the two newcomers to join them. They seemed a little livelier over lunch, than they had been at breakfast and there was more banter and joking between them. One or two of them started asking Billy about life as a volunteer when he had been on Tel Boker before. They listened politely as Billy described the highlights and lowlights of his time as a volunteer. At its highest level there had been close to a hundred volunteers occupying all the rooms in the volunteer area. With that number there had usually been some of them ready to party every night and the area where they had built a fire pit and set up the stereo speakers was usually buzzing until the early hours of most mornings.

As Billy was telling his story he looked around and noticed that whilst one or two of the volunteers were looking disapprovingly at the tales of drunken debauchery there were a couple who had an envious look in their eyes. Billy wondered if they had ventured out here with stories of drunken fun ringing in their ears only to find that life on kibbutz was not quite as wild as they had been led to believe. And now here they were sitting being told stories of exactly that kibbutz life they had been expecting. Their friends back home had not been lying to them. It appeared that this life was theirs for the taking if they could just make it happen. Billy had often had a theory about catalysts, people that could make things occur out of nothing, just by being present. He did not consider he was such a person, but he had met plenty of them over the years. It was too old fashioned to call them the life and soul of the party, because often they were the polar opposite, but around them and under their direction, things seemed to happen. Billy placed his cutlery on his plate and pushed it to one side. He relaxed back in his chair and lit a cigarette. He took a moment to look around the table. Some of the volunteers were talking among themselves, others were still watching Billy intently, vague looks of hope on their faces. Billy decided to see just how far he could push this thing.

"We could have a party tonight?"

"Tonight?"

This from one of the people who had obviously not fallen under Billy's spell.

"We have work tomorrow," added another.

There was a general nodding of heads around the table showing that a majority agreed with the speaker. Billy was about to give the whole idea up as a lost cause, when one of the others, someone who as far as he was aware, had remained non-committal and silent on the subject until now, spoke up.

"We could have a party, but we haven't got any booze and the shop doesn't open today."

This was something Billy could help them out with. Courtesy of Yossi he was still in possession of the Jeep and the keys. He pulled them out and dangled the ignition key in front of them.

"If you've got the cash I've got the wheels."

Billy wasn't actually sure how long he could hang onto the Jeep for, but he figured a little trip across the fields to the local petrol station, which had a small mini-market attached to it, would only take them an hour at the most and he could give the keys back to Yossi later on. They made the necessary arrangements and Billy agreed to pick them up from outside the dining room as soon as their shift finished at two.

There were three lads waiting for him, kicking their heels and looking furtive. Each was carrying a large holdall over one shoulder. Although the offer had been made in general Billy was secretly pleased that there were only three takers. This meant they could all fit inside the cab and there would be no need for anyone to ride out the back. Although most of the journey would be on Tel Boker land, there was one short stretch where they had to travel on the highway and Billy didn't want to get a ticket for carrying passengers illegally.

When Billy had pulled up in front of the loading bay at the back of the kitchen, they all glanced around as if to see who was watching them, before slinging their bags in the back and piling into the cab of the jeep. They found places among the detritus that seemed to fill the front and back of these kibbutz cars. There were old and broken bits of irrigation equipment, rusty tools, coils of wire and as usual a very large lump hammer. This was the kibbutzniks' tool of choice for most situations. If it was stuck then hit it hard. If it didn't move after that then hit it harder or get a bigger hammer and a cold chisel.

Billy didn't know their names, but they were friendly enough to introduce themselves. In the back seat there was Aaron, a dark haired and dark eyed north Londoner. With a name like Aaron, Billy guessed he was from one or other of the Jewish communities that populated that part of the capital. He was not wrong. Aaron said he was from Stamford Hill although he was quick to point out he came from a very secular family, not one of the strictly religious Hassidic families that seemed to pour onto the streets on Fridays. Beside him in the backseat was Henk, whose thick accent when he spoke English made him a little difficult to understand. Henk hailed from the Netherlands. His hair was dark brown and his eyes were blue. He was the only one without slightly damp hair as he had finished work much earlier than the others. The first milking shift of the day, at the Refet, finished at noon, so he had plenty of time to go back to his room, shower and change his clothes before meeting Billy. The last passenger was simply known as Dog. Billy didn't press for a real name, it wasn't necessary, so when Dog introduced himself as simply 'Dog', Billy had shaken the offered hand and left it at that. Dog was Australian, with Blonde curly hair that fell forward into his eyes all the time. He was short and very well-muscled and had forearms like small tree trunks. His biceps bulged out of the cut off sleeves of his t-shirt. Dog was relatively new to Tel Boker, he had only arrived a week ago, so he was still trying to find his feet.

As they set off it was Dog that was most effusive in his thanks to Billy for giving them a ride. He was also very much in favour of the party idea and he wanted to discuss the other preparations with Billy. He saw Billy as the man with the plan and was keen to pick his brains for ideas and inspiration. Billy for his part was not keen to impose any pre-formed ideas on them. He wanted them to plan and execute the party themselves. This would make it real for them and might mean that they would continue to have parties after he left them. Billy drove across the kibbutz heading for the back gate. From there it was possible to head across some of the inner fields and then across the main road and onto the petrol station forecourt. After they arrived, they climbed out and headed into the cool air-conditioned atmosphere of the mini-market.

This place was bigger in actual floor space than the shop on Tel Boker. It had a wider range of goods on sale, but funnily enough, now he could compare it, not as big as the kibbutz shop on Sde Avram. The four lads made a beeline for the alcohol shelves and began loading bottles into a shopping trolley. Aaron was working from a list and comparing prices with the amounts of money he had collected from people. This was obviously taking extra time but Billy was relaxed. He was sure Yossi would forgive him if he was a little late in returning the Jeep. He hooked a couple of bottles of Arac off the shelf and dropped them in the cart. Although he had mentally made a decision to take things a bit easier tonight, there was no point in running short of supplies. Henk was busy loading trays of foreign beer in cans onto the bottom of the trolley. Billy was amazed. These guys were obviously bent on going for it tonight.

He began to think about how he could ensure that the party really went with a bang. They would be battling against the 'single bottle of lager' group and the 'we want to go to bed early' team, but he felt sure they could make a go of it. He had a few ideas up his sleeve and a few people he could reach out to. Some of the younger kids had now grown up enough to be invited to the party, so he decided to drop by their block later and extend an invite. He would need to clear it with the volunteers, beforehand, but it was something they could discuss on the way back.

As they loaded their purchases into the back of the jeep, Billy brought up the subject of extending the invite to certain non-volunteers. He was surprised by the reaction he received from the other three. All of them seemed amazed that the youngsters from the kibbutz, would want to come and slum it with the volunteers. This reaction puzzled Billy, so as they set off, he started to probe for information. What he heard actually amazed him. It appeared that there had been a major schism, between the volunteers and the younger members at some time in the recent past. Although all of those present were very sketchy on the actual details, none could claim to have been present when the split happened, but he heard them using phrases like, 'they hate us' and 'they are so up their own arses', 'so elite', and 'they look down their noses at us'. This was not what Billy had experienced, on Tel Boker. There had always been a smattering of kibbutz kids and young members hanging out around the volunteer blocks in his time. He guessed, he was going to have his work cut out to get to the bottom of this. He had already seen a couple of familiar faces in the dining room at lunchtime. He would drop by the kids block later and get the low down; if fences needed mending then he hoped he had the skills and reputation to do so.

He dropped the three off at volunteer central, with their purchases, then parked the jeep back in the main car park. He handed the keys in at the office and filled in the mileage forms. When asked, he told the staff to charge the mileage to Yossi's account. This had obviously been agreed in advance, because there were no questions asked. Now free for the afternoon, Billy decided to go back to the room, try to link up with Anne Mette and see if she would accompany him on his diplomatic mission to the kids block.

When he approached the room, he could see there was someone deep in conversation with Anne Mette. With their back to him and partially in the shadows, Billy couldn't make out who it was? As he got closer, the person turned slightly. It was Mike. The two of them looked to be in the middle of an intense conversation as their heads were almost touching. If Billy hadn't known that Mike was absolutely crazy about Yara, he might have been more suspicious, because of the body language, between the two of them. He called out a greeting. The two of them turned to face him and then sprang apart, like they had just received an electric shock. This confused Billy, but he shrugged it off. He knew and trusted Mike, absolutely. Both were a little cagey as he walked onto the veranda, as if they had been caught with their hands in the cookie jar. Billy went up to Anne Mette and bent to kiss her. She turned her head and Billy's lips just brushed her cheek. This confused him too? He did not make a fuss in front of Mike, as this might end up embarrassing everyone. There was probably a very good reason for Anne Mette's reaction. He would ask her about it when they were alone. He had more important things to worry about right now, than whether he had said or done something to upset his girlfriend.

"Mike, I am glad you dropped by. I was going to come and find you later. I need to say sorry for last night. I overreacted. I was completely out of order."

Mike raised his hand palm outwards.

"Forget it, no harm, no foul."

He spoke the words, but Billy didn't detect any warmth in his voice. There was no forgiveness in his eyes, as Billy met his gaze. Clearly the events of the previous night, had left more than superficial scars on their friendship. They had been here before. It was impossible to have been friends this long without conflicts, some minor, others more serious. The two of them had always managed to resolve any past issues and to figuratively kiss, make up and move on, even from the most major of arguments. So, Billy didn't pay too much attention to this treatment from Mike. He didn't brush it under the carpet, completely. Again, it was not something to be discussed openly. Rather when the two of them were alone. That opportunity would come faster than Billy had reckoned.

"I have asked Anne Mette's permission to kidnap you for an hour. She's agreed."

'There you go', thought Billy, 'there was a perfectly reasonable reason for the two of them to have been in deep conversation. Mike was asking a favour.

"Let's go for a walk." Mike moved to leave the veranda.

"I just want to drop there off."

Billy held up the carrier bag with the Arac in it.

"And it might be a good idea to pick up some water if we are going far."

Billy pushed open the door and entered the gloom of the room. He placed the Arac bottles on the table, opened the fridge and pulled out a two-litre bottle of water that had been chilling there since before breakfast. He closed the door then re-joined Mike and Anne Mette on the veranda. This time, they didn't leap apart like scalded cats. Billy and Mike set off up the road that led to the top of the kibbutz.

At the top of the hill, the highest point of the kibbutz, stood the old watchtower. It had been one of the first structures built, by the founding members, as protection from incursions. It had now fallen into disrepair and the metal supports were coated with brown rust. On the top, the cabin was showing signs of age and weathering as one or two of the windows were broken or missing. Billy noticed that a safety conscious member had even thought it was a good idea, to wind some red and white tape around the rusted ladder about three metres up, vainly hoping, to stop people climbing up and thus avoiding the risk of an accident or serious injury. From the top of the tower, the view of the kibbutz and the surrounding countryside was spectacular. A favourite must-have photo for all the volunteers. Billy's photo album, had a couple of panoramic shots taken from the top of the watchtower and a rather stunning photo of a heavy red sun, hovering moodily, just above the horizon, partially shrouded by some darker blue-grey clouds. It was a shame to think that in a few short years the possibility to document such natural beauty might be curtailed if the whole structure collapsed. 'Still', thought Billy, 'it's all about progress and that is a train that cannot be stopped.'

He was mulling over the thought of progress when Mike suddenly stopped and sat down on a nearby rock. Even from ground level there was a breath-taking view below of the kibbutz fields. At this time with the strong afternoon light it was possible to see all the way to the border fence. When Billy screwed up his eyes, he was convinced he could see the sun glinting off the wire of the individual links making them shine like diamonds. The two friends sat in silence for a while. Billy tried to think of things to say. Nothing was springing to mind. He had already tried to apologise for the previous evening and that had led nowhere. He reached into his shirt, fished out a cigarette and lit it. He sat and puffed on it for a few minutes.

The overpowering silence was sucking all the joy out of his day. He couldn't take much more of this. He was going to have to say something and soon.

"How's Mel?"

'At last', Billy thought to himself.

"She was fine last time I saw her."

Billy's tone was flat and non-committal. Mike picked up on this and came straight back with another question.

"So you didn't part on the best of terms?"

"You could say that."

"So she wasn't too happy about you coming back out here?"

"Shit Mike!. Just spit out what you want to say. Stop pussying around."

Billy's voice had just gone up a notch.

"Have you been speaking to Mel?"

Mike looked over at his friend.

"I got a letter from her just before we left Australia. That was the last time. I sent her a card to tell her we were heading back here, but I haven't heard anything since."

That answer seemed to mollify Billy a little. He stubbed out his cigarette in the sand making sure the last glow of the embers were extinguished properly. At this time of the year, all the undergrowth was as dry as dust, like a tinderbox and ready to burst into flames at the smallest spark. Satisfied there was no danger from his dog end he cast it aside into the sand at his feet.

"Why did you come back to Israel Billy? You had a good job at home. Your own place. I thought you were on the way back up. You even had that young lady doctor, Saskia, in tow."

Billy suddenly realised that Mike knew nothing of what had transpired between him and Saskia. Mike could see the mention of her name caused a dark shadow to pass over his friend's face. The cocky smile disappeared and his eyes went cold. Mike tried to keep his enquiry friendly and light.

"So, what happened with her?"

"Seems like I wasn't her only patient." Billy's riposte was tinged with bitterness.

Mike took a moment to decipher what Billy was talking about.

"Ouch. How did you find out?"

"Oh, I went around there to surprise her and got a bigger one of my own. There was more than one doctor in the house and it looked like they had both been practicing their bedside manner."

Billy paused for effect.

"With each other."

"Oh man. That's a really shit way to find out. Don't tell me you threw it all in and came back here because of a broken heart? Not the Billy I know?"

"No Mike, you are right. There was a lot more to it than Dr Saskia."

Billy pushed himself up from the ground and began to pace back and forth in front of where Mike was sat. He didn't say anything, moving to and fro, taking time to gather his thoughts. He wanted this speech to be impressive. It was to explain once and for all, to Mike and also to himself just why he had packed everything in and plotted a course back here to Israel. On a couple of occasions he stood still and turned as if he was about to say something. Then stopped himself at the last minute, shook his head once and resumed pacing. Mike screwed the cap off the water bottle and took a long drink. He wiped his mouth with the back of his hand and waited patiently for his friend to speak. He was seriously worried. He had known Billy for a long time and he had never known him to be this lost for words. Whatever was troubling him was definitely effecting him profoundly.

This worried Mike. In a strange way, he felt guilty that he had abandoned Billy after all the years they had spent together. From their very first day in school when Mike had prevented Billy getting a real kicking from some other schoolkids, until the day when Billy had finally stepped up and repaid him, by clocking their works supervisor over the back of the head, with a shovel, to prevent Mike getting his face reduced to a pulp with a bunch of keys, they had always had each other's backs. Billy had taken the fall, when dope had been discovered in their room only a few hundred metres, from where they were sat right now. Mike had stood in the morgue and waited to identify Billy's dead body. There was no denying their lives had been intrinsically linked. Now after all this shared history they found themselves together here on this hilltop, both struggling to talk to each other. Billy was striding back and forth, unable to articulate his feelings. Mike was sat mute, equally incapable of encouraging his friend to unburden himself. Right now Mike was feeling a huge degree of separation and it bothered him. He opened his mouth to say something just as Billy did the same. They both paused. Mouths wide open, syllables rooted on their tongues.

"You first," said Billy.

"No, you can start". Mike made a sweeping gesture with his arm.

Billy crouched down in the dust and began to talk.

"Over the last few months, I have been feeling increasingly disconnected from, everything. Disconnected from people, the people I have always considered to be my friends. Disconnected from everything about my life. I was doing a job, and believe me it was a great job, but it brought me no satisfaction, no sense of belonging. The people I was spending time with seemed to matter less and less. They became irrelevant to me. They didn't understand me anymore. I just wanted them to leave me alone to live my life, but they kept interfering. It was as if they didn't understand. Now I don't know what happened to me, while I was living out here? Something changed in me and the people back home just cannot seem to understand, the new me. Even worse, they don't want to understand, this new me. I have to return to what I was before, to fit back in to their idea of who I am."

Mike sat, stunned to silence. He replayed Billy's speech in his head, trying to grasp the relevant points and wondering, which of these people Billy felt he was? He had noticed many changes in Billy in the time they had been away. When it came to his relationship with Billy, Mike was very rarely honest, even with himself, but he liked the old, the pre-Israel Billy. That Billy had been predictable, suggestible, and very easy to manage. Mike knew that a degree of that malleability had stemmed from their different social circumstances. Where Billy was often broke by mid-week, Mike always had a couple of crisp tenners in his wallet, usually courtesy of his dad. He had never used his financial superiority as a weapon or control mechanism over Billy or at least not knowingly. Now, was he one of those people, who Billy felt were trying to control him?

"Is that why you chose to come back to Israel?"

"That was part of the reason. It's true that while I am here I feel so much more alive, so much more of a real person, someone who counts and is valuable. Back in London I was just another body on the tube or the bus, squeezed into a metal can to be transported a short distance, before being spat out on the pavement at my destination along with all the other waste matter. Faceless clones, faceless drones, cogs in the machine. It was like back home, the whole thing was a badly lit black and white movie, one where the film stock has been slightly overexposed and the pictures are all cloudy. Out here, by contrast, it is glorious Technicolor, 3D, Cinemascope, Panavision, you name it, glorious rich colours, Dolby sound. It's the Wizard of Oz to the Jazz Singer and I mean the original not the remake."

Billy grinned at Mike. He was getting some of his old spirit back, warming to the theme.

"I mean there was one incident back home, at a party, where the host actually accused me of being a thief and threw me out. Well actually we left before they called the police."

"Why did they do that? What did you steal?"

"Nothing."

Billy suddenly sounded petulant like a naughty boy caught covered in chocolate.

"Well I lifted a bottle of scotch off the drinks table, but I was sharing it around," he added defensively.

Mike nodded his head in understanding. He knew that Billy didn't have a single criminal bone in his body and if he said he was sharing the scotch then that was what he was doing or had been intending to do. However Mike did notice that the argument had been over booze and its availability. He had also noticed the pile of empty bottles that had accumulated in Billy's room in the short time he had been back on Tel Boker. This was in his eyes a bit of a worrying development. Billy had developed a taste for the Arac during his last stay and there had been many drunken and crazy nights as a result of over indulgence, but Mike got the feeling now that Billy was not drinking to create memories, but drinking to forget. That was dangerous.

Mike knew only too well the perilous situations that such behaviour had caused, for Billy, as he had told him the whole story of what had happened on the fateful night in Eilat. That had been as a result of using alcohol to try and forget his life's troubles. The problem Mike faced was that he was unsure how he could broach this subject and get Billy to open up about his feelings without provoking a repeat of the scene from the previous evening. He knew that right now Billy was sober and that a 'sober Billy' might be less volatile, but nevertheless he still didn't want their conversation to break down and for Billy to storm off in a huff. He decided to put this subject aside for a moment and maybe feel Billy out slowly and then renew the discussion later on.

"So what did Mel say when you told her you were coming back?"

Billy looked over at his best friend and began to shake his head slowly.

"Oh man, she was not best pleased. Started yelling at me about not being ready for it and that this time I was going for all the wrong reasons. I can't really remember if the word 'coward' came up, but she was accusing me of running away".

"So she wasn't behind the idea?"

"Dead set against it."

Billy thought back to the exchange that had taken place between him and Mel in the flat on the day he moved out. She had gone as far as to accuse Billy of being a hopeless alcoholic. He would struggle to fit in back in Israel, just like in London, and that running back to the kibbutz lifestyle was not the answer. He didn't feel that Mel's analysis was justified and so he gave Mike a watered down version of their argument, focusing more on the criticisms that Mel had levelled against Mark and only touching briefly on Mel's feelings about Billy not fitting in. Mike listened to the account of the argument and Billy's description of his final few days in London.

"I bet you were glad to get back on the plane?" he said at the end of Billy's account.

"How are things working out with Mark?"

"He's okay, I suppose. He is a bit too keen to be a volunteer. I think he heard too many stories before he got here and now he spends most of his time trying to recreate someone else's kibbutz experience instead of having his own."

Mike nodded his head. He understood exactly what Billy was driving at. They had both seen their fair share of those type of volunteers. The ones who wanted to have the kibbutz experience their friends back home had told them about. Trying to follow this method usually would only lead to disappointment. Every kibbutz was different, every group of volunteers was different. You only had to look at the current group here on Tel Boker and compare them to the group from previous years to see that. As different as chalk and cheese, but both groups would return home with stories to share with their friends and family.

Billy's thoughts were the same at that precise moment. With his ideas for this evening's entertainment and how some of the volunteers might have a slightly different version of the story to tell after tonight was over. Billy smiled to himself. Mike caught sight of it.

"What's so amusing, Randell?"

"Nothing, nothing at all."

"Come on Billy. That was one of your evil, I have a plan for mischief, smiles."

Billy tried to wipe the smile off his face, but Mike was right he did have a plan for mischief and he hoped that it would all fall into place in a couple of hours. He decided to come clean with Mike and told him about the plans for the party.

"Christ Billy! What have we just been saying about trying to manufacture an experience?"

"I know Mike. These guys practically begged me to organise a party. I couldn't turn them down. In my defence, all I have done is driven them over to the gas station to buy booze, whatever happens or doesn't happen tonight, this will be all their own work."

"Or is this just another excuse for you to get shit-faced?"

Mike's words were harsh and they stung Billy, harder than he had believed was possible. He visibly flinched at Mike's accusation and Mike noticed the effect his words had on Billy.

"Look mate. I'm sorry. Didn't mean that to come out the way it did and to tell you the truth I am worried about you."

Billy nodded. He understood what Mike was saying, even if he didn't like the way he was saying it. Mike was not finished.

"Why on earth didn't you come back to Tel Boker?"

"Because I wanted a fresh start. I thought it would be good for me and fairer for Mark. We were both going to a place where neither of us had history."

"But why did you pick a kibbutz on the northern border? Things are getting out of control up there."

"We had a missile attack the other week, but that was no big thing."

"You haven't heard the news this morning?"

"No, why? What's happened?"

"They had multiple attacks overnight. Several missiles were fired over the border from Lebanon. The Northern Command are starting to rattle their sabres. They reckon it could all kick off in a week or so."

"Was anyone hurt?" Billy was concerned for the people left behind on Sde Avram.

"No reports of casualties but there was some local damage in places."

"Shit." Billy stood up again and began his pacing.

He turned back to face Mike.

"I am not about to run away because of a few fireworks."

"Billy, you might not have a choice. If things get really nasty they might evacuate all non-Israelis."

Billy folded his arms across his chest. He was no coward. He had never run away from a fight in his life, but he realised that in this case he might not have any choice. He suddenly felt an urgent need to get back to Sde Avram; find out what was really being said and what might happen. He was due to spend another couple of days here on Tel Boker, but he made a snap decision to cut short his stay and would return up north in the morning. He told Mike of his decision. It was not well received by his oldest friend. Mike of all people knew Billy best. He was not a coward, but he did possess a stubborn streak a mile wide. Secretly he admired his friend's courage.

"Well just so you know, Yossi asked me to talk to you about you coming back to Tel Boker. He told me last night that if the subject came up in conversation then I was to make you an offer of a place back here. The door is always open, just turn up here and he will handle all the paperwork".

Billy listened carefully while Mike spoke. At the end he threw his head back and roared with laughter. Mike pulled an annoyed face. He had made a heartfelt appeal and it looked like Billy was laughing in his face. Billy looked over at his friend and saw the disapproving look. He stopped laughing and managed to get a hold of himself.

"Maybe Yossi should wait until tomorrow before he makes me an offer to come back. When some of the vollies don't turn up or are hungover in the morning. He might have another opinion about offering me a place here."

Mike had to smile as he realised that Billy had not been laughing at him, but at the absurdity of the volunteer leader offering a place to a potential troublemaker.

"Well whether you decide to return here permanently or not, I am going to need you back here in a month's time."

"Why? What's happening in a month's time?"

"Yara and I are going to tie the knot."

Billy stopped in mid stride and dropped to his haunches like he had been hit right between the eyes by a stone.

"Whoa, where did that suddenly come from?"

"There was no 'suddenly' about it. We have been planning this for months now. It was one of the main reasons we came back to Israel. Yara wanted to get married here on the kibbutz."

"Do your parents know?"

"Yep, the whole family have already booked their flights and accommodation. They have decided to stay for a month and have a holiday at the same time."

Billy was silent. This was great news for Mike and Yara, even if it was another degree of separation for him from his old friend.

"Billy, I wanted to bring you up here today to ask you something, a favour. Would you be my best man?"

When he thought about it later Billy realised that Mike's request was the culmination of their many years of close friendship. For Mike to ask Billy to stand by his side and support him as he took this next step in his life was an outstanding honour. However his reaction when Mike dropped the bomb was less than honourable.

"Who me? Best man? I can think of a few people who might disagree with you on that score. Isn't there anyone better suited to the job? Am I your last hope?"

Each question, although delivered by Billy in an upbeat tone of voice and with a smile on his lips, was received by Mike as a stinging rebuke, causing him to flinch each time. Mike eventually lost it.

"Shit! For fuck's sake Billy! Do you ever take anything seriously? I come up here, lay my heart on the line. Ask you to be a part of the biggest day of my life. You rub my fucking nose in the dirt. Randell you're a cunt."

Mike pushed himself to his feet and stormed off back down the hill. Billy struggled to his feet and in a matter of a few metres had caught up with his friend. He made a grab for Mike's elbow, but Mike shrugged him off. Billy grabbed again, this time clenching the arm in a much tighter grip. Although Mike was taller than Billy by a head and bulkier in his upper body, Billy possessed a wiry strength with muscles developed from years of manual work. When Billy dug in his heels and stopped, Mike, despite his best endeavours was forced to a standstill too.

"Just hold on a moment mate."

Billy's voice was calm, like the soothing tone an adult would use with a frightened or terrified child. Despite Mike's recent outburst Billy wasn't about to take him to task about it. This was all about conciliation.

"I am sorry. Took me by surprise. No one has ever called me the best at anything apart from 'best at fucking things up'. Of course I will be your best man, even make an extra special effort not to lose the ring."

Billy's smile was lopsided, but he saw the anger drain from Mike's face. Mike released his arm from Billy's grip and aimed an open hand at the back of Billy's head. It was a friendly cuff, with no power behind it, just enough to mess up Billy's hair. The two friends squared up, fists raised in a mock fight, circling each other for a few moments shadow boxing with each other. They came together in a clinch, which turned into a back slapping hug.

"You know Randell, you can be a complete arsehole at times."

"I know mate, but I am your arsehole. No hang on. That didn't come out right. Ah fuck it! Let's go grab a beer and celebrate .My best mate is getting married and I am gonna be best man."

This last sentence was yelled out at the top of his lungs and the sound carried down into the kibbutz and echoed back off some of the buildings. The declaration probably woke a few people who were taking an afternoon siesta. A couple of the dogs tethered outside members' rooms started to bark and the general calm of the settlement was disturbed for a few moments. Mike had put his arm over Billy's shoulder and steered him back on to the track leading down the hill.

"Well if anyone didn't know I was getting married, they do now."

"Oh shit, Mike I am sorry. Was it still a secret?"

"You can never keep a secret on a place like this. You know that probably better than I do".

"You're so right, particularly in the summer when people sleep with their windows open." Billy laughed out loud.

## Chapter Fifteen

The bus pulled to a stop. Anne Mette was up, out the door and gone even before Billy had struggled to his feet and picked up his bag. Billy watched her back, departing, shrugged his shoulders and stepped down from the bus, into the afternoon sunshine.

"Fuck her."

He whispered under his breath and then realising there was no one around who could overhear him he repeated the statement in a normal voice. It felt good to vent his frustration. So he said the words again, slightly louder this time. The bus pulled away in a cloud of diesel fumes. Billy stood there for a moment and collected his thoughts.

"Fuck her," he said, one more time for good measure.

The wheels had come off their collective caravan of love soon after Mike had asked Billy to be best man at his nuptials. Instead of returning to the guest room and sharing that little nugget of information with Anne Mette, Billy had chosen to take a detour, around to the block of rooms occupied by some of the older teenage kibbutz kids. The invitation to the evening festivities had been well received by one and all and promises to turn up were made. He found no trace of any hostility towards the volunteers among the kibbutz youth, in fact there wasn't a single dissenting voice among them. Billy was therefore puzzled as to where this enmity had sprung from and none of the youngsters could shed any light on the subject. A few made comment about the volunteers being more detached than they were used to, but they had experienced enough transient friendships in their short lives that it didn't overly bother them.

After sharing a tin of Coke and a couple of cigarettes Billy set off on his way again. Now satisfied that he would not be the only person at the party Billy eventually made his way back to the guest room. The door of the room was firmly locked, from the inside and with the key still in the lock. This meant that from the outside Billy could not get his key in and therefore could not unlock the door. When he knocked a heavily accented Nordic voice told him to "go away" and no amount of pleading could get Anne Mette to change her mind. After ten minutes of pleading and knocking alternately, the knocking become progressively louder and heavier, Billy's knuckles were starting to hurt. He kicked the bottom of the door one last time in frustration, swore out loud when he hurt his toe and then turned on his heels and walked away.

He had nearly a whole packet of cigarettes but his Arac, all the bottles he possessed, were locked inside the room. He headed off in the direction of the volunteer block hoping that someone would be awake and he could cadge a drink off them. He didn't think Mike, after his long lecture earlier, would be happy about supplying the wherewithal for Billy to get off his face. The volunteers, on the other hand, who didn't really have a dog in this fight, might be a softer touch. That was of course if any of them were awake. He was lucky on that score. Not only were some of them not in the middle of their afternoon siesta, but they had decided to start the party early, so the Arac was already flowing. Billy explained briefly that he had been temporarily locked out of his room, without going into too much detail and was pleased when Henk one of the guys from the road trip earlier placed a bottle of Arac on the table and told Billy to help himself. Billy didn't need a second invitation.

When he returned to the room two hours later and found Anne Mette sitting outside on the veranda he was already pretty pissed. He said nothing to her, just walked past her and into the room. He made a beeline for the plastic bag containing the Arac bottles from the afternoon's road trip. He peered into the bag and saw that the two bottles were within, untouched. He grabbed the handles and then collected a fresh pack of Time cigarettes from the top of his daypack. He walked back outside. Anne Mette hadn't moved a muscle. She remained sitting on the green plastic garden chair, one tanned and lithe leg raised and her arms wrapped around the knee. Her cheek pressed close to her leg. Billy searched her face for any sign of distress. There were no traces of emotion, tears or even anger. There was nothing but an overwhelming Nordic calm. Billy placed the bag on the floor, leaned against the brick pillar that supported the roof and lit a cigarette. He remained silent watching the top of Anne-Mette's head. She looked up through her blonde fringe, her blue eyes looked cold and unforgiving.

"You've got what you came for?" She nodded at the bag on the floor at Billy's feet, "Although by the look of you, you don't need it."

"What do you mean?"

"Well if that pillar wasn't holding you up, you would be flat on your back. You are swaying like grass in a gale?"

She added something in her native tongue. It was obviously critical in nature, because it was delivered with a sneer and a twist of the upper lip.

"Are you going to give me the benefit of your Nordic wisdom, I am sure it was a worthy compliment and worth sharing."

Billy was beginning to get more than a little fed up with Anne Mette. This childish and needy behaviour was making him angry. He was starting to regret inviting her to come along on this trip. For the moment he completely forgot about the care she had shown him the previous night. It was as if that whole incident hadn't happened. Anne Mette looked bleakly at Billy. Her bottom lip was quivering slightly, a sure sign that tears would soon follow.

"You just abandoned me. Just disappeared off without a word."

"You knew where I was going. I was taking some people over to the petrol station."

"No after that."

"I was with Mike, you saw us both leave."

Billy was becoming exasperated now and his voice was rising in volume and sharpening in tone. The fact that Mike had been here and had most likely asked Anne Mette's permission to kidnap Billy for his special announcement seemed to have been conveniently forgotten?

"But Mike came back alone. There was no sign of you?"

"I had some other people to see. What did you think I was doing? Off shagging?"

"Well I don't know." The insecurity was evident in her voice. She knew Billy had a history on this kibbutz and she had witnessed, at first hand, the affection some members still held for him. It was quite possible in the intervening time for Billy to have paid a visit to Dafna's rooms and made love to her. The thought made her stomach hurt and she felt the emotion well up inside her. Tears started to slowly course down her cheeks, small twin trickles that caught the last of the evening sun and sparkled, alive.

"What is it with you and your petty jealousy? What do I have to do to convince you?" Billy was almost roaring with anger now and the intensity of Anne Mette's tears increased. Her shoulders were beginning to shake as the sobs wracked her body.

"I don't know?"

She bleated weakly as if it was some magic spell that could somehow deflect Billy's anger away.

"What don't you know?"

Mike's voice was loud enough to make both of them turn in his direction. He was standing a few metres away, his arms folded. Yara was at his side a worried expression on her face. Anne Mette sprang to her feet and rushed inside the room. She didn't want her distress to have such a public audience. Yara followed her through the door. She touched Billy's arm as she passed him. She wanted him to realise two things. She wasn't taking sides and that Billy should leave this to her.

"What was all that about?" Mike joined Billy on the porch.

"Lovers' tiff." Billy tried to pass it off lightly, then changed his mind.

"I got back to the room to find she had locked me out. She thought I was off shagging someone else?"

"Ah so your reputation as a lothario remains intact."

Mike smiled. Billy remained stern faced. He couldn't find amusement in anything right now. Yara came out of the room. The look on her face told them both that a crisis had been averted, but that it might take a little while to resolve the underlying issues.

"You two get off to the party, Anne Mette and I will join you in a bit. She needs to fix her makeup."

Yara held up her small make up bag for the two of them to see. Mike put his arm around Billy and steered him off the veranda.

"Come on Billy boy, let's leave the girl to their rituals."

Yara stuck her tongue out at Mike who laughed, loudly.

The party itself was a poor imitation of the wild nights that Billy and Mike had experienced the first time around on Tel Boker. Although the volunteers present had given it their all, they were to a large extent beginners at the game and not really sure of the rules. They had tried their hardest, but the result was a pale reflection. Billy had spent most of the evening chatting up one of the young volunteer girls and deliberately ignoring Anne Mette. She, for her part was trying to chew the face off of a young kibbutz lad. As Billy got progressively drunker, he started to loudly criticise Anne Mette for her behaviour and on one or two occasions, made lewd comments, about cradle snatching. The first time he got away with it. The second time one of the other Scandinavians present at the party provided a translation. This resulted in Anne Mette throwing a drink over Billy, before storming off into the darkness, hotly pursued by her new beau.

Billy guessed that he would again be locked out of the room or if the door was open then the bed might already be occupied. He had settled down and slept the night on the old hanging sofa that had stood outside his room in the old days. The lack of sleep had made it easy for Billy to spend most of the next day, while they crossed the country by the earliest bus, asleep. He awoke briefly when they changed Bus in Tel Aviv and grabbed a falafel at the bus station. He then slid low in his seat and slept all the way from Tel Aviv to Safed. For the last stretch of the journey, up to the kibbutz, Billy was awake. It was at the bus station in Safed, while they waited for their bus up to Sde Avram that Anne Mette, finally, broke the silence and announced that she thought it was a good idea if she and Billy parted. Billy was not about to disagree with her. He had already made up his mind that this was the only sensible outcome, though he had wanted, her, not him, to pull that trigger. He then endured a twenty minute lecture, on his failings as a potential partner, in complete silence. The bus then arrived and they were able to climb aboard. The change of situation seemed to quieten Anne Mette and they sat in a heavy silence, for the rest of their journey up to the northern border road.

Billy took advantage of the stillness to reflect back on what Anne Mette had said. She was clearly deeply troubled by Billy's behaviour over the past few days. It was only when she brought up the subject of her father and brother and their respective battles with addiction that Billy began to take anything she said seriously. The twin messages that the one life had ended in tragedy and the other, through tough love and rehab had had a happier outcome was not lost on Billy. The problem was he failed to see the connection between himself, a young man on the right side of thirty and an addled old man in his forties. With this image in his mind he could not easily identify with this tragic conclusion. He still felt he would be okay. If the end of the relationship with Anne Mette was a relief then the remainder of the journey back up to Sde Avram was the complete opposite. The shock came almost as soon as the bus left the Safed city limits. Billy was astonished by the change in the district, in the short time that they had been away. There was a marked increase in the number of military vehicles on the roads, most of them heading northwards and in some of the lay-bys along the route there were tanks and self-propelled guns parked up on their low-loader transporters. There was a general buzz of conversation on the bus and Billy welcomed the silence, between him and Anne Mette, because it meant he could listen in to some of the conversations taking place around him. He knew that for the most part it was just all gossip and speculation, but there were one or two worried passengers, voicing fears over a deterioration of the situation and the possible outbreak of war.

With these thoughts in his mind, he made his way down through the kibbutz to the volunteer's quarters. The place was largely deserted. This was to be expected this late in the afternoon, when volunteers were either sunning themselves by the pool or catching up on lost sleep in their rooms. Three hard-core drinkers were sitting in the shade of the first block of rooms downing bottles of cold beer, the dew of condensation visible on the outside of the glass.

"Got a spare one of those handy?"

Billy asked as he drew level with them. Adam, who was sitting with his back to the wall opened the top of the cooler box, he was leaning on, then popped the cap off a fresh bottle and passed it to Billy.

"Just seen Anne Mette go past breathing fire and smoke shooting out of her ears."

"You two fall out?"

"We broke up."

Billy took a mouthful of beer and folded his legs under him as he squatted down on the dry dusty grass and hard packed earth. He pulled a cigarette out of his pack, lit it, inhaled deeply and then exhaled the cloud of smoke.

"Apart from that, good trip?"

Paul was sitting next to Adam on the other side of the cooler box.

"Not bad. Caught up with my best mate. Hadn't seen him for about a year, so yeah it was good. What's been going on here?"

"Not much, same shit, different day." Adam sounded almost bored.

"They are getting their tits in a twist about the apple harvest, so it's all hands to the pumps on the orchard front."

David's heavy Welsh accent always made him sound gloomy.

"They're all worried we're all gonna leave, like."

Paul was quick to point out.

"If there's a shooting war then we might all have to leave."

Alcohol always made Adam's Scottish drawl more prominent.

"I wouldnae fass yourself."

Billy was intrigued by Adam's broad assessment and wonder why he had reached that conclusion. He felt he had to ask why Adam felt that way.

"What? You don't think it will get to that? I saw plenty of military hardware heading in this direction on the way up here, today"

"It's happened in the past according tae the locals. So it's no biggee." Adam responded as if this was the last thing to say on the matter. Others clearly didn't agree.

"So why are the diplomats visiting us, then?" Paul asked.

"Wait, what did you say?" Billy looked up at this comment.

"Yeah. We have had a couple of embassy officials sniffing around the place. No Brits, so far, just the Dutch and one from the Danish embassy, I think, but it might have been the Swedish, it's hard to tell with all that 'herdy-ferdy' they speak."

"So what are these guys doing?"

"Well according to Ari, the Dutch officials were doom and gloom mongering. They said if there is a war, then all flights from the Netherlands would be suspended and anyone left in the country would be stranded here without consular representation."
"Basically, a load of porky pies." Davey chipped in.
"Maybe we should wait and see what the blokes from the British Embassy have to say. They should be here any day now."

They all agreed they would wait and see what was said by their own people.

The message, when it was delivered a week later, was no different to the messages from other embassies, who had volunteers on Sde Avram. All these officials were touring all the northern kibbutzim and singing from the same hymn sheet. In the week, since Billy had returned from the south, circumstances had not improved, if anything they had deteriorated. There had been several prolonged missile attacks from over the border, with air raid sirens, alarms sounding and people hurrying to the shelters. The first couple of times these attacks had happened, they had been nerve wracking with people cowering, deep in the concrete structures, unsure of what they would return to, at the surface after the all-clear was sounded. When, after the first few attacks, the damage had been seen to be negligible, with many missiles either falling short of the border or flying wildly off target, the atmosphere relaxed. Retaliation from the Israeli side of the border had also been sporadic with only the occasional barrage of shelling or overflight by helicopters or fixed wing aircraft. This lack of a measured response was justified by the IDF, on the grounds that most of the attacks were being launched from populated areas like villages, the perpetrators using schools and hospitals, as launch sites. This meant that retaliation, without substantial collateral damage was very difficult. This lack of response didn't prevent the armed forces from deploying in large numbers. At times the road that ran along the border resembled a car park for armoured vehicles of all shapes and sizes as they were lined up nose to tail in ever lengthening convoys.

It was against this backdrop of a spiral towards open conflict, that the representatives of Her Majesty's Foreign and Diplomatic Corps arrived on Sde Avram to try and persuade any UK nationals, that now might be the appropriate time to make a run for home. Like all good imperialists, they adopted a divide and conquer approach. Instead of summoning all of the British nationals to a large gathering they dealt with them in smaller groups. They chose the middle of the afternoon to make their rounds, so found a number of the volunteers around the pool. Here, their light-weight tan linen suits looked completely out of place. Those not at the pool were taking advantage of the afternoon calm to catch up on some lost sleep; these volunteers were cornered in their individual rooms. Billy was awoken by a drumming on the outside of his door. He struggled into a waking state and when he realised the person outside the door was waiting patiently to be admitted he yelled out.

"Come in."

The door opened a crack and a face appeared. It was a face only a mother could love. The ears were sticking out, the nose was over large and red. Eyebrows like a pair of rutting caterpillars almost obscured narrow green eyes. The lips were fleshy and slightly wet with spittle.

"Michael Stevens, British Embassy, may I come in?"

Billy, who was now sitting upright in bed waved an arm to indicate his permission and reached for the Time packet and his lighter. Mr. Stevens, having been given permission had advanced slowly into the room. He looked around with a slight look of distaste on his face. Billy followed his eyes around the room watching his guest's look of disapproval. He couldn't see what the problem was. The room looked to be in a relatively clean and tidy state. Mr. Stevens had pushed aside a pile of dirty clothes and perched on the end of one of the unused beds. He was carrying a small leather attaché case, the one favoured by teachers and insurance salesmen with the single brass fastener on the front. He had carried it like his shield as he entered the room, but as he sat down he put it to one side and fiddled briefly with the catch. He reached inside and extracted a single manila folder. From the inside pocket of his linen jacket he pulled out a stainless steel fountain pen and unscrewed the cap. Opening the folder on his knee he looked up at Billy.

"Name?"

"Billy."

The civil servant gave him a slightly exasperated look.

"Family name?" His tone was very condescending.

Billy took an instant dislike to this official and decided there and then that he was not going to give, 'Mr. Stevens', an easy ride.

"Randell, with two l's" Billy said.

Mr. Stevens ran the nib of his pen down what was obviously a list of names and finding Billy's he made a little tick on the paper.

'Well', thought Billy, 'that's my card marked now.'

He took a long pull on his cigarette and blew out a thick cloud of smoke in the direction of Mr. Stevens, who caught a nostril full of the smoke and wrinkled his nose in disgust.

"Would you mind putting that out? The smoke aggravates my asthma."

"I could open a window," Billy countered helpfully and sprung to his feet to oblige.

"That won't really help much."

Mr. Stevens looked like he was about to start weeping and Billy wasn't sure whether it was from the effects of the smoke or some other emotion.

"Well we had better keep this short then. What do you have to say?"

Billy stood by the open window leaning against the ledge and continued to puff on his cigarette.

"Well Mr Randell, as you might know there are certain disputes currently taking place in this part of the world?"

'Typical diplomatic weasel words' thought Billy as he had been dragged from his slumber the previous three nights by the sounding of air raid sirens.

"And in the light of those disputes, we are strongly advising UK nationals, to evacuate the area ..."

"And where are these evacuees supposed to go?"

Billy cut in over the diplomat, but kept his tone level and conversational. Unhappy at being disturbed, Mr. Stevens tutted loudly. He clearly had a script that he wanted to stick to and any interruptions, he obviously considered, as the height of bad manners and treated them with disdain. Ignoring Billy's question, he continued with his scripted message.

"If the current situation escalates, becoming an all-out war, then it is likely that British and European Airlines will suspend all flights into Ben Gurion, so it will be difficult for foreign nationals to leave the country, if that happens."

Mr. Stevens paused and looked up to see if he still had Billy's full attention. Billy was watching him and still puffing on the cigarette, although he did reach across and stub the butt out in an ashtray. The diplomat remained silent, until he was sure Billy was again paying attention.

"We have been negotiating with all the main UK carriers and they have agreed that they will make seats available over the next week on all their flights, for any UK citizens who wish to leave Israel and we are strongly advising all nationals to do so sooner rather than later. Now?"

At this point he raised his pen and let it hover above the open file.

"Can I put your name down on the list for evacuation?"

"No." Billy's tone remained flat and non-confrontational.

"What do you mean, 'No'?" Mr. Stevens seemed almost incredulous.

"Last time I checked, no meant, no I am not interested in your offer, thank you."

"But I would strongly urge-"

"I am not interested in leaving."

Billy was remaining calm, but the diplomat was slowly losing his cool.

"You do realise the implications of your decision?"

"Yes I do."

"If a full war breaks out, then we will not be able to assist you. You will be on your own."

"I know."

"The Israelis will be too busy to help you out."

"That usually happens in a shooting war."

"You are aware that the payloads of the missiles could contain chemical weapons?"

"I had heard that rumour."

Billy was not lying there. He, like all the other volunteers had been briefed by the kibbutzniks about what they needed to do in the event there was a siren and part of that had covered the chance of a chemical weapons attack.

"And you will not be issued with gas masks or any of the emergency equipment." Mr. Stevens was almost smiling as he dealt out what he felt was his trump card. Billy bent down on one knee and reached under his bed. He slid out a large cardboard box and opened the flap. He held up his prize.

"You mean like this gas mask?"

The diplomat's mouth formed a large O.

"Where did you get that from? You do know you can be sent to prison for ten years for stealing military equipment. The sentence is considerably longer during times of conflict?"

The monstrous nature of Billy's crime was painted large on the diplomat's face. He had probably cut his teeth visiting convicted UK nationals in seedy foreign jails, all of them charged with capital crimes like drug smuggling and murder. Now he was faced with another case, another courtroom but this time it was for the minor charge of mis-appropriation of military hardware, and the contempt on his face clearly showed. Despite this he obviously thought Billy was lining himself up for an orange jumpsuit.

"Well then it's lucky I didn't steal it, isn't it? They were issued to us."

Billy like all the other volunteers on Sde Avram had been asked to visit the dining room one afternoon. There, laid out on tables, were rows of cardboard boxes, each containing a respirator and the necessary ancillary equipment. Each volunteer and member was issued with a box each. After the items had been signed for they were given a brief introduction into how each of the items worked and when to use the atropine injections. This was only to be used in the event of a chemical attack and they were given a lecture in the tell-tale signs to watch out for. With this Mr. Stevens seemed to deflate like a well popped balloon.

"You do realise things could get very dangerous?"

As a final appeal it was a woefully weak attempt, so Billy took pity on the diplomat. After returning the gas mask to its box and pushing it back under the bed with his foot, he stood up and stretched out his hand.

"Mr. Stevens, I am sorry to have wasted your time. I will not be availing myself of your government's kind offer. I am intending to stay here and take my chances."

As Billy had extended his hand towards Mr. Stevens, the diplomat had risen to his feet, so Billy was able to take the man's hand, place his other hand on his shoulder and steer him towards the door then out of the room. Once he was outside, Billy gave him a cheery "Good Luck," and shut the door firmly in his face.

'It's War'. The banner headline proclaimed from the front page of the red-top tabloid newspaper. The paper was already twenty-four hours out of date by the time it had arrived in Sde Avram. Probably purchased, by a traveller at a London Airport, it had been found discarded on a bench in Safed bus station, then brought back to the kibbutz for consumption. Being a Monday edition it had a full digest of the weekends sporting activities, but it was the headline from the front page that caused the most discussion. Accompanied by a rather dramatic photograph of a line of a dozen self-propelled guns all firing at once, the image struck all the right tones for the avid reader back home in England. However anyone, who knew even the smallest detail about Israel, might question the desert landscape that formed the backdrop to the picture. There was no conflict in the south at the Negev, where this picture had obviously been taken. Although it might be a live fire exercise by IDF troops, the image had probably been captured on one of the tank ranges that occupy large parts of the desert in that part of the country. It certainly was not taken in the much greener terrain of the north of the country. If the picture was a fake, a phoney, so was the actual war at this point in time.

There were still sporadic missile attacks from over the border as well as the interminable and rather inconvenient siren warnings that had everyone running for the shelters, but there had been very little actual damage done and there had certainly not been anywhere near the massive escalation in hostilities that had been expected. Historically, conflicts in this part of the world usually followed familiar patterns, where there was an initial period of mud-slinging, except in this case it was missiles that were being fired in one direction and the whole plethora of modern ordinance being dispatched in the other. Then at some point the Israeli's would tire of the incessant attacks and launch some form of military incursion into southern Lebanon. Everyone was expecting this to happen, the troops and armour building up in the border area indicated it was imminent, but it seemed that for the time being everyone was sitting on their hands.

If the conflict outside the kibbutz was a phoney war, the one raging inside the kibbutz was really on. The battle commenced as volunteers started to pack their bags and leave Sde Avram. Where there had once been an ocean of willing hands ready to participate in all the work assignments that body had now shrunk to something about the size of a muddy puddle. The remaining volunteers were therefore in increasing demand. As each week passed and the numbers fell, so the demands became more acute and the antagonism, between the various departments on the kibbutz became more hostile. It didn't help that at this particular time of the year the kibbutz needed to be full of volunteers to cope with the huge apple harvest. In a normal year a flood of seasonal volunteers would have been welcomed, but this year there had been a trickle, the flood had been in the opposite direction as volunteers, some under pressure from families and friends returned back home. Others, believing the doom merchants from their embassies and consulates, had packed their bags and left. The leaders of the apple growing teams were trying desperately to syphon off the majority of the volunteers to fulfil their needs, but other areas of the kibbutz were arguing just as vociferously for their share.

The plastic factory still had orders that needed to be fulfilled and their argument was that the apples could rot on the trees for one year, whereas customers, who were let down over orders, would be likely to take their business elsewhere. Council meetings in the evenings in the members club, were becoming increasingly fractious and on several occasions had deteriorated into screaming matches and on one memorable occasion had even resulted in members coming to blows. It was against this background of raging internal conflict that Billy first requested time off to attend Mike's wedding. In theory the kibbutz authorities could not refuse him. He had a contract, he had worked the days required to entitle him to time off. In practice it was a different story. To ask for time off at this busy time was viewed as an ultimate betrayal. At the time of the harvest, there was only one punishment befitting such treachery and that was to be sent to the cooler. This, like its namesake in the prison system, was a harsh punishment, reserved for those who were late for work or had committed some other infraction that had annoyed the management or supervisors in the apple business.

Billy, by asking for time off to travel south to Mike's wedding was found guilty of a most atrocious crime and therefore sentenced to time in the cooler. When the weather outside was hot, to be sent to work in a refrigerated plastic box might not always be seen as a punishment. You might think that people would be queuing up for the chance. This did not take into account the actual job required of the two individuals who occupied that lofty perch. In this enclosed plastic space, workers, sat astride the conveyor belt that took the apples from the fridges down to the packing lines where they were boxed up ready for shipping to market. In this respect it was desirable that only the best quality apples arrived at the packing stations. In order for this to be accomplished any imperfect or rotten apples had to be removed from the process, before they arrived at the packing area. Some of the more rancid ones fell through the grills by themselves, but others had to be helped by human intervention and individually picked from the conveyor belt. The tendency for these apples to implode in the hand into a pulp, along with the prevailing stench of rotten apples inside the cooler, was what made the place a living hell.

Coupled to this was the fondness for using the cooler as a punishment for late arrival at work. As most late arrival was due to overindulgence the night before it was a fair bet that any tardiness was usually accompanied by a hangover and therefore the occupants were likely to be suffering from their fair share of queasiness. Vomit, or the smell of it, added to the general atmosphere of the place, making it a punishment of nightmare proportions. It was usually left to the volunteers to appoint the occupants of the cooler and being such charitable individuals the victims were usually those who had partied the hardest and the longest the previous night, in order to naturally enhance the victims' hangover and make their night of debauchery even more memorable. From the moment Billy requested time off to travel, he became a permanent fixture in the plastic cage, by orders of the management and this was non-negotiable. If Billy was feeling victimised by the management in the apple factory, his personal life had also taken a turn for the worse.

Mark, whose girlfriend had been among the first to leave the kibbutz, being single again, now decided to get together with Billy's ex, Anne Mette. She became a full time occupant of their room and took great delight in noisy lovemaking with Mark in the night, often forcing Billy to find alternative sleeping accommodation. This should not have been a problem as there were plenty of empty rooms available? This was until he announced his holiday plans. Suddenly, no rooms were available for him. All the empty rooms were locked up, so when he went to request a transfer to another room, he was told that the rooms were closed for cleaning for the foreseeable future.

Feeling frustrated and that once again everyone was ganging up on him, Billy took his usual escape route and started drinking himself into oblivion every night. Of course that made his shift in the cooler much more difficult to endure, but at least he could usually beat his partner to the sick bucket at the start of the shift, if he even bothered to turn up. Mike was ringing Billy every other day pressing his friend for details of his arrival. He was keen to arrange a time for them to visit the tailors, so they could be measured up for their suits. Billy was miserable, hungover and sleep deprived. He had taken to sleeping outside of the volunteer block under the stars, but now it was beginning to freeze at nights. If he returned to the room, then he was subjected to overbearing displays of affection from his former girlfriend and his roommate. All in all Billy was coming to the end of his tether and he knew that something had to give. He had never been one to run from a fight, but this time he knew he had no way to win, so one morning about a week before Mike's wedding, he simply packed his stuff and then went in search of Rachel. He had pulled a double shift in the cooler the day before and had been begrudgingly allowed the morning free. He hadn't really been planning his escape, but he had now had enough of all of this shit. No one factor was responsible, they all were. So instead of a leisurely morning, he had been in the breakfast room early, stocked up on food, as it would be a long day ahead. He then returned to his room, packed his stuff and went to find Rachel.

He found her and informed her of his decision to leave, immediately. He was at the bus stop some thirty minutes later. Within fifteen minutes, he was on a bus heading out of the gates of Sde Avram. He had not said goodbye to anyone except Rachel and as the gates slid shut behind the bus he wondered if he would ever return? No one was there to say goodbye or to watch Billy's hurried departure. Mark was at work in the orchards. He had been out of the door at first light. Most of the other remaining volunteers were scattered about the kibbutz trying desperately to fill the holes left by their departed brethren. No one was on hand except Rachel. She had followed Billy out of her office when he had finished his little speech. He had turned left to head towards the bus stop and wait the few minutes for the bus to take him on his way. Rachel had turned in the other direction and headed along one of the paths that led from the administration area towards the front gate. She had spoken briefly to the two soldiers on duty, before climbing the concrete steps and entering the control room. In this air-conditioned space there were two more uniformed soldiers. Their duty was to watch the secure area, between the two gates and to operate the release controls. From the big glass window they had a commanding view over the approach road and the secure area between the gates. On the floor below their lofty perch there was a barrack room, where soldiers, fully equipped and armed waited to advance out and inspect any vehicle that entered the secure area. Rachel stood by the large window chain smoking her Noblesse. As she waited, the bus pulled away from its stop and entered the secure area. The soldiers made only a cursory inspection of the vehicle before giving the signal. The outer gate rolled back and the bus growled out and up the access road. Rachel reached over and stubbed out her cigarette in a nearby metal ashtray.

"Goodbye Billy Randell."

She muttered softly under her breath.

"I hope you find what you are looking for in this life."

In her heart she had wanted to keep Billy on Sde Avram. She was convinced that the lad had potential to be a long term volunteer or even make the switch, like she had, to become a full member. It was her head, the rational side of her personality that knew that before Billy was ready to make that kind of commitment, there were several deep-seated issues that he needed to deal with, first. She had felt that to keep him here in Sde Avram would not have helped him, even may have resulted, ultimately in his expulsion. She collected her cigarettes, lighter, then nodded a farewell to the two soldiers and left the command post.

## Chapter Sixteen

A steady regular electronic beep dragged Billy back to consciousness. This was not the electronic tone of an alarm clock, but it did sound vaguely familiar. Some part of Billy's sub-conscious was telling him he should recognise the noise. He opened his eyes expecting the light to be dazzling and for his head to explode with the onset of his hangover. Nothing happened. The light was muted as if the blinds were still drawn or it was the middle of the night. As for his head he felt nothing. No serious after effects of the previous night's debauchery. He took a moment to let his eyes adjust to the gloom. The ceiling above his head was pure white without pattern or motif, it looked almost clinical in its form and colouring. The bed beneath his body was firm, not uncomfortable, just a little un-yielding. He shifted his legs and realised that his body was trapped under sheets and a single blanket that were tucked in at the sides. He turned his head looking in the direction of the beeping sound. He could make out a machine with some red LED numbers on the front. 96, 102, was it a clock radio showing the wavelengths it was tuned into. The whole thing looked too large to be an alarm clock-radio.

He realised at the same moment that as well as the strange machine there was also a bag hung on a hook above his head with a plastic tube that snaked down towards his arm. He raised his hand higher and saw that the tube was attached to a plastic tap that was taped to his wrist. He opened his mouth to call out and realised that he couldn't speak because there was a plastic mask over his nose and mouth. He began to panic and thrashed around trying to sit up in bed, restrained by the sheets and single blanket it was difficult to wiggle out from under them and he pawed helplessly at the sheets to try and free himself. He was obviously very weak, because even this small effort left him panting for breath and exhausted. He lay back on the bed and considered his options. He was obviously in a hospital although a quick inventory of his body told him that nothing seemed to be seriously wrong with him. With the exception of the needle in his arm and the mask over his face there was nothing else apparently wrong with him, no plaster from broken limbs, no sore spots from any emergency surgery. He looked over to his right and saw that he was in a private room, alone.

Over by the window he could see his jacket was hung on the back of a visitor's chair. It was the jacket from the suit he had worn to the wedding the previous day; the white carnation in the buttonhole was still in place. All the guys had been given white carnations to wear in their suit lapels, although now twenty four hours later, Billy's had lost it colour and lustre and was turning a funny shade of brown. On this side of the bed someone had taken the trouble to raise the steel frame of the side. An electric cable was hanging over one of the cross struts. At the end of this was a plastic handle with a red button. Billy reached up and took hold of the handle and pressed the button. It was time to get some answers and then to get the hell out of this place.


On Mike and Yara's wedding day, Billy woke up and stuck his head out of the door. It had dawned sunny, clear and unseasonably warm for the time of year. It felt more like the middle of the summer, rather than mid-autumn. For the wedding he had moved back down to a room in the volunteer block as the guest rooms were being occupied by relatives of the bride and groom. He didn't mind being back among the volunteers. Although he had officially left Sde Avram, he had not yet spoken to Yossi about re-joining the volunteers on Tel Boker. That could wait until after the wedding. He didn't want work getting in the way of a good party. As long as he was just a guest, he would not be expected to sign on for any work assignments.

Tel Boker's location, in the south of the country meant that events in the north had had little or no impact on the volunteers. In fact, volunteers were still arriving in the country, so the organisers of the kibbutz programs were in need of safe locations to place them. This meant that numbers had been steadily rising over the recent months; Tel Boker now had close to seventy volunteers in total. Fortunately, one of these was the young lady that Billy had spent a very pleasant evening chatting with during his last stay. This time, things had progressed to the next level. As he turned back into the room he could see her golden hair was fanned out across the pillow, her naked body a delicious curve under the single blue bedsheet. He would have dearly loved to crawl back under the sheet together with her and enjoy a little morning fun, but, today, he had duties as Mike's Best Man.

The first of those was to be among the welcome party for the guests who would start arriving in the next hour or so. Before that he needed to assist setting up the wedding reception and be ready to help with any of the other hundred tasks that one or other of the organisers were bound to find needed doing. While he boiled some water for coffees, he poured a little lip-loosener from the bottle of Arac and water standing in the door of the fridge. He stepped outside, lit a cigarette, before savouring the cold drink and the quiet of the early morning. After putting out the cigarette and draining the last of the glass, he went back into the room and patted the curvaceous rump under the sheet.

"Time to get up sleepy-head."

The body under the sheet stirred and slowly came alive.

"Make me a coffee or I will die." The voice was thick from sleep, muffled by the bed sheet and the fold of an elbow.

"What did you say?"

The sheet was cast aside and the arm unfolded. Billy was treated to the sight of a single rosy pink nipple.

"I said make me a coffee, please." The eyes were still firmly shut, but there was the hint of white teeth from between her lips.

"One coffee coming right up."

Billy made the coffees for them both, then retreated again to the veranda to smoke and drink his in peace. Remaining in the room with this beautiful creature, would result in lust winning the day and he would get nothing done. He had to resist the temptation by removing her from sight. He was just finishing his coffee, when she joined him.

"Do you know if anyone has an iron I can borrow?"

"I might be able to find one or you could try the laundry, they'll have one."

"Good idea. What time do I have to be ready?"

"Well, the wedding breakfast is at nine, but if you don't want to get dressed up by then, the actual ceremony is at three, so we could meet up at the dining room, about two-thirty?"

"Okay."

She bent over and kissed him passionately. Billy felt a stirring in his loins. He broke off the kiss before things got out of hand.

"Out of here! Before I lose all self-control."

He pushed her gently away. She placed her hands on her very sexy hips.

"Go on then. Lose control ..."

She pouted sexily, then laughed, turned around and sauntered off.

"I could watch that ass all day."

Billy said rather too loudly then looked around guiltily to see if he had been overheard. There was no one around. Billy tossed the grounds from his coffee cup onto the grass and went back inside. He looked over at his suit that was hanging on the front of the wardrobe. It was still encased in its plastic wrapper, it had been made to measure by a tailor from the nearby town. The shirt and tie lay next to it on the table.

Visiting the tailor's had been one of the first things he had done on his return to Tel Boker. There had been five of them on the first visit, where they had been measured for the suits. Mike as the groom, Billy as best man, Mike's father and two of his uncles who were acting as ushers. The idea was that they would wear identical suits. Mike's with the added feature of a waistcoat, so that he stood out. Billy teased Mike that the waistcoat was to help him look less paunchy and Mike had been on the point of throwing a pair of sharp tailor's scissors across the room at him.

Billy looked at the garment hanging up. It was the first time he had ever owned a suit and it was beautiful. The women in the Spencer family had chosen the fabric and the colour of the matching shirts and ties. Billy had tried the whole outfit on, including the soft leather loafers he would wear on his feet, the previous evening and paraded up and down posing. He had never felt so grown up in his life. He had owned jackets and trousers in the past, but never a full suit and certainly not one that was made to measure. He ignored the suit for the time being, pulled on a pair of shorts, a clean t-shirt then slapped his feet into a pair of flip-flops and left the room. He spent most of the morning helping with preparations for the ceremony.

This was not going to be a traditional wedding in the true sense of the word because Mike, was not Jewish. This meant that a traditional rabbinical wedding was out of the question. The actual wedding had already taken place two weeks previously, when Mike and Yara and a couple of witnesses had flown to Cyprus, where they had been married in a civil ceremony. Despite the fact that this was not an actual wedding, both families were taking the event seriously and it meant that elements of both a traditional English and kibbutz wedding had been included in the day's events.

The first event of the day was the wedding breakfast. This was an informal but lively affair, with plenty of champagne flowing. After they had finished eating, people began to drift away and the tables in the members club used for the breakfast, were cleared away and preparations began for the evening party. Billy had to help the DJ carry in his disco equipment and then he stuck around to help set it up.

At one point there was a question about the location of the bar, which he couldn't answer, so he went in search of one of the family. He tried Mike and Yara's room first, hoping to catch Mike, but the room was locked and deserted. He didn't want to disturb Yara at her parent's house, so instead he went in search of Mike's parents. He knew they were staying in one of the guest rooms, so he went there and found the place deserted, but their room was unlocked. He went inside and looked around for something to scribble a note on. There was nothing obvious lying around, but in his search he came across a rather tasty looking bottle of single malt whisky. It was set out on a silver tray with a number of glasses beside it, so he pulled out the cork and took a sniff. The warm peaty tang assailed his nostrils and he just knew he had to have a taste. He took up one of the glasses and poured himself a generous measure. He sat on the edge of the bed and savoured the taste. It was so smooth he had to pour himself another good measure. Before he realised it, over half the contents of the bottle was gone and Billy was sitting there slightly buzzed from the alcohol. Billy couldn't recall how much was in the bottle, when he started or how many times he had refilled his glass but all that was certain was that the bottle was definitely looking rather empty now. Mike's dad had mentioned in passing that he had brought some good whiskey with him from the UK and invited Billy to share a 'dram or two' with him, but even Billy, by the wildest stretch of the imagination, didn't think he was supposed to down over half the bottle.

Guiltily, he rinsed out the glass and placed it back on the tray and then left the room. He forgot all about his original mission, so the question about the bar's location remained unanswered. Instead, in his confused and befuddled state, he headed off in the direction of his room to get cleaned up and changed for the ceremony. Part of the dressing process naturally involved a little attitude adjustment with a bottle of Arac and water and several cigarettes. As a result, when he returned to join Mike and his relatives outside the guest rooms, he was pretty loaded and in that wonderful place, where cares are removed to a safe distance and stress is something other people suffer from. However, Mike was clearly in the firm grips of stress.

"The bastards." Mike spat out as Billy sidled up to him.

"What's up?"

Billy was geed up by the Arac coursing through his blood stream and with the sun shining it was going to be a glorious afternoon. He was therefore genuinely interested in who had cast a dark cloud over the proceedings.

"Some bastard broke into Dad's room and polished off most of a bottle of Malt whisky. We were saving that for a special family toast. Now there might be a mouthful left for each of us."

Billy looked around guiltily. He realised immediately the bottle that Mike was referring to. The same bottle that had stood on the tray beside the crystal glasses. He was about to confess to his sins, but decided it would be better to try and brazen it out and deny all knowledge of the break in.

"Wow that's bad news."

He was trying to sound upset but was having difficulty

"Did anyone see anything?"

"No. We were all away at the time on a sightseeing tour of the kibbutz. I was showing the family around."

"That's too bad."

Billy put on a worried expression, but inside he was relieved that no one had spotted him in the vicinity of the room earlier. He wondered whether he should volunteer the information about his presence, just in case someone mentioned he had been seen in the area at a later point and his silence was taken as admission of involvement. Billy decided that discretion was the better solution, so he said nothing.

"Yeah dad is really pissed off as well."

"Any suspects?"

Billy tried to effect a concerned friend look. His mind was working at double speed, but the alcohol that was raging through his blood was dampening the thought process. He hoped that by sparking speculation around possible suspects, he could firmly shift any suspicion away from him. He didn't think that by encouraging Mike to consider who might be guilty he could ultimately reflect the suspicion back on himself. He should really have just shut up and let Mike vent his anger.

Mike stopped pacing and looked at Billy for the first time. He took in the suit, shirt, tie, shoes, the shades and smiled.

"Billy boy," he smiled, "Looking good."

Billy held open the suit jacket and did a slow twirl to show off the outfit. When he returned to face Mike the smile had disappeared. He wasn't sure what he had done wrong, but the smile had been replaced by a much sterner expression, one of outright disapproval.

"Are you drunk?" Mike's voice was harsh, accusatory.

"A little buzzed, why?"

"Come on Billy we talked about this already. I didn't want you pissed for the ceremony. At the party later would be fine, but not before we start."

Mike's voice had lost its harsh tone now and instead he sounded more disappointed.

"I'll be fine mate, no problem."

Billy was doing his best to convince his friend that there was no problem, but he could see he wasn't cutting much ice with Mike.

The arrival of Mike's parents diffused the situation. They were both smiling and obviously excited at the prospect of the event taking place today. They had both arrived in Israel over a week earlier, just before Billy had returned to Tel Boker and had spent the time making final preparations for the big day, whilst taking some time to play tourists. They had booked themselves into one of the big hotels in Tel Aviv for an extended holiday, once the ceremony, was over. They were both full of praise for Billy in his new outfit even if they had paid for it from their own pockets. Mike's father, pulling Billy off to one side, couldn't resist going on at some length, about how disappointed he was about the disappearance of the malt whisky. He railed against the kibbutz as a place, how untrustworthy it was. Why would someone go to such lengths to break into his room and steal the scotch?

"Did someone break in? Was the room locked?" Billy was trying hard not to sound like he was playing private detective.

"Yes, of course, well I think it was."

He saw a moment's hesitation cross Mr Spencer's face. He clearly couldn't be absolutely sure now, that the door had been locked when he had left it earlier. He shook his head, confused.

"I am pretty sure I locked the room before we left?"

This certainty surprised Billy who had walked into the room, but he was in sufficient control to realise that saying anything about his presence in the unlocked room earlier would give the game away; he kept silent. He did wonder, however, if he was solely responsible for the disappearance of the whisky? If someone else had actually broken into the room and helped themselves to a drink then he could stop feeling guilty? He just wished that in his befuddled state he could remember how much had been in the bottle when he had picked it up and pulled the cork out. He had been so desperate for a taste he had not bothered to check.

Mike's mother who was wearing a pale lemon summer dress that beautifully showed off her stunning, sporty figure came over to where they were standing. She spent countless hours on the tennis court in their garden at home and the exercise had honed every last ounce of fat off her tanned limbs. She overheard the last of her husband's comments.

"You are not still banging on about that damn whisky are you?"

"Darling you know it has been a family tradition for generations."

"Yes right back to the days of your Scottish ancestors. I remember all too well being engulfed in ripe whisky fumes at my own wedding. I think Yara might welcome escaping that."

Mike's father looked unhappy at his wife's revelation.

"Oh come on my sweet it wasn't that bad, was it?"

"Well to tell you the truth I was dreading the 'You may kiss the bride part'." she smiled mischievously.

"But it wasn't just you, it was your brothers, your father, your grandfather and all your uncles. You don't realise how many times a bride gets kissed on her wedding day until you are holding your breath every time. Anyway can't you start a new tradition?"

She turned to Billy.

"What's the national spirit drink of Israel?"

"That would be Arac, Mrs Spencer."

"And do you have a bottle of this Arac?"

"I am sure one could be arranged."

Billy knew where he could instantly lay his hands on at least six bottles of Arac and not the cheap stuff, the really good quality stuff. He had made sure a supply had been laid in for the bar for the night.

"Have you smelt that stuff?" This came from Mike's dad.

"No I haven't but I bet it smells better than 20 year old malt?"

"I wouldn't bank on it, but I am sure I can find a bottle from somewhere. I have a bottle in my room."

Billy was keen to make amends for his earlier mistake with the malt whisky, so he was even prepared to sacrifice a bottle from his own stash as reparation.

"Would you fetch it for us Billy dear?"

Billy returned to his room to find it deserted. He had expected Eva to be getting ready, but she had taken herself and her dress off to another room. The dress had been kept a secret and even Billy hadn't been given a glimpse of the gown. He had knocked several times before cautiously opening the door, he didn't want to perish by being impaled through the forehead by the business end of a stiletto heel. Seeing that the room was empty he simply swiped a fresh bottle of Elite Arac from the table and went back to the Guest area.

Mike spotted him approaching and moved to intercept him, Billy was making no attempt to conceal the bottle and was carrying it in one hand.

"What have you got there?"

Mike accusingly pointed at the bottle dangling from Billy's grasp.

"What did I say to you about drinking before the ceremony, you have responsibilities today, you're the best man."

"It's all right dear I asked Billy to fetch that."

Mike's mother had come over when she spotted Billy and her intervention shut Mike down.

"So do you drink this neat?" she asked holding up the bottle and studying the label.

"It's better over a block of ice or with a little water." Billy offered helpfully.

"It's better to avoid it completely."

Mike was not convinced cracking a bottle of Arac this early in the day was a good idea. He knew what Billy was capable of.

"Mike be a darling and get us some ice, will you, please?"

She smiled sweetly.

"Oh and don't forget the glasses." she added.

"I think that should be the best man's job."

Billy offered and was gone like a shot.

"I don't think you should be let anywhere near a drink ..."

Mike began but tailed off as he realised he was talking to an empty space where Billy had just been standing. Billy returned with the glasses, the ice bucket and together with Mike's mother began to serve the drinks. A number of guests were starting to arrive, so Billy was reliant on Mike's mother to direct him to the people, who should receive the special drink. The other guests were being offered champagne as a welcome drink and Billy wasn't surprised, when many of those designated to receive the Arac took one sniff of the contents of the glass and replaced it on the tray untouched, opting instead for the more familiar tasting glass of bubbly. Clearly it was obviously not that serious a tradition and besides, Arac was definitely an acquired taste.

At the end of the circuit there were still a half a dozen glasses left on the tray, so Billy placed it on a nearby low wall and helped himself to one of the glasses. He took a quick look around and convinced that he was not being watched he tipped the contents of another glass into his own before raising the now, almost full, glass to his lips and savouring the cool cloudy liquid as it trickled down his throat.

"Still drinking that stuff Randell?"

He jumped out of his skin, splashing some of the Arac out of the glass, onto the sleeve of his new suit jacket. He spun around, his anger flaring, and came face to face with a smiling Mel.

"Hello stranger."

"Mel, what are you doing here?"

"I was invited, just like you."

"Mike never said you were coming."

"I asked him to keep it a secret in case I couldn't make it, but here we are."

Billy noticed the use of the word 'we' and looked past his ex-girlfriend. A couple of paces behind her was the bespectacled and intense looking lad from the students union.

"Yes, here you both are. Are you going to introduce me?"

"Sebastian, this is Billy. Billy this is Sebastian. You two have met before at the Students Union."

The two shook hands briefly. Sebastian wiped his hand on his trousers after the shake and then used his index finger to push his glasses back up his nose. He was obviously not comfortable in the heat and his suit looked to be a heavy wool mix rather than the cooler silk that Billy and the others had on, as a result Sebastian was sweating freely and his shirt collar was starting to chafe on his neck.

"There's some people roaming around with refreshments, cold champagne and the like. Sebastian you look like you could do with a cold drink."

Sebastian nodded his head rapidly, so Billy scanned the crowd trying to find the person with the tray of drinks. The crowd was increasing now as the guests all assembled for the beginning of the ceremony. As well as the immediate family and friends there were members who lived in this part of the kibbutz all milling around. Elsewhere in another part of the kibbutz, where Yara's parents lived, another group were assembling. At a given time the two groups would leave and then make their way through the kibbutz to the area beside the members club, where the marriage ceremony would take place. As Billy watched the dense milling crowd seemed to part like the biblical red sea and strolling through the middle of the admiring group came a person in an electric blue figure hugging cocktail dress. Her blonde hair was piled in a messy bun on the top of her head, the loose strands flicking free like a leopard's tail. Her make up was tasteful, her blue eyes enhanced by a deeper blue eye shadow, her lips a scarlet gash. She saw Billy and made a beeline for him. Billy watched a hundred pairs of envious eyes track her progress as she drew closer to him. He smiled a welcome.

"Darling you look stunning."

He kissed the newcomer on the lips deeply and had the kiss returned with the same passion.

"Get a room you two," Mike's voice broke the two of them apart and they stood back facing each other. A rather dramatic cough from behind Billy's shoulder reminded him of his manners.

"Sorry, Eva, this is Melanie Bishop."

Billy presented the two to each other. He had conveniently and maybe deliberately forgotten Mel's partner's name, so he left it for her to make the next introduction. Mike had joined them and pecked both Mel and Eva on the cheek, chastely as was befitting a man soon to be wed to the love of his life. He was circulating among the guests suggesting that the procession start to form up and make its way to the assembly point. As such Billy was part of the lead party, standing, as he was best man, at Mike's right hand. Eva was of course hanging on to Billy's other arm and Mike's father was on the bridegroom's left hand side with his wife. They made quite a formidable and colourful bunch as they made their way through the houses to the Members club.

As they entered the large open area from one side, so the bride's party, with Yara and her father in the centre, entered from the other side. As this was not a full wedding ceremony there was no chupah and no rabbi waiting to marry the couple. Today, this ceremony, was more for show, officiated by the kibbutz secretary, with the couple pledging vows they had written themselves, in front of their friends and family. The plan had been to deliver the vows in both English and Hebrew, but even with intense coaching from both Billy and Yara, Mike had still not felt he was equal to the task. As a last minute compromise they had agreed that Mike would deliver his vows in English and Yara in Hebrew. It was the best solution and as most of the vows were extremely similar in content they felt nothing would be lost by doing it this way.

After this part of the ceremony was over and with cries of mazel-tov ringing out from around the square the happy couple made their way into the members club. Billy in his role as best man was required to escort Yara's maid of honour into the party. They had only met, briefly, the previous evening, so Billy was a little startled by the firm grip that she took on his arm. She was an old school friend of Yara's and the two had served in the army together. Like Mike and Billy, they had been inseparable and although she was now living and working in Tel Aviv, she had made time to come and visit Yara on numerous occasions since her return from her travels. Billy struggled to recall her name as they set off together. It came to him in a sudden flash, Ronit. There were strict protocols that had been drummed into all of the key participants. One of these was the order with which the procession would enter the members club. First in, naturally, was the bridal couple, followed by their parents. Next in the line up came Billy and Ronit as the best man and maid of honour. Once inside the lobby of the building they all formed into a receiving line. Then began the laborious process of meeting and greeting all of the invited guests.

There were some high points for Billy, like the arrival of his two old friends from the Eilat police department. Nurit was now a full sergeant and Gabriel was now semi-retired, enjoying his free time whilst still getting his hands dirty, as a part time consultant for the Eilat PD. There was not time for a full conversation, so Billy vowed he would catch up with both of them later. He then turned to offer his hand to the next person in the line. He kept glancing along the line hoping to catch sight of the end. He was starting to feel the need for a drink and he looked around the room hoping to find Eva and encourage her to bring him a drink from the bar, although drinking it might prove problematic as the maid of honour still had hold of his free arm. It was not that he objected to her attentions. At any other time, he would have welcomed them. She was yet another stunning looking Israeli girl with raven black hair and rich dark brown eyes. Like most girls of her age she had a tanned and fit body from the beach. She kept leaning very close to Billy to talk to him and each time she did this, Billy was engulfed in her perfume and treated to a brief glimpse of her ample cleavage.

On any other day it would have been heaven, but he already had another stunning beauty in the room and he still had to endure the first dance with Ronit, before his best man duties would be fully discharged. She seemed determined to make a show of it and when the moment came to make their way onto the dance floor and join the bridal couple in their first dance she made sure every eye in the room was on her and by extension on her partner. She paid particular attention to making all her moves seem as seductive as possible and the distance between her hips and Billy's was much smaller than that required in any manual ever written about how to waltz. She turned the rather formal dance into an informal grind fest and as they spun around the dance floor Billy tried to catch sight of Eva, make eye contact with her and offer her some form of reassurance. Eventually he managed to put in an extra spin, so he was facing in the right direction at the point they whirled past where Eva was sitting. Billy looked over to see that instead of watching his humiliation on the dance floor Eva was in fact deep in conversation with Mel. In the brief moment he had the two in view he saw that it was Mel who seemed to be doing all the talking and just as he span out of range, he saw them both look up in his direction. Eva gave him a look of pure hate, Mel merely registered a look of triumph. For the remainder of the waltz every time Billy caught sight of Eva she was staring daggers at him, while Mel sat demurely by her side occasionally leaning forward and pouring what appeared to be more poison in her ear. That she was not singing his praises was clearly shown by the increasingly dark looks he was getting from his girlfriend. Finally the last strains of the music died away and Billy moved to break away from Ronit and join his girlfriend. His last look at her before now told him, he might have to spend considerable time rebuilding his relationship. Far from smiling at him, as she usually did across crowded rooms, Eva had stared blankly at him and appeared close to tears. He thought he had escaped, but before he took two steps he was engulfed in a perfumed hug, by Ronit. He then had to endure a rather passionate and lingering kiss planted on his lips, before he could finally break free and leave the dance floor.

He had left the open space of the dance floor by the shortest route, anything to extricate him from the gyrating hoards that had flooded onto the floor as soon as the DJ spun up one of the latest pop tunes. The waving arms and wiggling hips made it difficult to see across the room to where he had last seen Mel and Eva sitting together. The record finished in a flurry of drums and the waving arms all dropped at once. Billy could see clear across the other side of the club where the two girls had been sitting. One of the chairs was now empty.

Mel was still sat in her place, but the seat beside her was vacant. Billy scanned the room searching earnestly for the tell-tale blue dress. There was no sign of it anywhere. He walked over to where Mel was sitting. She looked up at him her face a picture of innocence.

"Where's Eva?"

"I don't know."

"What did you say to her?" Billy flashed back at her angry at her insouciance.

"Nothing. Well I might have told her a few stories. You know, anecdotes from the old days."

She continued to grin at him like a Cheshire cat. It tipped him over the edge. He made a grab for Mel and got hold of her shoulder, she stood up quickly to try and shake him off, letting out a squeal as she did, overturning the table, she had been sat at in the process, sending glasses, and all the other table decorations crashing to the floor. Mel retreated backwards whilst Billy advanced towards her menacingly, cursing her out.

A few people tried to hinder his progress, thrusting arms out to halt him, but Billy pushed these aside. Suddenly he felt his arms being grabbed and pinned to the side of his body and a familiar voice in his ear.

"Billy, calm down or I will arrest you."

Nurit's warning in his ear bought him around. He stopped dead in his tracks giving Mel enough of a chance to skip out of his way. Billy looked down and saw that Nurit had hold of his arm above and below the elbow. It was a special police hold that meant if Billy tried to shake her off she could dislocate his elbow or break his arm. It was a no win situation and all the fight went out of him.

"Come on Billy let's get a drink and you can tell me all about it."

Nurit led the way to the bar and collected a couple of drinks for them before guiding Billy to a table on their own. In the meantime the overturned table had been set back upright and the mangled table decoration reinstated in the middle. Someone from the members club staff was sweeping all the broken glass into a dustpan. The party seemed to have returned to normal. Billy took a swig from his drink and nearly spat it out onto the floor.

"What the fuck is that?"

"Fruit juice."

Nurit sipped from her glass as if to demonstrate that the drink was not deadly.

"Are you trying to kill me?"

Billy pulled a face as he took a much smaller sip.

"I thought you could do with a change, you look like you have had enough alcohol."
"What are you now? My mother?"

They were harsh words, but Billy delivered them with a smile, so Nurit let them pass with a smile and a quick shot back.

"I am too young to be your mother and I am not sure I would want the job anyway."
"Thanks. Now can I get a real drink?"
"Not until you tell me what's going on."

Nurit had put a hand on Billy's wrist to keep him sat down. Billy could feel the iron grip through his jacket sleeve.

"I think if you want an answer you had better ask the queen bee."

Billy nodded in the general direction of Mel, who seemed to have recovered her composure and was in an animated conversation with one of the members of the kibbutz.

"What's happened to you two? You were the best of friends the last I heard."

Billy shook his head and looking down at the table answered in a rather gloomy voice.

"I don't know. I guess we just fell out."
"Over what?"
"Me, my life, my choices. My decision to come back here to Israel."
"What? Mel didn't want you to come back?"
"She said I was running away."
"Were you?"

Billy paused for a moment. He wanted to answer Nurit truthfully, not because she was a police officer, but because she was someone who had known Billy in both good times and to a certain extent in bad, or at least being an Eilat cop she had knowledge of the place that Billy had been in when he had been down on his luck, living and sleeping rough on the beach.

"I honestly don't know, maybe I was running away a bit, or running towards something else. All I knew was that I couldn't and didn't fit in back home."

"You're not the first person who has suffered from that. Plenty of people come to Israel and live here for a while then return to their home country and find they don't fit in. The question is are you sure you fit in here? You seem to be angry about something. Is it because Mike and Yara got married?"

"I think that you would be more upset about that."

It was a cheap shot but it scored a hit as Nurit blushed scarlet. She had helped Mike when he was in Eilat and searching for Billy and maybe she had grown fond of him back then. Billy had been surprised when he saw her name on the guest list for the wedding. Nothing had ever happened but Yara, had been a trifle prickly for a while whenever Nurit's name came up in conversation.

"That was a cheap shot Billy."

Nurit had quickly recovered her composure and her voice had a harder edge to it. Billy met her gaze and she could see there was contrition in his eyes.

"Sorry, it was nasty, but to be honest I have come to realise that Mike is not a part of my life anymore. He hasn't been for a while now."

"And that make's you sad?"

"A little, but it also makes me thirsty."

Before she could react Billy was on his feet and on his way to the bar. He ignored the drinks laid out on the top of the bar and went behind. Mike's father had made a fuss about buying a good bottle of whiskey from the liquor store in the nearest town. He had made a point of writing Billy's name on the label. Billy saw the phalanx of bottles lined up and sorted through until he found the one with his name on it. He hooked the bottle by the neck and unscrewed the cap. He chucked a couple of ice cubes in a tumbler and poured himself a generous helping. He brought the glass to his lips and let the spirit slide down his throat, warming him inside as it did. He leaned back on the shelf behind the bar and surveyed the room. Now the formal introduction dances were over, the DJ was spinning up the dance music and the floor was flooded with people enjoying themselves. He watched the smiling faces for a few moments and then poured himself a top up and decided to go and try and find Eva. He wanted to find out if things between them had been damaged beyond all repair.

He made his way towards the exit.

"Billy, where are you going?" It was Nurit who had intercepted him.

"I am going to see if I still have a girlfriend."

"Oh okay, good luck, see you later. I need to check that Gabe is not getting into trouble, he is not used to this kibbutz way of life, doesn't understand the ideals behind it."

She turned away looking for her friend and former colleague. Billy watched her for a moment then turned back towards the door.

"Where are you off to?"

Billy let out an exasperated breath at yet another interruption. Mike was stood between him and the door.

"Like I just told Nurit a moment ago I am going to see if I still have a girlfriend after Mel so brilliantly stuck the knife in."

"You can't leave, you have to give the best man's speech in a few minutes."

"Can't it wait?"

"No, it can't because after that we have the father of the bride and then my speech and I don't think people want to be listening to us drone on all night."

Billy was annoyed because the longer things went on the less chance he had of undoing the damage Mel had done. If Eva thought he was favouring Ronit over her, then his continued absence would just add to her suspicions. Mike's bulk was blocking his route to the exit. Billy had no other choice, but to turn around and go back.

Back in the centre of the members club, Billy looked around at the sea of faces all smiling, chatting, dancing, laughing together. He made a beeline for the bar and liberated the bottle of whisky with his name on the front and poured himself another large one. He had never stood in front of so many people and made a speech before and he was decidedly nervous about the whole thing. He had been briefed extensively on what would be acceptable subject matter for the speech and whilst they had not gone as far as to vet his every word they had drawn certain red lines in the sand over what he could and couldn't say. Billy had made some notes on little cards and these he had nestling in the pocket of his jacket. He patted the pocket and felt the reassuring shape of the card through the fabric. He was expecting the call at any moment, but a long time passed before he was called upon to grace the room with his words of wisdom and wit. By that time he had managed to make a serious dent in the whisky bottle and he was swaying alarmingly as he stood in the centre of the room and took hold of the microphone. It had been conveniently placed on a stand and Billy was grateful that it was, as he was able to use the stand as a crutch to lean on.

With one hand firmly clamped around the mic stand, helping him to stay vertical and his drink in the other he realised he had no free hand to remove his prompt cards from his pocket. He looked around for somewhere to place his drink down. There was nowhere close by so he bent over to place the glass on the floor. He misjudged the distance to the floor and the glass dropped the last inch or so, sloshing whisky onto the floor. Billy realising his miscalculation had made a swipe at the glass and missed, but the violent movement nearly unbalanced him. He grabbed frantically for the adjacent mic stand and clung on for dear life. He hauled himself bodily up the metal stand until he was back in an upright position. Nobody in the circle around him had made a comment, but Billy was suddenly conscious of the fact that a number of people in the room were watching him and he made an extra effort to stand up straight. There was still the gentle background hum of conversation in the room, so he didn't have the full attention of everyone in the room, which was just as well given his almost 'prat-fall' a moment earlier. He took a moment to compose himself. He wanted another mouthful of scotch to help settle his nerves, but the glass looked a long way off, on the floor at his feet. Instead he took a moment to check his appearance.

He looked down at his front and realized his tie didn't seem to want to hang properly, it seemed to be flopping to one side, so he made an effort to tuck it into his trousers and then straighten his jacket over it, to keep it in place. To restrain his tie and in an attempt to look smarter, he decided to button the jacket closed, but in his befuddled state he misjudged the placement of buttons and corresponding buttonholes and ended up with the jacket hanging crookedly, all skew-whiff. He straightened his shoulders and then realised his mistake and immediately attempted to rectify it. This took another few moments as he was forced to first unbutton the garment before myopically trying to see which button went into which button hole. At some point during this exercise his tie became untucked from his trousers and proceeded to flop over the front of his suit blocking his view of the jacket buttons. He swatted the tie aside in order to focus on the buttons, but the tie kept flopping back across the front of his jacket. He paused in his efforts, suddenly aware that the room had gone totally silent. He looked up and saw that everyone, without exception was watching him, in absolute silence. As is often the case when alcohol and human endeavour collide the desire to finish the task at hand becomes obsessional. This was the case with the battle of the buttons and the tie. Billy returned to the fray and continued his efforts to adjust his attire. There was an embarrassed giggle from somewhere at the back of the crowd and then another. Billy realised that his pathetic struggle was now becoming the subject of some amusement to the crowd. Someone laughed out loud and Billy abandoned his efforts with his jacket, pulled the microphone clear of its clip on the stand and raised it to his mouth.

"What's so funny? You think this is funny?" he pointed at the front of his jacket which was still hanging half unbuttoned, his tie was twisted around and facing the wrong way.

"You know what," he sneered at the crowd

"I was gonna tell you what a great bloke Mike was and what a lucky girl Yara was but I think instead you can all go fuck yourselves."

He dropped the microphone on the floor, which boomed as it hit the wood and started to feedback with a devilish squeal. Several people cried out in protest as Billy pushed his way through the crowd and out of the room.

He didn't stop running until he had made it to the top of the kibbutz and the lookout by the old watch tower. He was shaking with anger and it made it very difficult for him to light a cigarette. He dropped two before he finally got one into his mouth and managed to light it. He leaned against one of the concrete posts that held up the wire fence and smoked slowly as his heart and pulse rates slowly returned to normal. He had smoked three more cigarettes, before Ronit found him perched on a large rock.

"Mike said I might find you here." she said as she appeared out of the darkness.

"Here or in your room. I decided to look here first."

In one hand she was carrying the now half empty whisky bottle and in the other she was holding two glasses. She held up both hands in front of her.

"Care for a drink?"

Billy knew he was getting perilously close to his limit, but he thought that one more small one wouldn't hurt so he nodded his head. The drinks were poured and one glass was passed to him. Their hands touched briefly in the exchange and Billy was startled by how cool her hands felt. Her fingertips brushed the back of his hand, as she drew her hand away and Billy felt a jolt of excitement shoot up his arm.

" A toast?" she looked at him questioningly.

"To new friends,"

Billy held up his glass and then downed the contents in one. Ronit took a small sip from her glass and then let her hand with the glass in it drop to her side. She shifted uncertainly, wiggling a little as she transferred the weight from one leg to the other. Billy moved sideways and patted the rock beside him. Ronit turned and sat down carefully next to him. She placed the bottle on the ground between them. Billy was once more engulfed by her perfume. Somehow their close proximity made him feel safe and calm once more.

"What are you so angry about?" Her question, out of the blue, caught Billy by surprise.
"Nothing."

Billy snapped then paused considering his answer a little more carefully and honestly.
"Everything."

Billy was as confused by his recent outburst, as everyone else in the room had probably been. Weddings were always emotional affairs, but it was not usually the best man who made the big fuss. In Billy's very limited experience of weddings, most back at home in England, the trouble usually started, because after drink had been consumed, a member of the family from one of the sides in the arrangement made a disparaging comment about the principal from the other family and someone on their side took exception. This was usually a chance comment about the bride's romantic past or the groom being a loser. After that family honour was at stake and a fight usually broke out. In some rather extreme cases the result had been one of the bridal party ending up in hospital and the other ending up in police custody. Whoever ended up where, was usually a portend for the rest of the marriage.

"Can you be more specific?"
"No not really."
"Could I offer a little perspective?"
"Be my guest."

Billy topped up his glass and turned to face Ronit. He was interested in what she had to say.

"Well if you are feeling like me then maybe today you feel a little sad. You know that today is a happy day for Mike and Yara, but inside you are hurting a little bit."
Billy nodded his head in encouragement.

"Yara and me have been friends for a long time. I know it's the same for you and Mike. Now we are seeing two people start their lives together and we feel that we are no longer a part of that. They have each other and they don't need us anymore."

It was uncanny, but this woman whom he had met properly for the first time only twenty four hours earlier had managed to nail exactly how he felt, except Billy had been feeling this way for the best part of a year, since Mike and Yara had departed on their travels.

"I didn't realise you and Yara were so close."
"Yes we have been friends since before the army. My family used to live around here and we went to school together, then to the army."
"But you don't live here anymore?"
"No my father decided he wanted to leave our kibbutz and go and live in Tel Aviv a few years ago, just before I started my Army service."
"I thought I hadn't seen you around, I would have noticed you."

Billy's obscure compliment obviously struck home, because Ronit placed her hand on Billy's arm and squeezed it.

"That's very sweet of you."
She left her hand where it was and Billy didn't move to shake it off.
"So although I like Mike and I know he is good for Yara, I cannot help thinking that I have lost someone today and not gained anything. Is it the same for you?"
"Yes I guess that's how I see things too."

If possible their two bodies seemed to be getting closer together. Billy could now feel the length of Ronit's thigh pressing against the outside of his leg and their shoulders were also touching. It was not cold but Ronit shivered.

"Are you cold? Here take my jacket."

Billy slipped his jacket off and placed it over Ronit's shoulders. It gave him a chance to place his arms around her and she leaned heavily on him as a result. He could now smell her hair as she leaned her head into his chest. He absentmindedly brushed his lips across her hair. She looked up at him and then their heads came together and their lips met. This time, unlike the explosive kiss on the dance floor, it was a much more relaxed and less urgent event. Contact was soft and sensual and they took their time about it. The lack of urgency did little to diminish the passion and when they broke apart Billy was slightly breathless.

"Do you have somewhere we can go and be alone?" Ronit asked in a breathy voice.

The kissing had affected her in the same way as it had Billy. It was as if she was struggling to draw breath. Billy thought about his options for a moment. He had to come up with an answer and quickly or he felt the moment might escape him. He knew he wanted to be with this woman, right now more than anything in the world. She was a fellow lost soul and she had understood his feelings, so clearly, much more than anyone else including those who had known him the longest. He could feel her need was as great as his as she was struggling to her feet and pulling Billy after her.

Billy had one serious obstacle in the way. He didn't know where Eva had taken herself off to. If she had gone back to his room then turning up there with Ronit would be a serious mistake, for all concerned. If, on the other hand, she had taken herself off to her own room to sulk then he would be in the clear. His heart ruled his head on this one, so he decided to take a chance and the pair made their way down to his room. They took a roundabout route to avoid passing the members club and prevent any questions being asked. For once, on this very long day of catastrophic set-backs, the gods smiled on Billy and the room was empty. He looked both ways as he unlocked the door and then the two were inside and tearing at each-others clothes. Billy had barely enough foresight to lock the room door from the inside, before they were falling into bed together. It was to prove a good move. Sometime later he heard voices on the block and then someone knocked on the door. He lay quietly under the sheet beside Ronit and raised his finger to her lips. When he didn't answer, the person outside tried the door. Then he heard Mel's voice speaking to whoever was with her.

"Well he's not in his room."

After that the footsteps went away down the block. Billy waited until he guessed the coast was clear.

"They have sent out the search parties looking for us."

"Us? Or just you?"

"I should think we have both been missed by now."

"What time is it?"

Billy checked his watch.

"It's around ten-thirty."

"Should we go back to the party?"

"That depends."

"On what?"

Billy slid his hand up the inside of Ronit's thigh and she arched her back in response.

"Oh on that," she giggled and reached for Billy.

## Chapter Seventeen

They knew that after such a long absence it would be impossible to slip back into the party and act as if nothing had happened. They were both subjected to extensive interrogations on their return. Billy, who had still not been forgiven for his abortive best man's speech and his hasty disappearance was given the third degree by Mike and then by Mike's parents although the latter pair were kinder on him than Mike was. As he watched across the room Ronit was being questioned by Yara and a couple of other girls. Billy knew the drill, he had been there before. Once the friends got their claws into the relationship it very much hung in the balance. If they approved of you then it was green light and full steam ahead. If they didn't then there was nothing on god's good earth that could make the relationship last. It was already dead in the water. Billy waited to see which way the axe would fall. When Ronit was released and made her way over to him he held his breath. Ronit walked up to where Billy was standing and put her arms around his waist.

"Do you want to dance?"

The DJ had chosen that precise moment to slow things down and couples were forming up and moving onto the centre of the dance floor. This was the kind of dancing that Billy could handle, so he accepted the offer and moved together with Ronit.

"It wasn't too awful was it?" she asked as they moved slowly to the music.

Billy paused for a minute wondering what Ronit was referring to. Deciding that it was the interrogation, he shrugged his shoulders and said rather casually.

"I have had worse."

Then he panicked as he suddenly thought that maybe Ronit was alluding to their recent sojourn in his room. To answer that question in such a dismissive manner could get him his face smacked. Luckily for him she had been asking about the grilling and she nodded her head and simply added

"Me too."

Billy decided to push his luck and asked rather casually.

"Where are you staying tonight?"

Hoping she would agree to return to his room after the reception for a reprise.

"We have a bus taking a load of us back to Tel Aviv tonight. Some of us have got work in the morning".

"Oh right."

'Well that's put an end to that particular pipe dream', Billy thought. He focused on trying to come up with a Plan B. As if she was reading his mind Ronit suddenly said.

"There are some spare seats if you want to come back to Tel Aviv with me?"

Billy smiled as a Plan B dropped squarely in his lap. Now he could look forward to a night of passion, or what would be left of the night by the time they had made the journey back to Tel Aviv. There was always the ride itself, plenty of intimacy could occur on a darkened bus, particularly when most of the other passengers were exhausted and trying to get a little sleep. With that decision reached Billy found he was able to endure the last hour of the party without losing his mind completely. He had largely been shunned by Mike and the rest of his family, some of whom had already left the party and found their way to the guest rooms to sleep. Billy surveying the carnage of empty bottles behind the bar didn't doubt that there would be more than a few sore heads in the morning.

Mike and Yara departed for their honeymoon in a fanfare of confetti and noise. Although they departed in some style Billy knew they were only going as far as their shared room tonight, their big honeymoon adventure was scheduled to start in the morning. But tradition was tradition. Eventually it was the turn of the Tel Aviv contingent to depart and they made their way, in a noisy phalanx, down to the main car park where a tourist bus was waiting to whisk them, in comfort, back to the city. The noise ceased almost as soon as the bus engine started and the doors closed. People settled down to grab a bit of shut-eye and despite his hopes the same went for Ronit who was quite happy to cuddle up to Billy, who fell asleep almost as soon as her head hit his chest. Billy had to make do with a cheap bottle of local scotch, that he had hooked from the bar on the way out and concealed under his suit jacket, for company all the way back to Tel Aviv. Reaching the city limits the driver had a route that he followed winding through the suburbs and outlying neighbourhoods as he dropped the various passengers off. At one point someone leaned over him and shook Ronit.

"We are the next stop," the man said.

Ronit came slowly awake beside him. Her hair had stuck to the side of her face, so Billy brushed it aside for her. She smiled at him.

"Hello sleepy head, do you feel rested."

Ronit stretched like a cat and then rubbed at her neck.

"My neck is a little stiff, but I will live."

The bus pulled over into the car park of one of the local shopping centres and the doors opened. Billy stood up to let Ronit out of her seat and then started to follow her to the exit. She turned to him as she went to go down the steps.

"Where are you going?"

"I am following you."

"You can't."

"Can't what?"

"Follow me."

"I thought I was staying at your place tonight."

"I live with my parents, they won't let you stay."

"Why not?"

"Look Billy I can't explain this right now." She turned to descend the steps

"Wait. Hold on."

"Billy I have to go, the bus driver is waiting to leave."

As if to back this up the driver growled something unintelligible from behind Billy's back.

"When will I see you again?"

"Will you meet me tomorrow, on the West Beach, there is a bar there."

"What time?"

"Eleven?"

Billy nodded and then sat down in an empty seat and watched her leave. The driver closed the doors and the bus pulled away. Billy unscrewed the cap of the whisky bottle and took another long pull. The spirit was raw down his throat, he coughed. Well that was his evening effectively shot down in flames. Slowly he realised he had left Tel Boker with no more than a few shekels in his pocket, not enough to get a room at a hostel and he was not exactly dressed to sleep the night on the beach. Fortunately for him the bus was heading right for the centre of Tel Aviv and he was able to disembark only two streets away from the sea front. He walked down towards the beach taking regular nips from the whisky bottle and puffing on a cigarette or two.

He chose Rehov Gordan to make his way towards the beach and came out in front of one of the swanky hotels that lined the beach front. He looked longingly in through the smoked glass windows at the comfortable sofas that lined the lobby and thought that maybe, dressed as he still was, in his wedding suit, he might very well pass for a hotel guest. He looked over to the reception desk where the night manager and a night receptionist were both stood idly chatting to pass away the darker hours. His hand hesitated on the door, but he didn't push his way inside. He turned and headed down the slope towards the beach instead. He was no stranger to sleeping on the beaches of Israel. He had even slept a few times on Tel Aviv beach, but then he had been prepared, with a sleeping bag and not dressed as he was in a silk suit. He walked slowly along the esplanade looking for a suitable solution to his problem. There were a few groups of people still out enjoying the warm night, but with little or no money he was not even in a position to join one of these groups in a bar and buy a drink. He still had over half of the whisky left in the bottle, but that was disappearing fast as he nipped from it every few minutes. Asked later if he could recall what had happened Billy was forced to admit that he had no idea. One minute he was walking along the beach front and the next he was lying face down, the bottle had slipped from his grasp and smashed on the pavement, the contents splashing out in a starburst on the concrete. A group of local Tel Aviv residents, who were walking behind him when it happened who told the EMT technicians what they had seen. They had seen the person, smartly dressed in a suit, take a swig from the bottle he was holding in his hands and then fold over and collapse to the floor. One of them had run into a nearby bar and used a phone to call an ambulance. The EMT team had duly arrived and found a young male, unresponsive but still breathing, obviously intoxicated by alcohol and with a worryingly high pulse rate. They had put him onto a gurney and then loaded him into the back of their ambulance and driven him to the nearest hospital. Billy had been assessed and treated for advanced dehydration, alcohol poisoning and then placed in a hospital bed to recover. It was there, that Billy had now woken up.

Billy pushed the button a second time and then a third for good measure. He had waited for a few moments before pressing the second time, but when no one had responded he felt it was better to check that the thing was working. It was, as eventually a nurse entered the room. She smiled at Billy and spoke to him, in English, albeit with a heavy accent.
"Good afternoon, good to see you are awake. Are you feeling better?"
She approached the side of the bed and then reached up above Billy's head. She then reached down, fiddled behind Billy's ears and freed the mask from his face.
"It's difficult to talk with one of those things on. You shouldn't need it anymore. Just tell me if you feel at all out of breath. So how are you feeling?"
She stood back and waited patiently for Billy's answer. Billy considered the question carefully before he answered. 'Was he feeling better? Better than what exactly? What was the benchmark?'
"I feel okay, thanks. Where am I?"
"In hospital."
The nurse was busying herself taking readings from all the various instruments that were arrayed around Billy's bed and making notes on the clipboard that had been hanging over the end rail.
"I kinda figured that, but where, please?"
"Ichilov Hospital, Tel Aviv."
She paused and flicked over to another sheet on his notes.
"I see you were unconscious when they brought you in, which is why you are confused. I just need to get a few details from you; we don't even know your name."
"Err, Billy, Billy Randell, with two l's in both."
"Okay Billy, and where are you from?"
"The UK"
"And, what is your address in Israel? Which hotel are you staying in?"

Billy laughed out loud. While he had laid in his bed, waiting for someone to show up and tell him what was going on, he had tried to piece together his recent events. The last coherent memory he had was of standing staring into the hotel lobby and trying to summon up the courage to push his way through the door.

"What's so funny?" The nurse looked puzzled.

"I was only down on the sea front because I was too scared to try and blag my way into one of the hotels and sleep in the lobby."

The nurse was confused by the meaning of the word 'blag',

"What is 'blag'?"

"Pretend to be one of their guests"

Eventually, she understood him.

"So where are you staying, is it a private address?"

"It's a kibbutz."

"A kibbutz?"

"Yeah, kibbutz Tel Boker."

"Down in the Negev?"

"That's the one."

"So you're a volunteer?"

"You seem surprised?"

"I don't see many volunteers walking around in expensive silk suits."

She nodded at the suit jacket that was draped over the back of the chair.

"I guess the admissions people took one look at your clothes and assumed you were a businessman of some description. Oh dear this is rather embarrassing."

"Why?"

Billy had the sneaking suspicion, causing a horrible sinking feeling, that he was not being told something and he was unlikely to get the truth from this nurse. There probably wasn't anything seriously wrong with him, not medically anyway, but he wondered why the nurse's face had drained of all colour when he had mentioned that he was a volunteer? Maybe they had a special ward for volunteers or something similar? All sorts of possibilities were racing through his mind, each one slightly worse than the last. Why exactly was he not on a general ward with other patients? What had they discovered about him whilst he was unconscious? They would have had ample opportunities to run tests so what exactly had they discovered was wrong with him?

He was currently residing in a private room. He suddenly felt this was not the run of the mill treatment for volunteers in Israeli hospitals. He was not getting any answers from his nurse? She finished filling in the details then looked over at Billy. Her cheeks had coloured in shame and in a flustered voice she stammered.

"I will have to get the ward sister in here. Try to rest"

She disappeared through the door still clutching the clipboard to her chest. It looked like Billy's revelation had caused a bit of a stir, as first the ward sister appeared, before summoning someone higher up in the hospital administration, both then double checking his story by asking the same questions. It was almost as if they were implying that Billy had contrived to mislead them or had misrepresented himself? All Billy could say, indeed kept saying to each successive individual, was that as he was apparently unconscious when he had been admitted, how could any of this misunderstanding be his fault? However, worse revelations were to come.

It was understandable that the hospital were clearly looking to discover who would be responsible for paying the bill for Billy's medical treatment. When they contacted Tel Boker to inform them of Billy's whereabouts and to get their medical insurance details, the kibbutz claimed, quite rightly, that they had no one of that name currently registered as a volunteer.

The administrator relayed this information to Billy and asked him for an explanation. With a sudden swooping feeling in his guts, Billy realised that although he had discussed, with Yossi, the possibility of re-joining Tel Boker as a volunteer, he had not signed the necessary papers yet. So, officially, Tel Boker were right. He was not yet a volunteer with them. In a last ditch hope, he gave the administrator the name Sde Avram, but they had been unusually quick in removing Billy from their roster, so he was no longer registered there as a volunteer either. He had never thought he would need private medical insurance while he was a volunteer, so he now faced the prospect of having to find the money to pay the hospital bill from his own severely depleted savings. He knew he didn't have enough to afford the bill; probably not even a small part of it.

Sometimes, even the darkest clouds have a silver lining. Billy discovered this next morning when he was visited by Martin and Eve Spencer, Mike's parents. Apparently, the hospital contacting Tel Boker for payment had alerted the kibbutz to Billy's whereabouts. The Spencer family who, like everyone else involved in the wedding, had no idea what had happened to Billy after he disappeared at the end of the party, had quickly jumped into a hire car and driven up to Tel Aviv. The first indication Billy had visitors was when a cacophony of raised voices shattered the otherwise calm serenity of the hospital. Through the open door of his room Billy heard English voices raised in angry frustration; voices he thought he recognised. This was confirmed moments later when Eve Spencer stuck her head around the door.

"Hello Billy, please tell these people that you know who we are."

Behind Eve's bubble of blonde hair one of the orderlies was hovering.

"It's Okay, these people are family." Billy said to the orderly in Hebrew.

Relief flooded the orderly's face. Clearly he had not relished going toe to toe with the tenacious personality of Mike's mother. Like a queen in her kingdom, she immediately bustled into the room and began tidying. Martin Spencer sidled into the room a moment later with an apologetic look on his face.

"How are you feeling Billy? We've been very worried about you."

"I am feeling much better," Billy lied. He was actually sick to his stomach.

He still had the spectre of the hospital bill hanging over his head and he was now worried about what would happen to him, if he couldn't pay. He still hadn't seen the final bill and was unsure when they would discharge him. Also, how much larger the bill would be as a result of these extra days. He really wanted to get out of hospital as soon as possible, but he had been told he had to wait until the doctor had seen him before any decision could be made about his discharge. He felt certain they would not keep him in, unnecessarily, as it had now been established, that as a volunteer he was likely to have access to very limited funds.

By the friendly tone from both of Mike's parents, it seemed that any indiscretions that Billy had committed at their son's wedding, had been forgiven. They appeared genuinely concerned about what had happened to him and why he had ended up in hospital. So, they asked if Billy didn't mind, could they both stay in the room when the doctor came in on his rounds. Billy who was easy either way, said it was fine. This was to prove to be a blessing, because it seemed that while the ward staff were embarrassed to bring up the subject of payment of his outstanding treatment bill, the doctor had no such qualms. In fact it was almost the first thing out of his mouth after his initial greeting and the introductions had been made. The doctor had been briefed on Billy's circumstances and the fact that he was technically 'between' kibbutzim and therefore not covered under any medical insurance scheme, so the doctor was anxious to try and secure some form of reassurance that remuneration would be forthcoming. Billy was stunned and surprised at being ambushed in this way by a member of the medical staff and began to stutter his way through an explanation of his situation. However, Martin Spencer was having none of it. He stepped forward, held up his hand and interrupted both Billy, then the doctor.

"There is no need for you to be concerned over the treatment bill. It will be settled in full. I can guarantee that."

On hearing the magic word 'guarantee', the doctor immediately turned his attention away from Billy and then on to Martin.

"And you are?" The doctor sized Martin up.

"Martin Spencer.", he stuck out his hand expecting the doctor to want to shake hands.

The doctor eyed Martin's hand suspiciously. It was almost as if he was checking the hand for bugs and bacteria. Martin left his hand dangling for a moment and then removed it. He subconsciously wiped the hand on his trouser leg as if that might make it more presentable. It didn't. What it had done was give the doctor vital seconds to assess the net worth of the man. Martin Spencer was not an outwardly flash person, so any hint of personal wealth would not be demonstrated by cascades of gold jewellery. What the doctor was able to see in his brief moment's inspection, was the expensive Rolex watch that hung from Martin's wrist and the rather fine cut of the clothes he wore. His even tan hinted at someone who took regular holidays to sunnier climes rather than the tango orange of someone who spent hours languishing on a tanning bed. The doctor reached the conclusion that Martin's claim could be taken seriously.

"And your relationship to this patient is?"

"Who? Billy? I have known Billy, since he was in short pants, well just about. He is my son's best friend. He was with us at my son's wedding. Billy was the best man."

"I see."

The doctor said, although he was apparently not familiar with the role, so a puzzled look appeared on his face, as he tried to tie this expression 'Best', 'man', with the specimen lying in the bed before him. He had seen the state that Billy was in shortly after his admission and he shook his head at the thought that this was the 'best', 'man' or otherwise. Billy who noticed the confusion on the doctor's face uttered a single word in Hebrew.

"Shomer."

The doctor looked down at Billy as the light of understanding, slowly dawned in his eyes. Best man was not a concept generally known or acknowledged, at a Jewish wedding. The role of the 'Shomer' or guard, however was. The doctor smiled at Billy for the first time.

"Oh, so you speak a little Hebrew?"

He said in that language.

"A little."

Billy said and then switched back to English.

"But if it is not too difficult, can we speak in English as my Hebrew doesn't stretch to medical matters or words."

"A good time to learn then. Maybe?"

The doctor continued in Hebrew. Then smiled at Billy and switched back to English.

"Very well Mr Randell and for the benefit of your friends, we will continue this in English."

Now that the matter of the bill had been resolved he was prepared to give Billy's medical care his full attention. Whilst in the room, the doctor had been clutching the clipboard with Billy's notes and treatment plan on it. Now, he glanced at the notes written by the nursing staff. This included all of the treatment they had administered to Billy since his admission.

"I see that some blood samples were taken. Do we have the results back?"

This was directed at one of the attending hospital staff.

"I don't know Dr Fischer. Would you like me to go and check?"

The speaker was on the way out the door before Fischer had even opened his mouth. He returned a few moments later clutching a flimsy piece of paper, which he handed to the doctor. Fischer studied it for a brief moment. He made no immediate comment, but clipped the paper onto the board and then hung it back in place. He moved to the side of the bed and asked Billy to raise his top and expose his stomach. He prodded the area of Billy's abdomen just under the rib cage and asked Billy to breathe in and out a few times. He removed his hands and pulled down Billy's top and then pulled the sheet back over him.

"Right Mr Randell, I am sorry to say this but on top of the dehydration issue that saw you admitted here, you have a swollen liver. The blood test confirms this. We did a standard LFT screening: this looks at the function of the liver and yours is about to pack up and go on holiday. It looks like you have been over-indulging."

Billy looked up at the doctor, searching the man's face for some shred of a smile.

"I have been at a wedding and reception, so, of course we have been drinking."

Billy went immediately on the defensive.

"No, Mr. Randell, these results tell me you have been abusing alcohol for some time now. I can order another screening, but I think we both know the truth?"

He turned to one of the medical team.

"As a precaution, I would like to start Mr. Randell on a course of Clomethiazole, just to be on the safe side."

"The safe side of what?"

Martin Spencer had been following the conversation between doctor and patient closely.

"Mr. Spencer, what we have here is a classic case of alcohol abuse. Mr. Randell was admitted with an extremely high blood alcohol level, in fact dangerously high. According to our initial blood tests, Mr. Randell here should not have been capable of physical movement. After over twenty four hours abstinence, that level will be approaching normal again. This is where we are now, around the twenty-four hour milestone. We do, however, at this point face a very serious risk of withdrawal and in order to avoid any problems, it is best if we treat those symptoms before they arise".

"Problems? What problems?"

Billy was determined to get back into the conversation. It was, after all, his health that was being discussed.

"Oh I don't know?"

The doctor affected the air of an absent-minded genius as he looked around hoping to pluck answers from the ether, a vague look of wonderment on his face. He replaced it with a very stern gaze at Billy.

"The DT's, convulsions, heart palpitations, stroke, death."

The doctor had a worryingly straight face as he delivered this list, counting each condition off the fingers of his right hand. As he delivered the last one, he closed his whole hand leaving the thumb sticking up and in a dramatic final gesture, he turned it downwards. Billy absorbed the list and then reacted as any normal person would.

"But those are things associated with alcoholics."

"Precisely!" The doctor added with a self-satisfied smile. "There is light in the darkness."

Billy went quiet as he absorbed exactly what the doctor had just told him. Suddenly, the arguments with Mel in the flat back in London came back to him. Maybe what she had actually said was true? What if he really was an alcoholic? Of course he didn't see it, or at least he didn't want to see it, or admit it, not to himself or to anyone else.

Mike's parents had been listening intently to the doctor's explanation and Eve Spencer was quick to try and back Billy up.

"I am not surprised his reading was high, we have been having a bit of party to celebrate my son's wedding."

Billy moved to cut her off, but the Dr Fischer was quicker.

"My good woman, these numbers are not the kind of things that spring up overnight. In my professional opinion Mr. Randell has been misusing alcohol for a number of years."

"It's okay Mrs Spencer, the doctor is probably right."

"There is no probably about it, young man. If you don't change your lifestyle you will be dead in a couple of years. Now, we have a dependency nurse, who can come and talk to you about changing your lifestyle. Do you think that might be helpful?"

Billy nodded his head. Right now he was in a very bad place and anyone who could offer him a shred of hope was welcome to try.

"I think I had better explore all the options, don't you?" Billy looked over at the doctor.

"I think that is a very sensible decision, young man."

He finished up the rest of his consultation including writing up a prescription for the new drugs and then went to leave. He stopped in the doorway and turned back.

"I wish you all the best for the future. If everything works out then you can go home tomorrow."

He then turned to Mike's father who was by now perched on the windowsill.

"Mr. Spencer, I suggest you talk to the ward staff and they will put you in touch with the necessary people to organise the payment."

With that the Doctor turned on his heels and left the room. There was obviously some urgency about starting Billy on the withdrawal medication, because a nurse turned up a few moments later with a pill for Billy to take and a glass of water to swallow it with. The pill made Billy sleepy and he quickly drifted off. When he awoke later on, the Spencer's had left him alone. He didn't blame them. With so much of the country still left to explore, they probably didn't want to waste time in a hospital room, watching Billy sleep. They both knew he was in safe hands, so they could now get back on with enjoying their stay in Israel.

There was nothing for him to do except lie in bed and rest. Each time the orderlies turned up with his pills they seemed to send him back to sleep. He awoke briefly in the middle of the night and noticed that the IV line had been removed, along with all the other monitoring equipment, so he was able to go to the bathroom, then curl up on his side and get as comfortable as it was possible in a hospital bed. He quickly fell back to sleep.

At some point in the darkness he woke up. There was a dim light coming through the slit under the door. The overhead lights in the hallway outside the room were on, but with the door firmly shut, there was only a millimetre gap under the door, letting very little light into the room. He lay in the almost total darkness and tried to focus in on what had just drag him from his sleep. Something had intruded into the depths of his slumber and dragged him awake. Some noise, a sound, had woken him up, but right now all that he could hear was the roar of the blood in his ears.

"Billy are you awake?"

A voice spoke to him out of the dark. He turned his head in the direction the voice had come from, but there was no one there. He peered into the dark wondering if there was someone hiding in the shadows, playing a silly prank on him?

"Billy, come on man wake up."

It was another voice, a different voice. The first voice had been a woman's, the second a man's. Billy shook his head in an attempt to clear it of the last vestiges of sleep. The drugs they had given him to combat the alcohol withdrawal had left him sleepy and confused, in a semi-catatonic state. He had mentioned this to the nurse the previous evening and she had said that it was perfectly normal in the first twenty four hours, whilst the dose was quite high, to feel this way but after that, as they began to reduce the dose, things would slowly return to normal. He struggled upright in bed. The voices had both spoken to him, but as he went through the motions of sitting up so the voices seemed to fade away. They were still there, but it was if both the speakers had left the room. The door was still firmly shut, but the voices seemed to be coming from outside in the corridor. The fact that they were now coming from outside the door made it harder to hear exactly what they were saying. Billy concentrated on the voices. He thought it might help if he could identify the two people who were talking to him.

The male voice sounded like Mike, but with a much deeper bass tone than Mike's normal speech. The female voice sounded like Ronit, but when she spoke it was in clear unaccented English. There was none of the usual rich Israeli tone to her spoken English. The two seemed to be speaking together and only occasionally including Billy in the conversation. These inclusions were in the form of questions or exhortations for Billy to get out of bed and to follow them. Once Billy had sat upright it was if the voices outside in the hallway, through a closed door, sensed that he was beginning to comply with their requests and they started to move away, down the corridor. The voices started to fade as the two speakers walked away from the door. Billy hesitated on the edge of the bed. He had not called out to the two to wait for him. Maybe he should have asked for them to wait, while he struggled out of bed. He was no longer encumbered by the IV line and the bag of saline solution on its stand, but nonetheless nearly three days in bed with very little food had left him weak as a kitten. If his two friends moved too quickly they would leave him behind in no time and Billy had sensed from their exhortations that it was crucial that he follow and keep up with them.

"Are you okay Billy?"

It was the male voice, and it seemed he was back just on the other side of the door, to check if Billy was okay. From the nearness of his voice it sounded that way. Billy opened his mouth to answer, but felt somehow it wasn't necessary, just as long as he got out of bed and followed them.

"Come on Billy, the party's starting, everyone is waiting for you."

Those were the magic words Billy wanted or maybe needed to hear. It was the catalyst to spark him into action. He pushed himself off the bed and stood up, trying to ignore the weakness in his knees and the dizziness in his head. He grabbed the edge of the bedside table to steady himself and then paused briefly, to adjust to being upright for the first time in a while. When he had left his bed on the previous occasion to use the bathroom he had been helped by one of the nurses. This was the first time in nearly three days that Billy had been, literally, on his own two feet. He let the dizziness pass before setting out towards the door. He could still hear both voices talking to him from beyond the door. They were exhorting him to get a move on as the party was well underway and if he didn't hurry up then they would miss all the fun. He pulled open the door to the room. It was heavy so it took considerable effort to swing it wide enough, so that he could pass through and into the corridor. This gave access to Billy's room, the two adjacent rooms and lastly the bathroom that the three rooms shared.

This section of corridor was deserted, but Billy could hear the voices coming from around the corner at the end of the corridor. Billy set off at a slow shuffle in pursuit of the voices, convinced as he came to each turn he would catch sight of the two people in front of him. But every time he made it to where the corridor turned either to left or to right the section in front of him was deserted. The voices continued to talk to him, still exhorting him, to follow them, as they were just ahead of him, around the next turn. The rigours of the pursuit were beginning to take their toll. Billy was sweating profusely and his head was swimming. He turned another corner and entered a long corridor. This was clearly one of the main arterial routes through the hospital as it was much wider than all the others Billy had so far passed along, but also it seemed to stretch off as far as the eye could see. And as far as Billy's eyes could see, it was totally deserted. This was not unusual, even for a large hospital, as it was the middle of the night. The majority of the patients were asleep in their beds and most of the staff were taking the time to catch up on administrative tasks. Billy was puzzled. With a corridor of this length he had at least expected to catch sight of his two friends, but they had once again eluded him. What was more bizarre was that this corridor ran as straight as an arrow, no corners for them to have just turned ahead of him. The voices had also faded away and the place had fallen silent. His friends had just disappeared into thin air, or so it seemed.

    He leaned against the wall to catch his breath. Then, he tried to figure out what to do next. He glanced behind him back along the route he had taken. He couldn't remember how many corners he had turned, how many short sections of corridor he had traversed? In fact, as he stood there alone and in the silence Billy realised he was completely lost. He looked up at the sign above his head. The Hebrew words and the arrows pointing in all directions meant nothing to him. He couldn't read them and then it dawned on him that even if he could, he had no idea where he had come from. What ward, department or room number? He had no idea. Without that information, even if an orderly was to happen by, Billy would be unable to ask direction to get back to his bed.

    Another wave of dizziness overcame Billy and he clutched for the wall. He clawed his way along to where there were some plastic visitors chairs arranged in a row. He collapsed onto the closest chair, breathing heavily, then wiped the sweat out of his eyes. He noticed as he did this how badly his hands were shaking. His knees felt like they could no longer hold his weight. He might even have briefly passed out, as on rousing, he thought he heard the voices again. This time they were close, just across the corridor to be exact and coming from behind a door. There was a sign on the door, but like all of them, it was in Hebrew, so Billy had no idea what the room beyond contained. The two insistent voices were urging him to get up, cross the corridor, enter the room and join the throng. Party activities were being promised as it was approaching full swing.

    Billy struggled to his feet, paused to balance and with an enormous effort, shuffling and hobbling, he crossed the corridor. He reached for the door handle, leaning down using all his weight to move it. The lock released, he pushed the door open. The room beyond was totally silent and dark. This didn't bother Billy. He felt the party-goers were just playing a trick. In a moment, they'd throw the switch and all the lights would come on, everyone yelling 'surprise' and the music would start up. Billy ventured a little further into the room, tensing himself against the coming shock. Nothing happened. He felt resistance against his upper thigh. Something was in his way. In the pitch dark he could see nothing. He reached his hand down to try and push it aside. Then there was an almighty crashing sound as the object was overturned onto the floor. The lights above him came on.

    "What are you doing in here son?"

    Billy spun around at the sound of the voice, which had addressed him in Hebrew, not in English like the other voices. Spinning around so suddenly caused Billy to lose his balance. He tumbled into the pile of objects he had just upended onto the floor. He reached out and wrapped his hand around one of them. He lifted it in front of his face and peered at it. He discovered a plastic urine bottle as used by bed-bound male patients. Disgusted he chucked it aside. Shit, he was lying in a pile of them. He struggled to try and stand.

    "Relax son, they're clean. The unwashed ones are on that table."

The newcomer nodded across the room to the far side where there were more items stacked up.

Billy looked up at the newcomer, and concentrated on his Hebrew voice. As he was dressed in a simple blue t-shirt and white hospital pants, he was just a member of staff, so not invited to the party. This didn't deter the man from continuing in Hebrew.

"What exactly are you doing in the sluice room in the middle of the night?"

"I was invited to a party."

Billy replied in the same language. He was still struggling to sit upright amongst the rolling, rattling, plastic bottles.

"Here let me help you?"

Billy looked up. A tanned and calloused hand was extended down towards him. He took hold off it and it was surprisingly warm and dry to his touch. Powerful forearms easily hoisted Billy clear of the bottles, supporting him, as he got his feet underneath him and then holding onto his upper arms, as Billy regained his balance.

Billy, now upright looked into the fellows eyes. There was concern on the man's face. He was maybe into his fifth decade and his hair was cut short to his scalp, but showed flecks of grey across its entirety. Probably a regular silver fox if the hair was left to grow longer than its buzz-cut stubble. Under his thick dark eyebrows the kind eyes showed a deep concern.

"What's all this about a party?"

There was not a single shred of disbelief in the orderly's voice.

"My friends told me to follow them to the party."

"Where are they now?"

Billy looked around the room convinced that now the lights had been switched on everyone was going to come out of their hiding places, even if the surprise had been lost. The room was totally empty of people. It wasn't very large and most of the available floor space was taken up by large aluminium benches and several large, dangerous looking machines with rows of red lights and a large handle on them. Surely these aren't turbo-charged, extra steam, dish washers? He realised that the tray he had upset and all the others that were lined up around the room were almost identical to the plastic trays used on the kibbutz in their dishwasher, except these were stainless steel.

"So what do your friends look like? Maybe I passed them in the corridor on my way here."

"I don't know?" Billy admitted, sounding weak and confused. "I only heard their voices through the door and around the corner?"

Now not only did Billy sound confused, but also like a total nutcase. He was waiting for the orderly to rush off, summon the men in white coats with straight-jackets and then help drag him off to the psychiatric ward. But instead of suspicion Billy saw only concern in the man's eyes. He seemed unaffected by the bizarre nature of Billy's story. Instead he reached his free hand down and supported Billy under the elbow.

"Let's get you back to bed. What's your room number?"

"Dunno"

"Ward?"

"No idea."

"Can you remember the name of the doctor treating you?"

Billy searched the fuzzy fog in his memory, hunting for the elusive name of the doctor he had seen the previous morning. He had said very unpleasant things; that he drank like a fish.

"Fischer." Finally. He remembered.

"Goodness, you're a long way from home. Wait here and I will get a chair."

Ten minutes later Billy was wheeled, in some style, back onto the ward where his room was. He had been away for the best part of two hours and no one had missed him. His absence would have been noticed soon, because the day shift were beginning to arrive and as part of the handover someone would have been around, to check on the patients. This meant that so far his little outing, had not been discovered, but the orderly named Shmuel, reported Billy's return to the ward office. He had to do this as he needed a signed chit from the sister to confirm Billy's delivery. So his escape became general knowledge and with it came an explanation that the voices he had heard were hallucinations brought on by the strength of the medication he had been prescribed. Billy couldn't grasp that the voices were a product of his own imagination. They had seemed so real and convincing.

Billy took a shower, then dressed in a fresh set of pyjamas, he climbed back into bed. He didn't feel that tired, until he actually was in bed, had stretched his legs, rested his head on the pillow and closed his eyes. It was only then that the exertion of the night overtook him and he fell into a deep and dreamless sleep.

## Chapter Eighteen

Billy's wanderings around the hospital in the middle of the night and his hearing of voices was not even mentioned. He wondered whether the nurses had even bothered to report it to the doctors, or whether it was such a common side effect of the withdrawal medication, that it wasn't worth reporting. This both worried and shocked Billy. The full impact of what could have occurred or what he might have done under the influence of those drugs, finally dawned on him. The voices could have guided him to jump through a window or off a building. Something fatal, not just falling into a tray of plastic pee-bottles. Even though he had been assured that these hallucinations were only a short term side-effect, he was still shit-scared this could easily happen again. There was also the small matter of his mental fitness? Would this impact on his discharge? Were further tests or evaluations of his condition now needed? He needn't have worried, after the doctor's visit in the middle of the morning he was told that he was free to leave whenever he wished.

Now he was unsure about what to do or where to go. A return to the kibbutz would mean him reverting back to his old habits and the doctor's final warning, delivered during his discharge consultation, about the danger to his life, was still ringing in his ears. Where else did he have to go, though?

The staff were a little more relaxed on who visited him, now that his bill had been settled in full. He felt certain that Mike and Yara who had embarked for Egypt on their honeymoon would not be on the visitors list. He was unsure about Mel. After their last encounter at the reception he was not sure he would ever see Mel again. He found that despite all that had happened between them, he didn't blame her for how things had turned out. He felt certain that Mel would make an appearance even if it was only to chew him out his behaviour or maybe to just come out with an "I told you so", and to lord it over him. He resolved that he would be apologetic in the first case and acquiescent in the second. He was just sitting in his room contemplating the equivalent of his 'walk of shame', from the hospital, by bus, all the way back to Tel Boker, in his somewhat dishevelled wedding clothes, when the door flew open and in breezed Mel. She was carrying Billy's small pack and an empty suit bag.

"Thought you might appreciate a change of clothes and a toothbrush?"
She said cheerily dumping the holdall on the bed and draping the suit bag over the back of one of the visitors' chairs.

"I think there is some soap and a towel in there as well. I didn't pack it, Eva did."
"Probably arsenic in the soap and razor blades sown into the towel then?"
"Would you blame her? You behaved like a complete dickhead, again, didn't you?"
"For fucks sake, just say what you think, why don't you? Still pouring poison in her ears?"
"I was just telling her a few home truths."
"Whatever. She was already pissed off at me long before I started behaving like a 'dickhead'. So, maybe, just maybe, I started behaving like a 'dickhead' because she was pissed off at me, whichever way it's all your fucking fault isn't it?. I don't know what I did to piss you off in the first place, was it because I ignored your advice and came back to Israel?"
"No" Mel was immediately on the defensive.
"Then what was it? What got Miss Queen Bee so upset that she moved in on my girlfriend and started pouring shit on my relationship? Because like it or not that's what happened. You evil vindictive bitch. "

Billy was annoyed and there was a much harsher edge to his tone than normal. Mel, never one to be outdone in an argument met and matched this; the volume of their exchange, increased.

"Brilliant. So this is all about deflection. Shift the blame for your behaviour on to others. Classic alcoholic; it is everybody else's fault but mine."

"You have no idea what you're talking about, you stupid cow. Anyway I am seeking treatment for my problems. What the fuck are you doing about yours?"

"I don't have any problems." Mel looked indignant at the thought.

"That's bollocks and you know it. You're a fatuous ass."

"Are you calling my arse, FAT! You pathetic little wanker." Mel screamed.

Mel was on her feet now, her hands braced on the table. Staring daggers at Billy. He shook his head and slumped back down on the bed. For all her claims of being properly educated, there were clearly large gaps in her grasp of the English language. Before he could explain himself further a nurse stuck her head around the door.

"Will you quieten down in here! This is a hospital. There are sick people trying to rest."

Billy mouthed the word.

"Sorry."

The head disappeared.

"Listen Mel."

Billy dropped his voice to a normal conversational level and adopted a more conciliatory tone.

"I don't want to fight with you anymore. I don't want to fight with anyone. I have something much more important to struggle with. That is going to take all my energy. So if you are done with delivering your message I would like to get changed and get the hell out of here. Please."

"I will wait for you downstairs."

"Don't wait I am not coming back to the kibbutz, not tonight anyway."

"What? Where are you going? There are people waiting for you there. People who care about you."

"I know but right now I have to do something that is important for me."

"Like what?"

Mel was standing with her hands on her hips. Billy recognised the tell-tale signs of an approaching storm.

"Get myself to an AA meeting."

Mel opened her mouth to object and then the enormity of what Billy had just said hit her. At the same time she realised that any objection on her part to Billy's intentions would mark her out as a hypocrite. Her mouth snapped shut. She had missed or misunderstood what Billy had meant when seconds earlier he had claimed to be seeking treatment for his problems.

"Look. There." Billy waved in the direction of the table beside which Mel was standing. She glanced at the small blue folder lying there and reached to pick it up.

"It's in English."

Billy said as he watched Mel study the cover and then open the booklet up. The leaflet was for AA, Alcoholics Anonymous. One of the nurses had delivered it to him earlier and Billy had read the whole thing from cover to cover. It was not a big brochure and after the initial preamble, merely described the various types of meetings that were on offer and what were their stated aims. The last page was a list of these in the Tel Aviv area by type and location. Billy was not sure how serious he was about attending a meeting, but one thing he was certain about was that he should not return to Tel Boker, today.

There was a meeting taking place that afternoon in an annex to the hospital so it would not be difficult for him to attend. Although Billy was prepared to accept he had a problem, he did not know what to do next? He wasn't sure that AA would provide any real answers immediately, but maybe, being in a room with people, fighting the same battles, might give him some strength and maybe a little bit of understanding. Mel could see the common sense of what Billy was saying, but did not want to surrender control of the situation. She felt she had some personal stake in Billy's well-being and was reluctant to hand that over to a bunch of addicts. Billy could see the internal conflict written all over her face and he knew that it annoyed her. Secretly he was pleased, but he kept a straight face, he was following her advice almost to the letter and in doing so was causing her more grief.

Mel left the room to get a cup of coffee. Billy took a slow, leisurely shower and dressed in his fresh clothes. When Mel returned, later, it was to make sure that Billy was determined not to travel back with her. Even the promise of a seat in her car was not enough of an incentive. She made a big fuss over the fact that she had decided to rent a car for a few days so she and Sebastian could travel around the country on a whirlwind sight-seeing tour. Now that first day of the rental had been wasted travelling here. Apparently, Mel had left Sebastian back on Tel Boker. She was anxious to get back to the kibbutz, so they could start their tour in the afternoon. They were beginning in the south, in Eilat and then working their way slowly northwards, finishing up in Tel Aviv in a few days, just in time to catch their flight home.

"If I go now and you stay here, it might be the last time we see each other this trip. I am not planning on going back to Tel Boker."

Billy thought 'Neither am I', but he didn't give voice to this sentiment as he didn't want their last words to each other to be angry ones. Secretly Billy was quite happy to see the back of Mel as they seemed to have nothing much more to say to one another. She agreed to take Billy's suit carrier with the suit, shirt and shoes with her back to the kibbutz and she promised to hang it up in Billy's room.

They faced each other across the room. There didn't seem to be anything left for either of them to say and like their last parting in London several months earlier an explosive argument had left them annoyed with each other. Mel looked up at Billy. He was upright, clad in clean clothes and with his hair still wet from the shower. His arms were deeply tanned from the work outside and his hair had started to show blond highlights from daily exposure to sunlight. The biggest difference was he was sober, his eyes were clear and bright and he had a determined gaze. She wanted to cross the room and grab him and hold him close but her stubborn streak and some of the things he had said to her in the last hour prevented her. She stayed rooted to the spot, paralysed by her indecision.

"Well I had better be going." She started hoping Billy would say something nice to her and give her an excuse to stick around a little while longer.

"Yeah you had better, don't want to keep the nerd waiting."

"Fuck you." Mel spat and stormed out of the room.

Billy gave Mel enough time to find her way out of the ward before he grabbed his small pack from the chair, pocketed the money Mel had left for him and went to say his goodbyes to the nurses. It was just before lunchtime so Billy wandered out into the hospital grounds. There was a while to go before the meeting and when it got too hot for him outside, Billy sought out the cafeteria and got himself a cold drink. He realised it was almost time for the meeting to start, so he consulted the booklet, found the name of the place where the meeting was to take place, then set off to discover its location.

There were a few people milling around outside the meeting place. Most were smoking and chatting and it looked to Billy as if they all knew each other. As new arrivals wandered up, they were greeted like long lost brothers and sisters, with hugs and kisses. Billy hung back from the crowd, puffing uncomfortably on a cigarette. Mel had been also kind enough to bring him some Time up from his supply on the kibbutz, so he would not run out of cigarettes for a day or two. He flicked the butt into a nearby ashcan and took out another one from the packet, searching his pockets for his lighter.

"Could I bum one, please?"

The voice behind Billy startled him and he spun around. Standing facing him was a friendly smiling faced man, with longish hair caught up in a bandana. He was wearing blue kibbutz work shorts and a denim shirt. His dark tanned skin marked him as someone who had lived and worked outdoors for a while. His accent placed him as a foreigner. Billy offered the pack of cigarettes to him so he took one between his fingers and flicked it into his mouth, before patting the pockets of his shirt in search of a lighter. Billy lit his for him, so the stranger pushed his cigarette into its flame, whilst puffing on it, until it started to smoke. For a moment, they both stood in silence, smoking.

"Are you here for the meeting?"

The stranger asked, nodding his head towards the crowd of smokers across the path, which seemed to be growing ever larger by the minute.

"No, err, yes,"

Billy stammered, still not sure in his own mind if he was going to go through with it and join the meeting.

"Still not decided?"

The stranger had a knowing look on his face.

"My name's Dean and I am the secretary of this meeting. That means I effectively run it."

Dean's announcement prompted Billy to take a second look. In Billy's opinion, he was not sure what he was expecting to see, but if this man was an alcoholic he was hiding it well. No tell-tale signs of ill-health, no visible ticks or shakes and the eyes that met Billy's were smiling, bright and clear.

"What happens in the meeting?"

Billy asked as if something offered by Dean could be the grounds for him to object to attending and give him the excuse he was seeking to simply walk away.

"Well today we have a guest speaker, who will tell us about his life and then we open the floor up so people can share their own experiences."

Dean noted the discomfort that flashed across Billy's face when he mentioned the personal involvement.

"Don't worry, you won't be forced into a confession at gun-point. If you don't wish to share you can just sit and listen. There is absolutely no pressure."

This calmed Billy down a little and when they had finished their cigarettes he allowed himself to be led inside by Dean.

Inside the room there were rows of chairs laid out. In front of these there was a small space then two chairs, one of which was already occupied by an older man, the other was taken by Dean. Billy took a chair in the last row and hunched down in it, trying to make himself small, inconspicuous and as invisible as possible in the brightly lit room. Dean called the meeting to order and invited the guest speaker to tell his story. As Billy listened he heard the tale of a volunteer who had come to the country shortly after the war in 1967 and had been here ever since. He had fallen in love several times with various Israeli women, but his greatest love was the local cheap vodka and that had always won in any love war. The list of debauched and sometimes criminal acts that the guest had committed over the years in order to service his habit left Billy shocked. Personally he felt there was no way he would ever stoop that low and indulge in such depravity. This revelation came as a relief to Billy and he started to brighten up a bit. When the guest speaker finished Dean took a moment to reflect on what had been said. Billy listened intently waiting for some form of censure of the guest speaker's actions but none was forthcoming. All Dean kept saying was how he identified with certain parts of the story. Billy couldn't believe his ears. There was no way he could identify with any of what he had just heard. No way. If this is what being an alcoholic was about then he was definitely in the wrong place. He had never stolen money from a loved one to pay for his drink, nor had he poured Brasso through a loaf of bread and drunk the liquid residue. He was above these sorts of things. He was feeling very self-righteous and a little indignant that people could equate his small problem to the same magnitude as the depravities he was hearing.

Things only got worse when Dean opened up the meeting to the other people in the room and person after person thanked the guest for his share and then proceeded to share their own stories. Billy was on the point of standing up and leaving, when the baton was passed back to Dean. He then uttered a phrase which stopped Billy dead in his tracks and left him riveted to his seat in shock. Picking up on what one of the others had said Dean nodded his head and said.

"I totally agree with you, you should always look for the similarities and not the differences."

This particular piece of wisdom, one of a selection of what Billy would come to learn, were stock phrases around AA meetings, scored a massive hit on Billy. Up until that point he realised he had been looking around the room and seeing complete strangers, people he could and would not identify with. But after Dean's words of wisdom he began to take a second look and more to the point he began to listen properly.

He heard stories of kibbutz volunteers who had dropped out of or been kicked out of their kibbutzim and had headed to the cities around Israel either because they couldn't or didn't want to return home to their old lives. Stories of hand to mouth existences in the black economy and of nights spent in drunken stupors on park benches or beaches. As Billy listened he heard the story of his first trip to Israel, told through the experiences of others in the room. For Billy it was a truly humbling experience and in the end he was forced to clear his throat, sit up straighter in his seat and admit.

"Hello my name's Billy and I'm an alcoholic."

There he had said it. Now there was no turning back.


Billy knew he would have to return to Tel Boker eventually if only to pick up his stuff, but he was hoping to make it a flying visit and he needed time to summon up the courage to do so. It took him a couple of days to convince himself to make the trip and in that time he had attended several AA meetings and been occupying a shared room in one of the hostels, despite the fact that even that put some temptation in front of him. It seemed that wherever there were volunteers there would be alcohol and lots of it. He was sure that while he was still taking his meds, he would avoid drinking, but when the prescription finished and there was no incentive to abstain he was afraid his willpower would crumble. He regretted not taking Mel up on her offer as this would have given him the chance to visit the kibbutz and depart on the same day, or the next day at the latest. If Mel and Sebastian were sightseeing then they would be heading in the direction of one of the major cities and could have dropped him off. It was not the first time that Billy found himself cursing his pig-headedness.

He had resigned himself to taking a bus trip south and so as the day dawned he headed towards the central bus station. It was all very routine as he had made this trip so many times in the past, which was just as well as he was shattered. The previous evening had been a struggle as the hostel had an influx of new volunteers, who were intent on making a night of it. The balcony, adjacent to Billy's room that overlooked the street had been their chosen party venue and the party had gone on until dawn. At one point Billy had surrendered and gone out to the balcony to join them, but without an ability to indulge in the finer points of the party, he had, for the first time, realised how sad a bunch of drunk people, talking absolute nonsense really was. With this depression and the realisation of what a prat he had been, for most of the last three years, Billy took himself back to his bunk and even with his head under a pillow had been unable to fall asleep. As a result he was feeling very jaded and grateful that he didn't have to concentrate too keenly on the job at hand.

He had just bought his ticket and emerged back into the daylight and the general haze and noise of the bus station. He stood for a moment on the steps of the office and adjusted his small pack, moving it from one shoulder to the other. He felt a light tap on his shoulder and turned towards the source. A tall youth in full IDF uniform was stood beside him. He was young, probably only a recent draftee. His uniform looked in reasonably new condition and his beret was in it's usual place under his epaulette. His Galil was slung over one shoulder, the magazine attached to the stock by a thick rubber band.

"I think someone over there is trying to get your attention," the young lad said in very heavily accented English.

Billy followed the extended arm and looked across the road. He blinked. There was definitely someone on the other side of the road, leaning out of the cab of a Toyota Land Cruiser and waving madly in his direction. He couldn't make out the face, as most of the features were obscured by the shadow from the truck cab and the rest by a ridiculously large pair of mirror shades and a baseball cap. Billy wasn't even sure if the person there was waving at him. There must be fifty to a hundred people on this side of the street and the driver could have been trying to attract the attention of any of them. He glanced up and down the line of people. No one else seemed to be responding to the driver's signals. A bus passed, obscuring both driver and vehicle for a moment, but when it was gone the driver was still in place wildly waving his arm. It was impossible to hear what he was shouting over the general noise, but he was yelling something as Billy could see his lips moving. He decided to take a chance and crossed the road. As he got closer the driver got out of the cab and took off the baseball cap. It was Scouser.

'Great', thought Billy, 'the guy still owes me some money'.

Getting this back would mean that Billy, who had used the last of his cash to purchase the bus ticket, would be able to buy himself something to eat on the journey. At least he was in no position to lend Scouser any money, but a quick look at his old friend, as he crossed the street convinced him that Scouser was probably not down on his luck, in fact it was probably the complete opposite.

Scouser looked well fed, clean and was dressed in a smart pair of blue tailored shorts and a polo shirt, his feet enclosed in a pair of expensive looking leather moccasins. The two old friends enclosed each other in a firm hug. When they finished Scouser held Billy at arms-length.

"Bloody IDF useful for summit then, eh?"

He grinned, teasing Billy, his tongue in the corner of his mouth.

Billy looked puzzled.

"Why?"

"Bin yelling at you from here, before you went buyin a ticket, like. Got one?"

"Yes," Billy held up the ticket

"Goin'? Up north?"

"Nah, Tel Boker."

" Shame I'm off to Eilat, could've dropped you."

Billy was annoyed. With the shortage of funds, a free lift to Tel Boker would have been welcome.

"How come you didn't come get me?"

"Can't, could I, got all this stuff in the back."

Scouser pointed a thumb over his shoulder. For the first time Billy noticed that the back of the Land Cruiser was piled high with cardboard boxes. Some of them were plain brown, others were adorned with elaborate colourful logos and photos. Billy made a note of some of the brand names, Scubapro, Mares and Poseidon. With the stylised fish and trident the last was a bit of a puzzle, but Billy had at least heard of Mares, and Scubapro was self-explanatory.

"Where did you nick that lot from?" Billy nodded his head at the load.

"Not bloody nicked. Straight up paid for used cold hard cash."

Scouser folded his arms across his chest.

"New stock lines, the latest. For the dive shop. I'm the manager, like."

"Hang on?"

Billy had difficulty keeping the incredulous note out of his voice.

"You're managin' a bloody dive shop?"

"Fuck yeah." Scouser couldn't grasp that Billy was having such difficulty believing him.

"Very cool. Well done mate. So you got a real job at last?"

"Eh yeah."

Scouser paused. A sudden look of confusion passed across his face, replacing the smile momentarily with a frown.

"Told you all this crap last time. You loosin' it Billy boy?"

Billy opened his mouth to confess he thought he had been conned, but he never got to say a word. A blip from a Police siren snapped them both back to the present. A Police car had pulled up behind the Land Cruiser and a voice boomed out from the external speakers. Scouser looked over at Billy.

"What's 'e on about?"

"Rough translation?"

Scouser nodded his head.

"Move this vehicle along or we will be forced to tow it."

Scouser didn't need a second invitation. He waved at the officers who were watching them intently from behind their Ray-Ban aviators, as he rounded the bonnet and opened the driver's door.

"In you get."

"What about my ticket?"

"I'll buy it, like. Drop you back at Tel Boker?"

Billy didn't even need to think twice about his answer.

"Deal."

Billy threw open the door and slung his bag in the backseat. Scouser climbed in the driver's side and started the engine. He signalled right, pulled away from the curb and then turned immediately left into one of the streets that led away from the chaos at the bus station. Billy checked the side mirror. The police cruiser had made the same turn and followed them for a short distance before taking another left and doubling back on themselves.

"S'ok. You've lost the cops boss."

Billy hammed an American movie gangster accent. Scouser laughed out loud.

"Your actin's still shit then. Don't need to leg it from the cops these days. I'm totally, legit, like, Billy boy."

On the vinyl dashboard in front of Billy there was a large sticker with a cartoon of a scuba diver in the middle with the legend 'Dive Tribe' and an address in Eilat. Scouser had nodded at it. It was the same logo on the left breast of Scouser's polo shirt.

"Appears so."

"Wall's a mugs game. Alright for a while. But it's a total arse ache livin' always on the dodge. You can't own fuck all. Stuff just gets lifted. Really pissed me off."

"Was convinced you were running a scally scam. Blagging bus fares off gullible mugs, like me. On the hour every hour. Having a right laugh."

Scouser looked confused.

"Eh wot?"

"A few months back, you took me for twenty sheks. To get back to Eilat. Then buggered off instead of catching the bus."

Scouser went quiet as he focused on trying to recall the incident and why he would have borrowed the money and then done a runner. He suddenly thumped the steering wheel with his open palm.

"Alright. I did do that. I owe you that twenty."

"So what happened then?"

Scouser was quiet for a few moments, focusing on the street signs as if he was searching for an answer and hoping to find some inspiration in the road names.

"Fucked if I can remember. Oh yeah," the light of recollection suddenly lit up Scousers face as he remembered.

"Thought some bastard had nicked my wallet. Turns out, I had dropped it in the bus station. Anyway went to buy a ticket and it was only bloody sitting there, right inside the ticket booth. I had to fill out a bunch of poxy forms after answering a shit load of stupid questions. Finally get it back, but you were long gone by then. Jumped on the next fast one to Eilat. Never gave it another thought."

Scouser indicated left and turned off the main road into a side street which became progressively narrower and more choked with cars, parked on both sides.

"Shit! Thought this was a rat run to the highway."

"Unlikely ..." Billy remarked sarcastically as Scouser braked at the end of a cul-de-sac.

"Oh, bollocks." Scouser thumped the steering wheel before shifting into reverse gear for a three point turn, which turned into five as the road was very narrow and the pickup had a long wheelbase. He pulled over on to the side of the road.

"Grab that bloody map from in there, like." Scouser jabbed at the glove box.

Billy pulled out a larger map of the whole of Israel, on which some twat had ringed Tel Aviv and scrawled 'YOU ARE HERE' on in felt pen. Billy tossed this over his shoulder into the back seat and then focused on a large scale map of the greater Tel Aviv area. First, he pin pointed the bus station on the map before tracing their route to their current location.

"You went left one street too early. See?" Billy showed Scouser the map section. Scouser put the car back in drive and set off. Billy then continued to direct their route using the map.

"Right. What you been up to then? Playin' away in Tel Aviv? Why you heading for Tel Boker? Is there a party there?"

Billy was silent for a moment as he considered exactly how much of his current predicament to share with Scouser. It wasn't that he didn't want to share the truth, it was more about how stupid and pathetic the whole thing made him appear. Scouser sensed the indecision in Billy.

"S'ok. No need to get all touchy feely. Just the low down will do."

"Low? Down? Yeah. That's about right. I totally fucked up."

"Bit more detail would be useful? Those bastards kick you off again?"

"Nah. Got the hump with the kibbutz in the north, packed it in, after my now ex-girlfriend shacked up with my now ex-roommate, went back to Tel Boker for Mike's wedding. Yeah Mike tied the knot."

Billy waited for a reaction from Scouser to the big news, but he seemed preoccupied with ensuring they made the right turn this time.

"I was gonna sign up on Tel Boker again. Really not sure if it's right for me anymore though?"

"Eh? Thought this volunteer stuff was your big thing? What happened?"

'Good question', Billy thought to himself as he pointed over to the right and Scouser took the Land Cruiser around the junction and approached the on-ramp of the highway heading south.

The intersection before the ramp was cluttered with green uniforms and kit bags as today's crop of soldiers sought lifts to their various postings around the country.

"Are you gonna stop?" Billy asked, scanning the sea of faces for any that looked even vaguely familiar. He had made the mistake in the past of cruising past a group of soldiers without paying attention and totally missing two of the young members from Tel Boker. They gave him hell when they eventually made it home, several hours after Billy had. The situation had been made worse by a sudden unseasonal rainsquall that had left the two intrepid fighters soaked to the skin and freezing cold. Billy was persona non grata for more than a few days. He wasn't making that mistake again. He didn't see anyone he even remotely recognised among the throng.

"Nah," Scouser shook his head, "and stop ducking the question."

They joined the stream of traffic heading south and Scouser visibly relaxed. Billy knew that the journey time from this intersection to the Tel Boker gates would take about ninety minutes. It was a long time to spend evading the truth and giving obscure answers. He now faced a dilemma. Either he could shut Scouser down, claim he didn't want to talk about things and move on to other subjects, or he could open up to his old friend and tell him the whole story, or at least the story so far and see what he suggested. He had known the guy sitting next to him for the best part of two years and in that time they had shared a lot, both good times and bad.

Scouser lit a cigarette, handed the packet to Billy who also then lit one up too. He followed Scouser's lead and dropped the window a little to flick the ash outside. He inhaled a lung full of smoke and exhaled.

"No idea how to start really?"

"Reckon the beginning is favourite, like, Billy boy."

"Fair enough", Billy pondered where exactly he would consider to be the beginning, "Suppose it all started back in the UK really."

Billy felt certain that it was as good a place to start as any. Although he hadn't been aware of it at the time, there was a certain euphoria in being back home and a familiarity amongst his own. Telling stories about his adventures and people who wanted to hear them. They faded faster than his tan. After that he crashed back into reality. Accommodation. Job. Bills. These everyday necessities loomed large and eroded the remnants of any holiday spirit. Billy took most of it in his stride, but maybe the arrival home in the UK with a volunteer kibbutz mindset, was always doomed to failure. With hindsight his consumption of alcohol had not been acceptable in any location, even in the kibbutz. Yossi had at least made that much clear to him before he left, but then maybe the rosy tinted spectacles that he used to view his time in Israel with had coloured his memories.

Billy related his return to the UK, his job, his apartment and also mentioned the behaviour of friends and work associates. Mike's abandonment, Mel's desertion, his forced resignation, the party incident, his cheating girlfriend. Scouser let out a low whistle at the details of Saskia's betrayal. Apart from that he remained silent while Billy related the key events of the past year of his life. Scouser's only other interruption was a rather explosive,

"What a bunch of cunts!"

which he exclaimed when Billy was relating the incident involving the whisky bottle at the party. Billy nodded his agreement, even though, through his reflections over the past couple of days, he had maybe reached an alternative conclusion. Now was not the time to get into an argument. Therefore, he moved on to the slightly touchier subject of his showdown with Mel at the flat. He played it straight and told Scouser exactly what was said by both sides.

"No way man."

Scouser valiantly leapt to Billy's defence.

"You're no alky."

Billy would have liked to have agreed with his old friend, but unfortunately the body of evidence, particularly in the light of recent events, was firmly of the opposite opinion.

"Think I do have a problem."

"Really?"

"Yeah mate, don't wanna admit it, but I think Mel's right. Proven that these last few days, Sadly, I totally lost it, big time."

Billy then related the whole incident with the wedding, the reception, the stealing of the special malt whisky, the bus trip to Tel Aviv, his collapse, his admission to hospital and he ended with the doctor's summary of his medical condition. Another low whistle emanated from the far side of the cab.

"Not after a second opinion, like?"

"No Scouser I don't need one. This Doc gave me chapter and verse, which was what I needed to hear. Why would this complete stranger lie? No point to it?"

"No more boozing then?"

"Can't. Can I?" Billy was trying not to sound too gloomy about the prospect but it was difficult.

"What you up to, going back to the kibbutz then? That's just so mad mate. The kibbutz will swallow you whole?"

"Just getting my stuff. A change of clothes. This t-shirt will start walking on its own, otherwise."

Scouser wrinkled his nose.

"Thought that was my socks, like."

"None on, mate." Billy pointed out.

"Better get you a shower and shirt sorted, soon as, then."

"Fine by me." Said Billy sniffing.

After the seriousness of Billy's revelations, the conversation then turned to Scouser. When the film shoot finished, Scouser had, like many of the other extras returned to Eilat. Instead of embarking on a monumental bender and blowing all the money he had made, which seemed to be the most popular option among most of the extras, Scouser fundamentally changed his life. He had mentioned the details to Billy, before, at Tel Aviv bus station. Billy had just thought it was a front to scrounge money off people and he had largely forgotten most of it. Scouser quickly took him through the highlights and brought him up to date. In this job he was responsible mainly for the running and staffing of the Dive Tribe shop but he had his hand in other parts of the operation, and that was before he began to describe the beauty of the underwater world and the euphoria of the diving experience.

"I dive most every day, like, but it's all down to me, I am the Assistant Manager now, so I'm paid decent like. Even have a place of my own."

Billy nearly started taking the piss out of him, but at the last minute, something held him back?

"Sounds like a right giggle."

"You never been?"

"Scuba diving? Me? Nah. Never."

"You should give it a go. Right brilliant it is."

"Might just do that, sometime."

"Tomorrow then?"

"Eh?"

"Come back to Eilat, and I'll take you out, just you and me, up with the larks."

"Not sure."

"Ah, come on Billy, you can swim can't yer?"

"Yeah course I can. I was the fucking lifeguard at Tel Boker."

"Sound. Sorted."

"Is it?"

Billy wasn't so sure but they had moved on to other things and Scouser was updating him on the trials and tribulations of their other mutual acquaintances from back in the day. The subject of Billy and his introduction to the underwater world wasn't mentioned again.

It was mid-morning by the time they arrived on Tel Boker and they drove in through the unmanned and open gates of the kibbutz.

"Don't think anyone's home."

Scouser, whose very brief stay on a kibbutz had been on a settlement in the Golan Heights, was amazed at the apparent lack of any form of gate security.

Billy picked up on the vibe.

"It's like that here in the south. No bombs, no missiles, no tanks, no need for gate guards."

He made a peace gesture with his two fingers.

Scouser grinned at him.

"Where to now m' lud?"

Billy pointed to a small track that led away from the front gate.

"The volunteer blocks are down there."

The place was deserted as almost all of the volunteers were at work. Billy let himself into his room and began to sort out his stuff, throwing clothes and possessions into his large rucksack. He left some clean clothes and his towel out on one side. Scouser had collapsed into an armchair outside and Billy had thrown him a bottle of Goldstar to keep him company. After he had packed his stuff, Billy took a shower and cleaned himself up.

As if to prove to everyone that the kibbutz security was not as lax as it seemed, when Billy returned from the shower block there was another Jeep parked behind Scouser's Land Cruiser. Someone had obviously clocked their arrival. Billy slung his towel over the line to dry and then entered the room. Scouser was sat on one of the beds and leaning against the wall just inside the door was Yossi. The volunteer leader looked less than pleased to have been dragged away from whatever important job he had been attending to.

"I might have guessed it was you."

He pushed himself off the wall and came towards Billy.

"You gave us all a bit of a shock, just disappearing like that. It wasn't until we got the call from the hospital that anyone knew where you were. If the call hadn't come from the hospital when it did we were about to launch a search of the surrounding countryside."

Billy had the good grace to look contrite and then apologetic.

"Sorry Yossi, I just had to get away from here and I am afraid that I am not going to be staying. I just dropped by to pick up my stuff."

Billy actually surprised himself with his statement. While he had been standing under the stream of water, using the flow of warm water to help wash away some of the cobwebs in his head, he had been weighing up all the options available to him. He could stay on Tel Boker and battle his demons here. Up sticks and head for another kibbutz and try to re-invent himself as a sober and studious volunteer, or join an Ulpan program and learn Hebrew properly. Head for one of the big cities and try to disappear into the black economy and probably end up drinking again. Tag along with Scouser to Eilat and try his luck there.

"Where are you going to go?" Yossi asked a note of scepticism in his voice.

"I am going back to Eilat to work with Scouser."

"Are you?" It was Scouser's turn to act and sound surprised.

"Gotta a job for me mate?" Billy looked across at his friend.

Scouser paused for a moment, thinking.

"I am sure something will turn up."

Yossi still looked sceptical.

"Are you sure it's a good idea Billy? Mel and Mike have filled me in on what the Doctors in Tel Aviv said."

"That's precisely why I can't stay here, can I?"

Privately, Billy was annoyed that his medical problems appeared to have been the subject of general discussion. He made a note to chew Mel out about it, the next time they met.

"Won't you stick around and at least say goodbye to Mel. She will be back from Jerusalem later this evening."

"I can't Yossi. Scouser has to be back in Eilat tonight."

"I do?" Scouser sounded surprised again.

"Yeah. You said that earlier."

"Right, yeah, if you say so mate."

Scouser picked up the beer bottle and chugged the rest of the contents.

"Time to get our shit together, Billy boy."

He pushed himself up off the bed and crossed to the door.

"Nice to have met you, Mr Volunteer Leader."

"The name's Yossi."

"Bless You, mate." Scouser said over his shoulder as he left the room.

Billy grinned and then did his best to look sheepish under Yossi's withering glare.

"Look Billy, you are not registered as a volunteer here on Tel Boker, not yet. If you want to leave I can't do anything to stop you, and I won't. Just remember there are people here who care about you and we are looking out for your best interests."

"I know that Yossi, and I really appreciate it. Right now I think I need to do this; get away; sort my head out; see where things go"

"Get your head together? In Eilat? We all know how well that worked out last time."

It was Yossi's turn to grin. Billy stuck out his hand.

"Friends?"

Yossi took the proffered hand and shook it.

"You got it."

## Chapter Nineteen

Billy was fast becoming an expert on the rather informal Egyptian customs protocols as he had made these trips, with diving equipment, several times a month, over the last six months. He planted the dive bag on the counter and waited for the customs officer to examine it. The bag was heavy, it had two wet suits, a pile of other scuba equipment and a dozen t-shirts, still unopened, in their plastic wrappers. It was all brand new. None of it was Billy's. His scuba gear was safely stowed in his locker at the dive club, on the Egyptian side of the border. His equipment was second hand, except for two important and vital pieces, his buoyancy vest or BCD and his regulator rig. After much scrimping, saving and a hefty staff discount these were purchased, new.

He was effectively smuggling the bag's items across the border. It was no big deal. The customs officers were more interested in cigarettes, alcohol and the occasional tin of instant coffee, so Billy made sure, that at least on one trip, out of every four, he had one of those items in his luggage. The procedure was very simple. The customs officer would open the bag, look inside, poke around and see what it contained. If he found cigarettes then he would count the number of packets and extract a quarter as 'duty': with two hundred cigarettes, two packets were removed. It was the same 'rate' for alcohol. Four bottles became three. However coffee was higher. One in two tins, of the Israeli instant coffee would 'disappear' as import tax. The customs officer unzipped Billy's bag, pushed the two wetsuits on top, to one side. He was more interested in what might be lying underneath. The t-shirts were subjected to the same treatment. Today, Billy's bag also contained two tins of coffee; he was unconcerned, when one was 'taxed'. The tin of instant coffee was removed and stowed under the counter, and the customs officer pushed the bag away.

With this signal, Billy packed the stuff back down and zipped the bag closed. This was how the Dive Tribe kept their shop on the Egyptian side of the border stocked. Technically, this was smuggling, as there was no duty paid on the items they carried across. If they had been officially transported then they would have been liable for Egyptian Government import taxes and, as the goods were passing from a Tax Free Zone, also subject to Israeli Sales Tax.

The customs post at Taba was a row of huts with the Passport and Visa section on one side, Customs in the middle and the Money Exchange on the other. Three wooden shutters in a line, each individually manned by officials who seemed to bear a strong familial resemblance to each other.

As he had already queued up and had his visa form stamped, and these days he always had pockets full of Egyptian money, the best way to avoid the usury that took place at the exchange window, he was now free to head across the open ground to where the border guards were lounging on garden chairs, and pass through the gate into Egypt. The hotel right by the border fence had once belonged to an Israeli. Once the peace deal with Egypt had returned the Sinai to the Egyptians, he had threatened to blow the whole place up, rather than have it fall into their hands. Fortunately, he was talked out of this extreme response, so it was now the site of a blossoming dive business, operated by several Eilat clubs. It worked well as both a training school and a jump off point for jeep dive safari tours around the Sinai desert.

Although the guards on the main barrier at the border looked relaxed with their feet up on the railings, cigarettes dangling from the corners of their mouths the AK47's resting in their laps looked very lethal. Billy tried not to imagine one of them being pointed at him as he approached the guards. Occasionally one of them would smile and wave in which case Billy would smile back, but these two, this morning, merely stared at Billy as he walked past. Billy, kept his eyes firmly on the road ahead and didn't stare back. He didn't look up until he was past the red and white barrier, before crossing the car park towards the hotel's main buildings.

Billy's final task at the end of every working day was in its essence very simple, but still, even now, he found it a huge challenge. Across the hotel complex there were several restaurants and bars and it was not unusual for his charges to disperse across the site after they had finished diving for the day. This meant that he had a list of names and no idea exactly where the people on the list had ended up. So around five, he had to make a tour of each of the venues, search for the guests and remind them that they had to be back at the assembly point by six, to travel, as a group through the border back into Israel. Of course if people wanted to stay longer that was fine, but they would miss the lift from the border hotel to the Dive Tribe office at Coral Beach. Making that journey under their own steam was not much of a challenge as there were always taxis waiting on the rank on the Israeli side of the border and there was a bus service that ran until late in the evening. It was merely part of the club's service to paying guests that one of the Tribe minibuses would be waiting to ferry them back to the office.

Once back at the club then at some point they could take one of the Dive Tribe shuttle buses to return them back to their hostels or hotels in Eilat. The majority of the guests usually used the free minibus as it was not much fun lugging a heavy dive bag with you everywhere you went. Also the Club made it a strict policy, that any personal equipment was the owners' responsibility. Enforcing the club rules was not the challenge for Billy. It was having to enter each of those bars and check for patrons.

Sobriety was still a very new and fragile concept for him, so visiting drinking establishments was a real test. Most days it was a test he managed to pass with flying colours. Occasionally after a long and tiring day, when his defences were down, it was extra hard. These were the days when Billy had to focus on the good things that had come to pass since he had quit drinking. Not least among these was his job at Dive Tribe. He had thrashed out the details of his potential opportunities during the remainder of their journey down from Tel Boker to Eilat and he was surprised at how much Scouser had been prepared to offer him. He had to admit later, when challenged, that he had been a little sceptical that Scouser was in a position to make the offer in the first place, but after a half hour at the Dive Tribe the following morning he was made fully aware of Scouser's position within the company structure and how senior he, in fact, was.

Scouser had been able to make room for him in the equipment rental department and Billy had literally started at the bottom of the ladder ensuring that the compressed air tanks were all filled to the correct pressure and inspecting the used tanks, when they were returned for any signs of wear and tear. From there he moved up to learning how to maintain and service the equipment. Alongside his work he was taking advantage of the on-site training and was slowly working his way through the qualifications as a diver. He decided to stop his training when he too, like Scouser, had secured the Dive Master certificate. This meant that he was able to take experienced divers out on guided dives and that was exactly what he had been doing today. The road to qualification as a Dive Master had been relatively smooth. Billy had what it took to pass all of the exams and practical tests with flying colours. There was, however, one hurdle that Billy was dreading almost from the outset. At the Dive Tribe and according to stories he had been told, at other schools, there was a tradition that newly qualified Dive Masters were put through an endurance test after they passed their final tests. This 'passing-out' test usually involved copious amounts of alcohol, with the express intention that the newly qualified candidate would then be expected to lead the first deep dive of the day the following morning, irrespective of the state they had got into the previous evening. It was known affectionately as the "Passing Out Parade" or POP, but in the Dive Tribe mantra it had another name, The Beer Snorkel Challenge.

Billy had been present on several of these dives when the newly-minted Dive Master had been all but puking into his regulator on the descent. The residue vomit, drifting away with the current, attracted hordes of small fish, so if you spotted a diver swimming on the reef, their head encased in a cloud of swirling fish, there was a strong possibility that you were watching a newly qualified Dive Master at work. Billy, now given his estranged relationship with alcohol was dreading his own POP or Beer Snorkel Challenge. This was a slight misnomer as, although a snorkel was used, inserted into the mouth of the candidate for initiation, it was not just beer that was introduced to the funnel at the open end. The rules stated that any drink of choice, within reason could be poured into the funnel, the only proviso was that the candidate had to swallow as much as possible without choking. As the day of the final exam dawned Billy was feeling sick to his stomach about the coming trial. It wasn't that he was worried about making a fool of himself, everybody choked eventually, it was more what effect drinking alcohol again would have on him. He had built up robust defences against temptation and was worried that his strength and willpower would be breached and he would be back in the shit again.

He had not voiced his concerns to anyone during the training course preferring to bottle up his anxieties and keep them within. Given this he was very surprised when Scouser entered the exam room at the end of the final written test and took a place at the desk beside the instructor who was supervising the exam. When they were told to stop writing and hand in their papers Scouser asked for a moment of their time. The candidates, excited at the finish of their exams and anxious to find out their final test scores had taken a moment or two to settle back down. Once Scouser had their attention he cleared his throat. In his Sunday best corporate accent he said.

"On passing your final exam you will shortly be awarded your Dive Master certificate. There is however one final hurdle for you all to overcome."

He looked at the four candidates in turn. They all knew what he was referring to. It had been the subject of discussion at several points during the past few weeks.

"That exam module will take place at six this evening in the bar. I just want to say that Billy,"

He now looked at Billy directly.

"You will not be required to take this test."

The other three began to protest and Scouser raised his hands to quieten them.

"If any of you other three wish to back out of the Beer Snorkel tonight then we will think nothing less of you for doing so. We will make this a level playing field, but I will not expect someone who has to struggle daily with their sobriety, to have it challenged over some parlour game."

As the full impact of Scouser's words hit Billy, he realised what a true friend he had in the rangy Liverpudlian. The crew at the Dive Tribe valued his contributions, so now he had a real future. Billy had to struggle hard with the lump in his throat as emotion welled up inside him. For the first time, since leaving the hospital in Tel Aviv, he felt that he was maybe, just maybe, winning his fight.

In the dive group today he had four divers who were staying in the hotel on the Egyptian side of the border and four who had crossed the border with him that morning. It was these four guests that he was trying to locate now. He knew that he had eight very happy guests somewhere in the hotel complex. Both of today's dives had been superb, straight out of the top drawer, first class. If Billy could have taken an earlier dive and told all the wildlife to be in the right places at the right time, so they would appear on-cue like actors in a drama, then things could have not gone any better. The house reef, just off the beach, was teeming with fish and other sea life most of the time, but the divers he had with him were not there just to stare at the colourful fishes. They had certain things on their bucket lists. Wildlife that was particular to this part of the world and so to be able to point out the scorpion fish, the stone fish, any number of the highly dangerous, poisonous lion fish and a number of moray eels was a good tally for any dive in these waters.

The unusual attendee during the first dive was a rather large crocodile fish that had taken up residence on a part of the reef wall. Billy had seen it there before but it had been absent for several months and he had stopped looking for it. It was pure chance that he looked and spotted it, back in its usual place. During the second dive, the appearance of a large turtle, unusual in these waters brought a smile even to Billy's face. At the end of the dive, whilst coming across a patch of sea grass into the beach area and making a safety stop, his sharp eyes had located two miniature sea horses, camouflaged among the green fronds. Siting these rare creatures meant that even the most seasoned diver emerged with a smile that stretched from one ear to the other. He had caught a quick read of most of the log-books of the divers as they asked him to sign and stamp them. He was pleased with what he read there. To have had two such successful dives was not unique, but was nevertheless pleasing. He reckoned that the guests would be in high spirits tonight and when they went out into the city of Eilat later, they would be bragging about their diving today and singing the praises of the Dive Tribe and their dive guides. It was all good publicity.

He started at the furthest point of the complex, at the beach bar and slowly made his way from venue to venue looking for his guests. He located two of his charges in one of the beachfront restaurants. They were close to finishing their meals, so once Billy had ascertained that they would be travelling back with him he asked them to finish up and then make their way back to the dive club. The rest of the group, he found chilling out at the rooftop bar. Whilst it was hardly authentic, the decor and atmosphere was that of a Bedouin camp. There were carpets and cushions and low tables in brass. The walls were hung with carpets and silks. Open to the sky it was definitely a relaxing way to end the day. Most of the divers had opted for a tall frosted beer or a glass of wine. Billy hunkered down among the group and got comfortable. A waiter approached and Billy asked for a bottle of water in Arabic. It was among the few words and smattering of phrases he had picked up in the last few months. It was enough to impress the guests sat around him.

Most of them had heard him speaking in Hebrew at one point or another, either with Israeli guests or with other members of the Dive Tribe staff.

"Oh wow, you speak the language."

Said one of the other divers finding it hard to keep the admiration out of his voice.

"I know about four phrases, that's all."

Billy was loathed to make too much of his skills. He didn't like to brag anymore. It was a part of his new, more sober personality. Old Billy would have made a big play of his language skills, drawing attention to them whenever he could, new Billy was much more understated. He noticed that his reluctance had done more to impress the guests than he expected.

"So who is coming back across with me?"

There was a show of hands. He didn't expect those who were staying in the hotel to volunteer, but the last of his charges from the other side both agreed to accompany him. This was always more of a comfort to Billy. Although they were all adults he still felt better when he had returned all the guests to the club in the evening. This meant he had discharged his duty of care to the guests, so he could relax and enjoy his evening without worrying about late night phone calls from the Border police, informing him that some of his guests were wandering around lost in no man's land between Israel and Egypt. Thankfully these type of incidents were few and far between. The worst such incident had happened a few months back, when a mixed party of Brits and Danes had stayed on drinking in the hotel bar until late. Totally pissed, they had tried to come back through into Israel, where they had taken an exception to one of the questions posed by the security officials on the Israeli side. The resulting scene had only been resolved when the police had called him to come out to the border and vouch for them. Billy had arrived full of apologies and managed to sweet talk the security people into releasing his divers without charge or censure. This expended a large amount of his personal capital, built up over the months of almost daily trips through the crossing and he was not best pleased that it had been wasted, unnecessarily, on a bunch of drunken fools. What was worse was that, instead of thanking him for keeping their sorry hides out of jail, the group took Billy's actions for granted and then moaned in the minibus all the way back to Eilat about the 'Fascist' officials. What they had collectively failed to realise was that without Billy's timely intervention they would have spent the next three days in detention and missed their flights home. As it was only two days until they were due to fly home, they had to stop diving, so Billy never saw them again.

He was back at the border the next morning with another group where he was teased a little by the staff about the incident, a practice that continued for several days until the joke finally wore thin. It looked as if there would be no repeat of that unfortunate incident that evening. About an hour later Billy made the call to the Dive Tribe office and then set out to take the party back through the border and into Israel. There were no hiccups and as they emerged from the customs hall on the Israeli side, the Dive Tribe minibus pulled up and they all got in. Back at the club there were the usual post dive administrative tasks for Billy to perform. Fortunately he kept most of his equipment on the other side of the border, it was easier and safer that way, so he didn't have equipment to clean. This meant that once he had filed his paperwork he was free to go.

Most of the guests had already taken off back to their hotels or hostels, so Billy shut up the shop and went in search of Scouser. He found him propping up one end of the bar with a half empty beer glass in front of him. Billy hooked a stool and sat down. He didn't order a drink, he still had some of the water left from earlier. He did, however light a cigarette, before passing the packet and his lighter to his friend.

"Busy day?" Scouser exhaled a cloud of smoke.

"Not really. Same as."

"They sounded well happy when they got back here, like."

"Yeah. So lucky today. A bloody turtle and get this, some seahorses."

Scouser's eyes went wide at that.

"Really? No fucking way. Where?"

"In the long sea grass just in front of the club; still needs mowing by the way." Billy joked.

"Fuck. Been diving there for two years now. Ain't never seen a seahorse. Not even seahorse shit."

"Is there such a thing?" Billy looked confused.

"Dunno. Anyway, you're lucky bastard, Billy boy." Scouser punched Billy on the bicep.
"Tonight? Any plans?"

"Not really. It's the Yanks last night tonight so they are having a do at the Underground."

The Yanks were two American diving instructors who had been working in the Eilat for the past couple of months but were now shipping out on the next leg of their round the world diving tour. But before leaving they wanted to say a final farewell to all the friends they had made during their stay.

"You going?"

Billy didn't get a chance to answer as the two were interrupted by female company. Shari was suddenly between them plonking a large bunch of keys on the bar top.

"The office and the classrooms are all locked up."

"Ta Shari."

She gave Scouser a brief smile before turning the full warmth of it on Billy.

"I hear you had a successful trip today. Some very happy customers."

Billy demurred. He didn't like to blow his own trumpet. He would let the guests do that for him. Shari laid her hand on his forearm.

"I know you are a real asset to this operation." She squeezed his arm firmly. Billy and Shari had been flirting up a storm for the past three weeks, since she had arrived at work one morning and announced that she had split from her boyfriend back home in Jerusalem and this time it was for good. Their relationship since then had been very tactile but Billy was playing it cool as he didn't want to hit her on the rebound. She had given him plenty of encouragement over the past few weeks, always seeking him out if he was in the club and coming to find him in her breaks and making sure she was wearing the tightest, skimpiest of bikinis whenever she arrived on the beach after her shift finished, to sunbathe. Billy knew it was only a matter of time before something happened between them. The chemistry was all there.

"Are you coming to the Underground tonight?" Billy asked, trying to make it sound as casual as possible.

"I would love to," Shari gushed. "But I have an essay to write for my studies. Can we go out another night?"

Billy was disappointed but he covered it up well.

"Yeah, sure."

She pecked Billy on the cheek and was then gone.

"Blown out by the lovely Shari, but your still in then, Billy man? So what about tonight, you gonna hit the Underground?"

"I might, not much else to do is there. What time?"

"Nine-ish."

"Alright. Catch you there bit later."

The two bumped fists in farewell and Billy slid off the bar stool, stubbed out his cigarette and went out to the front of the club. He had managed to acquire a little moped at a knock down price from one of the instructors who had left now. It made a right racket, but it was a bit better than walking or waiting around for a bus. Billy stamped it into life and climbed on. He left the car park in a riot of noise and a cloud of blue smoke.


The regular pay-checks and the staff discount meant that Billy was able to afford a bed in one of the hostels in town. This hostel catered mostly for guests of the Dive Tribe and was partly owned by Schmulig the owner of Dive Tribe. His business partner in the venture was the hostel manager Orin. The sign outside the main entrance was the stylised blue scuba diver that was the club's logo and any further doubt about the main pastime of the clientele and their reason for being in the city of Eilat, was dismissed when you entered the main courtyard and found the racks for drying equipment and wetsuits alongside a large water tank, filled most of the time with fresh water and only occasionally with a drunken guest. The wooden racks were on wheels and one of the last jobs before bedtime was to roll the racks into the enclosed glass area on the opposite side of the courtyard. There they could be secured, under lock and key, to prevent any casual passers-by from helping themselves.

Usually Orin took care of this job and most of the rest of the time he kept a watchful eye on the hostel and its contents from a table in the corner of the courtyard, which was where Billy found him when he came in off the street. As usual there was a pot of rich strong coffee and a half filled ashtray on the table alongside any paperwork that Orin was working on. In the absence of paperwork there would be a newspaper or magazine open and spread across the table top.

Orin was a heavyset man, in his late forties, whose ham like forearms stretched the sleeves of his shirt to bursting point. His dark hair, greying in places, was curly and fell down over his eyes. He wore a pair of spectacles for close up reading, but was vain enough to remove them if any young ladies came into view. His English was passable but heavily accented making it difficult, sometimes, for non-native English speakers to understand. With Billy there was no problem, the two spoke Hebrew together and Orin was not averse to asking Billy for help if there was a particularly spectacular communication breakdown. Billy went over to the fridge and extracted a can of Coke. He wrote his name on the list on the door of the fridge, it was an honesty system where residents could take and sign for cold drinks and then pay their bill when they checked out. It worked well and it meant there was never any cash lying around for the unscrupulous chancer to get their hands on. Billy went over and sat down opposite Orin.

"How's it going?"

"It's going," Orin replied not bothering to look up from his papers.

This exchange between two friends, in Hebrew, was all that was required to know that the day had gone well for Orin, there was no stress in his life and he was reasonably happy with his lot. He finished reading the list he had been studying and looked up, removing his reading glasses as he did.

"The Americans they are leaving us?"

"Yep. In the morning. Early bus south to the border."

"But tonight?"

"Out on the town to celebrate."

Orin cast his eyes heavenwards. He was not puritan in any way and he accepted that occasionally people on holiday needed to blow off a little steam, but he didn't welcome overindulgence and drunkenness, particularly if it resulted in damage to property or extra work clearing up the mess afterwards.

"Be alright, They are Yanks not Brits. Might get a little messy, not carnage though."

"Are you going with them?"

Orin knew all about Billy and his new found sobriety; they had discussed it at some length over a number of late night cups of coffee.

"Might just show my face. Scouser's up for it later."

"He's a good lad." Orin smiled. 'If only you knew the old Scouser,' Billy thought to himself. It was true, back in the day, both Scouser and Billy had been drinking for England and many were the nights they had collapsed in a drunken heap on the beach not more than a few hundred metres from where they were now sitting. Billy also thought how things had changed for both of them now. Billy finished off his Coke and went through to his room to take a shower.

The heavy blue metal door to Billy's room was standing slightly open. This meant that at least one of his roommates was home. Billy pushed it open and walked in. The room was empty but the door to the bathroom at the other end was shut and from beyond it Billy could hear the sound of a shower running. So someone was home but they were in the shower at the moment. Billy would just have to wait his turn.

Billy slung his day pack onto the top bunk and then stripped off his t-shirt. This was rolled into a ball and then stuck in the large bin liner that also occupied space on the upper bunk. He slid himself onto the lower bunk and waited for the shower to become available. A few moments later the door to the bathroom opened and Grant, one of his roommates, appeared in a cloud of steam. He was wearing a pair of boxer shorts and had a towel slung over his shoulder.

"Righteo. You're good to go mate." His Australian accent was thick, pure outback Aussie.

Billy slid off the bed and grabbed his towel. He showered quickly and then wrapped a towel around him and exited the bathroom. Grant was partially dressed and was hunting around in his dive bag which was open on his bunk.

"Going somewhere nice? Somewhere special?" Billy asked.

Billy crawled back on his bed and propped himself up against the wall. Grant was dressed in a pair of smart black trousers. Billy watched as he pulled out a black silk shirt and pulled it on, leaving it unbuttoned. It was a totally over the top outfit for a night out in Eilat, where Bermuda shorts, T-Shirts and Flip Flops were the height of fashion.

"Nah, not really mate." Grant barked.

"Well who is the lucky lady?"

Billy was convinced that Grant was on a promise. He was making a real effort. As Billy watched, Grant poured himself a large handful from an aftershave bottle before splashing it liberally all over his face and neck.

"No one."

Grant was now squirming, visibly uncomfortable under Billy's probing questions.

"You wanna keep that sticky beak out, mate." There was a sudden flash of anger.

Billy held his hands up in surrender.

"Sorry mate. Sorry, didn't mean to pry. Nothing to do with me."

"That's about right mate."

Grant went back into the bathroom and Billy heard the squeaking as he wiped the mirror with a towel. Billy dressed quickly in a clean t-shirt and shorts. The t-shirt bore the logo for the Dive Tribe on the front and the word Dive Master across the shoulders on the back. Grant came back from the bathroom.

"Coming to the Underground tonight? It's the Yanks last night."

Billy pointed his thumb in the direction of the room next door.

"Nah. Meeting a mate. Can't."

Billy didn't want to provoke any trouble, so he didn't make any more jokes about 'lucky ladies'. Instead, he just nodded, clipped on his belt pack and slid his feet into his flip-flops.

"Right, off for some ciggies. Have a good one, catch you later, mate."

Billy left the room, pulling the door closed behind him. Once the door had closed Billy muttered under his breath.

"Or maybe not, if you get lucky ..."

He was still grinning to himself as he left the building.

## Chapter Twenty

Billy had to go further than he wanted to buy cigarettes as there was a long queue in the first shop, mostly people with shopping baskets or trollies stacked high with food. There was only one till open and the poor girl operating it looked totally stressed out. He didn't want to wait and he knew that there was another kiosk further down the street that just sold cigarettes, so he headed there. It was deserted. Billy bought his smokes and then walked back onto the street.

Checking his Timex, he realised it was a little too early to make his way to the Underground, even though he was halfway there already. He decided to return to the hostel and see if the two American lads, who were the hosts for the evening, were ready to leave yet. It would be much better to arrive in a group than for him to hang around on his own in a bar.

He puffed contentedly on his cigarette as he wandered back in the direction of the hostel. There were plenty of people out and about, most of them seemed to be heading downtown. Billy weaved his way through the crowds, being careful not to run into anyone. Up ahead, as the crowd suddenly parted, Billy spotted Grant crossing the road. He was looking around furtively, like he was worried about being spotted. His shifty actions intrigued Billy, who slipped behind a nearby palm tree, peering out from behind the trunk. As he peeped out, Grant stood at a bus stop on the opposite side of the street, peering intently up the road in the direction of the oncoming traffic. He kept checking his watch and glancing up the road. A bus pulled up, the other people waiting boarded the bus and it turned back into the traffic. Grant was alone. Still at the stop. He wasn't catching a bus. He was waiting to be picked up. Billy was intrigued as to who this secret date was? It didn't take long, before a small red car approached, indicated and pulled into the bus stop. The driver stopped the car level with Grant, who then bent down to open the passenger door and climbed in. The car was now level with Billy on the other side of the road. He couldn't see the identity of the female driver as she had turned her head away from him and towards Grant. After a brief exchange of words and what turned into a rather passionate kiss, the driver straightened up, flicked on the indicator, to pull back out into the traffic. Just as she was about to pull away, she looked over her shoulder for traffic. Billy saw the young lady's face for the first time.

It was like a hammer blow in his guts. Billy leaned on the trunk of the tree for support as he fought to catch his breath. The car in the meantime disappeared off down the road. Grant had just met, passionately embraced and driven off with Shari. She was clearly not writing any essays tonight. Billy took a few moments to compose himself. He was totally gutted. He was not the jealous sort. He had been making a special effort with her and felt that, given time, they would have got something going. This illusion was now completely shattered into pieces that were now slicing back into him, causing his old pains of rejection to well up inside of him. He crossed the road ignoring the blaring horns of the motorists and re-entered the supermarket. The evening rush had cleared now and the place was virtually deserted. He raced past the fresh fruit, the veg section, micro-wave meals, bakery, meats, fish market, dairy and arrived in front of the shelves containing all the wines and spirits. Standing there mesmerised, dream-like, by the colourful labels and the shapes of the bottles. He had more than enough cash to buy whatever he wanted and even reached out towards the shelves as if to pick up a bottle. No, something held him back.

On one level he just wanted to get drunk and ease the pain he was feeling right now. But there was another emotion. It was stronger. It was exerting itself now and he knew that to pick up that bottle, carry it to the checkout, pay for it, break the seal and taste the contents would solve, absolutely nothing. He reached out again towards, a bottle; ARAC. His hand halted. Halfway. He couldn't make his hand travel any further, no matter how hard he tried.

He was receiving intense scrutiny from the staff member behind the counter. He withdrew his hand. Walked away, up the aisle. Wines and spirits section ended then the beer fridges and finally the soft drinks fridge.

He selected a bottle of coke and then on his way to the till he picked up a couple of his favourite chocolate bars. He paid for these, then took the handles of the carrier bag and walked out of the shop, somewhat empty, but there, in the depth of his consciousness, he felt a reassuring pat on the back; a small, but significant, consolation.

He walked aimlessly back towards the hostel and was in a world of his own when his name was yelled from the entrance door of the hostel. Scouser was there tapping his wrist watch and yelling something about wasting valuable drinking time. Billy loaded his Coke and chocolate into the fridge and then re-joined Scouser on the street. The two set off up the road. Billy was deep in thought, still coming to terms with what he had seen.

"Eh, you alright, Billy? Not said a word, like. What's pissed you off, man?"

Everything was far from all right but Billy was not about to reveal the cause of his unhappiness. He forced a smile at his old friend.

"I'm fine. Honestly." He tried to sound convincing. He was not sure if he succeeded.

The Yanks, Alan and Brad, were already in place and with most of their friends, were now filling up one whole section of the Underground. Wishing them 'Bon Voyage' were most of the Eilat diving elite, so the conversations were a mixture of shop talk about new equipment or dive sites or tall stories about diving escapades, mishaps, close calls and close encounters of the marine kind. Billy had heard most of the stories before and after his third pint of coke he felt really bloated. At the same time the others around him, now on their third, fourth or in some cases fifth pint of beer were beginning to get a bit drunk and the volume of the conversation and the exuberance of the group was rising accordingly. At one point Brad came over and sat down heavily next to Billy.

"Hey Randell? Your very quiet buddy. You doin' ok?"

His eyes were shining, his cheeks were flushed. Both signs that the alcohol consumed was beginning to take its toll.

"That lovely Shari on a rain check? She's normally part of your crew?"

"No man, she's studying tonight, at home, some essay, she said." Lied Billy

Images of Grant with Shari intertwined in acts of love now danced across his eyes. He shut them tight, to banish them. Brad didn't notice. Just carried on about the plans he and Alan had made for their onward journey. They had been planning the next stage of their trip for the past few weeks, asking about the diving sites down the Sinai coast as far as Sharm and Ras Mouhammed. Billy had dived most of them whilst leading Jeep safaris organised by the Dive Tribe: so he was considered to be a bit of a local expert. The two Americans had been picking his brains for some of the must-see sites. Their plan was that after the Sinai, head off to the Far East, Thailand and Malaysia diving, before heading back to the US, in the autumn of the following year. It had all sounded exciting to Billy, but right now he was not in the mood for company and tales of grand adventures.

Brad pointed at his nearly empty glass of Coke.

"Get you something?"

Brad had just drained the last dregs of his beer and he was on his way back to the bar for a refill. Billy put his hand over the top of his glass.

"No mate, I'm fine, thanks." Smiled Billy.

"Okay."

Brad stood up and made his way over to the bar. Billy used his solitude to finish off the last of his Coke and he stood up too. He found Scouser talking to Andy, the other American. The two were both rather drunk and using each other to remain upright, by leaning heavily on each other like an A frame. If one of them should make a sudden move, they would both topple off their bar stools and end up as an untidy heap on the marble tiles below.

"I'm outta here mate." Billy announced, once he had got their attention.

"Right. Okay there, Billy boy." Scouser smiled.

"Oh, just in case I don't catch you, tomorrow, you guys have a superb trip."

This was to Andy. They shook hands, wobbling the A frame a bit.

"You heading to the hostel now?" Andy then slurred.

"Yeah, why?"

"Two of ours are missing in action, no shows. If they're at the hostel, send them this a-way, ok?"

"Okay, will do, if I see them. See you guys."

Billy turned on his heels and left the bar. He walked down the steps and then out on to the main road, turning in the direction of the hostel.

The city was buzzing right now. It was just before midnight and the streets were alive with revellers and tourists. The traffic was still heavy and the music was blaring out from every bar and cafe that Billy passed. He turned off the main drag and into the side street where the hostel was. Instantly the noise level and the intensity declined. Billy breathed a sigh of relief. He was happier away from people who were drinking to excess. So soon after he had decided to quit, it was still an effort and it left him feeling drained afterwards. A normal night was hard enough to endure, but a party atmosphere, like tonight, left him doubly exhausted.

He barely said two words to Orin as he passed through the courtyard of the hostel. He noticed that the racks of drying wetsuits were already inside. This meant that Orin was probably on his way to bed soon. He lived in a small flat over the main part of the hostel, so he was on site in case there were any problems during the night. Billy went through to his room and kicked off his flip-flops. He noticed the place was as he had left it, so Grant had not returned yet, but then he didn't expect it. Billy stretched out on his bunk and was asleep in a few moments.


The doors for each of the rooms in the hostel were made of steel, hung on steel frames. Whilst they provided an additional level of security and certainly were sufficient to deter a burglar, they did have one serious drawback. Their hollow steel shell meant that if you struck one with a single blow, with your closed fist, the resulting clanging chime was like the bells of doom, shaking the building to the very foundations, and certainly sufficient to wake even the heaviest sleeper. Multiple blows on a door, someone knocking several times for example, set up a serious of booming, reverberating echoes that harmonically intertwined into something approaching the roar of a wild beast. Now take this and multiply it out over the six doors in the corridor at the hostel and you had the unholy daemonic noise that wrenched Billy from his sleep. Someone had just passed down the corridor and systematically hammered on each of the doors to the rooms. Billy was out of bed in a flash and he yanked open the door and stepped out into the corridor ready for a confrontation. He turned towards his left, the direction leading from the dormitory area outside to the courtyard. Between him and the door to the courtyard stood Brad.

"Is that your bloody friends making all this fuckin' racket?" Billy growled.

Billy remembered Andy's request to keep his eyes open for their wayward friends and to send them on to the Underground. Billy looked the American up and down rapidly taking in the fact that he was clad only in a pair of faded boxer shorts and that his hair was messed from his pillow and he was knuckling sleep from his eyes. Clearly he had been as much the victim of a rude awakening as Billy had. The door opened and both of them turned on the newcomer. It was Andy, similarly attired to his roommate and with his hair plastered to his forehead with sweat.

"Friends of yours?" Billy enquired archly, folding his arms over his chest.

"Never seen her before in my life."

"Her?"

"Yeah her. There's some foreign chick outside, well she sounds foreign, heavy accent at least and she sounds crazy."

Billy muscled his way past the two Americans.

"Crazy, just got real."

He was angry now. Dragged from his sleep, he had noticed as he had come to, that the lower bunk on the other side of the room was empty. This meant, without any doubt that Grant was not back from his night out. His next action had been to check the time on his watch and it was approaching 2 AM, so there was a strong chance that Grant was going to be sleeping where ever he had ended up, if sleeping was even on the agenda. This realisation drove a fresh dagger into Billy's heart. This was one more reminder he could have done without, in the middle of the night. He had been tired earlier, but now with a couple of hours sleep under his belt, there was a real risk that he would remain awake for the rest of the night and as a result be exhausted in the morning.

He would have been happier if he had been left asleep and not had to deal with these emotions until the morning, when sunlight and a fresh cup of coffee could make anything appear in a more positive light. Instead, now, there was a certain person who was going to get the full force of his displeasure. Both barrels.

Outside most of the yard was in darkness. There was, however, a small pool of light, cast from one of the streetlights. In the centre of this pool of light, sat on one of the picnic benches, hunched over, was a figure. As the door clanged shut behind him Billy saw the figure straighten and swivel around to face him. In the limited light he took in her features. She was blonde, but her hair was scraped back from her face and caught in a pony-tail. Whilst this gave her a no nonsense business look, her face was soft featured with fine high cheek bones, flushed a little pink, probably from some recent excitement or exertion. There was one feature that almost stopped Billy dead in his tracks and if he had paused for more than a second, would probably have rendered him speechless. If someone had asked Billy at a later date to tell them what he remembered about this first encounter he would have been hard pushed to remember anything about her clothes, a white cable knit sweater and denim jeans, or anything else about her. But he would always be able to remember her eyes. Billy had seen blue eyes before, even Scandinavian blue, blue eyes, but these were a whole new type of blue. It might have been the limited light or something else but they seemed to glow with a steel blue laser-like intensity. They fixed on Billy and tracked him as he advanced across the intervening space. The eyes won the day and Billy stopped. He was not, however, rendered totally mute.

"What the blue buggering blazes do you think you are doing coming in here in the middle of the night and banging on all the doors, waking people up? People who were all sleeping peacefully. What the fuck do you think you are playing at?"

The eyes remained unflinching. There was an understanding in them. What Billy had said had been absorbed and while some of the more choice words might have got lost in translation, the general gist of his point had been delivered. There was a pause as a reply was formulated. The eyes scanned Billy up and down, taking in his attire and his general demeanour.

"Are you the manager?"

It was a perfectly reasonable question. Billy was stood in the courtyard of the Dive Tribe hostel, wearing a T-Shirt emblazoned with the company logo.

"No! I am not the fucking manager! If you want the manager why couldn't you press the button marked, manager!"

"What button?"

"This fucking button!"

Billy went over to the corner where the door which led upstairs to the flat above the hostel was. On the wall beside the door was a lit button which when pushed sounded a bell upstairs in Orin's flat. Billy stood to one side and rather dramatically pointed at the button.

"No. Don't get up,"

He said holding up his hand in a rather imperious gesture.

"Let me get that for you. All part of the fuckin' service."

Billy pushed the button twice and then unwilling to commit to any further discourse, or become part of any welcoming committee, when Orin turned up. He went back through the door, into his room closing the door behind him and climbed back into bed.

He lay in the dark for several minutes trying to master his breathing and calm himself down, hoping he would eventually drift off into the arms of forgetful sleep again. If he was lucky enough to fall asleep again he would be troubled by vivid dreams of a pair of stunning blue eyes following his every move and action. He had calmed his breathing and just closed his eyes when there was a light tap on the door and a voice called out in Hebrew.

"Billy are you awake. It's Orin."

"Am now!"

Billy replied ironically in Hebrew.

"I have a beautiful Danish girl to share your room."

Orin was obviously enjoying himself, even if Billy wasn't. The door opened and the hallway light flooded in. Billy could make out Orin's huge bulk framed in the doorway. He stepped aside and ushered his latest guest into the room. Billy had already correctly guessed who the newcomer was. The girl from the courtyard entered, balancing her hand luggage on the top of a colourful, monstrously large Mares dive bag. Orin wasn't hanging around in case there were any more fireworks. He beat a hasty retreat to his apartment upstairs and most likely his bed. The door slowly swung shut blocking out the light from outside and plunging the room back into darkness. This suited Billy perfectly, as it put the newcomer at a disadvantage.

"Is there any light in here?"

Billy reached out of bed and flicked a light switch on.

"Which bed is mine?"

Billy had his stuff spread out on the top bunk above his head and even though Grant had not returned, Billy didn't think it wise to offer his lower bunk to the newcomer.

"Top bunk there, is all that's left." Said Billy waving his arm dismissively.

There was the thinnest mattress up there, a single blanket and no pillow. It was the rule in these places. First in, got the most comfortable bed and bedding and so on; not in for a very good night, the new arrival, then. She stood and eyed, with a degree of distaste, the top bunk.

"Is this the bathroom, through here?"

"Yep."

She pushed open the bathroom door. It was in near darkness, too.

"Is there a light?"

Billy reached up over his head and flicked the bathroom light switch. Light from the bathroom spilled back into the room, so he switched off the bedroom light, before rolling around and hauling the sleeping bag cover over his head. Partially to block out the light, but really for the girl's privacy.

Within his cocoon he heard sounds of various bags being zipped and things being sorted out. Then the whisper of nylon on nylon: a sleeping bag from its carry bag was spread on the bunk. Through the covers Billy heard the bathroom door close and the room was returned to partial darkness and silence. Now noises of taps running, the toilet flushing and the bathroom door opening, again.

"I am sorry. I cannot find the light switch for the bathroom?"

Billy huffed and flapped his sleeping bag cover back again. Granted it was difficult to find, hidden behind his bunk upright, though. Reaching up behind the metal frame he flicked the light switch. As the light dimmed, Billy glanced across and was greeted with a fine pair of tight butt cheeks and firm upper thighs, when she climbed into the top bunk. As a final sight before lights out, that was definitely up there as one of his all-time favourites. He did eventually fall asleep and probably with a big smile on his face.

Billy didn't bother with an alarm clock. Most days he was sure that the early morning comings and goings in the hostel would be sufficient to wake him. Today was the same. Grant's bed was still unslept in. The huge and very colourful dive bag took up most of the limited floor space in the room. The night's events came back to him. Lying back in his own bunk he could see the nylon clad outline in the upper bunk on the other side of the room. He had dreamt of brilliant white, sun bleached ostrich shells, all lined up on the hot desert sand under a sky that was an unnatural shade of blue. Once awake he remembered the vision just before he went to sleep and realised the connection. Her eye colour matched perfectly that unnatural blue sky. He smiled once again. He was just contemplating the chances of another flash of buttocks, as this huge nylon serpent trembled and heaved when its contents stirred.

Billy, who had slept the night in his shorts and t-shirt tossed aside his own sleeping bag; preferring to sleep with it unzipped as a cover. He span sideways and sat on the edge of his bunk. Not looking, he probed around with his feet and eased into his flip-flops. He stood face now level with the recumbent figure in the opposite bunk.

"Good morning," he started brightly, "I am sorry about last night. I don't think we got off to the best start."

"Mmm phmph, mmm phmph."

The woman in the opposite bunk sat up. Her last action before going to sleep seemed to have been to release her pony tail and in her sleep her large mane of blonde hair, freed at last from the strict constraints of its bondage, had taken over her whole head, forming a sheer curtain of cascading blonde curls over her face. A hand snaked out from inside the sleeping bag and brushed the larger part of the hair away.

"Hi."

Now free from the encumbering hair, normal speech was possible.

"Did you sleep well?"

"Not really. Who was sawing the logs?"

"Ah, that'll be me, snoring. Should've said to use some ear-plugs. Sorry."

"It's a little late for that now."

Billy detected the first thawing signs of a smile dancing around the corners of her mouth.

"I'm Billy, by the way, Billy Randell." He stuck out his hand.

"Stine, Stine Pedersen."

The hand extended towards Billy. He took it in his own. It was soft and warm. They shook hands briefly. Warming to the theme of her discomfort in the night, Stine continued.

"I don't know how you sleep on these beds. It's like sleeping on solid wood."

"The Hilton, it ain't."

"Not even close."

Billy had no way to compare the beds at the Dive Tribe hostel with The Hilton, as he had never had the pleasure of sleeping at such a hotel. Stine's tone of voice suggested she had.

"Well if you think the beds are bad I strongly recommend you don't try the coffee. It's like varnish."

"Excuse me?" Stine had a confused look on her face and Billy had seen that look many times before. It was the look he got when one of his comparisons, analogies or jokes had got stuck in the translation trap. This usually took place when Billy was delivering his funniest one liners. When all he wanted was people to laugh so he could move on with his stunning repartee and, instead, the conversation foundered on a language barrier. In extreme circumstances he could be forced to return to the beginning and explain the whole joke in a simpler form, which usually killed the joke stone dead. Other times an alternative word could allow the conversation to move forward, even if the joke was severely wounded in the process.

He tried this option first.

"Varnish? Brown paint."

"Oh I see."

Clearly the expression on Stine's face told Billy she didn't and was just being polite.

"I thought you meant varnish." She held up her hand where each nail was painted with blood-red nail polish.

"Oh it probably tastes like that too. I have never drunk nail polish, so I can't be sure."

"And you have drunk paint before?"

Billy looked over in disbelief. He had forgotten how, 'literally', some of the Scandinavians could take things.

"Actually at some point in the past I probably have. Not my finest hour though. But anyway the point I was trying to make is that the stuff they try and pass off as coffee here is pretty undrinkable. I am on the way up the road to the local bakery where they do really good coffee. Would you like some?"

"How far is it to this bakery?"

"It's just up the road."

"Can I come with you?"

"Sure."

"Will you wait while I get dressed?"

"No problem. Do you want me to wait out …"

Billy got no further. Stine tossed the sleeping bag aside and dangled her long legs over the side of the bunk. She vaulted easily to the floor, reaching out her hand to grab Billy's arm and steady herself. He was only mere inches away from a rather attractive young lady, who was wearing just a thin vest and knickers. He looked away embarrassed.

"It's alright."

Stine had a slightly amused lilt to her voice, obviously sensing Billy's discomfort. She reached inside her dive bag, pulled out some shorts, wiggled into them then poked her head and arms into a t-shirt. Billy busied himself trying not to stare and hunted around in his own bed space for his money pouch and cigarettes. Stine strapped the sandals she had been wearing the night before on and tamed her wild mane with a scrunchy.

"Ready." She said.

They left the room together and went outside into the courtyard. The bakery was only a short walk away from the hostel. He used this time to try and find out more about Stine and her holiday plans. She had booked the whole trip through a travel agent in Denmark and had travelled here alone, although she had met with a group of other Danes on the flight. They were all coming to Eilat for diving holidays, although most of them seemed to have paid extra for one of the hotels. She had booked a package of dives with Dive Tribe. When she realised Billy had connections she was keen to get his recommendations for the best places to dive. With his Dive Tribe hat on he tried to be as charming as possible. The last thing he wanted was for Stine to sail into the club later on today and file a complaint about the reception she had received on her arrival at the hostel. Billy was therefore in full on service recovery mode.

The bakery was popular among both tourists and locals, so it was teeming with people stopping by to buy their morning coffees and snacks. The majority of the menu board behind the counter was written in Hebrew, but there was a small section, helpfully but badly translated into English. Billy waited patiently as Stine studied the board. In the end she turned to Billy.

"What do you recommend?"

Billy looked at her intently and then thought for a moment.

"Eh cappuccino for da senorita." Billy hammed a dreadful Italian accent.

"Cappuccino would be good."

"A breakfast sandwich, maybe?"

"Sounds good. What's in it?"

Billy described the ingredients.

"Yes please."

Billy waited to be served. He was a regular, so when it was his turn, the girl behind the counter gave Billy a big smile and a warm welcome. He ordered their coffees and two of the breakfast sandwiches. The girl went off to prepare their order.

"So you can speak the language?"

"I get by."

They waited patiently.

"Do you want to know something?"

Billy turned his full attention towards Stine. She pointed to a pile of pastries that were lying on a tray behind the glass counter.

"If you had made any comments about me being a 'Danish', I swear I would have slugged you one."

She grinned mischievously. Billy smiled back.

"Would've deserved it, too."

Their order arrived and Billy paid for it, refusing to take any money from Stine, by way of an apology for his rude welcome last night. They took their food and drinks and walked back towards the hostel, munching on their warm sandwiches.

In between mouthfuls Stine asked him what time the minibus came by to collect them and take them out to the dive centre.

"The bus is in twenty minutes. another at eight thirty. But, I can give you a lift on my scooter, if you're up for it?"

"With a full dive bag?"

Billy who had forgotten the bag, thought about it for a moment. The huge Mares dive bag which was dominating the centre of their room at the moment was a problem?

"Could chuck the bag on the minibus and then you can ride with me?"

Stine considered this option for a moment.

"Will my stuff be safe?"

"Yeah. Course. The driver can stuff it in our crew room."

"Cool. Let's do that then."

After a promise from Shimon, the driver, to place the bag in the crew room when he arrived the dive bag was safely on its way. So, Billy and Stine got ready to take the scooter.

Billy only owned one crash helmet, which he very rarely wore. Occasionally the police would stop him and tell him to put it on, but they usually had better things to do with their time. Gentleman Billy gave the helmet to Stine and she buckled it under her chin. Setting off, it felt very strange, when her arms tightened around his chest, before he twisted the throttle, indicated and his jumped up lawn mower screamed away from the curb. Bizarrely, it felt so right. After threading through the downtown traffic, Billy opened it up as they hit the beach road. It was always a pleasure feeling the warm morning breeze in his face when passing the Navy base, then Dolphin Reef. Today this was extra special. With her body pressed so close to him, he could feel her contours through the back of his t-shirt.

Over the engine's high pitched whine running at full tilt, conversation was completely impossible as the wind whipped the words away before they could be heard. Too soon they pulled up, breathless from the wind and the exhilaration of the ride, outside the Dive Tribe buildings. The car park was largely deserted. Just the two minibuses stood ready with their doors open. Nobody else was around.

Inside the club it was another story. It resembled the inside of a bee hive. People moving everywhere in an intricate and ordered dance, focussed on their common purpose. There was a method and form to this. The students who were taking diving courses needed to be assembled into their classrooms. The divers who were on guided dives had to be collected together, their equipment checked and then loaded into one of the minibuses waiting outside. Missing or damaged equipment had to be replaced or repaired. Air Tanks, lined up like patient guardsmen on parade had to be moved out to the minibuses or into the tank room to be refilled. People were even trying to snatch a bite of breakfast or a cup of coffee amongst all this hubbub. Billy skated his way through this turmoil like an ice dancer performing a well-polished routine, shadowed by Stine in his wake. His mission, to re-unite her with her dive bag, before he did anything else.

The crew room was an oasis of calm in a sea of commotion. Most of the instructors were already out in search of their students. The other Dive Masters were marshalling their guests and getting equipment loaded into the minibuses. Their own equipment was already assembled and standing waiting, their wetsuits and other gear in a crate, their regulators and BCD's already connected to a tank and lying wrapped together with the various hoses strapped inside the nylon protection of the buoyancy device. Stine's bag was stood alone against one wall. She was relieved to retrieve her bag, even opened it to check over the contents. Billy didn't take offence at her actions. He waited patiently while she assured herself that nothing was missing. She straightened up and looked over. Billy was leaning against the wall with his arms folded.

"Sorry."

She grinned sheepishly, wondering if her actions had caused offence?

"S'ok" Billy drawled. "I'd have done the same. Let's get you sorted out, registered and all your forms signed. Do you have your logbook and your diving certificate?"

Stine unzipped the front pocket of the bag and pulled out a plastic wallet.

"It's all here."

"Excellent. Leave that here or bring it with you. Up to you?"

"I will bring it. It's on wheels." Stine said and she pulled the bag behind her.

Billy took Stine over to the club office. This was usually Shari's domain but she was noticeable by her absence. Scouser was occupying her place behind the desk and he looked stressed. Billy knew he hated paperwork and also his spoken Hebrew was patchy at best and as a large number of the club's guests were Israelis this presented a problem. His eyes lit up when he saw Billy come through the door.

"Alright there Billy boy, right on time, you've saved me."

Billy was worried he might kiss him, as he looked so delighted.

"Morning Scouser, what's happening?"

"Need you front desk today, like. We are a man, well woman down."

"Yeah these all night essay writing marathons can be a bitch."

Billy was trying to keep the heavy drip of irony out of his voice. He failed and Scouser looked at him sharply.

"What's that?"

Billy shrugged his shoulders and took up a place at the other desk. He turned to Stine, who was now standing alone and abandoned.

"Any chance of grabbing us three coffees? Say they are for Scouser and they'll be gratis."

"Sure." Stine smiled warmly, pleased to be given something to do.

Billy looked up at the first person waiting in line and started to help out. After a while Stine returned with the coffees and Billy pulled over a stool, enabling her to perch behind him and watch him work over his shoulders. Scouser and Billy with months of experience working together, made short work of the queue of people. Sorted out all the questions, satisfied the complaints, registered the new students, assigned divers to their respective guides and paired those up who wanted to take a try dive with a willing instructor. As the last guest left the office Scouser drained the last of his coffee and tossed the Styrofoam cup into the trash.

"Need another shot?"

Billy asked, looking up from the last piece of paperwork he was filing into a plastic folder.

"Yeah, would be good."

Stine was already on her feet and heading for the door.

"The same again?" She asked, pausing in the doorway.

"Yeah," both of them said simultaneously, with Billy adding a

"Thanks" as an afterthought.

She was barely out of earshot when Scouser started his interrogation. Billy related the story of the previous evening and his part in the welcome Stine had been given. He admitted to feeling a little guilty and a bit foolish this morning and wanted to make amends for his behaviour.

"I thought maybe we could give her a discount and throw in her check dive for free?"

"You want to do her?"

"Yeah, but I know the rules."

The club had very strict rules about not fraternising with the guests. It was impossible to police one hundred percent and everybody knew things did happen, but it was still a club policy.

"Fair play to you Billy boy, but I meant do her check dive?"

Scouser grinned across the office.

"Checks have to be done by instructors?" Billy recited.

"Billy, my man, you can handle that, you're a sound diver. Read this form, sign it, take her into the water, do the exercises. Sorted."

"Okay. I'll do that after the next coffee. I think she wants to change some of her options. She has a package of dives she signed up for back home, but I have given her better alternatives. Anyway, what's the story with Shari this morning?"

"Dunno? Called her when she was a no show. Not picking up on her phone?"

"Bit Odd."

Billy kept his voice neutral. He didn't want to be the one to spill the beans and get her into trouble. She had certainly broken the rules by spending the night with a guest, although as it was the end of Grant's stay, she might be able to get off on a technicality. Billy reckoned that in Scouser's rule book, it was more of a crime not turning up for work, than spending a night of passion with a departing guest. He would not rat her out, no matter how bad he felt about being lied to.

"Too strange, alright." Scouser agreed. "I got a feeling earlier you knew something but weren't telling."

Billy looked the picture of innocence which only made Scouser more suspicious.

"Come on Randell, spill."

"I know nothing. But who needs Shari? We coped okay."

"We smashed it." Scouser high fived Billy.

Stine walked back in, balancing three more steaming coffees, which she proceeded to hand around. Billy introduced her to Scouser and they shook hands. Billy had taken a moment to sort out the registration and insurance papers. While they chatted, drinking their coffees, Stine sat at one of the desks, to fill in, then sign all the necessary forms.

"Billy man, what's the score with Shari then?"

Billy made a zipping and locking motion with his hand across his mouth. Scouser slammed his hand on the desk, which made Stine look up in alarm.

"Not gonna have to lean on you am I?"

Although he was a head taller than Billy, Scouser was of a wirier build. It would have been an interesting contest if the two of them ever came to blows in anger?

"Not on, Scouser. Play fair. I might have seen summit I shouldn't have, but not for me to say.

"On a hot date last night was she?"

"Scouser, I am no grass, you'll have to beat it out of me."

Scouser was about to rise up from the desk and move across to engage with Billy when Stine saved the day.

"Finished." Stine signed the bottom of the last form with a flourish of the pen and then waved the forms around her head like an excited student at the end of her final exam. Billy pushed himself away from the desk and snatched the papers. He read them through and then counter-signed the bottom of the insurance form. He found and corrected the date stamp and stamped the form.

"Right let's get you kitted out and then we can get the check dive out of the way."


Billy now dressed in his wetsuit shorts and a rash vest was standing with his BCD and tank rig slung over his shoulder. Stine had assembled her gear and it was lying on the stones at Billy's feet. She had gone off to the ladies to change into her swimsuit and as Billy watched she emerged from the dark doorway into the light. This sight of her emerging in a figure hugging one-piece swimsuit, was more enticing than the one in her underwear the previous evening. His heart leapt in his chest. As he tried to avoid staring he looked around and realised he was not the only person in the place who had been stopped dead in their tracks by this bathing beauty. Billy cursed the club rules on fraternisation under his breath. For Stine, he was prepared to go as far as to break the rules. He might lose his job though, so he knew he had to battle the temptation. He helped Stine on with her wetsuit and was on hand to help her with the zip at the back. He was consumed with a desire to plant a kiss on her naked shoulder just before it disappeared under the neoprene. Again he managed to control himself and resist the urge. After they were all buttoned and buckled up in their gear and had performed a thorough buddy check, he led the way down the beach to the enclosed area of ocean where they could go through the check dive. This was simply a repetition of each of the exercises that had been part of the skills learned during basic PADI training. Billy would explain the skill and then demonstrate and then watch while Stine performed the skill.

There was no doubt about it, despite the long interval since her last diving holiday, Stine had forgotten none of the skills. She passed with flying colours. At the end as they stood chest deep in the water Billy offered her a quick tour around the house reef, so they could use up the remainder of their air. It was not part of the usual schedule but he had very little else to do and he thought it would be fun. Stine eagerly accepted and the two of them set off into the deeper water. As he led the way, Billy kept checking on her progress and found that she was never more than a few feet away from his left shoulder, so it was easy to get her attention and point out some of the more interesting fish and other wildlife under the water.

Billy had spent many hours underwater with people from many different countries and with wildly diverse levels of competence, but there was something about diving with Stine that felt right, felt comfortable and felt natural. He couldn't put his finger on it, maybe it was the way her eyes sparkled at him when he pointed out something new, or when her teeth showed around the side of her mouthpiece when she smiled. Stine smiled many times as the short dive revealed many of the natives of this particular stretch of coastline. It was if they had all put in an appearance to welcome their new guest.

The surprises were not over quite yet. Billy had kept the dive shallow as they toured the reef and had left plenty of air in the tanks when they returned to the shallow water in front of the beach to make their safety stop. After the regulation 5 minutes of waiting Billy then cruised into the very shallow water and turned around and sat on the bottom letting the waves gently lap around his shoulders. He raised his mask and spat out his regulator. Stine did the same.

"Enjoy that?"

Billy asked, already guessing what the answer would be. It was written large on Stine's face. She nodded her head rapidly as she fought to catch her breath. Her eyes were shining with the excitement of a religious convert.

"Brilliant."

She finally managed to get the words out.

"Are all the dives here that good?"

Billy nodded his head.

"This was my first dive in the Red Sea."

By the tone of her voice Billy guessed it would not be her last and that the Red Sea had just acquired another new convert. They floated in the shallow water as they recapped on the highlights of the dive. This was mostly Stine singing the praises of the Red Sea wildlife, the Dive Tribe as a Club and Billy as a Dive guide. Billy payed special attention to the last part.

"You are definitely the best guide I have dived with. You don't swim too fast, you show me plenty of things and you keep in eye contact all the time."

Billy smirked to himself. He had a secret agenda with Stine and was slowly falling in love with her eyes, her smile, and even underwater, encased in neoprene, it was difficult to disguise her gorgeous figure. But Billy was trying to play it cool, smiling a lot at Stine's kind words and remaining calm at her personal praise, even if his heart began hammering in his chest when she pushed herself over towards him and grasped his forearm.

"And do you lay on a welcome committee for all your new guests?"

Billy obviously looked confused as Stine took a moment and pointed over his shoulder. He had been sitting with his back facing the beach so he was forced to turn around and face towards the shore. Coming down the beach from the direction of the dive club was a huge phalanx of running and whooping divers. In among the group Billy spotted most of the members of staff. Billy felt his stomach turn over in alarm. The last time he had witnessed such a movement had been up on the north Beach a few years earlier when a group of terrorists had come ashore and tried to murder the people there. Surely lightening couldn't strike twice?

As the group got closer and Billy could make out their features he realised that there was no sign of fear or anxiety anywhere among them. In fact it was the opposite there were huge smiles and shining eyes. He noticed people were hastily pulling on tanks, or running just carrying masks and snorkels. Billy stood up as the first of the group reached them.

"Whale Shark."

One shouted in Hebrew and pushed past Billy diving into the shallows and swimming quickly away in the direction of the deeper water. Stine had stood up now, fearing being trampled by the hoard.

"What did he say?" She asked puzzled by all the fuss.

Scouser reached them and stopped.

"We just got a call from the observatory, there is a whale shark on its way up the coast. It's following the deep water line."

He didn't wait but joined the others swimming out towards the marker buoy that indicated the spot where the seabed dropped off into the depths. Billy grabbed the air gauge on Stine's rig. It was showing 90 bar left in the tank. It was not ideal but it should be enough. He was not going to miss the chance to show her one of the largest creatures from the deep.

"Come on, follow me and keep close. If you get low on air grab my octopus. I have got enough air for both of us."

Billy already knew he had well over a hundred bar left in his tank. They both pulled on their masks and began to swim out towards the line of buoys that marked the point where deep water line. When they reached the line there were people with masks and snorkels circling in the water. Billy took Stine by the hand and they both descended into the deep. There were several divers hanging in the water, others, less experienced in controlling their buoyancy were swimming back and forth in lines. Everyone's attention was focused to the south, the direction of the underwater observatory. Billy set his gear up when they had descended to about eight metres and hung in the water. Stine bobbed up and down for a few moments as she fought to set her buoyancy correctly but eventually she got it right. Billy noticed that they were still holding hands and he looked around hurriedly to see if Scouser or any of the other staff had noticed. No one was paying him any attention. He decided to leave his hand where it was and Stine, for her part didn't seem to mind.

They didn't have long to wait, suddenly, from out of the gloom, a monstrous figure emerged, slowly finning its way along. The group in the water parted to either side allowing it to pass between them. Billy and Stine were at eye level as the beast passed them. Billy estimated the size to be a little over five metres in length. It was close enough to the surface that the sunlight was catching and showing off the dappling of yellow spots and stripes on its back. Billy realised that Stine was squeezing his hand, so tightly it was beginning to hurt and he looked round at her. He looked again and realised that she was crying. Her eyes were wet with tears, visible through the mask. Billy squeezed her hand back and she looked over and smiled. The whale shark move slowly, so the encounter took several minutes from first sighting until the creature disappeared back into the gloom. A few intrepid divers tried to keep pace but, one flick of its tail was enough to propel it away and into the deep.

Once it was out of sight they made their way back to the beach. As soon as they were able to, everyone started to talk at once. Billy by comparison was very silent. He had been deeply moved by the encounter, his first with this particular species. He had heard enough tales from other instructors about random encounters with whale sharks but it was his first. Stine, by contrast was gushing, with excitement and with praise. Billy got the impression she thought they had laid the whole thing on for her benefit. He smiled inwardly. He had pulled his mask off his face and it was dangling from his wrist. His regulator was looped over his arm and he bent down to pull off his fins. As he straightened up he felt arms go around his neck and hot hungry lips searching for his. He nearly tumbled over in surprise, but managed to maintain an upright position as he and Stine exchanged their first kiss. It was hot, it was passionate and from Billy's point of view, really rather nice.

When they broke apart Stine was breathless, but smiling. Billy got a whack to the back of his head with a fin.

"You're on a free pass Billy man, on account of that show."

Scouser passed him, lowering the fin to his side, on his way up the beach. He had obviously seen the whole thing and reacted as he saw fit. Billy grinned at his old friend.

"Won't happen again, boss, promise."

He looked over at Stine and saw a look of abject disappointment on her face.

"That's a shame." She said a slight note of sorrow in her voice.

Billy didn't like to see her upset, so he tried to explain the club policy on romantic involvement of staff members with guests. As soon as he started, he regretted using the word fraternisation as this was not a word that Stine had probably ever come across before and every time Billy tried to explain its meaning he was just digging himself into a bigger hole. Eventually he just shrugged as Stine asked him another question.

"It's their rules and I don't make them."

He said with what he hoped was a degree of finality.

"What about when we are alone in the hostel, in our room with no one else?"

That did sound tempting to Billy but he thought he would wait and see what had been arranged over accommodation before he made any promises. He had hoped that Orin had managed to sort out the bed allocations and moved Stine into the room across the hallway which was occupied by girls. That would make his life a little easier.

After lunch Billy got a bit of time to himself. Stine had signed up for an afternoon dive and Billy was able to finish off some paperwork and then took himself off to a sun lounger on the beach. He pulled a cap over his eyes, pulled out his sun glasses and put them on then lay back to soak up some sun. After a while he detected someone was standing over him, stealing his sun. He opened an eye and looked up. Shari was there standing over him. She had turned up for work but instead of the regulation Dive Tribe t-shirt and a pair of shorts, she was wearing an almost transparent sheer silk blouse and a fan belt of a miniskirt. Billy wondered how that little ensemble had been received by Scouser and the rest of the crew. Billy after an initial appraisal focused firmly on her face.

"Hello Billy, do you mind if I sit down?"

"It's a free country."

Shari sat down on Billy's lounger, pressing herself against his legs. Billy waited for Shari to speak. He was still annoyed with her for lying to him. He didn't really want her to apologise or explain herself. He had decided that he didn't really care that much. There was a rather long and pregnant silence.

"Is everything okay?"

Shari could feel the tension and she obviously wanted to talk about it.

"Fine."

He felt Shari's hand rest on his knee. She was clearly trying to make a connection. Billy wasn't sure he wanted to respond.

"Are you doing anything later?"

"No plans."

Billy could only be truthful. Secretly he was hoping that he and Stine would be able to go out and grab a bite to eat. They had not discussed anything yet, but Billy was conscious of the fact that Stine had set off on the afternoon excursion with three other Danes, people she had flown down here together with, so there was every possibility that they might have made arrangements to meet up later on. Billy hadn't really thought about it until after the minibus, with Stine on board, had driven off. At that point he had silently cursed himself for his reticence, cursed Scouser and the Dive Tribe for their bloody stupid rules and poxy regulations. He still held out hope that the connection they made that morning would have left some lasting impression on Stine. He was determined to make his suggestion as soon as she returned.

Shari seemed encouraged by his non-committal answer.

"Good. I want to cook you a meal, will you come round to mine tonight?"

"Can I get back to you on that please?"

Shari hesitated. She clearly wanted Billy to agree right here and now, but realised that this was all she could expect at this time. She seemed reluctant to press the point. She stood up.

"Okay Billy let me know later."

She wandered off up the beach in the direction of the admin office. Billy still held out hope that there would be someone else he would be spending the evening with, even if there was no chance of anything, romantic or otherwise, developing.

He was not disappointed. The afternoon dive, to a site known locally as Moses Rock, ended back on the beach in front of the club, so as Billy watched he saw all of the divers emerging from the shallows. He spotted Stine's purple and black wetsuit and he raised an arm in greeting. She had pulled her mask off and tucked her fins under her arm. She saw Billy's wave and returned it, but then she resumed her discussion with a rather tall and rangy looking guy with blonde hair. Billy didn't have to be an anthropologist to recognise another Scandinavian when he saw one, so he rightly assumed that the tall bloke was one of Stine's fellow travellers. The two were clearly recounting the events of the dive and they disappeared up the beach together still locked in deep conversation.

As Billy watched her departure he felt a sudden hollow feeling in his guts, a sense of loss. Had his discourse earlier on the evils of fraternisation done some damage to what might have been a blossoming relationship? Had Stine mistaken his desire to abide by the rules as dis-interest on his part? He knew that nothing he could say or do would repair that damage. Already her young head might have moved on to other potential suitors. He lay back on his lounger and closed his eyes. Billy was not a religious person, but as he lay there with his eyes closed he found he was whispering a silent prayer to himself, exhorting the gods of love, irrespective of their pantheon, to collectively influence Stine and bring her back to him. Fortunately, he was not to be disappointed. At least one of the deities was listening to his prayers. For no sooner had her equipment been washed and hung out to dry, her log book signed and stamped by this afternoon's dive guide, than Stine made a beeline for his sun lounger.

She had taken the time to change from her swimsuit into a rather fetching and rather brief peach coloured bikini. She spread out her towel on the next sun lounger and sat down. She asked Billy, rather sweetly, if he would help her to apply some sun lotion. Billy, ever the gentleman, agreed willingly. Her skin was soft under his hands but he could feel an underlying strength. She lay on her front and loosened the straps of her top. Billy smeared the lotion over her whole back trying hard to ignore the growing warm feeling he was experiencing in his very core. Stine was obviously enjoying his ministrations because as he watched she wiggled her bottom with excitement and then visibly relaxed as if there had been a sudden release of pent up tension. Her breathing which had been short and intense became more relaxed and deeper as if she was falling asleep. Billy wasn't sure so he decided to say nothing out loud, but he was convinced that the touch of his hands had been enough to give Stine a small orgasm. He finished his task and wiped his hands on his own towel. Stine her head on one side, her face pointing towards him, opened one eye, smiled and mouthed the words

"Thank you."

Billy lay back on his lounger and watched the proceedings on the beach through half closed eyes. After a while Stine was beginning to feel the heat, this time from the sun.

"Do you want something to drink?" She had stood up, fastened her bikini top and found her purse.

"A bottle of water would be great."

"Nothing stronger?"

"I don't."

"Don't what?"

"I don't drink alcohol."

"Wow, you don't?" There was a note of disbelief in her question.

Billy made a motion of crossing his heart.

"I swear."

"I thought all you Brits were drinkers."

Billy shrugged his shoulders. "I can't comment."

Stine returned a short time later with two bottles of water. She handed one of them over to Billy, who mouthed the word 'Thanks'.

"A non-drinking Brit. Who would have believed it?"

"Do you have much experience with Brits and their drinking?"

"My best friend at home has an English boyfriend. I get most of my experience from him."

"Is he a bit of a drinker?"

"He likes a drink yes. He is a medical student."

"Oh a student, that sounds about right."

Billy only had to think about his own friends who had chosen to become students.

"He's actually a nice guy when he hasn't been drinking."

"Meaning, you don't like him when he drinks?"

"He's a mean drunk. He gets very dominant when he has been drinking. It's not fair on her."

"I see."

Stine was on a roll and she seemed pleased to be able to vent her feelings on another British person.

She related the highs and lows of her friend's relationship and how she felt some of the demands that he was making were unfair. Billy paid close attention to what she said as it was giving him invaluable insight into how Stine felt on a range of issues. She was in full flow now about male dominance and she went into a long example of a recent conversation between her and her friend about the prospects for the future. Apparently when this British fellow finished medical school he was expecting Stine's friend to drop everything and move to Britain and become a doctor's wife.

"And that's not something she wants to do?"

"Not particularly. I mean when you have two people who come from different countries, where do you make your home? One of you has to move to the other person's country and give up their own friends and family."

"Unless you chose a third country and both move there?"

Billy thought his suggestion was a reasonable compromise. Stine nodded furiously, seeming to agree with him.

"What like Israel? Should we both move here?"

Stine gave him a broad smile and a wink signifying that she was more than ready for this as an eventuality. In Billy's eyes she appeared to have made a decision. Billy spluttered at her presumption. This discussion was going in the wrong direction rather rapidly.

"I was joking."

Stine moved to reassure him and remove the panicked look from his face. Billy having recovered some of his composure, along with his voice, now explained.

"You and me living together here wouldn't work. I would have an unfair advantage as I know people here, I speak the language, and have developed a network of friends."

"Oh good, are you going to introduce me to some of them?"

"Funny you should say that. Have you got any plans for this evening?"

Stine shook her head violently. Billy smiled. An evil plan was forming in Billy's mind and on the way home with Stine in tow he put the plan into action.

He stopped by the main office and stuck his head around the door. Shari was behind her desk staring at her computer screen, she looked up as Billy appeared.

"Hi Billy," she beamed, "have you reached a decision about dinner tonight?"

"I have. Dinner would be lovely, but can I bring a friend?"

Shari's face darkened. The invitation was out there and she had just renewed it, so it could not be easily withdrawn, but by the expression on her face, dinner had not been the only thing on offer.

"Who?" Shari was barely able to supress the ire in her voice.

Billy leaned around the door post and pulled Stine by the arm.

"Stine, I would like you to meet Shari. She has kindly offered to cook us both dinner tonight."

Stine would have had to have been blind not to have seen the flash of anger that crossed Shari's face, but she was all sweetness and light while accepting the kind offer.

"'bout seven then?" Billy was enjoying himself a little too much.

"Yes," Shari hissed through clenched teeth.

"See you then."

Billy took hold of Stine's hand and guided her outside the dive club and over to where the scooter was parked. Stine's dive bag was safely locked away in one of the customer lockers, so she was only carrying a small bag with her swimming costumes and a towel in it. They faced each other across the scooter's saddle.

"She didn't look very happy." Stine remarked.

"Who? Shari? Oh don't worry about her. Scouser has balled her out for being late for work this morning.

"If I didn't know better I would say she fancies you."

Billy laughed loudly.

"She is not my type."


The week had literally flown by and now it was time for Billy to say goodbye to Stine. They had not spent the whole week together. Stine had signed on for a three day desert jeep safari and despite Billy's best efforts he could not persuade Scouser or any of the other managers to assign him as one of the guides for the tour. He had however managed to be there at the dive club when they had eventually returned and had whisked Stine away on the back of his scooter as soon as the dive equipment they had taken on the tour had been returned to the store rooms. As they now waited in the departures area at Eilat Airport for the shuttle flight back to Ben Gurion he was aware of one thing. He had still not slept with this woman. He could still go into the club the next day with a clear conscience. The whole week had not been totally platonic. Orin had left them in the room together for the first two nights and it was only after Stine had departed for the dive safari that he had assigned other divers to Billy's room. On the first two nights, while they were alone, they had shared a bed but although things had got steamy and intense they had not had sex. Billy wasn't sure why that was and while Stine was away and the other beds filled up he began to hatch plans of taking a room in a hotel when she returned, so that they could be alone for their last night together.

Orin had also explained why Stine had been assigned to his room in the first place. Apparently, there had been a mix up over her name. A hastily scribbled note had mixed up two Hebrew characters so that instead of Stine, the name had been written as Steve and assumed therefore to be male. In the end he didn't book a hotel room and when she arrived back she was assigned a bed in one of the girl's rooms. Billy resigned himself to spending the night alone and instead focused on having an enjoyable evening out in the town. They did and it ended up with the two of them walking along the beach in the early hours. Funnily enough, when they got back to the hostel it was only to discover that Stine had been locked out of the girl's room. She had to come in and climb into bed with Billy, which naturally, he didn't complain about. As all the other beds were filled with sleeping divers there was no chance for intimacy.

Now as the minutes ticked down to Stine's flight Billy was left wondering what might happen next. The announcement came for passengers to go to the gate and Billy enfolded Stine in his arms and gave her a passionate kiss. She stood back and then took Billy's hand. She placed a scrap of paper in his open palm and closed her fingers over it. She stood on tip-toes and kissed Billy once more.

"Write to me." She said and was gone through the gate.

Billy opened his hand and extracted the piece of paper. He unfolded it and read the text.

"Please write to me Billy, I really want to see you again. Stine xx."

Below the text was an address in Denmark. Billy tucked the paper in the pocket of his shorts and pulled the sun glasses down off his head as he walked out of the terminal building and into the sunshine.

"Nice work Randell. Nice work."

# Acknowledgements

People say that writing and the job of an author is a lonely business and to some extent when you sit in front of a blank sheet of paper or a plain white screen you can feel alone and, at times, very afraid. This was certainly how I felt when I sat down to write this volume of the Billy Randell story. The Eilat Trap had ended on a hopeful note so where would Billy go next and what would he do?

But as I began to write, to weave the first strands of the story together, plenty of familiar faces began to show up to keep me company, because whichever way you spin it the stories of our lives are a succession of chance meetings, and it is how we react and what we achieve as a result of those meetings that make us what we are.

When the last full stop of the first draft was in place then I get to work with other 'real' people, and those are the folks who I really need to thank. I must start with my editors, Neil and Joules who took my humble efforts and shaped them into what they eventually became, whilst keeping both my feet firmly rooted on mother earth. The crew at Rise Tone who did such a superb job with the cover art and my family who endured the periods when I was not present with them in the here and now but a couple of thousand miles away and in a different century.

I would also like to thank you, the reader who has taken the trouble to buy and read my story, I do hope you enjoyed it and that you will not see the time you took to read this book as wasted. If you do then my most profound and deepest apologies.

I suppose the final thanks should go to our boy Billy who has allowed me to play with his emotions and strip his soul bare in front of the world. Life is not done with him just yet and there are still some parts of his story that need to be told, so Billy Randell will be back.

# Authors Note

As a self published author I don't have a huge publishing house behind my efforts so I rely very much on you, the readers to help me get the word out about my scribblings. One of the most valuable things you can do for me is to take a moment to write a review on Amazon and tell the rest of the world what you thought about the book. These reviews might help someone else to decide whether or not to buy the book and any reviews, good or bad, also helps me too.

You can follow me on Facebook for all the news about my work.
https://www.facebook.com/NickCreeWriter/